Praise for *The Above and Beyond Series* . . .

For *Hindsight*

"This is part of a series, and the best of the series thus far. The writing is exceptional, the dialog purposeful, restrained, important." — Rainbow Awards 2017

For *Untrained Eye*

"Jody Klaire manages to mix up a thriller crime drama with a psychic whodunit and an ever so slowly burning romance. Add in humour, great dialogue, brilliant writing and these books are just a joy." — Velvet Lounger, *LRR*

For *Blind Trust*

"From snow bound mountain rescues to the gentle rescuing of those locked in their own minds, you'll be spell bound and on the edge of your seat as Aeron does her thing. Loved this—gobbled it up in a few hours (hours when I should really have been sleeping...)—and can't wait for more." — Review, *Tales of a Librarian*

For *The Empath*

"I'm not giving anything away but, The Empath *is a taut tense thriller proving that there is two sides to every story and that everybody has their armour. How this series isn't in mainstream bookshops I don't know . . . Bring on book two!"* — *The Book Lovers Library*

"Jody Klaire's debut novel is an exhilarating rush, a cross between the best of X Files and Orange is the New Black. Fast-paced, sharp, and very, very smart." — Marissa Cohen, *She Magazine*

"The twists and turns kept things interesting and always moving forward. Even events that you wouldn't expect to be related to the crime were deftly folded into the plot and given purpose. It all made sense. It was crafted well." — Carleen Spry, *Frivolous Views*

NOBLE HEART

THE ABOVE AND BEYOND SERIES BOOK V

NOBLE HEART

JODY KLAIRE

BInk

Bedazzled Ink Publishing • Fairfield, California

978-1-943837-74-8 paperback
978-1-943837-75-5 ebook

Cover Design
by

DESIGNS

A Mindancer Book

a division of
Bedazzled Ink Publishing, LLC
Fairfield, California
http://www.bedazzledink.com

To,
Those who remain in my heart always and
remind me what it is to be loved,

For,
Mum and Em, who go above & beyond,

And,
For anyone who is that little bit different.

Acknowledgments

I could write a novel length of thank yous for all those who have helped me on my writing journey. You know who you are and, mentioned or not, I offer my deep unreserved thanks.

To the reader: it has been some journey so far and, knowing that there is someone waiting to meet Aeron for the first time or catch up with her does help what can be quite a tricky process. Thank you for allowing Aeron into your heart and cheering her on. I hope you enjoy spending time with her.

To those at the writers' workshop and online, colleagues, and friends who work equally as hard, all churning out those words and hoping someone will like them. Whether published or unpublished, it is a pleasure to know you, meet you in conferences and share our passion for the written word.

Thank you to Ann, Salem, Cheryl (and Lynn), and all my dear friends at the GCLS, thank you for your warm words, your kind support and for cheering me on.

To Lynn, thank you, once again for taking the time to produce a beautiful cover. I appreciate the hard work put in.

To Sui, who works so hard to do the typeset and make it equally as beautiful. I notice and appreciate all the concentration and focus needed to get it right. Thank you.

To Ian, Pat, and Siân who keep me able to type, but thank you, especially to Ian for igniting my imagination and teaching me so much about osteopathy in general. Your patience in answering my questions and suffering my thoughts on your wonderful profession is much appreciated.

A special thanks to Dr. Dhanjal who listened, fixed, and gave me the chance to feel once more.

To Team Truth, I still hold you dear to my heart and cheer for you as I know you do for me. In particular, Pam and Karen who shared their love of Baltimore with me. I hope my nod to your city is noted and gives you a smile.

To Beth and Joy who allowed me to share my love of writing

and then opening up your hearts and your friendship to me. It's such a pleasure to work with you and know you. Your kindness and your patience make it so much easier for me to smile. Thank you.

To Brie Burkeman for believing, for listening, for letting me walk smack into every mistake possible and not turning away. Thank you for steering me and stirring my love of writing. Thank you for the conversations and belief I wasn't too bad at stringing words together. It still anchors me. Thank you.

To Emma Darwin for gently guiding me and showing me all the amazing tools, tips, and ways to improve my writing. I hope that you see how much I've improved since we've been working together and how much I am set on improving. I never cease to be inspired by our conversations, and I'm sure that you understand just how much that means.

To Sue, for your honest thoughts and great eye for detail, your support of my work which helps me to know Aeron has friends, for lifting me by taking the time to remind me that my stories are enjoyed and looked forward to. I can't really express how much that makes a difference but it does. It really does.

To Claudia and Casey for taking a chance on my work in the first place and for cheering for me personally as well as professionally. Without doubt, *Noble Heart* became the book it is because you took the time to chat to me. I hope that it makes you smile as much as I.

To Katja, Melanie, and my German friends online and Dr. Hilary Thomas. Having the confidence to write even snippets in another language is always a bit scary. Although I'd already written *Noble Heart* when I met you, your kindness and patience with me attempting to talk to you made me very thankful that Theo shares your homeland and Frei and her family share your roots . . . And hopefully I got my German phrases right!

To Revd. Sue, Mr. B, Fr. Mike, Glenda, Revd. Jayne, Mr. H, Revd. Pauline, and all in the CNB parish (and beyond.) It is an honor to know you and a blessing to learn from you.

To Moira Spence (and Ian). May you always know how truly and deeply you shared in my journey and meditations. May you see how your dedication to guiding me helped me to find myself writing Aeron. May you see the light in my work and know your friendship is forever a strength in my heart and I pray that your heart grows stronger and the true Breath of Life replenishes, restores and grants you full healing.

To Sandra, I wonder sometimes if you shake your head with my thanks to you. I hope that you see your friendship, love, and compassion were well-placed. I also hope you don't mind me attempting to honor your idea for raising the bar and that you know how much of a blessing your friendship remains.

To my family, those here and in the next room. Your lives and stories inspire me. I hope that my work makes you smile.

Mum, thank you for doing all the small stuff, and all the things mums do that make a difference. Although your attachment to Aeron has changed, I hope my blessings still make you smile.

Em, for steeling me when I struggle, for smiling when I get something right, for worrying when I'm not looking and working hard to read, re-read, and proof-read . . . and for sleeping on the couch to keep me company while I work. Hopefully, you know how much it helps.

To THS: Thank you for your unfailing love, your gentle presence, your soaring joy, your comfort and your strength. You truly are love and the breath that breathes life into my heart. I pray that my works give you a massive smile, that they are acceptable in your sight. Thank you for the many gifts you have so gracefully given to me and, I hope, that you find I am preserving, retaining and being the person you intend me to be. I believe in you.

Jody Klaire
December 2017

Foreword

Cranial osteopathy is something that I have personal reason to love, and writing gives me the ability to explore and learn about so many things. It seemed quite natural that cranial osteopathy found its way into Aeron's story. Not only because osteopathy in general has its roots in Missouri, just like her, but because of the very nature of how cranial fuses logic and faith.

Noble Heart was a real challenge for me to get right, and I got it wrong a lot before it developed into the book you see. I wrote it between operations which saw incredible highs and lows. The quote that guides the book talks of perseverance and how that seed inspires others to believe. So, perhaps it was only right that I needed to focus my own perseverance in order to produce the story I really hope will entertain, inspire, and stir you into believing you can be who you were meant to be.

All things are possible . . . you just have to believe.

Big Smiles,

Jody

" . . . But the seed on good soil stands for those with a noble and good heart, who hear the word, retain it, and by persevering produce a crop."
Luke 8:15 [NIV]

Chapter 1

WHAT MAKES YOUR heart beat?

My heart was full of restless energy 'cause I'd been through a lot since I was sixteen. I weren't like a lot of folks: I'd been locked up in a mental institution for a crime I didn't commit; got released—over a decade later—Returned to my hometown and got targeted by somebody real mean who hurt young girls and got everybody thinking it was me. It took me hurtling up a mountain to prove I was innocent . . . and when I thought that'd earned me some peace and quiet, I was emotionally blackmailed into joining the Criminal Investigations Group—CIG.

It didn't stop there. I'd nearly frozen away in boot camp, been snowed in a Colorado town with a military grade lunatic and a commander who was out-to-lunch upstairs—Still weren't sure how I got through that one. Then, I'd been part of a team who brought down a slave academy in Texas—We'd rescued every child, but Jäger, another creep, lured out one of the children, Jessie, which saw us hurrying halfway across the States to get to her . . . and her mom. It was hard to process it all, especially as we were gonna head back into the slavery network to try and make sure Jessie, her mom, and her grandparents all stayed free.

Yeah, I'd run from tornados, avalanches, clung by the fingertips from cliffs and buildings; I'd been shot at, chased, driven to the point of collapse, half-drowned, half-crazy, and somehow scrabbled through. It had been some journey so far but folks close to my heart filled it with the strength to keep me dusting myself off.

Felt good to say that. Back in Serenity Hills—the institution I got locked in—I thought I had no one but, wow, had that changed. I needed a chart just to keep track of them.

First there was my family: My half-sisters; my mom and dad, who were the ex-head of CIG, now mayor of my hometown, and police chief respectively; Aunt Bess, also ex-CIG, and I was pretty sure might have been in charge too—Guessed it was a Lorelei tradition—who I'd just found out about. She was just like me, six foot and then some but she didn't have the bulk I did. Maybe she had been built like Samson a while ago but now she was *supposed* to be a respectable retired lady . . . made me chuckle just thinking 'bout that; and Nan—How'd I explain her in a nut stash? She was a whole load of love, heckling, and angel in a whispering breeze. She'd sweep on in from Etherspace to guide, chastise, and save my butt. When I'd been alone, she'd reached out and reminded me I was loved.

Some friends were a whole lot like family too. The current head of CIG, General Ursula Frei, was someone I loved as much as if she had the Lorelei name. She was so cool it gave me goosebumps. An ex-slave, now a general and mom of mini-Frei . . . Jessie. She had some sneaky skills and inner strength more steely than her mood. Sure, she had an impenetrable outer shell but inside, she was all hero.

And then there was my co-crazy person—a woman who confused the molasses out of me, shut me out, let me back in, rescued me, believed in me and then confounded me all over again: Commander Renee Black. She was my boss and an incredible woman who had more stubbornness than Mrs. Squirrel on a nut stash but she did something special to my heart. When it had been frozen with loneliness, she'd reached in and given me warmth; when I'd been locked up in mind, body, and spirit, she'd baby stepped me to freedom, and she'd needed every bit of that stubborn-headed heart of hers to help shake me from my shackles and get me moving again.

And me? Well, I'm a little bit different. Some people saw Aeron Lorelei—the ex-con, or Agent Lorelei—the CIG protection officer, or even Alex Riley—my cover when I'd been at the slave academy. They all saw sides but not many knew what lay at my core.

I was an empath: I saw the past and present of the folks around me; I read their moods, felt their feelings and, sometimes, when they asked, I could displace their ailments.

So maybe that's why my heart was restless. I'd been through a lot of different things at twenty seven, but mentally and emotionally, I felt a lot younger. I was institutionalized and being a protection officer with CIG weren't getting easier.

Nan talked to me a lot about it being a process. That I just needed to figure out what made my heart soar and what to let go but Frei was counting on me to be clear, to operate like an elite agent, only I weren't sure I could. I wanted to support her but since I'd got my burdens back in full, it was harder to control them.

That restless feeling kept nagging at me and, the more I shoved it away, the more it poked at me—an energy that prickled at me to be free. My heart seemed to know more than I did but, when faced with everybody else's feelings and under pressure to be that calm, controlled agent at Frei's side, how would I know, really know, if it was my heart speaking or somebody else's?

Chapter 2

FALL HAD BECOME a frozen winter. Ice encased everything making the trees look like they'd been turned into ice pops and the fields shimmer like jewels. Frei's place was built on the money she'd *earned* as a locksmith and Huber, her dad, had let her skim off the top of her work. She'd renovated a huge ranch and stables and turned it into a mini-fort with a lot of security and cameras. Somehow, it still looked humble with jig-jagged stone work and rustic-looking doors of reddish oak.

Inside, every inch was warm and homey—from the floors of rich wood and beams cutting into the solid stone walls, to the huge fireplace, fluffy rug, and a sofa my size. Yeah, I loved her style and I loved the warm. Warm was good. I really hated the cold and I was freezing my sizable butt off. If I'd thought helping to rescue Frei would have given me a break from being yelled at and drilled, I'd have needed to head back to Serenity—I was thinking about it just to get a rest.

I shivered and my breath billowed out like I was smoking a pipe.

"Slow breaths, you know that your throat contracts in the cold," Renee said, rubbing my back as I hunched over, spluttering.

I glared at her. We were in the middle of a white, frosty field near Frei's place and had been trekking around in minus something temperatures for what felt like hours. But, Renee's cheeks were rosy, her cold weather gear filled with so many gadgets that I made her crackle when I went near her, and still her gray eyes were filled with adventure. You'd think we were on vacation.

"It's colder than Colorado was," I muttered, trying to suppress a shiver. That was saying something, St. Jude's had been on a mountain for a start.

"This is nowhere near as cold, dimwit," she said, tapping her watch like she was scrolling through my readings, again. "And this time you're properly fitted for the cold weather." She scanned the barren fields around us and pulled out her binoculars. "I know you hate it but it's best we're certain that it won't hinder you."

"What, snow?" I pulled off my glove and scooped up a handful of the stuff—cold, wet, and stung my fingers. Sure, I healed myself in still water and washed away other folks' ailments in running water and snow was technically water but would it get in the way? I studied the pile of white mush, cold soaked through into my bones, and I shivered so hard my knees wobbled. Renee had rosy cheeks though. Why wasn't she shivering?

"You don't look bothered by it?" I mumbled as she glanced at me.

"I've undergone years of elite military training." She said it like she'd just been to the grocery store. "And I grew up in Colorado, remember?"

"If it was so elite, how come we been freezing our butts off in the cold for hours?" I scowled at her. I didn't care if she was the boss, Renee and Frei knew how much I hated the cold. Having hyperthermia once had been enough.

"Twenty minutes, Lorelei," she shot back, peering over her binoculars at me as I straightened up. "Frei is in position, so we need to run some checks." She looked at the watch on her arm again. "How am *I* feeling?"

"You?" I was trying to avoid reading her but her aura jiggled about like she was waving at me and my gut wriggled in response. It did that a lot since I'd gotten my burdens back. Sometimes it was when she popped into my head or I looked at her. Couldn't figure out what it was and I weren't planning on asking. "Fine."

"Hmm . . ." She furrowed her brow and stared at her watch again. "How are *you* feeling?"

"Cold." I scowled.

She "hmm'd" again like she was making mental notes then met my eyes. Her aura was hollering at me like I was missing something and the wriggle in my gut started again so I stared at the snow melting in my hand—Felt kinda tingly.

Renee sighed. "Alright, can you locate Urs?"

Her tone seeped through some of the pressure she was feeling. Yeah, we had to protect Frei and to do that, Renee had to know how I could perform in all situations. She'd said she had no doubt in me or my abilities with such belief that her lips shimmered with the truth.

My burdens were different and I hadn't long got them back . . . they'd changed in some ways—more intense? Yeah, real intense and my stomach ached thinking about it. Maybe that was the cold too, and I hadn't eaten breakfast.

Hmm . . .

Locate Frei? I could do that.

I shut my eyes. "She's about half a football field to our left and she's on her tenth coffee so far this morning."

I heard the relieved breath and peeked open an eye. Renee frowned up at me, hands on her hips. "If you could feel her that clearly, why didn't you say so?"

I mirrored her gesture right back. "'Cause you didn't tell me what we were doin', like always." She never told me nothing.

Renee narrowed her eyes. "I'm the commander. You didn't need to know. You're supposed to follow orders."

I raised my eyebrows.

She sighed. "Supposed to." She waved off my glare. "I worked hard to become a commander. Years and years of training. I didn't do it to get heckled."

I turned and marched to Frei's position in a mound of trees that were clumped together. I cleared the snow away and yanked open the door which led to the tunnel running underneath.

"I ain't hecklin', I'm just getting on with it." I motioned to the doorway. "Quit scowling at me and get in the warm."

Renee glared at me only for her aura to wriggle about, then her eyes to warm, and laughter to spill from her lips.

"Surprised you took so long," she said as she strolled past me.

I sighed and tried to fit my bulk through the door. It wasn't easy considering I was six five and built like Samson *without* layers of cold weather gear. Elite agent stuff was for short skinny folks.

"Why the delay, Lorelei?" Frei's bored tone greeted me before I could see her.

I squeezed myself in sideways and clanged my head on the frame. Short folks, that's what tunnels were for, real short folks.

"Delay?" I muttered, ducked my head, and rubbed at the bump forming.

Frei had her laptop out, as always, and didn't so much as look up. "You hate the cold." Her icy blue eyes caught the pale light from the peeking window she'd been watching us from.

I stepped into the room and the machines on the wall flickered so I sighed and stepped back—I made electrical stuff have a hissy fit on a good day. I'd blown the camera in the hallway back at Frei's place just by standing in the same room.

"You haven't had breakfast yet," Renee said with amusement dancing about in her aura. "Thought you'd have dragged me here."

"You *know* I can find you." I glared at Frei and yanked off my coat, smacked my elbow on the wall, and grunted. "I tracked your skinny butt half way across the States."

She raised a white blonde eyebrow. "Skinny?"

"Fine. Highly muscled butt which could break boulders. Happy?" She may have looked sinewy but she was a machine and could out bench-press me one handed.

"Better." She was unreadable on the outside—pale skin, white spiky blonde hair, and eyes that I swore could slice through stone. If her aura wasn't shaking about with laughter, the cool, unmoved act would have worked better.

"We know that. We just have to . . ." Renee paused while pulling off her coat as if searching for a word that wouldn't make me scowl. Her hair was blonde too but a warm golden color as it spilled out of her hat. "We . . ."

"We have to learn about how you work," Frei said, tapping on her keyboard. "You're training *us*."

"Yes, the thing is . . ." Renee sighed. "You're able to adapt quickly to your senses but we have to make sure that *we* can cope with any . . ." She looked to Frei.

"Curveballs." Frei kept on tapping at the keys. "However much I like popsicles, Lorelei, I don't want you being one mid-assignment."

And she did love her popsicles.

"Snow has been a problem before so we need to check," Renee said, slinging her coat over her shoulder. "You could feel her, which is as it was before you got all your senses back. We needed to know that."

"So why not just *tell* me?"

"Because it's our way of checking how your senses react when you're *not* told . . . like when someone is in trouble and you hear them?" Renee smiled at me. She didn't like keeping it from me but I guess it was logical to check. "We thought it would be quick because you love Urs, that gives you fuel."

Frei's eyebrow twitched like she was pretending she didn't hear a word.

I folded my arms, grunting as I smacked my elbow again. "Uh, huh . . ." Why'd I get the feeling they were skirting around something? "Who told you that you needed to check all this stuff?"

Frei opened her mouth—

I held up my hand. "Let me guess: smaller than me, same eyes, with a habit of meddling and driving me nuts?"

Mom was a pain in my butt.

Renee sucked in a breath. "We're on a Lilia sucks day, huh?"

I still had a tendency to want to poke her for leaving my dad and I, sauntering off to CIG and being some kind of hero, before sauntering back in and emotionally blackmailing me into taking her place in CIG.

Hmm . . . Maybe Renee had a point.

My stomach growled like it agreed.

"I'd say the mood is to do with that," Frei said, pointing to my stomach, eyes still on her screen.

"I can see you're laughing," I muttered. I could read her clearer than I could Renee now I'd learned so much about her.

Frei didn't acknowledge I'd said anything but her aura was chuckling for her.

"So, how is turning me into a popsicle gonna help us undercover?" I scowled. It weren't funny.

"In any other situation, you would have known what Renee wanted you to do, known where I was, and come straight here." Frei tapped away. If she was like my dad, I'd say she was playing that card game folks enjoyed so much, but knowing Frei, she was hacking into somewhere she shouldn't or monitoring my heart rate or something. "But . . . you were too slow," she said, frowning at the screen. "Snow seems to slow you down."

I shivered. "Because nobody told me we were looking for you."

"I was thinking it," Renee said with a shrug. She'd located the coffee machine and was on about her tenth cup too. The pair of them were too into coffee.

"I weren't paying attention, I was too busy trying to stop my teeth clattering together." Kinda. I was so close to Renee, I could hear her thoughts sometimes. She cocked her head like she could tell it wasn't really the truth and my stomach wriggled all over the place again. Was it an ailment? Was she sick or something?

I concentrated on my boots but I could feel her eyes on me and I tried reading how she was . . .

The lights flickered and groaned. I stared up at them. I'd always made electrics buzz, guess the lights had caught on.

Renee was healthier now than she'd ever been, and she was watching me, her curiosity bubbling. Correction: now *both* of them were looking at me and I was studying my boots till my stomach quit dancing around.

"You'll need to pay more attention in snowy conditions," Frei said in a gentle tone.

My stomach growled again. "I ain't a sniffer dog."

"No, they'd be cheaper to feed." Frei kept staring at me until I gave in and met her eyes. "Now we've checked, we know there's a delay in those conditions. It's important we understand that."

Renee and Frei liked to have every detail mapped. That's what soldiers did. I weren't real sure if I was a soldier, an agent or both and nobody was planning on filling me in.

"What difference does it make when we are luring out Jäger?" I'd spent months undercover as Alex Riley, who'd done time for crimes I didn't like to think about. I had been there to train the kids—who were slaves—to be thugs and make them more valuable to sell. I'd gotten into it to the point that Jäger, Jessie's father, had decided he liked my company. Considering what he did to Frei, even the thought of him made my gut twist.

"You'll be faced with people just like him, owners that you may need to read." Renee's soft tone made my stomach wriggle again. "We're targeting the owners he sold slaves to."

"If they are on the ropes, they'll snitch on him?" That made sense.

"Or at least give us something solid to send Sven's way." Frei closed the lid of the laptop. "If his brother is on his case, then Jäger will be off ours."

"You hope," I mumbled. Jäger didn't seem like the kind of guy that would stop. He wanted to cover up what he'd done to Frei by getting rid of her and Jessie. How would his big brother yelling at him change his mind?

"We talked about this," Renee said, sipping at her coffee.

Hmm. We had? I'd been kinda tired when they'd been talking 'bout it.

Renee sighed. "Jäger lured out Jessie and she was trapped in Sven's warehouse, yes?"

I nodded. Frei had gone to rescue her and gotten sick . . . and we'd tracked them halfway across the States . . . with a little help.

"And we're certain Jäger is using his brother's warehouses to sell off other people's slaves without his knowledge." Renee held my gaze, in teaching mode.

"Yeah?"

Energy faded in as she studied my eyes, along with music. She always made me hear music. "If Jäger is selling off slaves like that then he's making money for himself and not the family . . . which is an insult."

"And Sven will see it as a challenge to his authority," Frei said, icy eyes narrowed as she leaned back. Yeah, she was ready to make me do push-ups for forgetting. "So if he finds out, Jäger will either have to take him on, which he can't, or deal with the punishment."

I remembered this . . . sort of. "So Sven would hand him to the authorities or something?" I was sure Renee had said they might do something "barbaric" too. Guessed slave owners weren't the forgiving sort.

"No." Frei shook her head, exasperation in her eyes. "He'll become a slave to the person he owes money to."

"Who is?" I leaned against the wall, having to duck my head to fit.

"Huber," Renee said, exchanging a worried glance with Frei.

Renee kept on thinking boot camp should have turned a misfit into an agent. I didn't know why. Frei must have told her I'd sucked. Still, I felt like I needed to try for her. So Jäger would become Huber's slave, and Huber was Frei's dad . . . No, I rubbed the back of my neck. I still didn't get it. "Why?"

Frei rolled her eyes. "Lorelei, you passed boot camp, when did your brains rattle loose?"

I folded my arms. "Maybe when I was drowning trying to save you?"

Her aura waved about like she wanted to hug me. She wouldn't. That would break the tough act. "Jäger is selling slaves with Huber's mistress. He sold Huber's slaves, he sold my sister, and Suz . . ." She glanced away, pain glinting through her eyes and aura. "It's been going on for years and Jäger can't afford to pay up."

My head hurt. "And the snow . . . ?"

"Stealing owners' slaves won't make us popular and it's winter." Renee was staring at me again and my stomach was wriggling, again, and I weren't daring to look at her, again. "Escaping through snow is a possibility."

"Right," I mumbled. So we were targeting other slave owners to snitch on Jäger to his brother so he'd owe a load of money to Huber and become a slave. Great. Made me feel real noble.

"To protect Jessie," Renee said like she knew what I was thinking. "Otherwise he'll keep going until he gets rid of her."

Okay, now that made me mad.

"So we go in as owners." Frei shook her head at me. "You and I are business partners, thanks to our haul in Caprock, and that way Renee will be able to get extra support in and out. She needs to be able to move freely when we're there so we always have an exit route should we need it." Frei said it like that should bother me. "The best way of doing that is if she goes in as a mistress."

And that was why. "She ain't doing that, you'll put her in danger. What if the owner hurts her?" I shook my head. Nope, no way.

"I told you she wouldn't be comfortable," Renee mumbled, her tone filled with what sounded too close to hurt.

"What if they capture you?" Maybe they'd hit their heads? How come I was the only one who was confused? "What if they drag you off someplace and we can't come and help?"

She and Frei exchanged a glance.

They could look at each other all they liked. "I ain't having you kiss some creepy guy . . . or girl." I rubbed my hand over my face.

Renee cocked her head as the hurt in her eyes swirled into affection. There went that weird wriggle again. "Dimwit."

I waved it off.

Frei rolled her eyes. "I'll leave Renee to fill you in on the details."

Said like a general.

"Ma'am," Renee said like a soldier and I swore she would have saluted too if I hadn't shaken my head.

"Guess that means you ain't coming with us to breakfast?" I folded my arms, I weren't saluting Frei but she'd get a hug until she quit acting so detached if she weren't careful.

"I'm busy," she said, but I kept staring at her until she looked up. "I'll try and make lunch, okay?"

"You better or I'll set Nan on you." I nodded. Okay, so Frei shouldn't technically be able to see or hear Nan. When she swished in from Etherspace and nagged me, it took a lot of energy. I didn't think she could to somebody without blessings . . . Yeah, they were blessings more than burdens.

"I miss her conversations." Renee smiled, picked up her jacket, and drained her cup. "Well, when they didn't make me feel like I was talking to a . . . well . . . whatever she is."

"Angel if you ask me." I followed her out into the corridor and ducked as we headed through a load of concrete tunnels.

Renee walked in silence, her aura more jittery than Mrs. Squirrel without nuts.

"I don't like it, even if Frei needs you to be a mistress," I muttered, shoving my hands in my pockets. Didn't know why I looked around, Frei had stayed in the room we'd left her in— coffee was there. "You could get hurt. How is she gonna help you if you get in a pickle?"

"Urs is good at un-pickling things." Renee winked at me. "Now, come on, let's get you fed."

My stomach growled on command. "That's an order I'm happy to follow."

Chapter 3

FREI'S PLACE SMELLED of coffee beans and warm bread. I liked to stand in the kitchen to feel the essence of her cooking up her favorite meal—or since we'd arrived—chatting over breakfast and squabbling with Renee over who cooked.

The countertops were sleek, shiny, and some kind of stone. I ran my hand over it, smiling at how Renee and Frei were always bickering: good natured, sisterly. It made me feel at ease to hear it.

The floor was tiled but warm—Guess she had underfloor heating—and I closed my eyes, hoping it would relax me, calm me, but it didn't and I was gonna hide in here until I figured out what was making me feel so restless.

I leaned against the counter, trying to focus on breathing. In and out, nice and slow. Frei was where we'd left her and Renee was busy plotting escape routes in the living room. Weren't real sure why, had been too busy trying not to look at her.

Concentrate. I could do this. I'd meditated a lot. I was trundling my way through the readings but I couldn't . . . settle. It had been the same back in Oppidum before we'd headed off to rescue Frei and that had been some weird road trip. Reliving folks' memories wasn't new but I'd relived most of Frei's story.

How did Frei pick herself up after losing her friend Suz like that? The strength just shimmered from her. Yeah, it shimmered like the truth did when someone spoke from the heart. Real pure courage . . . And I still weren't relaxing.

"Hey," Renee whispered from the doorway.

And there was a big part of the reason. If I concentrated hard enough, maybe she'd think I was sleeping? She made me feel jittery; I didn't have my eyes open and my stomach was rolling but she weren't going nowhere . . . and now I'd piqued her curiosity, great.

"Hey," I mumbled.

"This about us checking how you coped in the snow?" Her voice held that undercurrent of pressure. "Because it was about making sure you were safe."

"I got that," I said, keeping my eyes shut, and smoothed over the counter. I couldn't read individual memories from the stone but I could pick up on moods, on moments. Frei cooked when she was lonely. Didn't like to think of her lonely.

"This about me undercover because I use vials," she said and I peeked open an eye to see her holding up her hands. "I'm trained."

"Least one of us is. Mom decided *I* weren't worth training up." I didn't know why mom sent me through boot camp if she was only interested in half an agent. Frei had heeded her request but she didn't agree. Nope, Frei would have drilled me properly.

"She didn't want you in that situation," Renee said, walking to the opposite counter and leaning against it. Energy buzzed between us, humming like electricity, prickling at my skin and giving me goosebumps. "You said in Serenity that you get confused with romantic feelings."

"Guess." Felt dumb that I'd told her about my worries. Didn't know why I had. Sure, it was tough being an empath 'cause I could never really know, when I was close to someone, if I was feeling my own feelings or just echoing theirs. Even with all I'd experienced since leaving the institution, sometimes it felt like, upstairs, I was still there.

"She didn't want you overwhelmed." Renee rubbed her bare right foot across her left calf and over the fitted, faded blue jeans—a habit from when she'd been hurt badly and couldn't walk without pain. "And *I* don't want you half-drowned just to get you back again."

"It was close with Frei," I mumbled, transfixed by the prominent shape of her calf. She'd always been toned but somehow, since I'd healed her, her muscles had strengthened and pulsed with energy. She pulsed with it.

"I know you were," she said with a sigh. "But I meant when your dad helped me . . . in the river."

How could I forget how much my dad had risked to get me back? He'd told me he loved me and, for the first time, I'd felt it. "Don't want you or Frei doin' that."

"If we have to, we will." She rubbed at her calf again, flexed her right foot. "But that's why we have to keep things from you sometimes."

"I'm not a kid." Even if I felt like one. I pushed off the counter, ready to skulk off back to my room and hide there.

"No, you're an agent under my command," Renee said, catching me by the elbow. "And a captain." She squeezed. "A CIG captain and my job is to keep you operational."

"So I am in the army?" Why that made me feel better, I didn't know. "How'd I get a rank?"

"CIG ranks are higher than army ranks." She blew out a breath. "It's complicated but you are in the army, yes."

"Don't get it." Why was it different?

"I know. Which is why I don't tell you and complicate things." Her eyes were steely, calm, and the overhead light bounced off the cyan rims as some thought or question rippled across. "Professionally, that's why I don't want you trained in using vials and hypnosis." She smiled but the ripples intensified. "Personally, I don't want you anywhere near that kind of situation."

"Because you think I can't handle it?" I folded my arms.

"Because it's not pleasant and the people we deal with are difficult sometimes." She dropped her hand away, guarded. "And, if they don't work, how will you get out?"

"How would you?" Was she saying they didn't always work for her?

She took my hand and held it with hers—

An ally? Yeah right. What ally cracks your cheek bone and dislocates your shoulder. Lilia must be wrong. There's no way Hartmann is the POI.

"Mom don't always see the full picture," I said, trying to shove away the flash of Frei breaking in to rescue Renee who'd been tied up and beaten.

"No, which is why she is in Oppidum and you are here with us." She massaged my hand. Her neat cut nails pinky, clean, perfectly shaped. "We need you. You're a wonderful agent, even without your burdens. You're a big part of the team."

Whatever she was doing made me calmer and more restless all at once. "I froze when we were getting fired at."

"You helped me to get us out." She soothed circles over the pad of my thumb. I had deeper lines on my hand, scars from all the nicks and scrapes. "We all get scared."

"You do?" I didn't think she flickered in those situations. She seemed ready for them, ready to conquer them.

"Yes, but years of training helps us place it away and focus on the job." She flexed my thumb around, my fingers, peering up at me from under her eyebrows.

"But I didn't get years of training." Boot camp had been bad enough. Didn't want someone like Frei screaming at me for years. No way; nuh, uh.

"Exactly. Which is where I come in." She smiled up at me, a shimmer of Commander Black pulsing from her eyes, from her, in a wave of energy. "If I don't tell you something, I've done it for a reason. I know what you need and when you need to hear it."

"You kinda give me goosebumps when you do that," I mumbled, hoping she couldn't see the hairs on my arms prickling. Hairs felt like the field by Nan's cabin in a swirling wind.

"The massage?" She raised her blonde eyebrows. "Or me being your boss?"

"Both kinda." I shrugged, and we both looked at my arms, which had pimpled up so much you could see each bump.

She cocked her head and her aura fired its lightshow. "If that gives you such a buzz, wait until I run through my extraction plan."

Static fired through her fingertips, she jumped, and each of her plans fired through my mind. "Kinda got them already."

"Then if you don't get them right, I can make you run drills?" Her eyes filled with teasing.

"You two are the heroes . . . I ain't the image of a damsel but I sure feel like it." I frowned as her aura laughed, filling with pinks and golds. "It ain't funny."

"So why are you smiling, Lorelei?" She gave me an innocent look but her smile grew, her eyelashes fluttering with it—

Renee closed her eyes for a moment and listened to the birds, to the river. Somehow all the colors had flooded back. She'd not realized how grayed out it had been for so long but, outside Nan's cabin in the warm summer sun, with the people of Oppidum who'd turned out in force for Aeron's birthday, the colors, the sounds were so vibrant. Their complete change in attitude toward Aeron was unexpected but somehow, in spite of every wall there'd been between them, both those gathered and Aeron herself had found a way through.

"I thought heroes did the saving." Aeron pointed to her jaw as they sat around benches. Her chin was still swollen and purple, the wires still in place to help it heal. "And you were the one in that role." She looked down at herself—in a set of clothes that fit—and chuckled. "Not quite the image of a damsel, am I?"

Renee held in her laugh but it wriggled inside, threatening to burst out with joy, with relief. Was Aeron really going to join CIG? She'd been through so much to get her freedom and she'd give it up for her mother?

Aeron cocked her head, like she could feel the locked up chuckle, and poked her in the side. "Don't you go picturing me in any dress," she said with a scowl. "It ain't ever gonna happen."

Which only made Renee picture it . . . vividly. The bubble of laughter squirmed inside and she clamped her lips shut to keep it in. "Sure about that?"

Aeron narrowed her eyes. Brown eyes, so big, so full of affection for everything and everyone around her. "Crystal."

Laughter rumbled, bubbled, creeping up. It was too tempting to tease, even though she should be civilized. Lilia was watching . . . watching with a quiet smile on her face. Yeah, she could probably tell what Renee wanted to do . . . Ah, well. She handed Aeron a burger and squirted a flower pattern on the top. "Shame it wasn't pink."

Aeron pursed her lips at the burger. "Don't think I won't dunk you in the river."

Life, color, feeling seeped through every pore, every dulled part and flooded her senses. Like she'd been released, like . . . like the lights had come back on. She hadn't acted like this in so long . . . but . . . she hadn't felt free enough to. Yes, free . . . like . . . like she could breathe again.

She cleared her throat, Aeron eying her as if she knew exactly what was happening, as if she was the one who'd crashed through the prison walls. Speak . . . don't just stare.

"You'd never catch me." She squirted ketchup at Aeron and hit her in the cheek. Frei, who sat observing everything nearby, exchanged a glance with Lilia and raised an eyebrow. "Besides, as the hero I'd more likely dunk you."

Aeron put down her burger and wiped the ketchup off with her fingertip. "You think so?"

Renee backed away from the table, catching the smile of pure relief on Frei's face—yeah, Aeron had pulled her free. "Oh, I know so."

She ran a few feet and let Aeron catch her. Two big, strong arms wrapped around her, warmth, care reverberating all around her. She pretended to struggle, ignoring the pain shooting down her spine. "Aeron, now be nice," she warned. "You need me to watch your back, remember?"

She squirmed some more and Aeron hoisted her off the ground. "In that case maybe we should get you all healed up."

And she meant it. Renee could hear it like an undercurrent. Aeron knew she was in pain and she cared enough that she wanted to help. How? Why?

"You did not *let* me catch you," I managed, tears clogging my voice. I hoped I covered it by putting my hands on my hips. "I got longer arms."

"Uh, huh," Renee's eyes held the same twinkle they had then. She leaned against the counter, right foot over left calf, intentionally putting her vulnerability on show. I hadn't known how special that moment had been for her. I'd felt something back then but I hadn't known myself or my burdens enough to click it into place.

She raised an eyebrow and pushed off the stone counter, easing herself back—feet shoulder-width apart, her smile filled with challenge.

I stepped toward her without meaning to. Why'd it feel like she knew I'd do that? Who was the empath? "Quit teasing or . . . Or . . ."

She flicked her eyebrow again, giving me a sneaky half smile. "Or . . . ?"

I glanced around the kitchen, to the table. Like that would help, what was I gonna do, threaten to hurl fake fruit at her? "I'll . . . tell Frei you stole her hair gel."

Or wax, or whatever she cemented it in place with.

Renee sucked in a breath, splaying her fingers across her chest, across the St. Christopher's catching the overhead light. "Scared you can't compete, Lorelei?"

I darted forward—heavy on my feet; she darted out of reach—
light on hers. I scowled, being all dainty weren't fair. "You're
short, I'll squash you."

She rolled her finger, leading me into the living room through
the cream-colored hall. "I'm five seven. That's not short."

"For a short person." I grinned, glancing up at the high ceiling,
thick beams cutting across slatted oak planks overhead. Made me
feel kinda normal sized. Go figure.

"Really . . . let's see how useful those arms are in self-defense."
She rolled up the sleeves on her fluffy jumper, kicking the rug to
the side.

"Uh . . . coffee tables don't make safe places to pounce . . ." I
put the leather sofa between me and Renee and wagged my finger.
"Frei is coming in . . . We should make her dinner . . . ?"

"Like I'm falling for that." Renee shot forward, up the sofa,
over it, before I blinked. I caught her. She snuck in a quick hug
but I tussled. I knew what she was up to. I tried to dunk her back
down, grabbing her bare forearms—

*Aeron carried her to the river, and Renee wriggled like a
hooked fish, her pistol dug into her side and she could feel everyone
watching. She pushed away, making a show of unclasping Aeron's
strong hands and dropped her pistol into a mound of grass at the
side of the cabin, then summoned her best stern voice. "Aeron.
Don't you dare."*

*"Too late." Aeron readied herself to throw her but at that
angle it would hurt. Better to adjust . . . She spun in Aeron's arms
and dropped to her feet, wincing as her spine jarred. She grabbed
Aeron's arm, used her bodyweight, bent, legs taking the weight
and launched Aeron over her shoulder.*

Splash.

*Well worth the extra painkillers she'd need. She glanced at
Frei who rolled her eyes. So she was having fun, doctors warned
her she shouldn't but she didn't care. Fun was good. Aeron sat in
the cold water and spat out the river. Fun was a sweet Missourian
with a smile like sunshine—*

Renee dropped to her feet. I tried to dodge but she had my
hand, my arm, I was off balance—uh oh—I hurtled over the sofa
and clattered onto it with a thunk.

Right. Nothing changed.

She grinned down at me and I grabbed her arm then yanked her over onto me—

Aeron held out her hand, full big brown eyes on show. Renee shook her head and took it. Aeron grinned. Her hand snapped shut, vice-like. Her eyes shooting an unsaid, "got you."

Sneaky!

Aeron yanked her, she lurched off balance, and Aeron's hearty laughter filled the air.

Splash.

Renee surfaced, hair plastered across her face. Laughter breaking free from her lips.

I cuddled Renee close, checking over her spine even though I knew it was healed up. I didn't care that I sucked at self-defense, I had my own set of skills. Renee gave up protesting and burrowed in, sighing like she didn't do cwtches.

"Nice to see you both hard at work," Frei said in a bored tone from the doorway.

Renee jumped, muttered something under her breath then sighed and poked her head up over the tall armrest. "We are, Aeron is running through how *not* to do self-defense."

I craned my head around to see Frei leaning against the doorframe with a bored "uh huh," look on her face. Her aura was sniggering though—She had me on the floor a lot faster but I weren't gonna tell Renee that, they'd get competitive.

"My parents . . ." Frei shook her head like it was weird to say. "They're on their way for dinner."

"Ah that's nice." It was good to see them—

"To talk tactics not taste my pies, Lorelei." Frei gave me her best icy stare and pushed off the doorjamb.

More tactics? I groaned, pulled Renee back, and buried my head in her fluffy sweater. "Can't you just talk about normal stuff . . . like hacking and picking locks?"

Renee rolled to her feet and yanked me to mine, pushing me toward the kitchen. "Says you who discusses flashes and burdens with hers."

"That's over chocolate . . . it's different." I pulled her into me, trying to shove the irritating wriggle away—

"That was sneaky." She flicked her hair back and splashed Aeron. Okay, she'd let her do it. It wouldn't do for the whole of Oppidum to see too much of her martial arts skills.

"I thought you were a doctor," Aeron said with a smirk, her brown hair slicked back. "You said you could read minds."

Oh, that was just cheeky—she slapped the top of the water and sent it crashing into Aeron's face. "Maybe I let you do it."

Aeron snorted out her laugh. "I know you didn't."

Renee folded her arms, watching Frei pick her gun up from the side and slide it inside her jacket. "Thought you couldn't see anything about yourself?"

Aeron opened her mouth and closed it.

Renee heard the carefree laugh fall from her lips. How long had it been since she'd laughed, really laughed like that? How good it was to feel, to see, to be alive again. "Besides, I'm a hero and it's my job to know these things."

Aeron met her eyes as if she understood how locked up she'd been, as if she had felt what it was to be in that hollow place and what it was to break free. Aeron pulled her into a soggy hug, and Renee relaxed into it.

Then Aeron met her eyes, pure affection in a smile flowing from her. "I can't argue with that. You've proved beyond doubt that you're good at your job."

I smiled down at Renee, tears bubbling up again. Didn't think I'd helped much. She'd fought her way free but I was glad I could be a part of it. The wriggle tugged at me and I bent to kiss her on the forehead. Not sure why, it just felt right.

Frei muttered something about "boundaries," behind us—Like she weren't as into getting hugs.

"You are a hero to me," I whispered to Renee then dragged Frei under my other arm and felt her give me a sneaky squeeze in response. "Both of you are."

Chapter 4

HUBER AND STOSUR: Frei's parents and some power couple—even if they weren't technically a couple. Stosur was the original locksmith; an escaped slave of Sven's, and I didn't think any of us apart from Huber had seen her real face. She went through disguises like Mrs. Squirrel did nuts.

Huber came from a long line of slave traders. He was as stoic and sharp tongued as Frei, and they both had piercing eyes. Not quite the same shade but they sure sliced through a person.

Some genes.

Renee had made me go change for dinner. I didn't know why but it seemed like a big deal to Frei so I did as told. The stairs creaked and groaned under my weight and I hesitated at the bottom, feeling over the metal edges inset into the wood with my toes. I checked my shirt again, not sure why it was missing the top buttons. Every time I moved, I kept seeing it flap at me. Renee had left it on my bed so I guess they had shops for folks like me in Baltimore—the collar flapped again—sure, they had shops but maybe they'd ran out of buttons?

They had heard me trudging down so there was no way I could just go back up and climb out the window. I didn't really do group meals.

"Lorelei, stop wearing out my stairs and get in here," Frei shot at me.

I sighed and lumbered into the room. Renee was busy stoking the fire, some thought swirling around her, almost as if she was tempted to start swishing the metal pole around like a sword.

"Smart shirt . . . interesting choice, Black." Frei raised an eyebrow, her gaze on the screen. "Only way you could get her *not* to button it up?"

I poked my tongue out and took a seat on the me-sized sofa—I loved that sofa—and Renee glanced over her shoulder, a half grin on her face. "No idea what you mean—"

"Jäger hasn't been fussy about where he sells the slaves," Stosur said, striding into the living room from the kitchen.

Renee gave a surprised, "ooh."

I'd only just felt Stosur before I saw her, and Frei scowled at her laptop—Guess locksmith Senior must have bypassed the security.

"That's good to know," Renee said, wiping up the ash she'd dislodged onto the wood floor. "We need to get dirt on him. They'll talk quicker?"

Frei tapped at her laptop, her scowl deep—She wasn't impressed with her security.

"Theoretically, but he's got enough of a reputation that they're unlikely to give anything away easily," Stosur said, squeezing Frei's shoulder. "I have a key."

Frei glanced up. "But you still bypassed the cameras."

"Because I taught you how to set them up," Stosur said with a smile. Her current disguise was auburn hair in a bun; a nose flattened to one side; a wart on her right cheek complete with fuzz and her left eyelid drooping down.

"Still unimpressed," Frei muttered, pressing a button with venom. "Huber, it's open."

I looked to Renee who shook her head. "It'll bug her for hours."

"It won't be easy to sell to Kiwi," Huber said, striding in and bringing a load of snow with him as he wiped his shiny shoes on the mat. "He is a twitchy sort."

Did anyone in Frei's family just say, "Hi, how are you?"

"Kiwi?" Renee brandished the ash sweeper. "Because they're from New Zealand?"

"No, he owns a company that imports the fruit," Huber said, his tone as bored as Frei's. His pants had creases down the middle of them though like CIG had tried getting me to do in boot camp. Frei had taken the iron away after I blew it and the electricity for the entire residential block.

"Oh." Renee smiled and scooped up the ash. "So, how do we gain his trust?"

"We let him spy on us," came out of my mouth. There it went again. It was always firing off without telling me.

"Why would he do this?" Huber eyed me. His aura skulked back like he wanted to keep me from seeing too much.

"Locks has a reputation herself," Stosur said in a tone like Nan used when I was being dense. "Anyone who has heard of Caprock closing will want to catch a glimpse of her."

"All the more reason to block their view," Huber shot back, sounding a lot like my dad when he got worked up. Maybe it was a dad thing although I doubted Huber's underwear had polka dots.

"What kind of spying?" Renee asked me. She was ready to veto and maybe note down the inflections in Huber and Stosur's voices. She loved languages.

"Selling," I said—or my mouth did. Why'd it never let me in on the ideas *before* it fired off?

"A dummy trade?" Stosur tapped her lip. "I like it."

"I don't," Huber muttered, standing opposite her like they would charge at each other. "She could be targeted."

"Jäger will be ready to pounce," Renee said, stoking the fire again. The flames jumped with a swooshing noise, casting an orange glow over her face. She was thinking about something but I couldn't see it. She could still block me reading her sometimes whether or not it was intentional.

"Sure, but I'll know if he is and Frankenfrei has got her trusty protection team." I grinned at Frei who was half-listening, half-trying to figure out how Stosur had snuck in.

"They're better than any mistress," Frei mumbled, tapping away, long fingers splayed out across the keys. "Get us in, we'll do the rest."

"You may have knowledge in some things but trading is an art that takes years of honing." Huber lifted his chin, still opposite Stosur, still with feet shoulder-width apart and hands at his side. "It takes subtlety."

Stosur raised her bushy eyebrow and looked him up and down. "I thought it took money and slaves?"

Huber blurted out a laugh. "That too."

Renee walked over to the chair opposite me. Maybe she was trying to get them to move before they started a self-defense session? Why couldn't I read her? She crossed her legs and studied the smudged ash on her fingertips then looked up at Huber. "Perhaps if you give us pointers?"

Huber flicked his gaze over her. He still wasn't convinced she wouldn't turn him into the authorities. I wasn't neither. When Renee was set on something it was hard to change her mind.

"It's not some high school sport," he muttered.

Stosur cocked her head like she'd seen a weakness. "Not a man I thought had ego issues."

Huber straightened his tie. "There is a lot of estrogen in this room."

Frei shut her laptop with a snap. "Huber, you are rarely useful." She gave him a withering look. "But if you're going to take up space, you may as well share your . . . expertise."

Yowch. I winced, Renee smirked, and Huber clapped his hands together, delight dancing in his aura. "Prickly as always but why would I bother?"

"Because otherwise I'll steal your car and sell it for parts," Frei shot back. She stowed her laptop on the table, got to her feet, and stood in the space between her parents.

He pursed his lips like he might tackle her too. "It's worth half a million."

What kind of car was it? I looked to Renee who rolled her eyes.

"I know, I made you the money to buy it." Frei looked him up and down and nodded to Stosur whose aura was sniggering for her, along with a lot of affection shimmering and some pride there too. Yeah, dad and daughter were two peas on a plate.

"Quite." Huber walked to Frei's side and gave her a smile.

Were they going somewhere? Were we meant to follow?

"Dinner," Renee said, getting up as Frei and her parents strode off down the corridor in silence. They looked like they were gonna parade or maybe duel or maybe both.

I joined Renee and shook my head. "And I thought my folks were crazy."

A slave owner, a locksmith, and a general . . . The Frei family were something else.

Chapter 5

IN THE SHADOW of Blackbear mountain, nestled alongside the river and in a clearing amongst the tall white-dusted trees, snow swirled around a stone building and its grinding waterwheel. Inside, Lilia Lorelei hunched over in the rustic-looking kitchen, her face illuminated by the oven light. She tucked her long dark hair out of her face and muttered to herself as she pulled out a batch of cookies.

She sniffed then sighed. They smelled delicious but, however hard she tried, she could *not* make them smell like Nan's. She placed them on the cooling tray, put her hands on her hips, and tucked the towel into her apron. It felt good to be in Nan's cabin, to hear the rumble of the wheel, to feel the essence of the love that filled it . . . and somehow, it didn't feel the same without Nan's cookies. She pulled her mouth to the side. Ah, well, the girls . . . and Eli . . . would enjoy them.

"Smells like chocolate chip with a hint of cinnamon," Nan said, leaning against the counter, her eyes twinkling as she sniffed the air.

"Got it in one." Lilia smiled, tucking a loose strand behind her ear. "You hear about my interesting mixing experience?" She rubbed at the bump on her head.

"Yup. Shorty and the girls are doing great but they're gonna need some old hands." Nan wafted the steam from the cookies at her nose.

"I was thinking of sending in Bess." Lilia tensed, waiting for the scowl. Nan wasn't best pleased with Lilia's older sister.

"You'd be right." Nan glanced at her and waved it off. *"She may be wayward but she knows when she's needed."*

"Aeron loves her," Lilia said, hoping she was hiding her smile. Nan couldn't stay mad for long and they both knew full well she was guarding Bess as much as any of them.

"Shorty is young an' impressionable."

Lilia leaned her hip to the counter. "Uh huh."

Nan chuckled, her white hair bobbing about. *"I got to admit, Bess was ready an' willin' when you called."*

"It wasn't her fault I joined CIG." They'd had this discussion before but Nan had been angry back then, or so she'd thought. Lilia understood now it was more worry than anger. "I had to."

"I know but she went an' worried me first." Nan tutted like she was still stewing. *"An' not to mention she went through all that pain and never once let me help her."*

Lilia pulled off her apron and went to her cell phone on the table. "Grief does funny things to people, Mamma, you know that." She couldn't bear the thought of Eli getting hurt let alone going through all Bess had, being widowed three times.

"Does. Now, tell her Icy's momma gonna need to fix her face up for this one." Nan chuckled. *"An' tell her . . ."* She sighed. *"Tell her she ain't too old to get hollered at for leading young men astray."*

Lilia raised an eyebrow. "Dare I ask?"

"That fella Grimes . . . She's wriggled into his affections without even tryin'. Woman her age . . ." Nan muttered under her breath but Lilia laughed. Bess did have an uncanny knack of getting people to fall in love with her. *"Tiddles is snoozing with your papa, I got to get a picture of this . . ."* Nan's presence faded and Lilia looked up from her phone. Did they take pictures in Etherspace? She shook her head. Aeron and her names for things, she was so much like Nan sometimes.

"Twig, if you call somebody, it's polite to speak," Bess's detached voice said.

Lilia jumped and looked at the phone. Right. She'd pressed call. "Sorry. Mamma was here." She switched ears. "The girls are going to need you to dust off some of your extracurricular skills. Mamma suggests you ask Stosur for help?"

Bess clicked her tongue. "Turnin' on my hunk of junk." Her computer, which was the latest Frei and Jessie special. Bess loved her gadgets even if she pretended she didn't. "Icy left a message, said that they need to lure out a chump . . ." She muttered under her breath much like Nan. "If you ask me that guy needs—"

"Pickle juice?" Lilia said, holding in her laugh as she was hit by an icy breeze. No doubt Bess was getting the same but she'd discount it, at least on the surface.

"Twig, I'm on my way." Bess muffled the headset as a male voice started chatting. "No . . . the cat feed is in the cupboard, man."

"Grimes?" Bess worked fast.

"Easy, Twig. He's here helping me look after all those strays you sent my way." Bess muffled the speaker again. The kids from Caprock needed somewhere to hide out, somewhere safe and who better than Bess? "That's the stuff for the litter tray." Her tone was almost official but a chuckle warmed it. "Worthington and Samson would have clawed you for that."

"Make a change," Grimes muttered in the background. "Next I'll be in an apron."

"Hey, don't give me ideas," Bess shot back. "It'd look cute on you."

Grimes cleared his throat.

"Anyway," Lilia said, trying not to laugh. "You have to get movin'."

"Yeah, yeah, Twig. I may be wrinkly but I ain't slow." Usual retort to any prompting. "Now, I got to drill Jed and Miroslav 'cause they ain't gonna be a lot of use if Grimes faints."

"Faints?" She had to hear this.

"If Jed Jr. decides he wants to be a free peanut." Bess sighed. She meant one of the teenagers, Miranda, giving birth. "You weren't this dozy before you started baking cookies again."

Lilia cocked her head. "How'd you know I was baking cookies?"

"You're still tryin' to crack Momma's recipe too, I'll bet. Now I got to go, got men to heckle." Bess blew a kiss and hung up.

Lilia put her hands on her hips and looked out at the snow. She was the one who saw things so how come Bess could see through her so well? She closed her eyes, soothed by the groaning of the waterwheel. Maybe she was just predictable? She liked baking. There was nothing wrong with liking baking. She opened her eyes and pursed her lips. She could crack it, she could. She tapped her finger to her lips. Maybe the cookies needed more cinnamon?

Chapter 6

WE HAD DINNER around the round kitchen table like normal folks did. Frei and her parents chatted like everybody else did, Renee fussed about getting drinks and filling up the bowls for extra helpings . . . and I sat there shaking.

I had issues with eating next to other people. Even being back at home with my family had sent me scurrying off to my room. Meal times in Serenity had scarred me and I couldn't shake them off.

It didn't help Renee was sitting away from me so I had Huber's energy to deal with and by dessert, my mood rumbled inside, bubbling higher and higher.

"Owners don't dine in kitchens often?" Renee said in a dry tone. Her energy fizzed. She could see I was struggling and was itching to help.

"No, formal affairs. Seating arranged accordingly," Huber said between mouthfuls. Hadn't noted him down as an ice cream and Jell-O man but he attacked it like Frei did popsicles.

"Owner in the middle, mistress on his left, wife on his right," Stosur said like it had been ingrained. "Sometimes, in large parties, an owner will only bring one." She smiled at me, trying to reassure me. "Normally the mistress."

My hands shook harder. I just had to keep calm enough to get through dessert and I could find space: quiet, alone space.

"Why not the wife?" Renee asked like she knew but, as everyone was watching me, I guessed it was something to say.

"The mistress does the protecting." Huber looked up from scoffing but he sounded as on edge as me. "Wives are a troublesome addition."

Renee laughed a strained laugh, her gaze on me. "I didn't get around to marrying Abby but, that at least, we agree on."

Huber chuckled, not the arrogant laugh I'd heard so often in Frei's memories, but a genuine one. "Whether you've married them or not, they are *all* troublesome."

Renee lifted her dessert spoon to him.

Stosur and Frei raised their eyebrows.

"When are men different?" Frei muttered, wagging her spoon at him. "They cause far more trouble."

"More?" Stosur asked, smiling at Frei. She knew how much Frei had been in love with Fahrer, a slave Huber owned. "You say this because . . . ?"

"Women assume they are right," Frei muttered, avoiding the question. Huber didn't know Frei had been in love with Fahrer. "But men *know* they are."

Stosur, Huber, and Renee laughed but I picked up my spoon and a cloud of anger rolled through me.

"Will Kiwi be as arrogant?" Renee asked as she studied me. "And does he have a real name?"

"Yes," Stosur said, her Jell-O wobbling on her spoon as she paused, eying me. "On both counts but it's better we focus on the face he is presenting . . . for now."

I pushed back my chair not sure why I was so mad but I couldn't stay there. My knees wobbled even though I was sitting. "I need air."

Stosur motioned to my bowl. "Don't you want the rest of your dessert?"

"Back off." I sprang to my feet, anger thudded through me, and I gripped the spoon, knuckles white.

Stosur didn't flinch, neither her nor her aura showed surprise.

"Aeron, put the spoon down," Renee said in a quiet voice. "It's the cutlery, that's all."

I threw the spoon away from me, my anger evaporated and cold sweat gushed over me. "I'm sorry," I mumbled. "I didn't mean nothin' by it."

Stosur smiled. "It's okay." She reached out and touched my hand—

Young. Too young to speak. Bike, small, shiny, big wheels, logo twinkling in the sun. He was handsome: blue eyes like a cloudless sky. His hands were warm as he held her shoulders, pushing her around the patio. "You can do it, that's a good girl."

I pulled my hand away as Stosur rubbed at hers.

Huber frowned at me. "Explain."

"It's a memory," Frei said like he should know. "It doesn't normally 'cause sparks."

Stosur shook her hand off with a soft laugh. "Some memory?"

I sighed. How did I explain? Huber was looking at me like I'd grown another nose. "You were on a bike. I think your dad was pushing you? Some fancy place anyhow."

"Can't be mine then," Stosur said, sadness in her eyes. "I was born a slave."

I looked to Renee.

"House matron?" Renee asked, nodding at me, her energy trying to send comfort my way.

"No. Mine was missing her front teeth and had a moustache." Stosur shook her head. "Those were the days when owners had mistresses and matrons in the household . . ."

"Yes, was more economical to make the mistress earn her money," Huber said like he was happy with the idea.

Stosur tutted at him.

"I need air," I mumbled again. What did I say? Flashes made me jittery and with my own jitteriness, I was close to wobbling over to the door.

"Aeron, we need to work out how we're going to tackle Kiwi," Renee whispered, smiling a warm smile at me.

Reassurance or not, I weren't staying at the table no longer. "He's got a thing for Frei. He don't need much luring just tell him she'll be there."

I turned and hurried out; out of the kitchen and out of the house. The cold hit so hard as I scurried across the yard that I had to stop. My throat ached, my chest stung.

"Coat," Renee said, catching up to me. "You'll freeze."

I took it off her, my hands shaking, and fumbled to put it on. "It ain't getting easier."

She sighed. "Give yourself a break. If you find it hard around your own family, it's not surprising you needed space." She bumped my hip, zipping her coat. "You did well getting that far."

"It was her memory," I said, fiddling about with the zipper. Couldn't grip it. Hands too cold.

"I know." She tapped my hands and zipped up the coat for me. "But she wasn't lying if I'm correct."

"Yeah, she believes she was born a slave . . . I ain't so sure." I shoved my hands in my pockets, puffing out my breath and making mist clouds. "This guy loved her so much it hurt . . . kinda like the feeling when my dad lets his guard slip."

"We'll let Urs know when they've gone." Renee looked up at the clear sky, stars twinkling away. "I used to camp out all the time when I was a kid . . . and when I was older."

"Yeah, with your dad and brother?" They were never far from her heart. I knew she was sharing to calm me but I loved it. I loved hearing about her.

"I found family dinners hard . . . well . . . impossible when I lost them." She shook away some thought. "So I'd sneak up the mountain just to be close to them. Used to drive my mom nuts."

I pulled her under my arm. "This is my version."

"Of?" She cuddled in.

"Making myself feel better," I mumbled, soaking up the warmth from her heart as much as through her coat.

She burrowed in and gave me a squeeze. "Likewise."

Chapter 7

STOSUR DROVE US into Baltimore to use one of the warehouses for our dummy slave trade. We passed by the row houses, the mansions, and out to a warehouse that had once housed some kind of food if my twitching nostrils were correct, something spicy. At least it had food and other wares whoever owned it wanted to keep from prying eyes. I took in the same half windows—like the building had sunken into the ground—that signaled somewhere slaves were kept, worked in, and were sold.

"It's harder for them to use the places now," Stosur said, her focus on the road. "With so many derelict or abandoned, it's more difficult to cover up the machines working."

We stopped at a set of lights and a huge water rat looked up from foraging. He met my eyes through the window, sniffed at the air as if to say, "You're not from 'round here," and went back to his task.

I turned back to inside and watched Renee check her pistol. She loaded bullets not tranquilizer darts which were still on the clip on her belt. She slid the pistol into the holster strapped to her thigh and slid her skirt back down, then she pulled out a smaller pistol from her back, loaded a few darts and placed it away, covering it with the bottom of her low cut top then flicked her eyebrow when she caught me looking.

"He knows we're not local," I mumbled.

"That is one huge rodent," she said with a curious smile.

"Some cities have cats, some have those," Frei said, her tone bored as she checked over a set of tools in a leather roll. "You aren't going to let Lorelei pick up more pets?"

Renee scowled. "I didn't let her, she does what she likes." She sighed and pulled her mouth to the side. "You try arguing with two Lorelei ladies set on something."

I nodded. Weren't worth it. Aunt Bess loved furries as much as me.

"Task?" Frei shot at me, in full Frankenfrei mode.

"To fool some fruity guy into believing we sell slaves." I couldn't manage military but that was my attempt.

"Group dynamic?" Renee said, all Commander Black.

"Er . . . Frei steals stuff and we follow her around?" I didn't know. I'd wandered out to find the left over Jell-O and ice cream but Huber had eaten it all.

"Lorelei, unless you want to run the field when we get back?" Renee fixed me with a look.

The field was cold. I didn't want to run in no cold. "Frei and I are business partners. Same cover as Caprock. I'm Alex Riley, you're Roberta Worthington and Frei is Locks."

Frei rolled up the leather toolkit. "Who is Renee to you?"

"No idea." I shrugged. I didn't. In Caprock I'd told Jäger we were kinda involved and in Huber's, Renee had kept to that cover. "She's there to look good?"

Stosur roared with laughter. "I like that . . . that's good enough for me."

Renee poked me, pursing her lips. She had that pale lipstick on that Roberta Worthington wore.

"Your role?" Frei said, trying not to smirk.

"To buy slaves off somebody . . . and er . . . that's it?" I really should have paid more attention but this stuff just went over my head.

Renee shook her head at me, narrowing her eyes. She had dark eye-paint on and stuff that made her eyelashes black. I liked that they were blonde. What was wrong with blonde? "We'll talk about this."

Sounded like I weren't gonna enjoy that chat.

"Just remain in cover," Frei said with a cheeky smile. "If you think *I* drilled you, you haven't seen Renee taking boot camp."

I shuddered. That sounded like fun.

DIRT, DUST, AND the rank eggy stench of something gone off filled the air. It was so cold, biting cold, that I felt like my nose was gonna fall off as I trudged into the warehouse.

Inside, the scent of some kind of oil coated the inside of my nostrils and mixed with all the stink from outside until my gut curled. Renee and Frei had sent me in alone. I didn't know why but they were confident I could handle it. I guessed that meant buying slaves? Why'd they think I could handle buying slaves? Wasn't Frei the owner or something?

I never remembered this kinda stuff so hoped whoever was lurking at the back of the warehouse could tell me what I was meant to be doing.

"You coming out or just loitering?" I muttered, trying not to show how much I was shivering.

"You're alone?" The guy answered. He sounded and felt uneasy. He had a nervous edge about him that rattled my overloaded senses.

"Unless you seeing double." I folded my arms. "I ain't gonna waste my time with cowards."

He crept out of his hiding place—bald head, beard, gun bigger than needed. He looked nothing like he did out of disguise. Fahrer had been the guy Frei was head over hind in love with but I didn't think she'd have been as into beards.

"I'm no coward," Fahrer muttered, sloshing through a puddle of something. It didn't sound like water, looked more like oil.

"No, but a lifetime of being told you ain't worth nothin' makes you act like it." I looked him up and down like I didn't much care for him, ignoring whatever was fluttering about in the rusted up girders overhead. "And the reason you can't so much as look at me."

"I know my place." He turned and nodded in the direction of a black car. It opened and a huge guy got out with a bushy gray beard and energy I knew so well I had to hide my grin. Aunt Bess made a mean looking guy.

"You got something I wanna see?" I grunted like I didn't want to wrap her in a hug. Man, I'd missed her.

"Depends if you have anything I want." Her voice was deep, the accent Canadian—because that was the word that flashed in my mind—but she sounded French to me. What did I know? Maybe there were French folks in Canada too.

Aunt Bess scanned the warehouse behind me. "I'm here to meet Locks."

"She'll be here." I hoped. Would she? Where was she? Where was Renee and what was I meant to be doing with Aunt Bess in man-guise? I looked up at brown smeared windows, some cracked, hoping it'd make me look unbothered and give me thinking space.

Were there tactics for buying slaves? Huber had said it was an art, that it took subtlety, so I guessed, "give me people to order around," wasn't gonna work.

"You didn't say your name," Aunt Bess said, moving closer. Her eyes weren't the brown we shared usually but a pale blue that matched her real pale skin. How'd she managed to change the color of her skin? Cool.

"You didn't say yours." I jutted out my chin, hoping I looked rough and tough.

Aunt Bess's eyes hardened and she pulled her thick brown coat aside enough to show one big rifle but her aura waved about like she was saying hello. "Mladenovic." She pointed to Fahrer. "This is Garcia."

"Riley," I shot back, folding my arms like guns didn't give me the 'eebies. "But most folks call me Samson."

Her aura wriggled with laughter. "I've heard a lot about you."

"Most of it is true." I tried to act all bored and nonchalant and looked up again, whatever furry that was flapping up there was mad. I weren't sure if it was crazy mad or just mad at us for trespassing on their snoozing time. "Some of it ain't even close to showing my temper." I met her eyes. "I don't like waiting."

"Calm," Frei said, striding in—turtle neck on, tight black jeans, boots, and that jacket she wore like armor. She looked every bit the hardened criminal and nodded to Aunt Bess, ignoring Fahrer and his nervous twitching. "Mladenovic, I've left your fee where you wanted it."

I heard the echo of heels on concrete and my jaw unhinged as Renee swept in: Long coat, shorter than decent skirt, heels higher than was safe, and a top low enough I could see lace. How come she weren't freezing?

"Good." Aunt Bess spotted her and I swore she was thinking about telling her she'd catch a cold but instead, she cocked her head. "Shame I didn't see you before. I would have raised my fee."

Renee winked at her but I didn't miss her gaze track every crevice, her posture ready for action, her aura like steel.

I grabbed her 'round the waist and pulled her into me, giving Aunt Bess my best glare. "She ain't for sale."

Renee ran her hand over my stomach and I tried not to flinch at her tickly nails. Not Renee's neatly cut ones but Worthington's long manicured ones. False, like every part of the cover. It bugged me. Her covers always bugged me.

"Shame," Aunt Bess said, her aura radiating love and reassurance. "I could make a lot of money with her."

She was giving me a pointer. My cover: Alex Riley was in it for the money. How'd I get myself out of that? "She got skills I appreciate more."

She did? I did? Huh?

Frei raised an eyebrow, slinking onto one hip, and looked over Aunt Bess's car with disinterest but her energy fired a warning at me. I'd gotten myself in a pickle . . . again.

"And what are they?" Aunt Bess looked intrigued but she sent more reassurance my way, like every part of her was saying, "You can do this, kid."

"Yeah, there ain't a lot of folks who pay me enough attention and don't irritate me." I gave the kind of smile that send goosebumps up and down my arms. "It takes a lot of skill to stay on my . . . better side." I laughed the kind of laugh that made me shudder.

Renee's hand stilled. Well, I'd succeeded in freaking myself and Renee out, would Kiwi buy that?

Aunt Bess's energy swirled around me, giving me some kind of energy hug. "So I've heard." She turned back to Renee—who was trying not to stare at me—and her phone went off. "You were good to your word, Locks. I look forward to working with you again." She nodded to Fahrer who went to the car and ripped open the door. Three people got out but I didn't have one iota who they were.

I glanced at Frei.

"Alex?" Frei asked, texting on her phone like she was bored. "What do you think?"

I shoved Renee forward. She'd know what to do, she paid attention. "She can check them out. Don't know where they've been."

Was I classed as an owner? Frei was and she'd said . . . I was her business partner? Yeah, that sounded good so . . . Renee was a . . . matron, right? I hoped so. Was that the same as a mistress? Either way, Huber wouldn't have gone checking slaves over, would he?

Renee flashed a dazzling smile over her shoulder and strode

over to the slaves. They were trying to keep their chins up but they were shivering, maybe shaking, fear looming over them as Renee circled, pulled at them, her eyes cold and hard. "Good quality even if this one needs less to eat and more work." She pinched the fat on one slave's arm.

I nodded like I was happy we were buying people, and Frei clicked her fingers. A car screeched into the warehouse. Stosur—in another disguise—got out and Renee took the kids over. Stosur frisked them in a way that the guards in Serenity would have been proud of and shoved them into the back.

"Nice doing business with you," Aunt Bess said, turning back to her car. "When the blonde loses favor, Samson, I'm happy to talk."

I nodded, stepping around some broken parts of machinery. "If you got that much money."

Stosur, Renee, Frei, and Aunt Bess all fired enough, "you got yourself in a pickle," energy at me that I had to fight not to tense up.

"High value?" Aunt Bess asked.

"Nah." I turned away, wanting to run over and hug her and really wanting to impress her too. "I just prefer to have fun."

The tone in my voice made my hairs prickle again. I'd spent way too much time with unhinged folks.

"You'd make a mess of her?" Aunt Bess grunted.

"Depends how well she keeps me entertained. Besides, I can clean up after myself," I shot back, clicked at Renee and then at the car. Renee followed like I did it all the time, like she didn't mind.

Aunt Bess laughed. "Shame, when you train them so well." She knew that unlike Worthington, Renee would have floored me for clicking at her. In fact, I'd have floored myself first.

I shrugged, suppressing a shudder. The place was coated with pain, worry, hurt. Aunt Bess nodded and got into her car, Fahrer followed suit, and they screeched off.

I pointed to our car, and Frei did the same but I glanced around the warehouse. It was a place slaves were sold regularly. Its essence: terrified kids, angry slave owners, hostile guards, dirty, grimy, merciless industry, now abandoned and hollow. I got in the car just to shut it out and we screeched off.

Being in those places made me feel so blessed I'd only been locked up in prison. I glanced back at the shattered windows, the stench still lingering. At least you could get released from prison.

THE STREETS BUZZED with rush hour traffic and sleet peppered the windows as we drove back through the city. I wasn't sure who the three slaves were so I kept quiet even though I wanted to help them, to tell them we'd keep them safe. Undercover was exhausting.

"Text came through," Frei said in her usual emotionless tone from beside me. "Kiwi wants to talk."

Stosur glanced in the mirror at us—guessing that wasn't normal.

"He interested in merchandise?" Renee asked in her fake English accent.

"We shall see." Frei looked to me. "Slaves will join the others. If they are useful, we'll keep them."

I could feel that the three slaves were hoping they weren't going to get sold for parts. Again, I wanted to reassure them but Frei, Renee, and Stosur were saying nothing so that must mean they needed to keep it from them until they were safe.

"Whatever, as long as I don't have to touch them." I looked out of the window so I didn't have to see their worries. We were on some big busy street and I didn't get how so many folks could be crammed in cars waiting at lights . . . and why did they have to honk? The light was on red. What did they want the person in front to do? Where were they gonna go anyway? Stosur cut across the traffic, through the red into a side street—guess they could have done that.

"Pull over here," Frei snapped at Stosur.

"Yes, Miss Locks." Wow, Stosur sounded like Fahrer talking to Huber. She pulled us next to a familiar-looking sleek car.

I got out without knowing why, then went to Frei's side, checked the street and nodded, then pulled open her door and guided her over to the sleek car.

Renee got out of her side, tapped the top of Stosur's car which screeched off as I ushered Frei inside her car; once again I checked the street and nodded to Renee who nodded back as she reeled in something she'd used to check under the car.

We both got in. Frei hit the start button, the car rumbled into life, and we screeched off, darting out in front of two cars.

I rubbed my head. Okay, I'd been a part of that but I didn't have one iota what I'd been doing.

"Perfect extraction, Lorelei," Renee said from the passenger seat, her tone back to the warm lilt I loved. "Observations?"

"Two cars at the bottom of the street. Pulled into motion. We have a tail," I said then blinked a few times. We did?

"I agree, orders?" She looked to Frei.

Frei smiled at her and slid on her aviators. "Let's see how well they keep up."

She floored it.

I clung onto the handle, while trying to click in my seatbelt. Needed one of them safety bars they had in theme parks not a belt.

"Stosur will debrief the slaves?" Renee asked, checking over her shoulder, gaze hard, focused.

"Yes, she likes to observe them first. Gives her an idea if she can help them." Frei switched lanes and zipped through a red.

"And the contact?" Renee pulled something out of the glove compartment, looked to Frei who nodded, and lowered the window.

"Not procedure." Frei slowed the car. "On three."

"Three," Renee said and threw whatever was in her hand out the window. "He our tail?"

"No, they're Jäger's men," I mumbled, turning to see a load of smoke fill the street. The cars following swerved and one hit a parked car. "Yowch."

"He'll be watching the city," Frei said and yanked up the handbrake.

I clattered into the door as we screeched into a turn. She hit the gas, and I got flung back into the seat as we hurtled down an alleyway.

"Good thing I ain't had lunch," I mumbled.

Renee frowned into the mirror. "Tail is still wagging."

Huh? It was?

"Blow their tires," Frei ordered.

Renee pulled a box out from under her seat and clicked a gun together in seconds. She loaded it and leaned out the window. "On your order."

"Fire at will," Frei said, swerving to avoid a dumpster.

Renee sighed. "Unless you want me to hit the radiator?"

"Your head works better attached," Frei shot back.

I turned to look at the car. There were two guys and one was equally weapon-heavy.

Renee fired.

The car lurched to the right, clipped a dumpster and the guy with the gun had to hold on not to fall out of the window.

Renee fired again.

The car lurched back to the left, hit a load of trash cans that flew up into the air and crashed onto the hood. Sparks shot out of the sides and the car skidded to a stop.

"Hostiles getting out," Renee called.

I ducked forward, pulled her darts in a gun clip from her belt, and held them up for her. She smiled, ejected the bullet clip into my hands, and rammed the darts into place. "On your order."

"Fire at will," Frei shot at her, slowing as we headed toward where the alley met a busy road.

Renee fired.

First guy gripped his arm, dropped his gun, and slumped to the ground.

Renee fired again.

The second guy pulled the dart from his thigh, lifted his gun, then fell forward in a heap.

"As expected," Frei said as I pulled Renee back in. So she could do it herself but I didn't like her hanging out of windows at high-speed. "Any more tails, Lorelei?"

I shook my head as Renee broke apart the rifle, ejected the clip, and stowed everything away. My hands were trembling as I sat back. I hoped Renee couldn't see. Didn't know if I was trembling with adrenaline or awe.

"Nice work, Lorelei," Renee said, beaming at me.

"You did the shooting and Frei did the driving . . . I just clung to the seat." I shrugged. They were the soldiers and I really did need safety bars.

"You handled the dummy trade efficiently," Frei said, meeting my gaze in the mirror as we headed onto a road, leaving the city behind us. "It made us look good."

"It did?"

Renee nodded. "You have a way undercover." She exchanged a glance with Frei. "Unnerving."

"Freaked myself out." I rubbed the back of my neck. "Don't get why I gotta say all that mean stuff."

"Training," Frei said, as she had a load of times. "Trust it."

I shrugged. "I trust you guys, that good enough?"

Renee smiled at me, and Frei roared us down the road. I looked out at the snow-covered fields. It was snowing here unlike the sleet back in the city. Big white flakes swept at the windows, swirled through the air, making it hard to see anything. The lights from cars were bright against the wintery evening light.

I did trust them, even if I didn't love them so much, it was hard *not* to trust them. Yeah, they made some team.

Chapter 8

DEEP IN THE isolated countryside, in a barren field blanketed with drifting snow, Ursula Frei took a long slow breath. Her lungs burned, her fingers numb, her nose forming icicles.

"Again," she grunted out, perspiration dripping from her nose.

She and Renee dipped into another set of push-ups. Renee's fitness had improved—Frei glanced at her—even if her lips were trembling from the strain.

"You were quiet at dinner." Renee groaned, holding the push-up, one arm behind her back.

"I was re-running the dummy trade." She couldn't understand why Kiwi only wanted to talk. Talking meant he still was unsure; talking was for unknown buyers. He knew her. She'd stolen from him countless times.

"She concerns me." Renee's gaze was locked on the mist covering the tips of the treetops in the distance. Her hair was tucked up under her cold weather gear but strands feathered her sweaty face.

"Why?" Frei asked and gave a curt nod.

They sprang to their feet and sprinted through the thick snow. Another five minutes at full speed then five hundred more push-ups.

"She coped with Serenity, she can cope with undercover," Frei said.

Renee contorted her face as she tried to keep up. Frei was only at two thirds her full speed but Renee liked to feel competitive.

"Coped?" Renee puffed out, cheeks inflating. "You think throwing palettes off rooftops and locking herself away for months is coping?"

"That was a response to change and grief." Frei watched Renee's body position and the angle of her spine. It was a habit since Renee had been hurt but she was healed now—all thanks to Aeron.

Renee pushed harder, her breath steaming from her in clouds. "And being locked in a situation she couldn't control."

"Which makes her human." Frei checked her watch. A couple more minutes to sprint but Renee's body was struggling.

"Yeah, but other humans don't blow up electrics, do they?" Renee glanced at her, her face rosy, healthy, good to see. "And I'd never put anyone who had been locked up so long in her position."

"Why?" Frei upped the pace, her body responding. She'd run in worsening pain for years but it was gone now—again, thanks to Aeron.

Renee followed even though she was panting. She was good in the cold weather conditions. Years and years of training had honed her, something they both could count on—Frei checked the heart monitor on her wrist and scrolled through to Renee's readings—Elite, yes, but she was no locksmith.

"She's institutionalized, Urs," Renee spluttered out, her shoulders rising. "She got cranky when you made her skip breakfast." She gasped and grunted as she dodged around a fallen tree. "And one minute she can't concentrate on the briefs, the next she's pulling off cover like she's been doing it for years."

Aeron was unpredictable, they both knew that. Her moods were up and down, her focus either zoned out or heightened like the soldier they knew lay underneath. She was coping with the situation in the only way she could, the way she would have in Serenity.

"She keeps hiding away . . . I don't know what she's thinking," Renee mumbled, her movements more pronounced with fatigue. "Then there was dinner. How do we control her reading the cutlery?"

"It's part of her. It works with the cover." Frei upped the pace again, enjoying the feel of her muscles really working. It was hard to feel it stuck in an office.

"And what if we get an invitation?" Renee slowed as her body reached the point of collapse. "What if she acts like she did inside?"

"Play the violin?" Frei hopped over a mound of something . . . whatever it was, it shouldn't have been there.

"No." Renee stopped, threw her hands behind her head, and took gaping breaths. "Withdraw, flip, trash the dinner party." She bent over, her entire body shaking. "That kind of thing."

Frei halted, checking all the readings—Renee had improved,

adding to her personal best by at least a half. "It works with the cover."

Renee glared up from under her eyebrows, her blonde hair plastered to her dripping brow. "Only if she doesn't resort to telling the owner things about himself she shouldn't and couldn't know. Do you want him freaked out?" She shook her head, cheeks rosy. "Imagine the value they'd see in that."

She had a point. "That's where you come in."

Renee gripped her knees, spitting as she tried to control her nausea. Frei didn't need burdens to know every move Renee made. She'd driven her to collapse enough times. "Because you think me pretending to have a relationship with her will help?"

"It's not a relationship." Frei squeezed an energy sachet into her mouth and handed one to Renee.

"But she'll still get the brunt of all my feelings on top of everyone else's." She smiled, hope in her eyes, then stared up at the sky and let out a long groan. "It'll overload her."

"You said she can't feel anything to do with herself. She'll be fine." Frei checked the levels again—Renee would pass out if she kept standing.

"I doubt that'll work if I'm throwing myself at her, will it?" Renee shook her head as if to clear the wooziness and staggered to the side.

"Still an hour to go." Frei knew Renee would be lucky to wobble over to the chopper she'd just called.

Renee sucked in a few long breaths and straightened up, blinking. "Ready to go again."

Frei doubted it. "Aeron will cope."

"Urs, I think . . ." Renee shrugged, that half-smile creeping back. "I think Aeron is . . . well . . ." She rubbed her hands over her face. "Well . . . she's paying more . . . attention." She blinked again as if shaking off the symptoms of her blood pressure plummeting. "Which is distracting her. She needs to be focused."

Frei hid her smile by looking in the direction they were supposed to be heading. Renee would remember the route, she'd have memorized every detail. "She'll deal with it, you'll deal with it, in a professional way." She heard the distant sound of the rotor blades. "You know the rules, Renee."

Renee stumbled, dropped to her hands and knees. "Because

that works with the rest of CIG?" She heaved as she tried to
control her body's will to pass out. "And most of us have at least
had some experience of relationships and feelings."

"And like the others, I expect you to follow the rules and be
a professional." She watched as Renee fought to get to her feet.
"Besides, she'll have you to guide her and talk to."

Renee rolled onto her back and held up her hand, admitting
defeat. "You have way too much faith in me, Urs."

Frei smiled, went to her and pulled her to her feet as the
chopper came into view. "I know you. You'll get the job done and
Aeron through it."

Renee clasped onto her arm for support. "Then why are we
training to escape on foot?"

They ducked under the rotor blades, and Renee slumped into
her seat. Frei stepped back, jumped down onto the snow, and gave
the thumbs up to the crewmember who started to shut the door.

"Wait." Renee held up her hand, stopping him. "Aren't you
coming?"

Frei shook her head. "I still have recon to do."

"Urs, you know you're not meant to do that. It's dangerous."
Renee held out her hand, worry in her eyes. "We've been in sub-
zero temperatures all night, we haven't slept, we've kept moving.
You need rest, hydration—"

Frei signaled, and the crew member shut the door. Renee
carried on yelling through the window even as the chopper rose
into the air.

Frei shook her head, inserted her earpiece, and turned back to
her heading. "Renee is in the chopper, all clear, over."

"Adequate," Stosur said, her voice held a hint of being
impressed. "But she's not you."

"She spent her childhood doing normal things." Frei moved
into a sprint, dodging the barbed wire wrapped around another
suspicious mound in the snow. Stosur would demand full pace. "I
had Huber."

"Good thing he paid attention to some of my methods." Her
tone filled with warmth. "Kiwi rents his estate off Sven. He rents
his slaves for security too, so we practice . . . and perhaps find
some information along the way."

Frei checked her map. Stosur didn't mind technology but the

order was that she reacquaint herself with traditional methods. "Security?"

"Heavy," Stosur said, the sound of a muffled "oof" in the background. "Sven prides himself on it."

"You and my sister broke out, that makes two," she said, taking a run up, hitting the tree next to a tall fence at speed. Up it, foothold, main trunk, balance, legs coiled, leap . . . cleared the buzzing fence . . . land without a sound. "That's not something to be proud of."

"We were the only two." Stosur didn't sound like she was offended. "And getting out is far easier than getting in."

Frei spotted the telltale give away of an outpost. A copse of trees in an otherwise barren field. She flattened herself into the snow, covering herself in it. Her suit would use it to mask her body heat. She crept through the snow, paused, smooth metal next to her fingers: pressure plate. She adjusted, kept her position low, and was at the door to the outpost in seconds.

"No movement," Stosur said.

Frei picked the lock and snuck inside—long, dark, winding, narrow tunnels that dripped and shimmered with puddles of melted ice and water. Bare pipes ran overhead, doors veered off at angles, and she turned left, straight to the observation room. Stosur was busy dealing with the snoring guard, rolling his chair out of the way and placing a bottle of spirits in his hand.

"What are we looking for?" Frei asked, hacking into the computer system.

"Weaknesses. Plant the tester and we'll retreat back." Stosur pulled the guard's key off him and pocketed it with a satisfied smile.

"Done."

Stosur lifted her eyebrow.

Frei smiled. She was efficient, what could she say? "Practice."

Stosur nodded, and they crept out of the outpost and across the field to a safe distance, concealing themselves in snow.

"Usual response time?" Frei asked, pressing the button on her watch to activate the tester. She glanced up as men poured from the outpost like army ants.

"Seconds," Stosur said.

"Where were they?" Frei cocked her head.

"Where there's one guard, there's a nest of them." She met Frei's gaze. "They don't ask questions before firing either."

"How welcoming."

Stosur smiled. "Some people are impolite." She pushed up. "We move."

Frei followed her, creeping, silent, calls from the men behind, her heartbeat slow and steady in her ears. They reached the electrified fence without any of the men so much as looking in their direction. "Sloppy. I'd say that is a weakness."

Stosur nodded to a thick wooden pole with the circuit box for the fence attached. She sprinted across the snow, ran up the smooth surface, grabbed the footrest embedded up high. She yanked herself up, coiled her legs, sprang out, up, over the fence and landed with perfect body position. She turned and winked at Frei through the buzzing mesh. "They had heat vision on too. Technology can be most disappointing."

Frei grinned. She sprinted to the pole, up, footrest, hoist, coil, leap . . . and land with ease. "They don't make slaves like they used to?"

Stosur sped off and would outsprint her, just like she outsprinted Renee—Something she loved. Frei set off after her, dodging the pressure plates, the mounds of darts, the tripwires, enjoying how it made her calves tingle.

"Quite." Stosur glanced at her as she had to Renee, watching her monitor on her wrist and a warm smile broke out across her face.

Frei couldn't help but smile back. It felt good to be near her again. Especially now she knew Stosur was her mom. She grinned wider. A really, really cool mom.

Chapter 9

WHEN I GOT locked up in Serenity, I'd had to learn the rules there: which guards to avoid, which inmates to dodge, how to build myself up, how to hold myself so folks didn't challenge me and how to keep my head up when everybody told me I was crazy.

Didn't matter that I was released now, that enforcement lingered. Empath or not, I'd been conditioned that everything I felt wasn't right, wasn't normal and how I reacted was just as messed up. Sometimes, I could wrestle that down and convince myself I could cope . . . and sometimes, like now, I was ready to hold my hands up and let somebody take me back to a shrink.

Renee and Frei had been out overnight. Frei had told me that they would be, that I didn't have to get worked up but I was. I'd paced up and down the living room, kept the fire crackling, worked out on the rug, mopped the floor, dusted and polished and then paced some more.

I could cope . . . maybe. I lay on the sofa and stared up at the ceiling, focusing on the beams. I loved how they were bobbled and knotted, raw and real. It was almost like they were still part of the tree, still breathing somehow, that Frei had rescued them and restored them.

"It gets better," Renee said.

I stood up so fast I got stars in my eyes. "Doc?"

A hand on my arm told me I wasn't hallucinating but the blood pulsed through my ears like I'd pass out. My vision cleared and there was Renee, the woman who'd reached me, the woman I felt so attached to, she'd given me the belief to get on the bus home.

My mom had only wanted her to get me out; Frei had called her back to CIG and Renee didn't go. Instead she'd come to find me. I'd needed someone who understood me, who could reach me, who cared enough to try.

I sat up and stared at the fire.

Renee's belief in me had sparked something. I hadn't ever felt that kind of connection to anyone. It was so profound. Considering I didn't know her when we were in Colorado—Not inside and out—I'd believed in her when she needed me right back.

"I need you to know that no matter how far I have to separate myself from you . . ." Her pale gray eyes gazed up at me, the cyan rims caught in the light. I could see her forcing every wall she had down. "I meant what I said back in Oppidum. I am not playing with you . . . and I do care about you."
The truth glistened as it fell from her lips.

I shook the picture of it from my mind and headed to the mop, dunking it and swishing it across the floor—Just needed to keep busy. Thinking too much wasn't good for me. I started humming only to stop and stare at the mop handle. *Moonlight Sonata.* Somehow that tune did something to me, pulled at me. It had filtered in without me realizing, like it was fading up, slowly, gently, lulling me into a daze—

Blue light washed everything with a silver shine. The trees twinkled like they had lights on them. I felt the need to capture the moment somehow or maybe play it on my violin. I could hear the strains of Moonlight Sonata in my mind then wondered if she could hear it too the way her eyes twinkled at me.
The dim moonshine illuminated her, making her almost shimmer. Renee was one of those women whose beauty shone from within her. Not in a flashy way, but a quiet, gentle pulse. She always inspired me and somehow, in the doorway, I felt the itch to compose something just for her.

The wriggle filled my stomach and tickled through me, right to my toes. Energy, music, and now that weird wriggle. I groaned. Why was it rolling around and around in my head? I scrubbed at the floor like it would stop the restless feeling building.

Renee sighed. "I'm horrible. There's no excuse. I say things I don't mean but please, please, don't ever think I don't care about you." She touched my bruised forehead. "I mean it, I adore you, you great big dimwit."

And there went any chance of staying mad at her. "You do?"

"Guaranteed. Even if I yell at you, act like I don't, or we argue." Renee smiled, stroking her thumb over my cheek. Music floated from her to me, energy wrapped around me and released all the tension I'd felt. "You're a part of me."

I ditched the mop and paced. Why was I running over it so much? Frei told me she cared about me too. I didn't spend hours thinking about it. Didn't give me the wriggles either.

I headed to the fireplace and stoked at the fire, then stared at the metal in my hand. I could feel Renee's energy throbbing through it but I couldn't see the memory. There were parts of her that were unreadable: Her own private spaces? Like the space she held for whoever she loved. The way she talked about them changed her aura, her energy. It lifted her and flattened her all at once—

I rubbed my neck again. I didn't know how to help. I couldn't make no one love her. I didn't think she'd want me to. Love was a prickly subject I guessed. Folks got hurt. "You know, you always make me hear songs in my head."

Renee raised her eyebrows.

"I like that." I shrugged. "I ain't sure why it is, but I like it." I looked up to the stars. "Guess that ain't much but . . . well . . . you'll always have me around."

"I hear music too."

I left the fireside and headed to the window. It was crowded in my head. Too crowded.

Something made a ringing noise nearby and I jumped. I was crazy and on edge. One night on my own and I was back to Serenity.

I shuddered out a breath. I could do this. Baby-steps, just like Renee always said. I could cope. I'd eaten dinner, I'd gone to bed and, sure, so the phone had rung a few times and I couldn't pick it up without knocking out the power, and it wasn't starry outside anymore but pale with white clouds, and I was jumpy, and ready to look for liquor, but I'd coped just fine. Kinda.

The phone rang again.

It was Huber. Why didn't he just ring Frei's cell or something? "I *can't* pick it up!"

I need help.

I stared at the phone. I was sure that was a flash. Maybe I was overtired?

Cold . . . hurt . . . help.

Good enough for me. I hurried to the closet and pulled on my coat—Renee and Frei would get mad if I froze. Then grabbed a lock hanging off the coat hook.

"Don't blow up on me," I pleaded and held it to the door.

It opened. Phew.

I grinned and hurried out into the snow, shut the door, and ran down the long drive. Would have helped if I'd stopped to find snow shoes. How come I could see stuff and still leave my brain indoors?

"Just move," I muttered and slid my way to the gate. I unlocked the little door inset, and tried to squeeze myself through, grunting and shoving, then it or my coat gave way with a rip and I sprawled into the snow on the road outside.

Who made a gate only small folks could fit through?

I clambered to my feet, shut the gate and skidded my way down the road. It was icy under the snow and I was shivering already. Just had to focus, Huber was a lot colder.

Too cold.

"I'm coming already," I muttered, picking up my pace. It was better than driving myself crazy with memories anyhow.

Chapter 10

SNOW FELL, HEAVY and thick as I hurried down the icy stretch of road. At least, it had been a road. Now there was just a load of white in front of me punctuated by powerlines. My chest tightened up until I coughed and spluttered with each breath and I couldn't make out Frei's place through the flurry.

Where was Huber? I couldn't feel him enough to pinpoint him. I couldn't feel nothing but cold seeping into my bones and freezing up my brain cells.

Need to get back to the car.

I stopped. I heard that. I scanned the road in front. Why wasn't he in his car? How was I gonna find him? I couldn't see any tracks, any shapes of cars anyhow . . . it was all just white. I looked up at the sky. It was snowing hard. Enough that it would bury it already?

What did I do?

I took slow, deep breaths like Renee always told me. Think with logic. I was following the powerlines so I was on the road. I'd tracked folks back in St. Jude's in the snow. It was harder. I remember that. I'd had to do something . . . I shivered. Maybe he'd passed out? I couldn't feel folks when they slept since I'd gotten my burdens back. I couldn't even feel their mood when they were dreaming. Either I was getting better at blocking it out . . . or . . . I couldn't remember.

"Focus, come on," I yelled at myself. "What did I do to find them . . . I'd . . ."

I took a deep breath and tried again. I pictured the scene, the flash I'd had.

Nothing.

I got to my feet, Renee looking half as though she wanted to shove me back on the ATV and half like she wanted to throttle me.

*Her aura rolled about like waves in a storm but I closed my eyes,
one last time, as the roar of the other parties met my ears.*
    "Charlie, where are you?"

It was worth a shot. I closed my eyes, trying to picture Huber.
"Where are you?"
    Nothing.
    "Huber?" I scrunched up my eyes.
    Nothing.
    "Useful." I kicked at the snow, trying to vent the panic. Renee
said baby steps, she'd be logical. She'd look for options, things
around her that were useful . . . Useful . . .
    I stared at the snow. Snow was water. Frei thought it slowed
me down but it was water . . . and I healed in it . . . worth a try. I
dropped to my knees, yanked off my gloves, and shoved my hands
into it.
    "Huber, where are you?"

Here.

"Yeah!" I scrambled across to the side and slid into the ditch.
Huber was in it, blood gushing from his head. He was colder than
my hands were.
    "I need you to wake up," I muttered, trying to shake him. "You
gotta ask or I can't help."
    He didn't respond.
    "Come on!" I shook him harder. His suit—battered, ripped,
blood-stained. He was real strong just to be holding on.
    Nothing.
    "Don't fade on me," I muttered. Frei hadn't fought so hard to
get hit by losing her dad. "Think . . . think . . ."
    Useful . . . er . . . snow . . . water . . . healing . . . I picked up
more snow. Shoved it in his ripped shirt to his side. He snapped
his eyes open.
    It'd do.
    "You need help?" I focused on him, hoping he'd get it. If
he was like Frei, speaking another language was fine when he
was with it but not so much semi-conscious. German . . . he was
German-speaking like her. "*Hilfe?*"

I was pretty sure that was help. Didn't know if it was the correct form or whatever Renee had tried explaining but help was help, right?

"*Bitte,*" Huber managed.

I knew that was please so I placed my hands on him.

Pick up . . . he retried her cellphone. He had a tail. He couldn't get rid of it. He didn't dare stray near her house with them behind. It wasn't normal to have snow this bad but it was coming down thick and fast. Like a blizzard. Hard to see. Crossroads. Needed to lure the tail away.

Slam.

A car hit side on. Wheels skidded. Ice. Car flipped.

Smash.

Head hit the windscreen.

Crunch.

Pain . . . ribs.

Screech.

Metal on road. Grinding. Skidding.

Crunch.

Upside down. Snow in the car. He fought to release his seatbelt, slammed at the door. Crawled up the banking. Dropped down.

Jäger's men cruised near.

He hid, covering himself in snow. Woozy.

They laughed as they sped off. Jäger may have paid well but not enough for them to make certain the job was done.

He crawled up onto the road, cellphone was cracked. He dialed her house number. She wasn't there but maybe it would reroute.

He kept crawling, kept ringing. More tired, more pain . . . cold.

I winced as I relived him rolling off the road into the ditch to hide himself as a car drove past. The snow was too thick for them to know anything had happened. He was sure it had been Jäger.

Huber gasped and opened his eyes. Steel shone in them.

"Your car got cleaned up," I mumbled through the flashes of Jäger's men and their trucks. "You were lucky you kept moving."

He pulled himself up, then wobbled. "I slashed my head."

I nodded, staggering to my feet . . . and it felt like somebody was flicking the lights on and off with my heartbeat . . . Felt exhausted. Not normally this tired.

"Where is the gash?" He touched his face. "I've got slashes in my clothes, blood but no wounds."

"You heal quick?" I offered, catching him as he lurched to the side.

"Then why do I feel like I'm going to pass out?" He glared at me. "And what did you do?"

"Nothing. Just stuck ice up your shirt to wake you up." I was trying to shake off my own wooziness. Felt kinda drunk. "Maybe you got concussion."

He nodded like he was happy to go with that . . . for now.

"Where is Ursula?" he shot at me. "And when did you learn German?"

"She went out." Why was he getting mad at me? "And I managed one word, that ain't really speaking it."

"You picked the right one." He stopped and offered me a smile. "So here's two more."

I tensed. I was sure, even though I didn't know a whole lot, that I'd know cussing.

"*Vielen Dank*," he said with a nod, holding me up as much as I was him.

I smiled as we staggered our way down the snowy road, barely able to see for the snowflakes. "You're welcome."

Chapter 11

HELPING FOLKS GET rid of ailments was one thing but getting rid of the hurt that stored up in my hands was another. When we got back to Frei's place, I could just about manage to let us in with the lock and get Huber inside to the fire.

Before my burdens were dimmed, I'd go to the bathroom, shove my mitts under the running water, half-drown as I relived their hurt again, then pass out on the bathroom floor.

So far, since I'd gotten my burdens back, everything seemed more potent . . . and I'd promised Renee that I wouldn't go washing without a spotter.

Huber eyed me, sprawled on the sofa like he could sleep for a week. "What is it, girl?"

I sighed. As much as I hated admitting I couldn't wash anything away by myself, Renee spoke sense sometimes. "I kinda need your help."

He nodded, groaning his way upright, leaving a load of snow which lost the white sheen as it melted. "How can I assist?"

"I got to wash the pain away," I said, bracing for the "huh" look.

He raised his eyebrows, pulling his mouth to the side.

There it was.

"Look, I just need you to come to the bathroom and pull me away from the sink when I say so . . . You with me?" I didn't have to read him to see the confusion so held up my hands. "Please . . . just humor me?"

"If this helps you." He nodded, and I led him to the downstairs bathroom. Frei had a whole room for a shower with no divide. Maybe it'd be easier if I just stood under the shower? I looked back at Huber who stared at the sink like it would give him answers. Maybe he'd get nervous dragging me out of a shower? Best to stick to the sink.

I pulled out a towel from the cupboard and tied it around my belt. "When I tell you to, you need to yank me away from the sink but don't touch me."

"Then what?" He sounded worried, irritated, and curious all at once.

"You just observe me until Frei or Renee show up, okay?" I gave him my best smile. "And don't go freaking out."

"Freaking out?" He jutted out his chin.

I turned on the faucet and shoved my hands under, getting slammed to my knees in the process. "Yeah, freaking out."

I yelped as I relived the car hitting him again. Why'd I have to relive it twice? I didn't used to see it when I healed folks before only when I washed. Getting smacked around all over again was just plain mean.

Huber edged forward.

"Don't. I told you to stay put," I managed, gripping onto the sink with my chin as I relived Huber flipping in the car and the water sucked away my air.

"What do I do if you pass out?" Huber muttered, lifting onto the balls of his feet.

"You stay put." I grunted—the car rolled into the ditch—My heart lurched. "Now . . . pull."

Huber darted forward and yanked the towel.

I didn't move. Rooted. "Pull."

"I'm trying." He yanked again. He was strong but the water was stronger.

Uh oh.

I shut my eyes—air sucked away, fuzziness took over. Couldn't breathe. Air, desperate, clawing need for air.

"Renee!"

She'd heard my thoughts before. I could feel her close by. Close enough?

Huber dropped the towel and yanked me by the shoulders. "What is happening?"

I opened my mouth but my voice caught like I was underwater. Couldn't breathe, needed to breathe, lungs burning, sucking in, can't breathe.

"Renee!"

For all Nan's attributes, I didn't think she could physically drag me from the sink. I couldn't hold on much longer—my vision blanked.

"Renee!"

"I'm here." She gripped my waist. She and Huber pulled together. The water let go. My hands snapped free and I slumped backwards into Renee's lap as Huber landed in a heap by the doorway.

"I've got you," she said, holding onto me.

My teeth were clattering, my heart was pounding but the room faded into view as did Renee's face. Her smiling, rosy-cheeked face.

I clung to her, shivering. "You heard me?"

She squeezed, affection in her gray eyes. "I heard you."

"Heard you?" Huber frowned, pulling himself to his feet. "She didn't say a word."

"Of course she did," Renee said, meeting his eyes. "Why else would I know where you were?"

He frowned deeper, then rubbed at his head. "I need to lie down . . . You may be right about concussion." He wandered off, mumbling about not seeing any wounds and me not talking.

I sighed. "This is what happens when you leave me on my own."

Renee leaned over and kissed me on the forehead. "Why were you washing?"

My eyelids drooped and I cuddled into her. It was relief just to feel the warmth from her. "Long story."

"Then let's get you to bed," She said with a yawn. "And you can tell me about it when you've slept."

She pulled me up and steadied me as she led us to my room. She'd taken to sleeping down the hall but I held onto her hand as she went to leave.

"You need me to keep an eye on you?" she asked, her eyes gentle.

I nodded like the big kid I was.

She yawned again. "Then we can sleep it off together."

I got a flash of her and Frei in the snow. "Boot camp?"

Renee sighed and helped me into bed. "With Urs, who knows. Think she just likes drilling people."

I nodded. "She does."

Renee flopped down beside me. "Thought so . . ." She groaned in relief. "Bed is good."

I smiled, as her relief washed over me. So was company.

Chapter 12

I DIDN'T KNOW what it was about displacing ailments or washing them away but I always felt like I'd argued with a grizzly, stolen his fish, and he'd football tackled me into a boulder. It was just aches, some grogginess but now it hurt to move too. Was that new? I was sure I'd have remembered it hurting this much.

I wiggled my toes, forcing open my eyes. Ouch. The light was dazzling, burning, and made my vision blur up with tears. Why was it so painful? Had I hit myself? Hadn't Renee helped, Huber too.

Was I sick? I wiggled my nose around—no sniffles. Jaw was fine, hadn't broken it; no scratchy throat . . . Guess I had just been football tackled by a grizzly then.

"He's only just waking up," Stosur said in a hushed voice. Was she in the room or outside the door? I couldn't tell. "Jessie didn't have the same problem."

I'd helped mini-Frei fix her asthma before she left Frei's, yeah . . . I'd been sleepy after that but not as drained as I felt now and that had been after I got my burdens back. I didn't get it.

"No," Frei said, her tone flat. "Aeron didn't either."

"Maybe it was the extent of his injuries?" Renee asked. I could see her chomping away on her lip in my mind's eye. She always gnawed on it when she was worried—normally about me.

"We don't know what happened," Stosur said, her tone sharper: concern. "Where is his car?"

Okay, I needed to shift butt and tell them. I tried moving but my body was on vacation. Had Renee glued me to the bed?

"There's nothing much on camera," Frei muttered. "The snow was too thick to see distance and . . ." She sighed. "Aeron blew it when they got close."

I had. Oops. They weren't cheap by the tone of her voice.

I should explain or call to them but I couldn't make my tongue work. Maybe I could signal to them, tell Renee by focusing on her? I closed my eyes. Pain split through my temples. Nope, I weren't trying sensing nothing until someone screwed my skull back on.

Maybe they were near enough to see me? I lifted my pinky, maybe they'd see the pinky?

"You checkin' wind direction, Shorty?" Nan asked from next to me. Now she'd spoken, I could tell she'd been watching over me awhile.

I tried to speak but my tongue felt glued to the roof of my mouth.

"Did you get yourself in a pickle by helpin' when you weren't asked again?" She tutted at me.

I scowled. I *had* asked and wiggled my pinky in protest.

"You did, huh?" Nan sounded like she was knitting up something. Maybe they could speak "pinky wiggle" in Etherspace? *"Hmmm . . ."*

Hmmm? She was meant to know this stuff and I flicked my pinky at her to say so.

"Your grandpa was on the ropes," she said like she was smiling. *"So close to drawing level."*

Cards? If I could have rolled my eyes, I would have.

"You washed it away?" she said, click-clicking away. She knitted faster when she was thinking.

I nodded—Hey, I could nod.

"Ah, it's snowin' out." She sounded excited. *"I do love that pretty white stuff."*

"Cold," I managed—words were good. Slurred, a bit like a squeak but good.

"Sure, but you remember how we'd build up a snow mound and you'd charge right through it?" She chuckled. *"Same as your grandpa."*

"Cold," I grunted again.

"You get the shivers quicker now," she said, clicking away. *"Explains all the aching."*

"How?" I rolled enough to sit up, then gripped my head and slumped back down. Yeah, it was gonna fall off.

"Sure, it's water." A cold breeze tickled my forehead. *"Guess your energy is a lot like electrics . . . gives a kick in water."*

"Painful?" I kinda did feel like someone had fried my circuits.

"Guessin' it is." She sniffed. *"Cookies are smellin' tasty."*

"Why . . . is it . . . like that?" Tongue was moving but I weren't sure it made sense.

"More amplified means you couldn't control it, so same thing happened like when you didn't ask." Nan swooshed to my side. *"An' now you feelin' it."*

"Am I gonna get hollered at again . . . 'cause I tried." I asked. Slurred words but they were joined up so that was something.

"I didn't holler. Dimming things was to help you understand how blessed you are. You learned that lesson already." Felt like she placed her cold hand on my forehead. *"It just makes you feel like Blackbear sat on your hind."*

It did. I nodded, then gripped my pounding head. "I didn't mean to take too much away."

"Don't you worry 'bout that," Nan said, cooing to me like she did when I was sick. *"If you took it, you were meant to."* She wrapped me in an icy hug. *"Trust in that."*

I did. I did a lot more than I'd realized.

"Quick thinkin' to use the white stuff to find Icy's dad. Even Tiddles was impressed." She chuckled and a cat meowed nearby.

"Hey, Tiddles," I said, managing a wave, then frowned. "Wait, didn't you say you were playing cards?"

Nan chuckled again. *"I was, one eye on you, other on your grandpa but Tiddles was sticking."*

I pulled myself upright, fighting the urge to eject whatever was left in my stomach. "To?"

She chuckled harder. *"Cards, Shorty."*

It was lost on me. Did cats play cards? Nan faded before I could ask, and Renee poked her head around the door and waved at thin air. "Did I miss the chat?"

I looked over at whatever she was waving to.

"You were talking to Nan, right?" She cocked her head. "Or . . . yourself?"

My stomach wriggled and I flopped back to stare at the ceiling. I was aching too much to have wriggles in my gut.

"Who knows?" I stretched out my neck. "Jäger hit Huber's car."

"He did?" She strolled into my line of sight, peering down at me. "You blew the cameras."

"Yeah." I cracked my vertebrae back into place and groaned.

"Not Jäger personally . . . He sent chumps to do it for him. Took Huber's car."

"So how did you get back?" She placed her hands on either side of my neck and eased it side to side like she was tapping in cards.

"We kinda staggered back." My neck loosened and I groaned with relief. "Surprised he stayed awake."

"He passed out in the hall," she said, making me sit up and flexed my back about. "Had to explain the bump to Stosur."

"Great. You go help a guy and he dislodges his own brain cells." My back muscles loosened and released and I groaned again. "Hey, that's good."

"I know. When it comes to spines, I have a lot of experience," she said like she found it hard to say. "I know backache."

Best I didn't think about how bad she'd been hurt.

"Huber says that he was attacked." Frei strolled into the room, looked from Renee to me, and cocked an eyebrow. "Must be Megan."

"Megan?" Renee asked, working my shoulders, her hands rolling the muscles, squeezing out the tension, the aching, the stiffness. "Why? I know she's sly but if he gets hurt, she's out of a job."

"Yes, but . . ." Frei fiddled with the ring on her finger. "Maybe she knows he's onto her?"

"Although I'd like to agree," Stosur said, strolling in so much like Frei—even in disguise. "She's loyal in that sense but someone let slip to Jäger where Huber would be."

Renee dug out a knot and I winced. I liked the gentle stuff better. "Maybe Jäger's men just followed?"

Stosur shook her head. "No, Huber would have noticed."

"What's to say he didn't?" Renee asked, digging deeper and I yelped. "Sorry . . . tense."

Her or me?

"If he was being followed, he would have turned around." Frei tapped her lip. She strode to the window and yanked open the curtains. Light flooded in and my head pounded. "They'd have been waiting for him."

"Aeron," Stosur asked, eyes tracking over my face. "Do you have any . . . ideas?"

"It don't work like that," I muttered, then groaned again as Renee ran her hands over my head and massaged away the ache. "I ain't—"

If I tell him, he'll get me out. He'll get me back to Caprock.

I sighed. "Kevin."

Kevin had been a prickly little kid back in Caprock. Jessie had been into him but he was nasty. I'd tried stopping him falling off a roof, then he'd tried yanking my fingers away. We'd tried getting the kids out and he'd tried blowing their cover and their escape. Didn't know why Huber had bothered.

"I suspected as much," Huber said, his forehead with one big purple bump on it, his steps careful as he wandered in. "I've been too soft."

"Soft?" Stosur eyed him like she'd poke him. I guessed they had different views on slaves.

"Yes. I learned from Fahrer that some mentalities needed breaking." He dropped his gaze to his shirt and did his cufflinks up. "Boy took a long time to fix his violence issues."

Frei stared at him. "Fahrer?"

"Yes." Huber looked up at her. "Boy was volatile to the point I thought of committing him." He rubbed at his purple forehead. "He would do as expected one minute then something regrettable the next."

Made sense why Huber would be wary of him but Fahrer had been gentle with Frei. Maybe Huber's methods had helped?

"Regrettable?" Stosur asked, not sounding one bit impressed.

"Yes, like shooting at me or his temper getting the better of him," Huber said it like it was all nonsense and fiddled with his cufflinks again.

"He disliked being a slave perhaps?" Stosur asked, leaning against the window frame, gazing out, white light illuminating her.

"He didn't know he was one. No, he was very . . . hormone filled as a teenager." He sighed and turned back to Frei. "Whether or not you approve of my methods, *I* was once a hormone-filled boy . . . I know what they need."

Stosur pursed her lips, glancing over her shoulder at him. "Bully tactics?"

Huber laughed. "Hard labor and setting definite boundaries."

I looked to Renee who'd stopped massaging. "Positive re-enforcement versus hardline . . ." She stared at him like it was fascinating.

"You're more of a shrink than you let on," I muttered, squeezing her hand until she started massaging again.

"Suz was like that, you didn't do that to her," Frei whispered, fiddling with her ring, moving closer to Renee and I like we were comforting her. "Or me."

"Suz had Megan to discipline her," he said with a sigh and adjusted his collar. "And neither of us knew how to cope with her." He cleared his throat with a sad smile. "You were rational."

Stosur sighed, her eyelids fluttering like she was trying to blink the tears away. "Suz was too much like him."

"Like who?" Frei scowled, hands on hips, glaring from Huber to Stosur and back.

"Sven," Stosur said with a sad smile. "She didn't even listen to me when I tried reaching her."

"Why would she?" Renee asked like she wanted to record the whole thing and study it. Sometimes she was a lot like a shrink but as long as she kept massaging, I didn't care.

"I was her mother," Stosur whispered like it broke every fiber of her heart.

"You were?" Frei stared at her then Huber. Renee stopped and took her hand.

"Yes," Stosur said, lifting her chin. "Which may be why you always felt so close to her . . . I'm glad you were close."

Frei turned, pulled free from Renee's grasp, and strode out.

"Go after her," I whispered, urging her off the bed.

"She won't talk to me," she whispered back.

"She will." I took her hand from my shoulder, squeezed it, and smiled at her. "Go."

Renee nodded and hurried out of the doorway.

Huber and Stosur looked to me.

"She needs time to process it," I said like I was sure of it. "We got any other family ties that we ain't shared?"

"None," Stosur said, staring at the door. "Our girls and Suz."

"They were *all* our girls," Huber said, pulling in his chin. "No matter about the genes."

"Good thing Suz had your jacket, huh?" I said, rubbing the back of my neck. Renee had skills. I didn't feel in pain at all.

"Yes." Huber smiled, fiddling with his cufflinks again. "Looks better on her than it ever did on me."

"And good thing I was cold enough that you parted with it." Stosur's tone softened and she hugged herself. "Best not tell her that or it may lose the shield-like feeling for her."

Huber looked to me and shrugged. "Manners, that was all."

"Nonsense," Stosur said, her smile tender. "It was your way of telling me you loved me."

He nodded, forcing back his shoulders. "Still do."

"Ebenfalls," Stosur whispered, kissed him on the cheek, and walked out.

Huber touched his cheek, smiled down at his fingers, and followed her.

I flopped back down and smiled. I knew that much German. *Ebenfalls* . . . it meant likewise.

Chapter 13

IT TOOK AN hour before I could really move and I headed downstairs to a glass box that overlooked the courtyard complete with a fountain and what, I guessed, would be grass in summer. I could see flickers of Frei meditating out there with a peaceful smile on her face. It was real different to the worn look in her eyes and worry swarming round her like bees as she sat there with Renee.

"You doin' better, Shorty?" Aunt Bess said. I grinned, searching for her until I spotted her in the kitchen flitting about. "Bet you need some good ol' feeding up."

I lumbered over to her and launched into a hug. "When you get here?"

"I rolled on in this morning. Your momma got the feeling you'd need some looking after," she said, pulling back and ushering me out of the kitchen. She cooked like Nan did. Didn't like to tell her 'cause I got the feeling she and Nan didn't get on so well.

"You baking . . ." I sniffed and my stomach grumbled with joy. "Cookies?"

"You know, I got the itch to," Aunt Bess said, lifting up a plate to show me. "But you got to eat your greens first."

"Oh, she will," Renee said, smiling around her cup. Her eyes were puffy like she'd been crying, but from her energy it was out of sympathy for Frei. "I've heard a lot about Lorelei cookies and that they are something to be savored?"

Frei nodded, staring out at the view, her aura buzzing at her.

"Nan made the best cookies," I mumbled, joining them at the table. I ran my hands over the grained surface. It was a fallen tree that Frei had found, dragged here, spruced up, and varnished to give it back its sparkle. I could feel how it shone with the care and attention she'd showed it. "Nobody in town knew what Nan did that made her cookies so . . ." How'd I put it? "So . . .?"

"Mouthwatering," Aunt Bess said, bringing in our plates, all balanced on her arms. She slid them off with ease then wagged a finger at Frei. "Eating gives you energy, no arguing."

Frei blinked up at her like she was speaking another language.

"You ain't gonna look so slick if your hair wilts." Aunt Bess pushed the plate under Frei's nose. "Energy."

Frei touched her hair in a daze.

Renee sighed, her aura patting Frei on the back. "It's best you keep your strength up."

I didn't want to ask out loud so reached for Renee's hand and hovered mine over it—

"He's attacked Huber." Frei threw herself at the dummy, kicking lumps out of it. "What if he hurts you or Aeron?" She smacked it with a powerful kick and the dummy shuddered around as it recoiled. "Jessie will fall for it, she did fall for it . . . What if Lilia hadn't seen?" She slammed the dummy again. "She's too much like me. He'll lure her out and . . ." She stopped, bent double, and gripped her stomach.

Renee went to her, rubbed at her back. "He won't . . . Lilia did see it and alerted your mom. She'll pick her up."

"I can't bear it." Tears dripped off the tip of Frei's nose, splatting onto the plastic safety mat. "I can't breathe."

"You're a mom, it goes with the territory, right?"

Frei gave her a watery glare.

"So I've heard anyway." Okay. So she wasn't a mom herself. What did Frei want?

"If you think I just meant Jessie then you don't know me."

Smack.

Frei roundhouse kicked the dummy.

"I didn't say that." Wow, she was cranky. "I meant that kids are supposed to worry their moms, it's part of the job." She ducked a woodblock Frei hurled. "We, as your friends, are meant to do the same."

"You're more than friends," Frei spat at her, hurling another woodblock—hopefully the wall bars didn't need them. "You get that? You feel more like family to me than . . ." She threw another block.

Her own family. Yeah, Renee knew that feeling well. "Because we spend more time with you, that's all." She ducked again.

Frei picked up a stick, the kind with multiple bamboo rods bound together. "I get that." She smacked the dummy. "I'm so worried about you, about them . . . I . . . It gets to me."

Smash.

"You bug me too, Urs," Renee said, vaulting Frei's attack. She rolled, ducked, grabbed for the spare stick, and blocked a second attack. Guess self-defense was in session.

"I was sick, you knew I was sick. I didn't worry this much about myself." Frei parried the block. Renee rolled out of the way.

Thwack.

Bamboo to the buttock.

"Too slow," Frei shot at her.

"I know," Renee muttered, rubbing at her butt. "When you love people, they override your common sense." She narrowed her eyes. "And give me a break, you drilled me to exhaustion."

"Jager won't." Frei caught her in the stomach. "He's faster, fitter, unhinged . . . And he disarmed me."

Renee blocked the strike to her head. Frei lunged in, smacked her off balance, and she crashed, flat on her back on the mat.

"And no one disarms me." Frei's voice wobbled with her tears.

Renee swept her leg out. Frei smashed forward and landed face first beside her. "That's because he scares you. It tenses you up, narrows your attentional field and you miss the cues."

Frei lay there, head in the mat. "Yes."

"I get scared too," she whispered, staring up at the ceiling: high, wooden, like a lodge.

"It stops me thinking. He makes me freeze. I do stupid things." Frei growled. "Anyone else and I'd wipe the floor with him."

"Hey, I've been there," Renee said with a sigh. Her butt stung. "Took Aeron to break me out of my head, remember?"

"But at least you shot him first." Frei turned to look at her. "You had the reactions to pull the trigger."

Renee nodded. "So will you. You just need to use the stuff I gave you even though you hate shrink stuff." She ignored the scathing look. "Relaxation, visualization, picking a point nearby." She flipped up onto her feet. "Confidence . . . you just have to find a way to unlock it." She picked up the stick and smashed the dummy with a swing attack. The stick split, bamboo splinters spraying out as the dummy slammed to the mat. "You're not alone anymore."

She held out her hand to Frei.

"Which means he can hurt you too." Frei sniffed. "And that'll hurt me."

Renee yanked her to her feet and into a hug. "No, it means that if you can't beat him . . ." She drew her pistol, pulled the trigger— Click. Click. *"I will."*

"Make sure you got darts loaded then," I mumbled. "He needs jail time in some place like Serenity."

Renee smiled at me. "Oh, I know. He could do with a nice friendly roommate too."

Aunt Bess looked up from her food. "Ain't askin'."

Frei's lips twitched, her aura calming, the snow outside reflecting in her misted over eyes.

"Imagine his face?" Renee bumped Frei's shoulder with a smirk. "Wouldn't be so rough and tough then."

Frei nodded, her thoughts somewhere over her head.

"So Kiwi contacted you?" Renee asked, ducking to catch Frei's gaze.

Frei blinked, a tear dribbling down her cheek, and prodded at her food. "Yes."

I shoveled mine in, trying to fight through the prickle of panic. It was just dinner, why was I being such a baby? I liked Aunt Bess, Frei and Renee . . . maybe it wasn't my worries? Maybe it was Frei's? I couldn't tell. Why couldn't I tell?

"Eat, Shorty, you're getting pale." Aunt Bess tapped my hand with her fork.

Had I stopped . . . and why did I want to go bake cookies?

"He's trustworthy?" I mumbled around my mouthful. Aunt Bess had cooked up some dish: vegetables, sweet sauces, succulent tastes of meat . . . or fish? I weren't sure, and I didn't care. Tasted so good.

"No." Frei tucked in, one mouthful turning to scoffing. She groaned at Aunt Bess. "Delicious."

Renee nodded, licking her knife clean with a satisfied grin. "Lorelei special?"

"This Lorelei anyhow. I learned it from a fine chef." She smiled like it hurt to think about. "Always helped when I needed to find my smile again."

I got the flash of her taking off her wedding ring, tears blurring her vision.

"Guess Grimes will have to up his cooking skills," fell out of my mouth. Grimes? The detective my dad had taught? Nice guy, sure, but he was . . . well . . . he was a lot younger than her.

"He ain't touchin' my kitchen," she muttered. "But he cleans dishes good enough." She winked at me.

Renee chuckled.

I just stared at her. "What about Baltimore?"

He'd lived in Baltimore and worked in D.C. Was he gonna move states to keep her company? I didn't want her having to travel all that way.

"Quit worryin'. He's got vacations stacked up. I'm too wrinkly for settling." She tapped Frei on the hand. "Only useful when they can reach the top shelf."

Frei managed a smile. "Or pick locks quicker than me."

Aunt Bess "ah-hummed" her agreement.

I looked to Renee who rolled her eyes. "I believe they are pretending that they don't pine over the menfolk."

Frei scowled like she'd fence her with her fork. "I do not pine."

Aunt Bess held up her hands with a grin. "Oh I pine but they're still only useful to take out the trash."

"It's okay," Renee said, squeezing my arm, a cheeky smile on her face. "They don't really mean it."

"Oh *I* do," Frei muttered. "You don't have to put up with them."

Aunt Bess ah-hummed again.

"No, I get double PMS and perfume up my nose," Renee said with challenge in her eyes. "How do we know if Kiwi will actually meet us?"

Did they like folks or didn't they? I couldn't read nothing off them.

"Stubble rash." Frei pointed to her face. "We don't know if he will."

"And dirty clothes that don't get nowhere near the basket," Aunt Bess added with a nod. "Which is why I'm staying to keep an eye on you."

"Wardrobes full of shoes, pot puree in every room, and flowers . . . everywhere." Renee huffed out a breath. "Will Stosur be assisting?"

"Muddy boots, sport on TV, and beer clogging up my fridge." Aunt Bess grunted. "Course she will, she fixes up faces."

"Fluffy cushions covering the sofa, cheesy movies on TV, and *diet* food clogging up my fridge." Renee looked to Frei. "So, why are we going to meet him? Can't we just hack his computer?"

"Hairy armpits," Frei said, wrinkling up her nose. "He's our shot at proving Jäger is selling. He doesn't do computers. The other buyers have closed ranks."

"Hairspray coating your throat." Renee chewed on her lip. "I don't like it."

I held up a pinky. "Meeting Kiwi or hairspray?"

"Both," Renee said with a chuckle.

"Takin' an age to change a tire," Aunt Bess said. "I'll need to keep an eye on the screens, make sure he hasn't brought Jäger's men too."

"Communal showers with crazy folks," I said.

They all stared at me.

I shrugged. I didn't really have anybody but Renee changing tires and she seemed pretty good at it. "You'd better keep an eye from here, it's safer."

"You get irritated by showering?" Renee asked, laughter in her eyes.

"Nope." I cleared my throat, trying not to pay attention to Frei's aura which was howling with laughter. "Showers were more prickly than dinner . . . glad we don't got to shower with folks outside."

"You had a hard time inside, Shorty." Aunt Bess looked all kinds of concerned.

"Yeah." I shuddered, best not to say that I'd been attacked in them. "Aimee kept stealing my soap; Tiz was always trying to rip the shiny pipes off the wall; Yasmin sang . . . real bad . . . and Nora picked at the grouting so much she kept forgetting to wash."

I missed my Serenity buddies. I wrote to them a lot. Couldn't say much and nothing about CIG so I just told them little stuff.

"Lorelei, you definitely win," Frei said, her smile wide and her aura had lost its worry-bees. "You're right." She looked to Aunt Bess. "We could really use your backup here . . . in case we need an alternate extraction."

Aunt Bess nodded. "You got it, Icy."

"Icy?" Frei sighed. "You too?"

Aunt Bess shrugged. "Lorelei nuts sprout strong." She got up, went to the kitchen, and pulled out a plate. "And we sure rock cookies."

Well, Aunt Bess and Nan did. I was pretty sure my mom might too but I didn't have one iota . . . but I could eat them. That had to count.

Renee, Frei, Aunt Bess, and I took a cookie each and I raised mine. "To folks that drive you crazy."

Chapter 14

FREI HAD GONE off to meet Stosur and retrieve Jessie; Aunt Bess had locked herself in the "hunk of junk" room, as she called it, and I tried meditating only to feel too distracted.

It was close to dinner so I thought I'd be useful and make Renee something to eat. Ham and gherkin, or pickles as Nan had called them, sandwiches weren't much but I'd chopped and peeled the pickles. I washed them too for good measure . . . then spent fifteen minutes trying to spread the butter on the bread.

Why was it so difficult? It just kept on sticking to the bread. Didn't help Frei had used the knife so I got her mood enough I'd wanted to roundhouse kick something.

I left the kitchen and wandered out to a converted cattle barn to one side of the yard. Renee was there in overalls, tools in hand, some muck on her cheek and her blonde brow dipped in concentration as she fiddled and fussed with the tail of the helicopter.

It wasn't the one Frei flew—too small—but the place had been converted to a workshop and made a pretty cool place to stow mini-bugs.

I leaned on the divide and got the picture of some animal chomping on feed. The place had a calm energy and so did Renee. Her aura was rich in color, happy shimmers and gentle flecks of light. She picked up some kind of wrench and mumbled to herself.

I sighed, enjoying the relief wash over me. Relief from the restlessness wriggling in my gut.

Renee turned, caught me staring, and cocked her head. "Quit it, dimwit."

"Quit what?"

Her nails were short, neat cut; her hair shoved up in a band. "Smiling at me like that," she whispered, her eyes twinkling.

"Sorry." Although I wasn't.

"If you're sorry then why are you still smiling?" She chuckled and sparkles of light flickered around her.

"I like you," I mumbled, holding onto the divide. Sounded dumb.

Renee beamed with smile and aura. "Back at you."

"No . . . I mean . . ." I couldn't figure it out myself so how'd I explain? "I like *you* . . . as you are." I motioned to the mini-bug. "I like watching you fix stuff, and cook . . . and look like you."

"This your way of saying you're hungry?" She wagged her wrench at me. "That's not liking, that's just cupboard love."

I chuckled as relief washed over me some more. "I made sandwiches."

She still wielded the wrench. "Uh huh."

"I made you some too." I held up the box. "Ain't sure if you're into ham and pickles but it tasted okay."

Renee lifted up the see-through box. "Aeron, they're cucumbers not pickles."

I shrugged. Made sense. Thought they'd tasted funny.

"Did you butter the bread?" She eyed it.

"Tried to. The knife kinda got stuck." I screwed up my mouth. "Couldn't figure out what I did wrong."

"The butter was too cold." Renee headed to a sink on the side and washed up.

"Don't forget your cheek," I mumbled. She looked cool with it but the oily stuff smelled off, like it could seep in and cause trouble if she weren't careful.

She used her overalls to scrub at her cheek and turned. "Better?"

I nodded, pretty sure she got more awesome the more I watched her. She could do loads of things—fixing bugs to speaking to folks in other languages.

She studied me and energy rippled into motion. She gave me a half smile, a quiet smile, then she turned back to towel off.

A wave of cold washed over me. How could I miss her not looking at me? Dumb. I was just dumb.

"So, what were you doin'?" I asked as she headed over and pulled out her lunch.

"Wire locking," she said, chomping off a piece, wriggling her face about as she chewed. "You washed and chopped the cucumber?"

I nodded, even if I had thought it was a pickle. "Wire locking?"

"Yeah, it was loose." She nodded toward the chopper. "Not a bad effort at all, Lorelei."

I grinned, feeling a whoosh of joy hit me. "Really?"

She smiled and I was sucked in. "Really."

"Wait . . . loose?" She'd been on the tail. "They come loose?" I was never getting on a bug again—

"Not the tail," she said, affection in her eyes. "Just a bolt. Sometimes the vibrations shake them loose so you tighten it with a torque wrench and wire lock it back on."

"Oh." I kinda got it. Sort of. I still weren't sure about getting on one.

"Running repairs . . . better?" She inhaled her sandwiches and started folding the wrapper.

"Sure, so the gunk on your cheek?" I reached out and flicked over it, getting a shot of energy.

"Itchy." She caught my hand and rubbed at it, then smiled up at me. "You know, even deep undercover, I'm still a wire-locking genius inside."

I stared at my hand in hers. "Static shock?"

She shook her head. "More how smiley you are."

Oh. Yeah. I was being dumb again. "It's . . ." I rubbed the back of my neck. "It's . . . er . . . nice . . . to be around you."

Renee leaned on the divide beside me. "And it's . . . nice . . . to know I'm appreciated." She tapped my arm. "And even nicer when you brought lunch to show it."

I nodded.

She leaned on her fist, watching me. I was gonna stare at my hands till my cheeks stopped throbbing. "Nan said I should . . ." I sighed. How did I say this out loud? "Nan says I should talk to you . . . about stuff."

She had, back in Oppidum. She'd also said stuff about shaking cans of soda. I weren't though, and it was pop.

Renee leaned in to catch my eye. "Stuff?"

My stomach wriggled and I pushed back off the divide, making it creak. "I guess . . . it's just . . ." I blew out a long breath. "I left Serenity in some ways but . . ." I stared up at the ceiling—well, the loft above the section I was in. "I guess . . . I ain't left it in others."

Renee leaned in further, into my peripheral vision. "Others?"

I turned and stared at the ladder. I couldn't look at her when I was saying this stuff. I didn't know why but I couldn't. "I can't . . . I can't sleep. I ain't settling."

"Are you worried about something?" she asked, her tone soft.

"No . . . it's 'cause . . ." Nan had said to talk it out. Renee could explain why I was all kinds of crazy then. "'Cause . . . 'cause . . ." I sighed. "'Cause . . . *you're* not there."

I dared a peek her way. Renee's aura fired its lightshow, her eyes filled with affection and amusement. "I'm only down the hallway."

I nodded. I was a big baby. "An' like I said. I'm still Serenity upstairs." I cleared my throat. "So, anyway, glad you liked your lunch."

I turned to leave but Renee caught my hand. "Come back." She pulled me toward her, that half-smile back in place. "I'm your commander." She gave me a stern look. "Professionally, it's not okay for me to be anywhere near your room."

See, I was crazy.

She dropped my hand and fiddled with her trash, tying it up like always. "The fact I'm in your room when we're in Nan's cabin is . . . not really allowed." She chewed on her lip.

"It's okay, I just . . ." I turned to leave again. I should have just kept it to myself.

Renee grabbed me by the hips and turned me around. "Don't go scuttling off." She smiled up at me and slid her arms around my waist. "Professionally, I'm not meant to hug you or have any kind of physical contact either."

"You ain't?" I didn't get it. "But I hug Frei too."

Renee nodded.

"So she's gonna get told off?" Everything was so complicated outside Serenity. It was simple in there: You liked a person, she was as crazy as you were, and you just took her as she was. Outside, there were so many rules, I felt like I'd done something wrong just breathing.

"No." Renee smiled up at me. "Our personal love for you outweighs any professional protocol." She squeezed me, and a burst of warmth and love flooded up through me. "We just do it when no one is looking."

"You don't mind that I'm crazy?" I was figuring that's what she meant.

"Will you stop calling yourself that?" She poked me.

"Can't help it. Serenity does what flying does to your bug: Rattles your screws loose." I tapped my head.

"Then it's a good thing I have a wrench." She flashed me a cheeky smile.

I rolled my eyes and picked up her toolbox.

"I can carry my own toolbox," Renee muttered, trying to take it off me.

"You're short. It could stretch your arms." I chuckled, knowing she was gonna poke me before she even lifted her finger.

"My arms are perfectly in proportion, thank you." She ran her hand up my bicep and squeezed it. "You just have big guns."

"Yeah, and you said you like choppers with big guns." Didn't know why I'd said that but I couldn't help teasing.

She raised an eyebrow, something flashing across her eyes. "Depends how they handle."

"They could bench press you, any good?" I flexed my arm, leaning in.

Her aura filled with pinks and her eyes filled with some emotion I couldn't read. An energy around us made the room shimmer. I weren't sure what it was but like everything faded out but her. Energy hug? What was it?

She squeezed my arm again, clearing her throat. "We . . . We should go find Aunt Bess."

Why was it hard to speak? The energy throbbed and I shuddered.

"Aeron?" Her voice was softer, lower than normal.

I looked down at her hand on my arm. Was it that? "Uh . . . Sure."

My head felt fuzzy.

Renee stroked her thumb over my arm, squeezed once, and dropped her hand away. "Why did you think it was better she stay here? We could do with a closer extraction."

"Huh?"

The energy calmed but fuzzed there in the background.

"When we meet Kiwi, you asked her to stay here," she asked like she was having trouble speaking too.

"Er . . . Yeah." I rubbed the back of my neck. "Just fell out of my mouth."

"You do that a lot." She met my eyes and the energy faded in more. "You're a natural."

I didn't know what the energy was but it kept prickling at me to do something. I pulled her to me and gave her the squishiest cwtch I could.

She relaxed into it and hugged me right back. "That makes you need a cuddle?" she asked in a half-chuckle.

"No, can't figure out what all the energy is so I'm hoping this will help." It did, a little. She smelled of oil and soap.

"Energy?"

"It's so vivid, it's making the room fuzz." It was making my stomach fuzz with it.

Renee leaned back and looked up into my eyes, like she was trying to figure something out, and a gentle smile spread across her lips. "We should go and find Aunt Bess."

"Why, will she know what it is?" Aunt Bess was good with a lot of things. It was worth a shot.

"Best we don't mention it . . ." Renee pulled away, far enough that all the energy faded and I got a cold feeling again. "Better?"

"Kinda liked it," I mumbled. It was warm.

Renee blew out her breath, making the strand of hair falling into her face jostle about. "Best you don't mention that either." She muttered something to herself but all I caught was "professional," like she was telling herself off.

I stared down at the toolbox. Maybe I'd messed up?

"Don't worry about it," she whispered. "You're just picking up on me. We need to get you sleeping, or you'll be feeling everything."

I nodded. "Sure . . . That mean you got to sneak in?"

"Lorelei, I have countless years' experience having to avoid detection in these kinds of situations." She pulled her mouth to the side. "I even managed an engagement like it . . . ish."

"Why'd you have to sneak around to see Fleming?" I didn't get it.

"She's a woman. In the military that wasn't allowed." Renee shrugged. "It doesn't matter. Just know that it gave me some extra-curricular skills."

"Shifty skills." I held up the toolbox. "Should I give you the wire-lock or Frei's lock picks?"

Renee chuckled. "I'm not climbing through windows so I'll be happy."

I got the flash of her falling into a kitchen sink in the dark. "You got it." I turned to walk out.

"Aeron?" Renee whispered as she fell into step beside me, snow swirling around us and crunching under our boots.

"Yeah?" I glanced down at her. Her aura was doing a happy dance.

"I like you as you are too," she said, bumping my hip. "You understand that, right?"

"Not really." I studied her. Her eyes were more piercing in the pale light. "You do?"

"Yes," she leaned up and kissed me on the cheek. "Very much."

Chapter 15

I HAD A real uneasy feeling as we got into the SUV to drive to Kiwi's. Sure, we had bullet-proof vests on; Frei and Renee were armed; Stosur had packed the trunk with survival gear; and Aunt Bess had given us some cookies for the journey, but I was still . . . anxious.

I hoped I looked composed like the others but I was glad they couldn't see my aura. It would have been buzzing like a beehive for all the panic. Maybe I wasn't cut out for being in CIG 'cause I'd frozen before when Renee and I were trapped in a warehouse, Jäger's men close to finding us. I'd panicked, led us into a room full of fuel, and Renee had only just gotten us out.

"Change of location?" Renee asked, looking up from checking her assault rifle as Frei muttered in German at her phone. "Why there?"

"Don't know," Frei said, tapping away at her screen.

Her bullet-proof vest made her jacket rise up while she sat and she rested her chin on the seam as she frowned down at her phone. She was a Frei-sandwich between me and Renee while Stosur was up front driving.

"Kiwi shouldn't have any ties to quarries," Frei muttered, shaking her head, like the phone was spinning tales.

"That's more Hartmann's property now," Stosur said, glancing in the rearview at us. Her bullet-proof vest rose up too, but less so than Frei's. "Doubt she's aware he's using it for meetings."

"Quarries?" Renee leaned around the seat to look at Stosur. "She was into higher grade business when I was there."

I looked to Frei who pretended she couldn't see me looking.

"Oh, she's far higher," Stosur said, slowing us as we headed onto a road clogged up with mulched snow. "She's a shark."

I looked up to the pinky sky; it was gonna snow again soon. How were we gonna get through if it did? Road was bumpy enough now.

"As in . . . ?" Renee asked, sounding fascinated. Her hands

looked real strong holding onto the material, her arms were defined even through the leather jacket she had on.

"Hunts owners," Stosur said. I could feel she was curious why Renee wanted to know, and even more curious how Renee knew Hartmann.

"Tracks them down, takes their companies bit by bit, circles them with dinner parties, rips away their money, their property, and, if she's in the mood, their freedom." Frei fiddled with something that beeped, then frowned at it. She looked to me and moved it over to Renee more, holding it up. "Not the kind anyone with sense annoys."

"Yet Kiwi is?" Renee's hackles were up to the point I hunched too. "I don't like it, Urs."

"Me neither." Frei tapped at the device again and sighed. "Can't get a signal." She gave it to Renee who held it up. "But he's the only lead we have, all the others closed ranks."

My stomach clenched, and I gripped onto the handle. Motion sickness? No, the SUV was making ground over the slippery snow-littered road.

In the fields on either side, it lay as high as the first two planks of the farm fence—at least up to knee level. Guess they'd tried clearing the roads but the snow just kept on falling.

"There will only be one route in and out," Frei said when Renee handed back her device. "And plenty of places for them to hide."

The nausea grew, and I gripped my knees.

"Aeron?" Renee reached across Frei and squeezed my leg. "You okay . . . ? Talk to us."

"Sick . . ." I managed, trying to shove down the bubbling inside. "No . . . I'm gonna be sick . . ."

Stosur slowed.

"Got eyeball on the target."
"Wait. Jäger wants it flipped."
Like he was waiting. He slammed his foot to the gas.

"Brace!" I yelled. I stuck my arm out, yanked Frei and Renee down by the scruffs, and covered their heads as gunfire erupted.

Ding, ding, ding, smash. Glass sprayed across the SUV.

"Hit the gas!" Renee ordered, snapping something into the rifle between her legs. "Hit the gas!"

Renee ducked up. Opened fire.

Burrrr.

Her gun shook the seat as it spat bullets through her smashed window.

"Trying," Stosur yelled back, ramming the drive stick around. "Ice trap." The tires screeched, the burning rubbery smell filled the SUV. "Stuck."

Clink, ding, ding, ding, smash. More glass flew at me. Head stung. Right eye stung.

Renee leaned over to yank up the handbrake. "Watch!"

Smash. The door folded in at me. Smacked my head on something hard. Gripped Frei to keep her head down. Passenger seat buckled at us, caught my head.

Groaning, spinning, crunching.

Burrrr. Renee's gun spat into life. "Hold on!"

Smash, groan, screech. Frei fought to sit up but I held her head there, covered it.

Ding, ding, smash. More glass. A lot of glass. Must be the front windshield.

"Stay," I snapped. "They're waiting for you."

"Mom," Frei slurred at me, fighting to sit up. "Need to help her."

"She's unconscious," I said and looked up at Renee, her gun shuddering through the seat. We were side on with the car. She was firing out of her window, they were firing back.

Slam. Renee grunted as the car smacked into us. They were trying to ram us.

Slam.

"Hostiles?" Frei snapped.

"Alongside, spun us 'round." I yelped as the sharp metal from the door sliced my arm. "Renee took out a tire."

"I have to get us moving," Frei shouted over the gunfire and met my eyes. Blood dribbled down the side of her face but she squeezed my knee. "Aeron, I have to. We need to move."

I nodded and let go. She leaned over the middle console, head in the foot well.

"Ditch," Renee grunted, firing another round to cover Frei. "We're heading for the ditch."

The SUV shot forward. I smacked into the seat in front. Guess she found the gas.

Burrrrr. Renee kept on firing. "Taking out back tires."

"Can't see!" Frei called out. "Where are they? Need some direction!"

Crash.

It wasn't us. At least I couldn't feel nothing but it was loud. Nearby?

"Hostiles are in the hole!" Renee shot back, a nod to me. Then she gripped on. "And we're heading for the other ditch."

"*Rechts?*" Frei muttered in German. Something sparked from the dash. I launched forward and covered her, wincing as hot searing pain hit my head. *"Rechts oder links? Rechts?"*

"*Nein, links!*" Renee said, then pulled my head back down. "We're still heading right, we're gonna hit the ditch."

Frei yanked at the wheel but it weren't working. I reached up and yanked with her but it was stuck. "It's jammed."

"Brakes are flooded," Frei muttered. "Trying pumping." She clunked away at something.

"Not working." Renee tapped my shoulder, shook her head. "Need to exit. Now."

"Ma'am." I pulled back, bringing Frei with me.

Renee slammed open her door, firing as she did so, and yanked Frei out with her. "Move!"

"Trying," Frei slurred somewhere outside. *Ding, ding, ding.* Gunfire erupted.

"Down, keep your head down!" Renee ordered.

Burrrrr. Her assault rifle rattled through my aching ears.

I leaned over, trying to yank free Stosur's seatbelt.

Jammed.

"Alex, you gotta move!" Renee barked from distance.

More gunfire. *Ding, ding, ding.*

SUV still sliding, slipping. Had to get Stosur free. I punched at the seatbelt, ripped at it.

"Come on!"

Ding, ding, ding. I grunted as something sharp sliced the skin on my forearm. Lodged in the seat next to me.

Burrrrr. "Covering you. Get them out!" Frei shouted, her accent full of its German sounds.

"On it!" Renee appeared in the doorway, then shifted her position. *Ding, ding, ding.* She grunted. "Out, now."

I slammed at Stosur's seatbelt again. It pinged free.

"Lorelei, move!" Renee grabbed for my arm.

I threw myself out. Slipped on the ice, smacked my hip to the ground. I righted myself as Renee yanked at the driver's side door. Bullet holes riddled the SUV, glass all smashed in.

"Hostiles aiming!" Frei called out. *Burrrr.* She had Renee's gun.

"I'm going as fast as I can," Renee muttered, desperately yanking at the door.

I glanced at the car in the ditch. Guy took aim at Renee.

"No!" I threw her to the ground.

Ding, ding, ding. Bullets hit the metal above us.

"Get the pack," I said, gripping the handle myself. "Get the pack and get to Frei."

Renee met my eyes, nodded, and sprinted to the trunk. I ripped at the door. It groaned, strained, and peeled open.

The SUV tipped. I grabbed for Stosur. Clasped her shoulders. Renee gripped my belt. Keeping me upright. The SUV fell away from me, crunched into a deep ditch, roof crumpling as I clung to Stosur.

Ding, ding, ding. Renee threw us forward. *Clunk.* The pack clattered to the ice. She opened fire. *Bam, Bam, Bam.* Pistol. "Eyes on cover. Focus on it."

A guy let out a guttural grunt.

I slid and slipped but Renee kept me upright, kept me moving.

"Taking aim!" *Burrrr.* Frei opened fire.

Renee threw us over a clump of snow next to her. *Ding, zip, zip.* Bullets smashed through the top of the mound.

Renee covered my head. *Bam, Bam, Bam.*

I peered up at her. We were behind some rocks, an entrance to a field, big boulders marking out the space. I tapped them with relief.

"Breadcrumb?" Frei slurred at Renee, blood still oozing down the side of her face.

"Way ahead of you," Renee said, her voice thin like she was in pain, her face speckled with glass gashes. She pulled out something. "Giving us a head start."

Frei nodded. Renee hurled it high overhead and pulled my head down. A high pitched *wheee* split through the air.

"We move." Renee dragged me up, and I put Stosur over my shoulder. Was it snowing in my head? I could only see smudges.

I walked smack into something and grunted.

"Watch the fence," Renee said. "Pass her to Urs."

I did as told, feeling Stosur being taken off me more than seeing her. "Can't see."

"Calm," Renee said, and I felt someone move my foot and place my hands. "You're with me. I've got you."

I scrambled over the wire, wincing as the barb caught my leg. My foot stuck in between the wood below and I clattered into the snow, getting a mouthful.

"Stay still," Renee whispered. "We'll untangle you."

I felt someone move my boot.

"Free," Frei said, helping me to my feet and handed Stosur back to me. "Hostiles?"

"Starting to recover," Renee said, and I felt someone take my belt in front and someone behind.

"They ain't looking to share supplies," I mumbled. I could feel how mad they were.

"Neither am I," Frei said from in front of me. "I've left them a few surprises."

"Keep a steady pace," Renee whispered to me, her voice thinner still. "They will scope the area first then spread out the search and we'll be in the cover of those trees by then."

I couldn't see no trees. I couldn't see nothing but fuzzy white.

"You're doing great," Frei whispered to me. "Keep going."

I was trembling from knee to nut. Felt so cold. The ground hardened beneath my feet, stumbled over something.

"Tree stump," Frei said. "Good place to stop."

"Check injuries," Renee said and tapped my back.

I lowered Stosur to the ground and slumped to my knees.

"Mask acted as a barrier," Frei said to my right. Zippers and Velcro—must be opening the pack. "Looks like it has some kind of heat resistant quality."

"Your forehead doesn't though," Renee muttered.

"Lorelei stopped it meeting the windshield, I'm fine," Frei

slurred back at her. Something beeped. "BP low, but normal, pulse seventy five, steady." I saw a light flash. "Out cold but bloods show no abnormalities. We'll need to get her back to check injuries."

Something touched my cheek and warmth spread from it. I smiled. Renee. "Glass in your wound . . . You are definitely going to need stitches."

I shrugged. Felt like I'd tried shaving my head with a chainsaw.

"Can you follow my finger?" Renee asked, her voice faint.

"What finger?" I put my hands out and found her shoulders then frowned. "You're hiding something."

Pop.

"Hostiles have found the trap," Frei muttered. "How did they find it so fast?" I could feel her scrambling near me, pulling Renee from me. "No wonder."

"I'm fine," Renee managed. "It's just a flesh wound . . . a really . . . really big flesh wound with friends."

"You've lost too much blood. Renee, there are at least three bullets through your vest." Frei's voice filled with hoarseness. "They're following the blood."

"Then I'll hide here, you move." Renee said it like she wasn't close to collapse.

"No chance." I held up my hands. "Where?"

"Renee, please. If she doesn't help, I can't fight them off alone." Frei's voice wobbled. "Please."

"If you don't ask, I'll do it anyway and then you can explain to Nan." I felt too detached to feel anything, to cry or get mad. I just needed to get her fixed.

Warm hands took mine. "Fine, only the bullet wounds . . . please."

I placed my hands to the oozing blood seeping out from her back. How was she breathing at all?

Got to get back to get them out. "Stay there," she shot at Frei. "Cover me."

Frei nodded to her, slamming a clip into the rifle. "Covering you. Get them out!"

"On it!" Icy, watch the gouges in the road. Check hostiles:

Reloading. Sprint, faster. the SUV slid toward the ditch, screeching, groaning.

Aeron yanked at something: Stosur's seatbelt? Must be trying to free her.

"Renee!" Frei yelled.

She glanced over at the hostiles, guns raised.

No, not Aeron.

She dived into the gap.

Bam, bam, bam.

Three in the back. Didn't matter. Had to get her out.

I slumped forward into the snow, pain throbbing through my head. "Better?"

"Stopped the bleeding," Frei said with a sigh. "Good work."

"Good, now move." Renee's voice was strong, clear, controlled.

I tried but my body wouldn't, and I was lifted up by the belt.

"I'll carry my mom," Frei said to my left.

"No, I can do that." I shook off the wooziness. "Better, in case you got to fire."

"Agreed," Frei said, and I felt Stosur's limp weight on my shoulder. "Take some of this." She placed something to my lips. "Energy sachet."

"Thanks," I mumbled, wincing as the sugary stuff stung my gashed lips.

"You too, Renee," Frei said. "Anywhere else you're hit?"

"Don't ask and I won't have to lie," Renee shot back from my right. She'd been specific about only the bullet wounds but she'd taken the full brunt of the crash and the attack. "Your head wound a problem?"

Frei let out a sigh as I stumbled along with them guiding me. "Concussion most probably . . . if the pounding is anything to go by."

I stopped. "I can—"

"No," they said in unison, and I was shoved into motion again.

"We need you awake," Renee whispered. "We need you moving."

They didn't have the energy to carry me. I could understand that. "So how do we lose our tail?"

Renee let go of my hand. "By making it too hard to follow."

Chapter 16

BESS LORELEI GUNNED it along the snowy road, ignoring the breeze heckling at her to slow down. Her dear mother could holler all she liked but Aeron needed help and she *was* going to get there to help.

"There's a signal!" Jessie's shrill yell filled the car.

"Mousey?" Bess glanced at the dash. Where'd Mousey come from?

"Speaker phone," Jessie said, her voice squeaky. "Turn left!"

Bess waggled her jaw as tinnitus bounced around her head. "That left?" How did Jessie know how to activate the auto pickup? It needed a code.

"Yes!"

Bess slammed the SUV back down through the gears, slid into the bend, eased through, straightened it out, then switched up the gears with fluid motion. Sure, it was an SUV but it was one of Frei's SUVs. "Mousey, I got a ranch exit on the left and wilderness on the right."

"Up ahead. There are two vehicles in the ditches . . . or were." Jessie muttered away to herself in Dutch.

"Kid, I can't see no ditches. The snow is falling kinda heavy." She squinted up at the sheets of white floating down. Made her eyes funny. Twenty-twenty vision was long gone but she could still make out a rock in a rockery—wonder of laser surgery.

"On your . . . right . . . yes, just ahead." Jessie muttered away in Dutch again. "Just there."

Bess slid to a stop and got out, pistol pulled and searching. On the left, tailgate sticking out of the ditch. She headed over, blinking away the snowflakes. Riddled with bullet holes and an average make of car. She used her boot to clear away the top layer of snow and winced. Two mashed up guys and one crushed up windscreen. "First car rolled into the ditch."

She searched the expanse. Misty white blurred sky from ground and the snow didn't look like it was stopping. She scanned the ground, kicked back the sludge on the road—gouges. "Shunt?"

Jessie didn't answer so she headed back to the SUV and dug in the console for an earpiece. "Mousey?"

"Here!" Jessie sounded like she was bouncing on her mini-toes.

"Left car ain't them, searching the right . . ." She followed the gouges to a ditch on the right and swallowed. Trunk was open but the SUV looked like a crushed can. She dug away the snow.

"Ain't in the SUV . . ." She felt something sticking into her knee on the ground and picked it up. "But there's a breadcrumb."

"Are they okay?" Jessie sounded like she was peering between her fingers.

"Left a message . . . You know how to download these things? My mitts don't work as well in the cold." She peered at the slot in the phone and attempted to jam the breadcrumb in.

"Download what?" Jessie asked. "I can only see dots on a screen."

Ah. She pressed send on the phone and her gut dropped as she read through the statuses. "You ain't hacking nothin' I should be worried about?"

"No?" Jessie didn't sound all that sure about it.

"Uh huh. You want to try locating a breadcrumb for me?" She shook her head at the phone. She'd suggested the breadcrumbs had transmitters in them years ago. The tech guys always whined about it being hard because the things were so small. Typical but then they couldn't cure the sniffles yet either.

"Mom left one in the warehouse . . ." Jessie mumbled. "I didn't know they had trackers." She let out a sigh, and tapping filled Bess's ear. "I can't find anything."

Bess narrowed her eyes. "Wait . . ." She walked back to the first car and peered at the guys' uniforms. "Same motif as in the warehouse . . ."

"Sven?" Jessie asked then grunted. "Or Jäger . . . I can hack his system."

"Careful, Mousey. He may be your papa but it ain't wise to go stirring the termites when you're on a mound of dirt." She left the car and headed to a load of stones marking the entrance to a field. Bullets littered the ground. She glanced up at a group of trees in the distance and climbed over the fence, locking the car remotely over her shoulder. She hurried through the snow then dodged to the side as something about the snow looked . . . off. In front of it was a huge ditch. She cocked her head at the black soot-like substance seeping through the snow.

"He's not my papa. He's an idiot," Jessie grunted. "And I'm with grandpa so my mound has guns . . ." She sighed. "Even if he is eating lunch with Megan."

"Don't let her get you on your own," Bess said. Megan was all kinds of sneaky and slippery.

"I know. I remember her," Jessie said like she'd karate chop her given half a chance. She was a lot like Frei.

"Your mom do soot traps?" Bess stepped around all the traps laid out.

"It's an irritant . . . Grandma uses it." Jessie tapped away. "Makes people dizzy . . . or pass out . . . I can't remember."

Or didn't want to and she didn't blame her.

Bess crept into the line of trees and knelt down at one. Blood soaked the ground . . . a lot of blood. She found a breadcrumb in the tree trunk and her heart skipped—Renee was in real trouble, Frei weren't much better, Stosur was out cold but stable, and Aeron—she closed her eyes and crossed herself—she only hoped she was near water.

A breeze tickled her and she smiled a sad smile. Her momma wasn't as mad as she liked to show, it seemed.

"Mousey?" Her voice sounded miserable to her own ears.

"I've intercepted a call . . . two of Jäger's men. They've requested back-up . . . um . . ." Jessie tapped away. "One man down in the trees . . ." She sounded close to hyperventilating. "They're heading for . . . the ranch . . . a ranch near you!"

Bess spotted the guy in the trees. Cool but not cold yet. There was still a chance to find them. She put her fingers on his eyelids and slid then closed and limped her way back across the field—knee didn't much like the cold. "Any ideas why the guy hit the mulch?"

"He made them go the wrong way . . . something about setting off a trap." Jessie's voice wobbled. "Jäger told them to shoot him." She gasped in her breaths. "You need to find them . . . please."

"Calm, Mousey," Bess said as she got in the truck, slammed it into gear, turned, and headed back toward the ranch. "You got two Lorelei's around . . . We're good at fixing stuff."

A breeze fluttered through her hair and she smiled. Yeah, make that three Loreleis.

Chapter 17

STOSUR WAS EITHER getting heavier or I was getting weaker. The white fuzz in my vision had become a blank screen and my nose or head was dribbling something warm and gooey, my ear too. I guessed that weren't something I could blame on the cold.

"Keep going," Frei whispered, her breaths sharp. "Renee, are they following?"

"Yes." Renee's voice sounded so tired, like her injuries were getting worse. "Trap didn't work."

"It did," I muttered or slurred. Was I slurring? "Jäger told them to head our way."

Frei muttered a whole load in German.

"I agree," Renee said, sounding out of breath. "But we can't take them on. You can't even walk in a straight line."

"I know," Frei snapped. "It's infuriating."

"At least you can see," I said or slurred. "Snow keeps getting in my mouth."

Frei slowed me by the belt and Renee walked smack into the back of me. "Renee?"

"Sorry," she muttered. "Woozy."

"Can you pick the lock?" Frei asked.

"No . . . tendon in my hand is shot," Renee said with a sigh. "You?"

"One handed and concussed?" Frei said with a cockiness in her voice. "Easy." The door clunked open, and cattle stench hit my nostrils.

"In," Renee ordered and I heard the door close behind us. "Lock it."

"Who is the general, Black?" Frei muttered but the door clunked like she'd done as asked.

"Who is the only one who can see without swirls?" Renee shot back. "Ladder to the left. Looks like the hay loft."

"Aeron, can you climb steps?" Frei asked in such a gentle tone that a shiver ran through me. She was beyond worried. "I need you to keep her safe."

I patted Stosur. "You got it . . . and you're trying to keep me out the way while you two try taking on those guys."

"Yes." Renee wasn't going for gentle. She was trying to figure out how to get us out safe. "How many?"

"Nine." I fumbled with the ladder as someone placed my hands to it.

"Nine?" Renee sounded like she'd swallowed wrong.

"Yeah. Two on our tail and seven in fake uniforms pulling up outside the ranch house." I placed my boot to the metal, hoping I could keep Stosur in place as I climbed. "You need to use darts."

"I don't have that many darts," Renee muttered.

"So, when we run out, we'll just use hand to hand." Frei patted me like she wasn't wondering how either of them could shoot let alone fight.

"Aunt Bess is in the SUV," I mumbled, grunting my way up the steps. It shouldn't be this hard to climb. "Don't shoot her, she'll get mad."

I reached the level and felt wood, hay. I placed Stosur onto it and slumped down, not sure why I had known about Aunt Bess. I couldn't even feel Renee and Frei now.

"Keep safe," I whispered, hearing them hurry off. "Please."

ICE COLD HIT Renee's stinging face and she held in her yelp as her shattered knee shot so much pain her teeth tingled. She'd tried to bandage the shard of glass in place but it had been too hard with one hand. Frei's attempt to tie it hadn't been much better. They needed to get rid of Jäger's men and get Aeron help.

She nodded to Frei as they navigated the outside of the barn. Metal building, colder than the snow falling so hard it was impossible to see any distance. She could just about make out the ranch house across the yard.

"I'll get the family to safety," Frei slurred, motioning to the house. Blood dribbled off her chin from the gash on her head. "I'll see if I can take down a few of them."

"You have double vision." Why was she bothering to say it? Frei would fight, shoot, without a care for her own safety. They were too much alike. Frei met her eyes, held her gaze. Sadness, guilt, pain glinted in her icy blues. She opened her mouth but Renee placed her blood soaked finger to quieten her. "I know. Just get her out, okay? Keep her safe."

Frei blinked as tears brimmed, soaking her white blonde eyelashes. "Maybe she can help? Maybe . . ." She took a shuddering breath and looked down at Renee's oozing wound. "I . . . I can't lose you."

Renee kissed her on the cheek. "Do your job, general. Free your family."

Frei pulled her into a desperate hug. "You are dribbling blood all over the ground again," Frei muttered, one long lingering look, and staggered off in the direction of the second barn adjacent to the ranch house.

Renee hugged the corrugated metal and slid her way to the front of the barn. She ripped open an energy sachet with her teeth and downed it. Wasn't going to do a lot but it might keep her going long enough. Her vision wobbled—maybe.

Two squad cars parked up outside the ranch house. They looked like genuine police cruisers but something about the men getting out made her uneasy. They didn't move like officers and she didn't think she'd ever seen five in one car before. The way the farmer stood in the doorway, his stance, his frown, told her he was having the same doubts.

She glanced behind. The two remaining men following them were fighting their way across the field. One was dragging the other out of Frei's trap. Renee crept across the space between the barn and a snow covered fence. She half-climbed it, using some of the blood to flick it into the snow beyond, and retraced her steps.

She headed back to the rear of the barn and took aim with a trembling hand. She'd lost a dart clip somewhere in the trees. Three had snapped so she only had three left.

She held her breath.

Zip.

The man trying to help his friend dropped to the snow.

Zip.

She fired again and the second man slumped forward.

Raised voices filled the air and she turned to see the farmer protesting about something. One "officer" was gesturing back at him as three headed her way. There were two staring out from the cars and one was headed Frei's way, walking around the back of the ranch house. She looked down at her darts, she only had one left.

FREI SNUCK IN through the kitchen door to find three kids and a woman staring at her and she held up her hands. "My name is Agent Frei. Those men outside are not police officers."

"Told you," the boy muttered to his sister beside him. They had coats on, hats, like they were going somewhere.

"Never thought they were. Police officers don't carry machine guns." She folded her arms.

Frei hoped her face didn't show the lurch her stomach had performed. "I'd like to take you to the barn and hide you there until it's safe." She pulled out the clip on her belt. One dart left. Helpful. "I have bullets but we like to bring people in without too much damage."

"That include you," the older boy said, looking her up and down. Brave, considering his chin was wobbling. "'Cause your face is pretty messed up."

"Quiet," the mother—at least she resembled them—muttered. She looked frozen: keys in hand, jacket half on, torn between getting the children to safety and helping the man. "There's a place in the nearest barn, used to have a workshop in it with a pit."

"Good." Frei held open the door. "Unless you're sure it's clear, please remain there." She led them out and closed the door, hoping it made less noise than it felt to her throbbing ears.

She glanced across the yard as they ducked across the snowy gap between house and barn. Three of Jäger's men were heading Renee's way.

She hesitated as the family moved ahead. Her heart wanted to charge across and help Renee, rescue her. She needed help, urgent help, even then the way her leg was bleeding was too much.

Frei gripped her stomach, that ache, that helpless ache that had buckled her when Suz died crept over her. She had always had the ability to shut off and slice duty from feeling but Renee had always forced her to be . . . emotional? Yes, to feel more. There was no logical way Renee could make it, not with her wounds, not with Aeron critically injured but, somehow, her heart refused to believe it. She wouldn't—couldn't—No, focus on the job.

She turned back to the family and followed them into the barn to a corner. The mother helped the children down into the mechanic's pit and Frei pulled some tarpaulin over them, placed a trough across the gap, and covered it in hay.

She snuck back out to the house and crouched as she heard footsteps. One of Jäger's men turned and spotted her. She pulled her gun. Her vision wobbled.

Zip.

He gripped his side and slumped onto the ground, mouth open. She staggered to him, clumping into the wall. He had a police uniform on, a genuine one, but his sidearm was definitely not police issue. She checked the clip—armor-piercing bullets—and peeked around the corner. Two men were loitering next to the cars.

"Why would anyone hide here?" A man muttered, worry lacing his voice. He had the same accent as the family—must be the farmer. "I haven't seen anyone."

"Maybe your family has," another man said. "Why don't we just go in a talk about it."

"They're at her mother's," the farmer said. "I don't want you spooking the cattle."

Frei loaded the bullets in her gun. If he was lying, he was worried. They'd see it. She couldn't risk them shooting.

"We need to check your property," the officer snapped. "Stand back."

An engine roared. Frei peeked out. An SUV hurtled at the two men by the cars. They scattered.

Frei raised her gun as the window slid down. Aim—Wait. Aeron said Aunt Bess was in the SUV.

Frei lowered her gun.

A hand shot out, gun raised.

Zip. First guy dropped to his knees.

Zip. Second guy gripped his chest and slumped down.

Zip. The officer next to the farmer collapsed before any of them could so much as call out.

Aunt Bess was out of the car and motioned for the farmer to get inside. "Icy, get in."

"Who are you people?" the farmer mumbled, covering his head.

"FBI," Aunt Bess said and flashed a badge his way. "Go join

your family . . . ?" She looked to Frei: an unspoken question, where's Aeron?

"In the barn, mechanic pit," Frei slurred and scowled at the farmer. "Go."

"Ma'am," he mumbled and scurried off.

"Icy, move." Aunt Bess took her arm and dragged her to the SUV.

"Three heading for Renee," Frei said, got in and ripped the back compartment open. She kept a med kit in there. "Aeron's in the barn with my mom." She turned and met Aunt Bess's eyes. "They're badly wounded."

Aunt Bess turned and strode off and Frei grabbed the med kit. She let out a long sigh. Shame she didn't carry spare blood around.

Chapter 18

BESS CREPT THROUGH the thick snow, trying to see through the thickening blizzard. Two of Jäger's men had headed right toward the fence side of the barn and the other had gone left. She followed the two men, dropped to her haunches, and loaded more darts. Why she'd decided on darts, she couldn't explain but it was an urge. She'd learned long ago to listen to her gut.

"Blood," one guy said to the other and they walked over to the fence.

Bess caught something move in the distance and her mouth went dry. Renee stumbled out of cover and raised a shaky hand.

Zip. Zip. Bess fired twice. Both men dropped into each other and slid down the fence.

She hurried to Renee as she dropped to her knees, breath shallow, eyelids drooping.

"Glad to see you," Renee rasped.

"Kid, you gotta stay with me." She hoisted Renee up and carried her back to the SUV.

"Aeron . . . have to . . . help . . . barn . . . please." Blood pooled at the corner of her lips. Internal injuries, major wounds to the right leg. Venal, not arterial but the bandage attempting to cut off the bleed wasn't working. Bess felt something ooze through her hands as she placed Renee down—glass wound in the side. Too deep, probably hit the spleen and kidney.

"Icy, med kit? Where's the med kit?" Not that it would help. Not even a surgeon ready in a theatre was gonna be a lot of use. "I have to get Shorty."

Frei nodded as she placed Renee inside, heartbreak in her eyes. "Stay with me, please . . . Aeron needs you . . . I need you."

Bess clamped her tears back and half-jogged, half-limped across the yard, wincing as her knees jarred her. Doctor had told her not to go running around—Doctor was talking crazy. She hurried to the left. A door was halfway along and open.

She pulled her gun, ducked inside. The guy was most of the way up the ladder, a grin on his face.

Smack. He yelped, fell backward, and clattered to the ground. Stosur disarmed him with one mean move. Bess threw her the dart gun and scrambled up the ladder over to Aeron.

"Oh no . . . please . . . no." Her heart stuttered like it would stop and she dropped to her knees. "Shorty, please . . . you gotta wake up."

She tucked the blood-matted hair out of Aeron's face. The wound was so deep the skull was showing, cerebral fluid dribbling out of her nose. "I can't take losing you, you hear me?"

"Ursula will have a med kit," Stosur said from the ladder. "She'll have supplies."

"Ain't much use for them." Bess swallowed back the nausea seeping up her throat as Aeron spluttered for breath. "Momma . . . I know you're mad but . . . I need you."

A breeze hit her and an idea shot through her head.

"Go get them. Go get Frei and Renee. Meet me in the other barn." She felt the urge and she was going with it.

She pulled up Aeron into her arms as Stosur sprinted away. "Shorty, you was a big peanut. Shoulda known then that we'd have that bond." She slipped down the ladder, clattering her chin on the rungs, Aeron's head rolling loose and limp. "I didn't get to see you learnin' stuff or get to be there when you needed me before . . ." She swallowed down the tears, carrying Aeron out into the snow. "But you seem pretty okay with finding me now . . ." She held on tight, heart aching with every step. "I don't want to miss out on you no more."

The snow fell like it was crying for her, each icy tingle hitting the back of her throat. She wouldn't give up, she couldn't. "Your Nan used to say a good idea was inspiration from above."

Tears clogged up her throat, her knees throbbing from the extra weight but she kept moving, kept going. "An' don't tell her this . . . but she's always right."

Aeron's breathing got shallower, slower, gaps between breaths. Bess looked up to the sky, into the white, blinking back her tears. She carried her into the barn and stopped, hurt amplifying until she spluttered out a sob.

Frei had Renee on the floor, pumping at her chest. Furious CPR. "Please . . . Renee, please . . . come on." Tears dripped off her nose. "Please."

"What do you need us to do?" Stosur hurried in, med kit on her back.

"Trough," Bess mumbled, not knowing why. "We stick them in the trough."

Frei met her eyes, hope igniting in hers. "Yes!"

Stosur grabbed Renee as Frei staggered to her feet and they hoisted her into the half-full water trough. Frei climbed in, continuing CPR.

Stosur hurried to the side, fought with the tap, and grabbed a bucket. "I don't know why, I just know I have to fill it."

"Follow your gut." Bess managed to get Aeron in, trying to ignore all the blood in the water, trying to ignore the breaths, shallower, slower, fading.

"What now?" Stosur said, pouring water into the trough and hurrying back to refill.

Frei climbed in and met Bess's eyes. "Wake her up."

"How?" She dunked Aeron's head under the water without thinking. Aeron opened her eyes and she pulled her back up. "Keep with me, Shorty."

Frei took both Aeron and Renee's hands and placed her own over them. "Renee has to ask." She wheezed out her tears, her own blood dripping from her. "It'll set off the process. I know it will." She shook her head, sobbing. "How can she ask when she's not breathing?"

Bess shut her eyes, praying, begging. They needed help.

A breeze swept through, rattled the barn with a fierce bullet. Icy, sharp. Bess gasped in her breath and snapped open her eyes . . . did she hear that?

Yes, Renee gasped. Murmured something. Blood trickling down from her mouth.

"You can do this . . ." Frei begged, shaking her. "Ask."

A rattling gasp fell from Aeron's lips.

"No!" Bess dunked Aeron again. Held her there. "Stay with us, Shorty. Please."

Aeron didn't respond.

"Shorty, don't quit on me." She held her there, not sure why drowning her would help. Gut instinct. Trust it. Believe. "Please."

Something tingled inside her, through her, around her, from her hand, shot into Aeron who jolted.

Aeron's eyes snapped open. Focused. The energy shot from her, rippled through the water. She gripped Renee's hand. Renee's eyes snapped open, and Frei yelped.

"Please," Renee groaned.

Slam—water sucked downward, hard. Bess clattered her chin on the trough but held onto Aeron's head, held her under. Stosur kept pouring water in, blood swirling around, mixing with the mud and grime.

Frei grunted and was pulled in deep.

"Please." Frei shut her eyes.

Renee's eyes closed.

Frei was sucked under.

"Shorty . . . ?" Bess strained. Aeron's pulse weakened. "Come on . . . Don't make me take your cookies away." Tears salty in her mouth, she held on, begging, praying, she couldn't lose her . . . Please. "You can do this."

Pulse faded, slower . . . fainter . . . slipping . . .

"Please," she whispered feeling her heart throb with her words.

Water lapped against the side, her own sharp breaths, Stosur's panting, so loud against the silence.

A breeze, warm, unlike anything she'd ever felt swirled around them, gaining speed, momentum, swept up like it was over Frei, overhead, poised . . . and hit the trough, shooting a wave of water over the side.

Jolt.

Aeron focused again. Bubbles rolled up from her mouth to the surface. One hand gripped onto the side the other held Renee . . . Renee responded with her hand, gripping on, her other held onto Frei who strained against the water. Stosur reached in and pulled Frei's head above the surface and she gasped for breath, pale, trembling.

Breeze picked up strength, rippled through the water, through Bess's hair and built, warmed, swept up, poised, then shot at the trough. Water crashed out either side. Energy crackled.

Jolt, once—Frei grunted; twice—Renee yelped; three times— Aeron stopped breathing.

No.

"Shorty!" Bess ducked her head in, gripped hold of Aeron, and hauled her up to the surface, clinging to her, straining against the sheer ferocity as the breeze swirled and the water hummed with potent voltage. "You can do this!"

The breeze swirled, swept up, poised . . . Hit the water with a crash. Current slammed her back down, pulled her under, sucked the air from her. Crackling, buzzing, building, humming from her through her but she held on.

Her lungs burned, tightened, desperate for air but she focused on the warmth of that breeze, pure love, like the joy of seeing Aeron as a woman, of seeing how incredible she was, how brave and loyal Renee and Frei were, how they were a team, a team built on love . . . Love.

Building, rolling, swirling, up, up, up . . . *Crack.*

Aeron grunted, energy shot into her, from her, into Frei, into Renee, into Stosur and Bess. She yanked with all her strength, surfaced.

"Now!" Aeron met her eyes. "Tip it!"

Bess and Stosur hit a leg each, the trough tipped, sending clear water over the floor and into the drains. Bess toppled with it, holding onto Aeron who slumped into her arms with a shuddering gasp. Bess clung to her, gripped on, like somebody would tell her she was crazy and that hadn't happened.

"You scared me, Shorty," Bess mumbled, hearing her tears as she rocked Aeron gently. "You ain't meant to go scaring old ladies."

"Sorry . . ." Aeron gripped on, squeezing back. "I didn't mean to . . . I'm sorry."

"Faucet is frozen," Frei said, her voice heavy. "How'd you get water from a frozen faucet."

Stosur stared at it, then at the bucket discarded to the side.

"Renee, you there, you hear me," Frei said, brushing back the hair from Renee's face.

"When did I try out-drinking you?" Renee groaned back.

Bess clung to Aeron, squeezing her again. "You fixed them up. You did it."

"*We* did," Aeron whispered back.

Bess hoisted her up to her feet and carried her to the SUV. Stosur carried Renee as Frei nestled close, holding onto Stosur's elbow. A lot of drooping eyelids. They all looked ready to snooze for a good while.

"Good thing I'm drivin'," Bess muttered, carried Aeron to the back, and slid her in. Stosur placed Renee next to her—out cold but breathing—and Frei slumped in next to them, cuddling in, her shoulders shuddering from her tears.

"You got folks to fix up the mess?" she asked Stosur.

"Yes, Jessie will know what to do," she managed, buckled her seat belt, and then passed out.

"Mousey, you read me?" Bess said, shaking her head, and started the engine.

"Are they alright?" Jessie sounded like she was hopping. "Are they?"

"Yeah, what you worryin' for?" Bess hoped her tears—now in relief—weren't showing through her voice. "I need you to get Stosur's guys to come and clean up. They got two cars to tow, two more to take and wipe, two cold ones in the first car, one in the wood and nine more dotted around the farm." She sighed to cover more tears. "You reading me?"

"Making notes," Jessie mumbled. "Mom, grandma, Renee . . . Aeron . . . they are really okay?"

"Yep, snoring in the back." She let out a long breath of relief. "Now I gotta get us back before we get snowed someplace."

"You got it. I'll check the weather statuses and the maps and plot a good route." Jessie was tapping away again. "Check back in a minute."

Bess nodded and rested her head back, focusing on the snow-packed road. Her windshield wipers were struggling to keep up but she felt a soothing breeze so knew Mousey would get them home.

She smiled and said a silent prayer of thanks then blew out another shuddering breath. Her momma always told her to remember to say thanks—she gripped the wheel—and she was thankful for a lot right now, and real thankful her momma was with her.

Chapter 19

BESS LET OUT a long sigh of relief as she shunted the truck into Frei's yard and shut the engine off. The snow had made it difficult to keep moving as they approached the house. She pinched the bridge of her nose, trying to unwind her shoulders. Now she just had to carry a load of sleeping folks inside and her back wasn't happy about it.

The door to the house flew open and Bess pulled her pistol, only to lower it as Jessie and Huber hurried out into the snowy yard.

"Mousey?" Bess shook her head as Jessie ripped open the front door. "How'd you sneak your way in?"

The kid had been the perfect navigator but she should have been in Huber's not out on the road herself.

"Mom gave me a lock," Jessie said, hugging Stosur then went to the back, clambered in, and hugged Frei, Renee, and Aeron. Then she dived at Bess and hugged her too. "I knew you'd find them."

Bess cleared her throat. Now Jessie was getting her teary. She needed something stiff to wash it off. Getting all sentimental in her old age, that's what. She'd be as soft as Lilia at this rate and start baking cookies. She frowned. Had she already baked cookies?

Jessie tried to pull Frei upright to carry her out and Bess held up her hands. "Whoa! She got muscle and it ain't light."

She nodded to Huber as he ducked his head in, relief pulsing from every movement. Then questions filled his eyes like he had so many he didn't know where to start.

"Better you just carry the ladies or make the coffee," she grunted at him. "An Irish one for me."

"I can do that," Jessie said and grinned up at her as she climbed out. "Nan said you would help. She said you were the best."

Bess waved it off. Her momma really thought that? There went the teary again. "It's a Lorelei thing. Scrapes and scratches are badges that matches."

She hadn't heard that one since . . . when was it? Was it the O'Reilly boy? No, no, that was her first kiss . . . or was it? She was sure things like that were supposed to stick but then she'd kissed a few since then. She chuckled to herself, pulling Aeron into her arms. Yeah, there'd been some fine fellas.

"I'll put her upstairs," Huber said, eyeing her as he carried Frei. His voice was quiet, concerned.

"Stop sweating on it. You were just fine, they'll be fine too." Guess folks who hadn't grown up with Nan, Lilia, Aeron, or any of the Lorelei clan might get rattled. "Best if you just act like we do this a lot."

"It's not that," Huber said as they climbed the stairs. She hoped Frei didn't mind snow and mulch on her shiny wood floor. "It's the fact that, if it wasn't for you . . . and Aeron . . ." He studied Aeron's peaceful expression as her head lolled over Bess's arm. "Jäger would be smiling."

"But he ain't." Bess put Aeron on the bed in the first room and re-joined Huber in the hall. They both took a breath and headed back down the stairs. "How'd we get him to back off?"

"I don't know." Huber's shoulders lifted as he braced himself against the snowy wind. "I'd like them to find new identities, to walk away . . . but they won't."

"No, 'cause that's running," Bess said, pulling Renee into her arms. Her color was coming back. Good. "And when you run, guys like that just run after you."

"Yes, but engaging them, trying to strike at his allies?" Huber asked, lifting Stosur into his arms. "Has only shown how he will use them to land his blows." He stomped inside and up the stairs. "The tactics need to change."

Bess nodded, climbed up the stairs, and placed Renee next to Aeron. She smiled as Renee, still out cold, found her way into the nook of Aeron's arm and cuddled in, and Aeron pulled her in closer. Cute as a pair of kittens.

"Your Irish coffee," Jessie said, presenting it like it was a trophy. "Had to check mom's recipe book."

"Every woman needs a good recipe book," Bess said and tasted the drink. Oh yeah, Frei knew her drinks. "Just what I needed."

Jessie grinned up at her. She'd grown since she'd seen her a few months ago. Her skin was darker than Frei's, her hair a mousey brown but her shoulders were starting to widen. Glimmers of Frei, the smile, the nose, were peeking through. She was more expressive though, more animated in her movements.

"Mom said about getting Sven's attention so Jäger *couldn't* attack," Jessie said, chewing on her lip and looking to Huber.

He sighed. "Irritating a bigger idiot doesn't seem wise."

"But he's the only guy that makes Jäger sweat?" Bess sipped her drink. Strong stuff. Good to know that Frei had the right amounts in her drinks.

"Yes." Huber flexed his jaw. "But he's known for his temper . . . and I'd like to avoid it being directed at them."

Sounded like good reasoning. "So we figure out some way to make sure it's directed at Jäger instead?" She pulled Jessie under her arm before she got any ideas. "For now, let's rustle up some food and get some rest." She grinned down at Jessie. "Then . . . I'll show you how to play snow mounds."

Jessie pursed her lips in a true teenage pout. "I'm too old to play in the snow."

Bess smiled and sipped on her drink. Oh, she'd get her playing . . . and Huber. "Take it from a wrinkled peanut." She winked at her and Jessie laughed. "You ain't ever too old to be joyful."

Chapter 20

I PULLED THE blanket around me as I sat on the window seat, warm and toasty, watching Jessie and the others out in the snowy yard below. She sprinted full pelt and hurtled into a waiting snow mound as Renee cheered like it was a football game. Frei clapped, a grin on her face, as she extracted herself from a nearby mound and Stosur and Huber were busy building more.

It was a Lorelei tradition that Aunt Bess was overseeing and, if I just looked with my heart, it could just be any family having fun in the snow. It looked so beautiful now, stars peeking through breaks in the clouds.

"Shorty, you went and got yourself in a pickle . . . again." Nan muttered it half-hearted as she faded in, the seat beside me dipping.

"Jäger kinda has a habit of keeping me busy," I managed. I was too tired to be heckled.

"Figured." I could feel Nan watching me as the competition below heated up.

. Huber had smashed his mound and Jessie giggled at him, shaking her head. *"Helping when you ain't got the energy to stand ain't wise."*

"If I hadn't, Renee wouldn't have made it." I shivered at the thought. I didn't know how Aunt Bess had got me back after I'd helped Stosur. "I did as told."

"This ain't about that. You know it's draining you and you know it's taking longer to recover." Nan tutted. *"You ain't a medic. You need to rest up."*

"I know but we ain't playing snow mounds." I smiled as Renee crashed her mound with a football tackle and got heckled by Frei. "Jäger got a lot of issues . . . guess he's like Sam in that way."

"Ah. Don't mention that boy to me," Nan muttered. *"I got pickle juice to throw at him."*

I looked at the space where I could feel her. "You got a thing for pickle juice too?"

"*'Course,*" Nan said, her energy flickering. *"If I tell you to rest up and try not to go helping . . . would you listen?"*

"Nope. I get that from you." I nodded, feeling my heart fill with the thought. "You work harder as an angel than you did before."

"Got to keep an eye on my girls." Nan's face filled my mind and I could see her smiling, see her eyes twinkling; her whole face beaming with light and love.

"So then I guess we'll keep on working hard." I shook my head as Jessie hurtled at Frei *not* her mound. Frei caught her easily and hoisted her, feet first, into the air. "She needs us to keep her safe."

"Mousey is soaking up a lot from you," Nan said with a chuckle. *"She's got a fine heart. Like yours, it's itching to help."*

"Which is what Jäger is counting on." I leaned my head back against the wall, wrapping the blanket tighter around me as Aunt Bess looked up and waved. "We'll need to figure out how to stop her getting lured in."

"Yup, an' your Aunt Bess got plenty of wiles that'll help but it'll be better for the ticker if she don't need thawing out." Nan chuckled. *"An' she thinks she can't feel a thing."*

"You sayin' she can?" I couldn't make out the detail of Aunt Bess's face but it was like she was searching, hoping for a glimpse of Nan.

"She's been roughed up a lot but she's like that wily squirrel." Nan chuckled louder and I felt a cold breeze on my arm.

"She got a crazy thing for nuts?" I grinned as I got an icy prod in my side.

Nan tutted. *"She loves her family and she will break through most walls to get to them if she has to."*

"Yeah," I said, wanting to reach out to Nan as she faded. "That's the thing about love." Stosur tackled Frei to the ground; Huber tackled Stosur, and Renee, Jessie, and Aunt Bess pelted them with snowballs. "Love is strong enough to break any wall."

Chapter 21

THE SNOW STOPPED falling after a few days and Huber decided that we'd take up an invitation to Sven's Ocean City estate to show Jäger his attack hadn't worked. That was the bit I got amongst all the whispering and discussing everybody did. My mind felt like it had hung out the "gone on vacation" sign and it weren't planning on coming home any time soon.

We'd flown out of Frei's place in a helicopter and landed in Huber's estate, in the private residential area, in Ocean City. The air was salty and bitter when we stepped out and headed for a long limo. Didn't look like much snow had visited but the ground was hard and slippery.

"Mladenovic gonna be here?" I asked, hoping I'd remembered Aunt Bess's cover right as I got into the back of the limo.

"Along with his entourage but they'll be visiting the neighbors." Frei held my gaze for a moment. "Shame for the neighbors that they will be at the dinner party with us."

"I don't want Roberta eating nothing that will upset her stomach." I was real worried about Renee and Frei. I didn't think I could read food and Jäger was sneaky.

"Good thing that all your prison training made you immune then." Frei gave me a wry smile. "And Roberta's stomach is even more concrete than yours."

Renee nodded. "But Locks's is like steel."

Good to know. "So this chump Sven gonna cause me bother?" I wasn't sure why I was acting like Alex Riley already but somehow it gave me armor. I could look out at all the mansions lining the roads and the line of cars snaking up toward a huge mansion in the distance and pretend it weren't really me. I was Alex and she didn't get worried.

"Sven is not the kind of guy to get his hands dirty," Renee whispered to me. "He should be all charm."

"But don't think he isn't stewing after we bankrupted Caprock." Frei tensed her jaw so much, I winced as the jolt of pain hit me.

"We just need him focused enough on you not to notice I've wandered off."

"Roberta going with you?" I didn't want Jäger—and he was sure to be there—following her.

"No. I don't desire your mistress's company, Alex, but thank you for the offer." She turned to stare at the house, and the folks all getting out of their cars.

We stopped and Stosur held open the door for us—I tried not to flinch—she was hyper alert and I didn't need no more nerves.

The salty air prickled at my face as I took in the house: Grand, imposing, floodlight whitewashed walls much like Caprock. Big windows and guards everywhere. I wobbled, getting smashed by emotions to the point I wanted to grip my head.

Renee moved to me, her heels making her reach the level of my chin, and she placed her hand on my back. "Baby steps."

I nodded, thankful she was close as we were greeted by slaves in suits.

"Miss Locks, Miss Riley," one said, checking his list and scanning down it. He wore thick earrings, scar cut into his neck, creating a bald patch in his stubble all the way up to his mouth. He frowned and glanced up at Renee.

"Watch your eyes," I snapped. Sure, she looked stunning in her long gown and hair all fluffed with hairspray but she weren't for drooling on.

"Pardon, Miss Riley," the suit said, staring down at his list, his hand shaking as he held his pen there, poised. "But . . . madam doesn't seem to be on the list."

Frei's aura tightened even though she looked bored.

"Madam don't need to be on it. She ain't worth nobody noticing unless they want to see me mad?" I moved closer to him, trying to ignore the fear prickling over him. "She's with me."

He nodded. "Understood."

"I earned my nickname," I growled down at him. "Use it."

He scribbled out Riley and stuck Samson in, then added Worthington in too. So he'd known who we were? Why push us?

"Good. Now get out of my way or I'll knock your teeth out." I didn't know why the words fell out of my mouth but the slave scarpered and I motioned to Frei. "Baby steps."

She smiled and nodded, striding in through the huge double doors, her tension washing behind her.

"Obstacle one down." Renee squeezed my arm, flashing me a dazzling smile. "Well done."

I shrugged, fiddling with the flappy collar on my shirt. "I learned from the best."

CRIMINALS, IN JAIL or free, seemed to be a lot alike if the dinner party was anything to go by. Now, I didn't mean that as an insult but they had ways of communicating that were on show everywhere around us, ways I knew well from my time in Serenity. The setting might have been fancy: Big chandeliers hanging from high white ceilings and big long rooms decked out in marble and cloth. But, dressed up or not, a criminal in a cocktail dress was still a criminal. That helped me relax for the first time in a while. I knew prison. I understood prison.

"Samson," one guy called out. A false grin in place, gold dripped from every available piece of skin. "Nice piece of playing in the gala."

Which really meant, "You stole my goods," so I laughed at him, knowing it would rub at his ego.

"You think that was me playing?" I laughed harder, really taunting him. "Took three months for me to figure out which was the bow and which was the fiddle."

His laugh sounded like he was ready to burst into tears. "Convincing. You should have been an actress."

Said more like I should have been a slave.

"Nah, I get more fun with Locks." I motioned to her a few feet away, knowing he was doing anything not to look at her. Instead, the guy looked Renee up and down, then up and down me like it would bother me.

"You look like you already know how to find fun." His smile was smarmy as if he was trying to stir my temper.

"He's trying to distract you." Renee's thoughts filled my head. She could do that sometimes and I didn't know how but it was good to hear her real accent.

"I know. Sending you in." I glanced over at Frei talking to Huber. She was in a pant suit, top buttons open, looking as icy as

always but she didn't have a bullet-proof vest on. "Roberta, go ask Locks if she minds me finding someone to entertain myself."

Renee winked up at me, tottered off to Frei, and moved her away from the guy loitering nearby with a gun.

"You're still sticking around?" I shot at the chump next to me. "It was even more pathetic than your slaves. Had to sell them cheap."

He flinched and scurried off.

I strode over to the guy with the gun and tapped him on the shoulder as he followed Renee and Frei. He turned. His eye level at my chest. He raised his eyebrows, glanced higher, until he craned his neck to meet my eyes.

"You want to bug me, chump?" I smiled down at him. "Locks pays me real good money to keep her healthy."

He shook his head, gold clinking about as he did so.

"You lost your slaves. Suck it up. Find something more . . ." I looked him up and down. "You . . . like hairdressing or ballet."

Why those two suggestions?

The guy glanced around him as if to check anyone had heard.

"You'd look fetching in pink." I held his gaze, hoping my mouth knew what it was doing. "Need me to share the pictures I got?"

His frown dipped further and panic bloomed into his aura until I felt edgy myself.

Then he bolted.

I stared after him. Huh?

"Don't ask," Renee whispered, a hint of laughter in her fancy English accent. She took my hand and ran her thumb over it. "Huber wants a word then Sven wants to meet us."

I nodded and followed her. "Never made someone backup by threatening them with ballet before."

Renee smiled up at me. "I'd have run."

I chuckled and squeezed her close. "Imagine me in tights."

She clamped her mouth shut, her lips losing all color as she tried to stifle her laugh. It still bounced through her energy, twinkled in her eyes.

Baby steps and a pirouette. I was on a roll.

Chapter 22

IT WAS SOME experience being at Sven's dinner party. The guy had a ballroom the size of the canteen back in Serenity and folks danced over it like they were at a theatre. Renee tensed under my arm as we loitered near Megan, Frei, and Huber. Jäger's allies were all around, watching us, waiting for a chance to strike.

Megan draped herself over Huber, watching Frei like a hawk as she chatted to him in German. She was doing it to irritate Megan, and Megan was sure rising to it. The way her eyes glinted, I was sure she'd try attacking her with those long nails of hers.

Renee kept as close as she could, trying to help me calm and block out the energy of the nasty ambitions swirling around us. A lot of the attention was drawn to Renee and her top which was competing with Megan's for who could get the lowest . . . and Renee's was so low, I could count the lace stitches.

"Eyes up, Lorelei." Her thoughts trilled through my head as she caught me staring. So I looked to Megan who jutted her chest out and winked at me. Mistresses were kinda strange.

"Samson," Huber said with enough force that I snapped my gaze to him—tux, neat hair, sharp eyes, unimpressed scowl. If I hadn't seen him building snow mounds, I'd wonder if he ever smiled.

"Huber?" I shot back.

"When I have your attention?" He fixed Megan with a glare. She just looked pleased she'd riled him. "Sven is approaching."

Frei tensed, so I pulled her to me, keeping her close . . . and there was the reason why. Jäger limped along behind his brother. Not as tall as me but he walked like a hunter. His dark suit, boot polish stubble and rugged features. Even though he was limping because Renee shot him in the thigh when he was trying to hurt Frei back in the boathouse, limping only meant wounded and dangerous in my eyes but how'd I keep him focused on me and keep his eyes off Frei?

"Ah, you must be Samson," Sven said somewhere in front

of me. He sounded more cultured than Jäger and I could see the picture of him in my mind's eye: watery eyes, skin that was so thin you could see the dark veins riddling his forehead and I could feel how tight his chest was.

"Sure," I muttered like I weren't impressed and kept my eyes locked with Jäger's. His sharp eyes tracked over each of us, probing. He was trying to figure out how none of us had any scratches from the attack.

Sven wheezed—He didn't like not being the center of attention—while Jäger's dark eyes bored into mine—he didn't like that we were all healthy and breathing—So, I stared right back.

"Jäger felt you had potential. That sneaky little move in Caprock proved him right," Sven said like I was a naughty school kid. I could see him wag his finger out the corner of my eye.

"Locks appeals to my sense of adventure," I grunted. That, and I loved her like she was a Lorelei. How could they treat someone like her—or anyone—so bad? Pickle juice, that was what they needed.

Jäger's eyes glinted, the corner of his chipped lips twitched. He thought I was a challenge and he wanted a challenge. He wanted to wriggle his way into my heart so he could rip it from the inside. He wanted to take me away from Frei right under her nose so she'd be alone, abandoned and he could enjoy the victory.

Chump.

I squeezed Frei, making sure she knew Jäger wasn't getting anywhere near her.

"And this is the mistress?" Sven's voice held a hint of, "Look at me. I'm important." He laughed a raspy laugh. "Bankrupting an entire academy; stealing property; helping Locks buy her way free. It was some debut."

Renee slid her hand along my back, found Frei's hand, and held it. Yeah, Renee wasn't letting Jäger near her either.

"Yeah, she likes sticking bullets in people who bug me," I said to Jäger, making sure he saw me looking at his leg.

His nostrils flared, eyes flashed with some nasty thought, and those roughed-up lips twitched again like he was ready to smile. He found being shot funny?

"Smyth is still running," Sven muttered, his energy poking at me to look at him.

"Yeah? He could stand to lose some pounds," I said with a smile, hoping it wound Sven up. He was stewing that Jäger couldn't find him, but then he didn't know Jäger had been running around trying to stop Frei.

Jäger's eyes glinted. Yeah, we'd snuck a whole lot of kids out from under his nose *and* Frei and Jessie had gotten out of his trap. Bet that really bugged him. I gave him my cockiest smile as Renee pulled Frei until she stood behind me.

I had their attention now, I could feel it. Both Jäger and Sven were too busy watching me to notice Huber pull Megan off some place and Frei start to sneak away.

"Well, I'm pretty smart," I said to Jäger, my gaze lingering on his leg once more. "Got to say though . . ." I looked him up and down. "I expected more."

Didn't that intensify Jäger's stare.

"Aeron, be careful. Don't bait him." Renee's thought flashed into my mind. Frei had slipped into the crowd unnoticed.

"Present company excluded," I said, letting through a smug smile. "One of the perks of the job."

Jäger's eyes glinted as if I'd given him gold.

"No flattery." Even Renee's thought sounded exasperated.

I turned my attention to Megan who had somehow wrangled her way free from Huber. "Pleasant company is always worth a challenge or two." My mouth was firing off again.

Megan's eyes twinkled and she winked at me. Jäger cleared his throat, glaring at her. Oh, so he didn't much like not being my focus? All three of them were vying for it. Go figure.

"Mistresses are always worth the challenge," Sven said in a tone that made me want to poke him in the eye as he looked Renee up and down.

I fixed him with the best "back off" glare I had. "Some challenges really ain't." I squeezed Renee close. He weren't getting his mitts on her, no way.

Renee responded by rubbing her hand over the top buttons of my shirt like she was fixing them.

"Women rarely have the strength to be a worry." Sven's bored tone didn't mask the bulging dark veins in his forehead and the prickle of fear running through him.

"Brains, strength, and long memories make them more of a

challenge than any chump." I went back to glaring at Jäger. It was hard not to focus on what he'd done to Frei.

"Why are you baiting Sven?" Renee's mental prod was as good as her poking me. I loved that she could do that. Energy fuzzed through me as she stroked her thumb across my skin. *"Focus, you're shooting eyes at Jäger."*

I was? Oops.

Jäger cocked his head, lips slid into a sneer, bushy eyebrows twitched, and his eyes turned even more shark-like than usual.

I flicked my gaze to Sven, boring into his watery eyes until he couldn't hold it. "You don't get called Samson if you can't crush somebody real easy."

Sven fumbled in his pocket and took his inhaler—same type Jessie had used.

"It's hard to find decent protection these days," Sven muttered, his gout-riddled fingers puffy but white as he clenched his inhaler and glared Jäger's way.

"Locks found the best." Meaning Renee. She was the best.

"So I'm starting to see." He glanced up and down Megan 'cause he felt real uncomfortable with my attention and nodded to Huber who'd stalked to Megan, looking ready to yank her away by the hair. "You look older every time I see you, Huber."

Huber met his gaze with a smug satisfaction. "And you are more irritating."

Sven laughed his wheezy laugh. "You always find women with slick tongues." He looked me up and down, watery eyes full of curiosity. "It's a talent, that much I will give you."

"Oh, I'll take the credit but Samson knows how to play," Huber said, oozing confidence. Feet shoulder-width apart and his belt buckle on show. Looked like he was gonna duel again.

"Yes, she's quite the asset." Sven sounded like it was painful for him to say and turned to me. "I'm looking forward to hearing where Locks found you."

His smile was smarmy and I fought the urge to groan. I sure had a way with the Jäger family. Renee squeezed my arm in support as Sven led us to a quiet area. They hadn't paid any attention to Frei's absence, if they'd even noticed.

As talented and dangerous as she was, she was just another piece of property to them. Well, they were soon gonna see what happened when property decided it weren't gonna lie down.

Chapter 23

BEYOND THE PARTY, the guards crawling over every entrance and exit, the house grew still. A prohibited area sported teams of guards with an extra glint in their eyes, harder features. Not one noticed Frei slip by as she crept along an empty narrow corridor, dodging around marble statues and stone benches as cover. She put her earpiece in and scanned behind her. Sven's place looked as overstated as every other owner's—deep colored carpet set into stone, paintings and wealth draping from every surface.

"Loop in place," Jessie said in her ear. She and Stosur were with Aunt Bess in a neighbor's house. They needed to be close. Frei didn't like it but Jessie was better than anyone at systems . . . and that way Aunt Bess could sit on her if she tried sneaking off.

"All clear," Stosur added.

Frei hurried to the room leading to Sven's databases and archives. Stosur had the plans in her memory and knew most of his buildings well. The database should give them an idea of how to hit him hard enough that he would pay attention.

She swiped the key card Stosur had liberated from Kiwi's outpost in the lock. It was modified now to copy the electronic code on the door—Jessie's idea—She placed it in the slot concealed in the back of her cell phone.

"Downloading," Jessie mumbled.

She was so full of energy now that Aeron had "relieved" her of her asthma. Yes, Frei was so proud to be her mom. How did that fill her up so much? Jessie was a gift. Jessie made the scars worth it. She made taking on Jäger worth it. She rubbed at her face. Must still be emotional from the trough with Aeron. She still felt emotional. Oh get a grip.

Her phone vibrated, and she shook free her thoughts.

"Code is stored," Jessie said.

"Don't forget the signal will disappear when you're in the

room." Stosur couldn't help be a mom herself. "The signal will be scrambled."

Frei smiled. She had parents and a daughter. It was still hard to process. She headed inside—Jessie would be scrambling the camera loops and sensors in the room which would only be active for minutes—minutes more than she needed to break a lock.

She swiped the card and placed it in her phone. Sven prided himself on his security programs and his company was by far the biggest: Cold Lock. It would freeze the system of anyone hacking in, copy it, disable it and Sven would have every bit of detail he needed to send his security team around to make sure the hacker couldn't try again.

The phone buzzed. She took out the card and swiped it and the door opened. Yes, Sven loved to boast about his impenetrable systems which just made it all the more satisfying to break in.

She hurried over to the monitor and inserted the drive into the port. It buzzed once to let her know it was copying the system and she scanned the room. The buzz of electricity hummed all around her and she smiled, imagining the firework display if Aeron poked her head through the doorway. If Aeron wasn't looking so pale then she'd feel better. She hadn't seemed . . . Well? Maybe.

The drive pulsed, she retrieved it, strolled out of the room, and peeked out into the corridor: Empty. She stepped out and closed the door behind her.

" . . . incoming. Move!" Stosur's tone sounded like she was repeating herself.

Frei responded, hurried down the corridor, picked the lock of one room, ducked inside, and relocked it.

"Stay put," Stosur ordered. "Guards are checking the door to the database."

Frei searched the room around her: An office; One desk, one chair, surveillance screen showing an empty corridor.

"Jessie, the loop," she whispered.

"Right. Altering to show the guards," Jessie fired back.

Frei hurried to the window and looked out. Spikes on the window sill—one of Sven's more welcoming additions. To outsiders, they stopped birds landing but they were filled with venom and an electrical current. Not a wise escape route.

She glanced at the screen. One of the guards had something in his hand. He was following her exact movements.

"You have a guard heading your way," Stosur muttered.

Frei glanced up at the ceiling. No air ducts.

"Opening the door," Stosur said.

Frei used the ninety-degree angle between the two walls to scurry up and hold herself above the door.

The guard walked in, eyes on his screen. Military haircut, tall, dark but no marks on his ears. He wasn't a slave. Younger slaves, like Jessie, had worn bands with a chip in them but the guy was around Frei's age—he'd have had an earring.

The guard moved, walking to the monitor—as she had, and over to the window—as she did. She dropped down, silent, and scurried out of the door, along the corridor. How had he been following her trace?

She reached the landing—where she was permitted to be—ducked into the ladies' rest room and blew out a breath.

"Still following," Stosur muttered.

Frei rubbed her hand over her face. "Any ideas?"

"None." Stosur sounded worried and she was never worried. "He's following something."

"There's no other feeds. No secondary cameras," Jessie fired off as if she was hacking every system she could find. "There's no way he can be following anything."

"Fall back," Frei muttered. "Get to the extraction. Now."

Jessie blew out a breath. "But—"

"On it," Stosur fired and cut the line.

Frei pulled out her earpiece and glanced at the door.

"Now, Roberta, don't look so worried," Aeron said, bursting into the rest room. "I just need to use the bathroom."

Frei whimpered with relief.

"Hey, Locks. You got a phone I could borrow 'cause mine ain't working and I want to check how the . . ." She looked at Renee. "Broncos are holding out."

Renee shut the door and locked it, hurried to Frei, took the USB drive, and shoved it in her bra then glanced at the window as if to suggest it.

Frei shook her head.

"See, now windows let out all the warmth. What kind of crazy person would have a window open in the winter?" Aeron held her gaze, nodding.

Frei climbed up onto the sinks, opened the window, pulled herself out and up to the next window ledge: white hot agony ripped through her hands as the spike sliced through her skin—she groaned, fighting the urge to snap her hand away as the jolt hit her. Then she climbed back in, wiped her blood off the sink, turned, and reached for Aeron—

The door opened and the guard wandered in, eyes still on his monitor.

Aeron pulled her hand back, ducked into the toilet, flushed the chain, and slammed the door of a cubicle.

The guard startled, fumbled not to drop the device in his hands.

"Hate to tell you," she grunted. "But you ain't pretty enough to be a girl."

The guard's gaze rolled up until he met Aeron's eyes.

No, he wasn't like a woman at all—Low brow, kind eyes, stubble, broad shoulders, tall . . . the zing through her was far too close to attraction. It had to be the blood loss. She glanced over her shoulder. A *lot* of blood.

The guard met her eyes, his darkened or maybe she was imagining it?

"Hey, chump," Aeron muttered. "You got hearing problems?"

He snapped his eyes back to Aeron. "Pardon, Frau Samson. I'm trying to locate an intruder."

So he was German? He was no slave and his voice was smooth.

Smooth? Must be lightheaded. She exchanged a glance with Renee as the venom shot through her system, her hands sweating, her skin, her throat burning.

"In the girls' bathroom?" Aeron laughed as if she'd flatten him any second.

Renee moved her hand to her back, to her pistol.

Frei shook her head.

"Now, if you start saying they're hiding under the cubicle doors, I'm gonna have to drown you in the toilet," Aeron continued like her temper was fired up—Frei and Renee both flinched. Aeron's soft tones added another level to the threat.

The guard swallowed enough that his neck flexed—Strong neck. Rugged. There was another zing—Venom, it had to be the venom.

"No, there is an intruder," he said. "They climbed out of the window."

He pointed to it and Aeron walked over, leaned around Frei, washed her hands—and the blood—down the sink, then rested her hand on the back of Frei's neck.

Their eyes met: An unspoken question, "Did she want help?"

Frei nodded. The searing pain in her hands faded, the room stopped swaying and her heart stopped pounding.

She wheezed out a breath, hoping her knees would stop wobbling.

Aeron looked up at the window. "I don't see how nobody could fit through that."

The guard strode over, and Frei moved to the side but Aeron glared at him.

"I would like to check," he said. Polite but a statement that Aeron wasn't getting her way. Frei admired his courage. It took a lot to stand up to her when you didn't know she was an overgrown puppy.

Aeron turned to the side, not backing off but allowing him to see there was no blood in the sink.

He frowned like he'd been expecting blood. He climbed up onto the sink, stuck his head out of the window, and Frei looked anywhere but him as his aftershave filled her senses.

Renee raised an eyebrow.

It was the venom, that was all.

"They climbed out." He frowned at his screen, then eyed her. His eyes tracked over her. "They would have been hurt."

"An' I care?" Aeron's voice held an edge to it.

The guard climbed back down and looked over Frei, worry in his eyes. "I need to check, please, Frau Locks."

His politeness was far too cute. Frei held his gaze, hoping her odd reaction didn't show. "Check what exactly?"

"Your hands." He held out his, not threatening but worried. Was he really worried she was hurt? Frei let him lift up her palms. They were trembling. Must have been the effect of Aeron helping her.

"Happy, Chump?" Aeron's voice held a hint that she could read Frei and was trying everything not to.

"Yes." His eyes tracked over Frei's face and he turned back to Aeron. "I will tell the security team that they must be on foot."

"When you find them, tell them to quit using the girls' bathroom or I'll stick them through a window myself." The sharpness through Aeron's tone made the guard move onto the balls of his feet.

"Of course, Frau Samson." He strode out.

Aeron blew out a breath, turned on the faucet, and stuck her hands under the water. "What kind of crap is that?" She grunted as the water clamped her in place.

Renee hurried to the door and relocked it, then held Aeron's arm as Frei held the other.

"It's new. I've got a sample. We'll all need to immunize ourselves against it." She glanced at the door. "Not pleasant."

Aeron's knees buckled. She yelped, whimpered, and nodded. "Worth it?"

Frei and Renee pulled her free.

"Worth it," she said.

"We'll need to keep an eye on him," Renee whispered. "He didn't buy it."

"He's more likely to find a squirrel in his trunk." Aeron held Renee's gaze then Frei's.

Squirrel in a trunk? Mrs. Squirrel was always in . . . Eli Lorelei's trunk. A cop? The guard was a cop? She glanced at the doorway. Interesting.

"He's trying to figure out how you hid the cuts and dealt with the current," Aeron whispered. "Oh, and he appreciates your hair."

That fired a huge zing through her and she ignored it. She was going to forget Aeron's words, she was.

"Who wouldn't?" she mumbled as Renee and Aeron looked at her, affection in their eyes. "You want a picture?"

She strode around them, pulled the door, only to remember it had been locked. She glanced over her shoulder, seeing Aeron and Renee exchange a look.

"I'm still groggy, that's all," she muttered, unlocking the door. It was just the venom. Weird effects of the venom that made her find random men attractive.

She caught sight of the guard at the bottom of the stairs, the zing firing through her again. She rubbed her stomach. So, she wasn't remotely attracted to anyone else in the room, it didn't matter. It was the venom . . . it was.

FREI WAS ALREADY looking sleepy as we headed back down to the party. Jäger had spotted us and was coming our way and I needed to give Renee an excuse to get Frei away from him.

"Roberta, why don't you escort Locks to Huber." I rubbed my stomach, making a show of it. "Ask him how long I gotta wait till food."

"Of course, Samson," Renee said, helping Frei to walk steady. Frei wasn't sleeping yet but she was close.

"You do a remarkable job," Jäger said as he reached me, casting a scowl Frei's way. "I have to admire your dedication."

I met his eyes—steel and about as warm. "She pays real good."

He wagged his finger. "I doubt if I offered you more, you'd change your mind?"

I smiled. "You'd be right." I couldn't cope being in the same room as him, knowing what he'd done to Frei.

He laughed and placed his hand on the small of my back as we walked. "So what does she have that ensures such loyalty?"

A heart? A conscience? Cool hair? "Simple really."

"It is?" He led me to a room with a huge dining table. Folks were taking their seats around it but it was only a portion of those who'd attended. Guess the rest hadn't been hungry.

"Yeah. Locks gives me the route to do what I want and covers my tracks." I slowed, making sure Renee could get Frei to her seat. Wait. Did I sit on Renee's left or right?

Oh no.

"And only she could do that?" I didn't get why he sounded so surprised. He'd seen me shield her from a bullet he'd fired. Chump.

"The fun I like to have takes talent to cover." Sounded like I knew what I was saying. "She gets points for looking good as she cleans up." I looked at Frei in a way I knew Jäger looked at me. She smiled like she was used to it. I didn't. If my mouth weren't firing off, now my eyes were at it.

He leaned in closer. "I could do anything she does and more."

It was official. I was a magnet for the viciously unhinged— mom must be so proud. "Maybe. I ain't seen none of your skills."

And I wasn't planning to. I stared at Renee, hoping she'd turn around and come save my butt because the twinkle in Jäger's eyes made me want to crawl under the table. Yuck.

"Samson, you look tense." Renee was on her feet and at my side like she'd sensed my panic. Had she felt it? Who cared, she was there and rescuing me, again. "She always gets so pent up when she's hungry."

Her tone sounded like she'd just fired an insult at Jäger and she'd poke out her tongue just to emphasize it.

He ran his gaze over her. "Then maybe she needs better stress relief?"

Smack—it sounded like he'd taken Renee's pitch and hit it into the open field.

"This *is* her stress free, Mr. Jäger, but then it takes an expert touch to understand her needs." Renee caught his hit one handed, with a yawn.

Jäger smiled at her like he was planning to hit her across the head with the bat. He turned, limped over to the table, and took a seat.

I raised my eyebrows at Renee. "Verbal baseball?"

"I prefer cricket," she said in her English accent. "He'd have been out for a duck."

Duck? What did ducks have to do with it?

"I ain't arguing," I mumbled, pulling her close. She pushed me to her right, like she was playing. Right, I sat on her right.

I yanked out her chair and lifted it under with her on it and took a seat, nodding to Frei who was next to Renee. Then I turned to Megan who I'd either married or Huber was gonna sit the other side of her.

"Crespo," Sven rasped from the seat at the head of the table. "How's business?"

I remembered Crespo. Nasty little scumbag, a slave trader, bought students who failed in Caprock. He was bald, greedy inset eyes and pock marks riddling his cheeks . . . wait . . . I scowled. *He* was Kiwi. No wonder he'd helped Jäger attack. He was mean enough and crazy enough to do it.

Caprock slave academy and my group stood in the beating Texas sun. It was mid-term assessments and any kids that failed got sold to Crespo. It had been my job to keep the group safe, help them pass but Miroslav, a boy with a rare heart condition, stumbled to his feet and joined them. He couldn't stand up without passing out when I'd met him and even now, after all the rehabilitation, he'd barely manage a few minutes.

The school matron, Harrison, knew he was sick and was planning on him collapsing. She could fail him then, sell him to Crespo.

My heart started to pound in my chest and I knew it was from Miroslav. My legs were shaking. My heart got faster. Harrison was a quarter through reading out. She was taking it real slow.

Miroslav's gaze locked on mine. He was scared. I could feel his fear pulsing through me. I was terrified for him. My knees creaked like they'd buckle.

"Hold on," I mouthed to him. "Hold on."

His shoulders rose and fell as his breathing got more labored. My chest ached. Any second he'd have to bend over. His body couldn't hold him up.

Harrison glanced over at Crespo with a snide smile.

I blinked away the memory. The kids had stood by Miroslav and kept him from Crespo's clutches. It still tightened up my stomach as I glared at him. Some blonde woman sat to his right, young enough to have been a student herself, and a chubby woman sat the other side of him with frizzy brown hair.

"Best haul in years," Crespo said with a sharp grin. "Some academies know how to keep their standards," he added with a pointed stare at Jäger.

"Why plough money into students who are less than adequate?" a guy to the right of Crespo asked—black hair, curly, his fingers covered in gold. "Ms. Harrison has been instrumental in ensuring our goals are met."

Harrison? The matron in Caprock? I looked along the table and, sure thing, she was next to the guy who'd spoken. Same pointy nose, scraped back gray hair, and that scowl.

"We all learned lessons from Caprock." She glared at Frei. "I am better equipped to keep the children safe."

"Safe?" The guard who'd been in the rest room took a seat near Sven, and Frei tensed enough that *I* gripped the table.

"Theo is a curious sort," a woman near him said. "That's security for you." She laughed and everyone else around the table burst into laughter like it had been hilarious but it wasn't. Why did it sound like everyone was terrified?

Renee dug her nails into my leg as she tensed. I bit back the yelp and stared at her. Frei felt like she was trying to stick her shoulders in her ears and now Renee? I touched her hand—

Hartmann always had an easy charm. Powerful, successful, confident. Underneath, she wasn't pleasant company; Underneath she had a temper that made Renee's hairs prickle. It hadn't taken long for that temper to stir when she said she wasn't interested. It only made Hartmann more focused in her pursuit, and it felt like a pursuit. Lilia had said she'd be an ally, that she'd find a trusted friend. Maybe Hartmann would thaw?

Hartmann . . . great, that's how Renee knew her? And she was the shark? So who was she circling?

"Safe, Theo," Hartmann said like she was talking to a kindergarten class. "As in safe from ruthless criminals who want to abduct them and use them for their own means." She glared at Frei. "Locks would be able to tell you all about them."

Theo's energy switched from curious to suspicious. "I have heard much about you."

Frei's eyes hardened. "Good."

"Won't help much if she's got her eye on you," I said, hoping to draw attention from Frei as her eyelids were drooping.

"But now you're in business, surely the goal is to protect what you have?" Hartmann met my eyes. She didn't like me one bit. She had decided I was someone she needed to put in my place or shove out of the way so she could get to Renee.

Good luck trying that. If she went anywhere near her, I'd shove pickles up her nose.

"Squeeze Frei's knee, she's gonna fall asleep in the starter," I thought, hoping Renee would pick up on it, and flexed my thigh, giving Hartmann a pleasant smile.

Renee poked Frei in the leg.

"I have Samson," Frei said, pulling herself up straighter. "She's more than a match for anyone who wants to cause trouble." She sounded as bored as always. "You've met Roberta too. You know how much of an asset she can be."

Hartmann's gaze lighted on Renee. It prickled with the kind of creepy energy that Jäger had when looking at someone. "I recall . . . vaguely . . . how she can be tolerable."

I slid my arm around the back of Renee's chair. I needed to give Frei a static shock or something to wake her up but my arm brushed over Renee's bare shoulder—

Hartmann was dashing. It was hard to ignore it. She was trying to, really trying but everything about her was so smooth, so easy to like. She was attractive and she knew it. Renee couldn't help find herself drawn by it. So she was a lot younger but the way Hartmann smiled at her made her feel . . . what? Special, interested? She needed to keep her onside as the POI, but she didn't need to be that close.

Avoiding her wasn't working. Hartmann had experience, about twenty years more experience, and knew exactly how to get around her avoidance. Did she enjoy the challenge?

Hartmann sat across from her and flashed another smile: disarming, flirty. Renee shoved her unwanted response away, locked it up. Hartman knew she could have anyone she pleased. Renee was just another challenge. She didn't want to be just a challenge to anyone.

No. Lilia needed her close. She needed to do her job. She felt in her pocket for the sleeping vials. Temper or no temper, Lilia wanted Hartmann onside. Renee flashed Hartmann as shy smile, the kind of smile that would make her think she was getting somewhere. She thumbed over the vials. Better Lilia didn't know about her . . . feelings.

"Roberta is a whole lot more than tolerable," I snapped. "An' she likes to keep busy."

Hartmann locked eyes with me like she'd throw her fork at me. "I see she's found you to occupy her."

"Helps when you can keep her interested." Yowch, now I sounded like I was playing verbal baseball. If I could figure out what I was saying, it would help some.

Renee stroked her thumb over my free hand—

How can she be the POI? Even the thief laughed. Everything works out but something is just . . . off?

She flicked off her shoes, clutching the vial in her hand. Hartmann shoved open the door, downed the drink Renee gave her, and slammed it down on the table.

"You found her interesting?" Hartmann snapped. She stank of drink. Renee tried to hide how much she was tensing. It was harder to calm her when she drank.

"Not as interesting as you." It was a lame attempt and they both knew it.

"I give you attention, luxury, and what do you do?" Hartmann gripped her by the shoulders. "You waste it on some useless nobody."

The thief. How could she tell Hartmann she was trying to keep her safe? There was something about the thief. Something cocky and familiar in some way. She had the arrogance to show up at Hartmann's dinner party with a man and act like she hadn't stolen anything.

"She was asking about you." Renee smiled a sweet smile.

"You think I buy that . . . ?" Hartmann raised her hand, her eyes rolled, and she slumped to the floor.

Renee let out a long breath. POI? Really? The woman was vile. What could she do? Tell Lilia, the head of CIG, that she was crazy? How could she explain why Hartmann kept getting angry? No, Lilia would think she'd crossed lines. She'd look into her history. The military would find out. She'd lose her career.

Renee hoisted Hartmann onto the bed. It was better she sucked it up. She glanced at the door. She wanted to go and find the thief. Somehow she felt like she needed to. How would she explain that one? The thief found her amusing.

She slumped onto the bed next to Hartmann. Yeah, she was funny, really freaking funny.

"Some women need tags on them," Sven said in his raspy voice and raised his wine glass.

Most around the table laughed but Theo scowled, his low brow wrinkling. "I don't agree."

"Oh, lighten up," Hartmann said and smiled as she lifted her glass of wine to him. "He gets far too intense about things." She tapped Theo's hand. "Surely your new toy should be keeping you happy."

"New?" Sven asked, leaning onto his puffy hands, a greedy look in his watery eyes.

"Oh yes," Hartmann glared at Renee and Frei, but her smile grew surer. "To keep sticky fingers at bay."

Huber laughed. I hadn't seen him take up his seat next to Megan. He tapped the table with his finger. "Sounds like a challenge any good locksmith would enjoy."

"My system is impenetrable even to a locksmith," Sven muttered, greedy gaze still on Theo. His aura wasn't as convinced by the way it wriggled.

"Hmm . . . didn't you say this of Caprock?" Huber's smile was cocky as he leaned back in his chair and opened his dinner jacket.

"Human frailties," the woman next to Sven snapped. "An error."

Jäger's temper rumbled from him. I didn't need to look at him to know he was scowling.

"We've learned from Smyth's mistakes, dear," Sven said like he was groveling. "Technology is far more effective."

She glared at him. I guessed she must be the wife.

"Technology and experts," Hartmann said, patting Theo's hand. "Are a perfect team."

Sven beamed.

"Humans can be replaced but a machine is always . . . harder to clear." Huber waved his wine glass around, dismissive. His words sounded like he didn't care much for anyone but he didn't mean what he was saying. He meant that everyone was worth something. That a machine was one thing but a living, breathing person held value.

"A person is *always* valuable," Theo said, his eyes intense like he'd throw his fork at Huber. "A person is always worthwhile."

I had to give it to the guy, considering he was with a bunch of slave owners, he wasn't scared to make a point.

"Said like a good security chief," Hartmann cooed like he was a pet puppy.

Smoke. Move. Smoke coming out of the vents.

I sprang to my feet, yanked Renee up, Frei up. "We're leaving. Now."

Everyone stared at me.

"Problem?" Renee pulled her pistol. She moved Frei in between us. Now I knew who the mistresses were as every one of them around the table did the same.

"I smell smoke. It ain't a barbeque." We moved Frei over to the door. Huber was behind us, Megan at his side, gun drawn.

"Theo?" Hartmann snapped, as he fiddled with some gadget.

"She's right. Smoke . . . downstairs?" He frowned at me.

"Try again." I pointed to the vent in the hall, which started to spew smoke." I got a flash of Huber letting in Stosur, and her setting it off.

"Let's move," Renee ordered, marching us to the door and glancing out. She nodded to me. "Chopper is ready."

"Megan, flank us," I shot, like I knew why I'd said it.

Megan ran her gaze over me, nodded, and filed in, placing Huber behind me.

"I see *they* have it under control," Hartmann muttered as I shoved Frei out of the door.

Renee hurried to the chopper, the door opened. Aunt Bess was inside, although she had another disguise on and another male one to boot. I was starting to wonder about her.

She yanked Frei onto the chopper in one move, Huber followed, Megan glanced back at the house.

"Ladies first," I said, picking her up and throwing her in. I wasn't giving her time to check if Jäger was okay. Megan squealed, then flashed me a flirty wink as she sat beside Huber—another admirer, great.

"Ladies first?" Renee said so low I swore it was a growl.

"Yeah." I picked her up and threw her in, climbed in myself and Aunt Bess shut the door. Her aura looked like it was ready to howl with laughter.

I nodded to Stosur, trying not to wince at the temper shooting at me from Renee, and the chopper lifted free of the ground.

Jäger yelled into his radio, Sven was being yelled at by his wife, and Hartmann was climbing into her own helicopter.

"Now we've missed dinner," Megan muttered, her gaze lingering on me again.

"Relax, the kitchen will find you a nice salad," Huber snapped.

Renee leaned into the cockpit as if she was asking Stosur a

question. I didn't miss her hand over the phone Frei had off-loaded in the bathroom too. Hopefully they'd find something to help us get Sven's attention.

Frei nodded to me as I sat opposite her and then did the same to Renee as she sat beside me. That had been one fast extraction that was for sure. We'd even beaten Hartmann.

I glanced at Huber. His face was as stoic as always but his eyes twinkled. If I didn't know better, I'd have thought he was impressed. I knew I was.

Chapter 24

THE CHOPPER RIDE was bumpy as the wind smacked us around. I watched out the window as Baltimore came into view dusted with snow, its lights twinkling up at us. I didn't know a whole lot about the city but it felt industrial, a city hard at work but there were sections that felt . . . abandoned? Maybe city life was like that for some? Surrounded by thousands of other lonely folks. I was more for the open expanse of green or hulking great mountains sprouting lush forests.

We landed, Stosur shut down the engine, and I stooped over to fit my bulk through the door Aunt Bess slid back. Was she staying in Huber's place with us? Was Stosur?

Aunt Bess brushed my hand as I clambered out—a picture of her baking cookies in Frei's with Jessie tied to the chair and Stosur judo-folding the washing.

I smiled but really didn't want to leave her. Renee helped Frei off the chopper with difficulty. I wasn't meant to care enough to help so I folded my arms and stared out at the icy grounds, hoping I just looked bored.

"You know that a woman like you shouldn't be scraping scud from the bottom when there's far richer places to discover," Megan whispered, leaning up to my ear. Her spicy perfume tickled my nostrils.

"You don't think Locks is able to get me what I want?" I whispered back, holding Megan's gaze. My voice held an edge to it, and her aura prickled with fear.

"I think you'd enjoy a more mature vintage." Her smile was sultry as she stroked over my arm—

"You keep your eyes on her. The other one was shot . . . a waste. I don't want to be disappointed again."

Megan flinched with the static shock and frowned at her ring laden hand.

"It ain't so much the vintage but the quality of the wine that makes it," came out of my mouth but I knew nothing about wine. Then I felt warm fingers brush across my back and Renee winked up at me, acting like she'd pulled something from my pocket, and tottered off.

"Quite," Megan whispered, her lipstick so greasy and thick, it shimmered in the yellow glow of the up-lighting around the house. "You won't find it here." She glanced over her bony shoulder along the icy stretch of grass to Huber who was eyeing us. "Don't make my mistake by entertaining the disreputable."

The chopper lifted off, the gust buffeting us as it roared free of the ground. "What is reputable to you?"

I glanced up. Clouds looked full like white flakes would break free again but the air felt too bitter. Hoped Aunt Bess and Stosur would be safe and landed if it did snow.

Megan shivered with the cold. Would have helped if she'd worn a coat . . . or clothes that covered her.

"Families who know where their loyalties lie and don't make money from stealing other's slaves." Megan pouted out her lips like she never did nothing of the sort.

I trudged across the hard ground toward Huber's back door— white washed house, rich wood door with glass inset, and a roof that looked like a snowy hat. "Why would I care?"

She stroked her nail up and down my arm. "If you want to build on the entrance you've made, it helps to have experienced friends."

"And you can show me them?" I leaned in closer as we reached the door.

Renee and Frei had hurried in. Huber's irritation was rising as he strode along behind us, and I was hoping my hands didn't look as blue as they felt.

"Megan," Huber snapped as I held open the door. "I don't remember giving you permission to talk to Samson."

She gave me a crafty smile and turned to him. "I was just telling her about Eis and how three families profited when they went missing . . ." She wiggled her hips as she walked in front, heels clattering on tile as she went. "Two in the right manner and the other . . ." She looked him up and down over her shoulder. "Like a common thief."

"Which is more class than a tramp like you will ever have." He sneered, gripped the back of her neck, and shoved her down the corridor.

I slowed to watch them go, glancing right at Huber's office. Renee had convinced him to help us find Frei when she'd been missing. I still weren't sure how and she wasn't giving details.

I placed my hand on the door, ignoring the odd look from the slave guarding it. It had a sad energy, a frustrated energy—

"You better not have been stupid enough to fool around with his slave," his father snapped, storming into the office.

Even now, as a man, a fully grown man, his father could still make him hunch like a scared child. "Do I get an explanation or am I just to guess what you are talking about?"

"You know full well." His father's eyes blazed, his stern face cut with deep wrinkles. "That slave is a locksmith, boy, and she's not yours to play with."

"I don't play with people," he snapped, slamming his hand to the table. "And I would never play with her."

"So it is true." His father studied him, those razor-like eyes cutting through every layer. "You got her out."

"Yes." He didn't care. "She deserves her freedom . . . everyone does."

"Then let us hope that she can find it and not walk straight into a Jäger trap." His father sighed. "You know better than to assume that family will let a prize like her go."

"That may be so but I believe she can do it." He stuck out his chin. "In fact, I know she can."

"Love blinds you, boy. She is a woman. The second they target her children, she'll come running." He hung his head. "They always do."

"Alex, is there a reason you're listening to the door?" Renee asked in her fake fancy accent.

I dropped my hand from the metal door handle. "'Bout time you found me. It ain't polite to leave somebody waiting in the corridor."

Renee held out her hand. "I was sweeping our room. However much I like Locks, it's always best to be thorough."

I went to her, trying to process Huber's memory. Huber senior seemed like he'd had plenty of firsthand experience of Jäger and his family. We turned a corner and passed a room on the right with a bare wooden door.

"You're a beautiful . . . child . . ."

I pushed the door open but Fahrer wasn't inside. I'd seen the room a lot in Frei's memories but it looked so much smaller to me. A bed, a desk, a lamp, and a chair. Frei always said that was luxury for a slave but it looked like a cell.

"Does she sleep in one of those?" I asked as Renee pulled me back, closed the door, and led me to a huge set of stairs.

"Not anymore," Renee said, helping me up. Feet felt kinda heavy. "And it's best we get you your rest."

Guess Frei was already out cold then.

Renee led me up and to the right, along another wood paneled corridor until she stopped, pulled a lock from inside her bra, and held it to the door.

Weren't gonna ask so I stared up at the high molded ceiling—swirls and flowers in plaster.

"Lock is the key." Renee's thought floated into my mind and she dragged me inside a huge room with a desk—office space more so—a floor-to-ceiling window facing the grounds and white-painted panels on the walls. It had a huge bed, forget king-size, this was a football field size compared to that. Looked kinda comfy too.

"Bugs scrambled, you can talk freely," Renee said in her own accent, pulled me around to the other side of the huge bed, and pushed me onto it. "We have an internal door to Urs, and I'll keep an eye on her while you sleep." She tapped a laptop on her table. "And I have her on camera curtesy of . . . Mousey."

"Yes, ma'am." I saluted and groaned at the relief of a soft bed under my tired body. My spine ached with a dull ache.

"Dimwit." Renee kissed me on the forehead and perched on a sofa facing the door. She unstrapped her pistol from her thigh and placed it on the table, winking at me. "Sleep."

"Stretch your back out," I mumbled, fending off more bubbling energy. I was too tired to think on why it was there.

Renee flicked off her high heels, groaned, and massaged her foot. My feet tingled too, and I watched her rolling out her shoulders. She looked up, her smile soft. "Quit staring and sleep."

Sleep. I closed my eyes, feeling sleep suck me under. Yeah, I just needed to sleep.

Chapter 25

RENEE HEARD A noise outside the door, snapped her eyes open, and sprang to her feet, ready to take on whoever was trying to break in. The room was in darkness, only a dim glow from distant streetlights shone through the tall windows.

Her heart pounded in her ears and she crept to the door dividing their room from Frei's. She ducked inside but Frei was sound asleep in a ball, her smile innocent and sweet. Renee strained, listening for any kind of noise and hurried to Frei's door. Locked, with the intruder-guard across.

Renee frowned. So what woke her?

She went back into her own room and double checked their door. Locked and the intruder-guard across. Hmm.

Maybe she'd just heard one of the slaves?

She curled up on the sofa and placed her pistol on the table again. Hypervigilant, that was all. She closed her eyes.

"Blondie, you getting yourself in a twist?"

Renee jumped, yelped, and gripped her chest. "Nan?" She got up, looking to the door then sighed, because angels always used the door? Dimwit. "I'm not supposed to hear you anymore."

"Uh huh." Nan sounded as amused as ever. *"An' who told you that?"*

"Aeron has her burdens back. That meant I lost my share." She rubbed slow circles over her chest, hoping to ease the palpitations.

"Now, I don't remember tellin' you that." Nan's energy sparkled as she flitted over, then the glitter cleared until Nan appeared as vivid as if she was standing there. Her eyes, much like Aeron's, twinkled with her big beaming smile.

Yup, she was *still* seeing Nan, still hearing Nan. That had to be some kind of mental health issue. "I need sectioning."

"Blondie, you think Shorty gonna let some shrink get her hands on you?" Nan took a seat on the chair next to her and, yes, there appeared the knitting. A stocking stitch if she was correct.

Maybe she could section herself? Doctor Serena Llys—

her cover as a psychiatrist—could have. She pinched her nose. Yes, Doctor Llys could section Renee Black and then Roberta Worthington could teach her English while she was committed.

Yeah, she really did need sectioning.

"She should. They would be correct to lock me up," she muttered.

"They would be and they wouldn't. All folks are crazy. Only some are better at hidin' it is all." Nan winked at her. *"An' if you're crazy, then you're calling Shorty crazy too."*

"Shorty, everyone, they think I can't feel anymore." She tutted at Nan. "And she's *allowed* to see you, she's the empath."

"You're worried about her tripping her fuse?" Nan knitted away: back through middle, catch the loop, flick the stitch off the left needle. She looked like she was making a woolen hat. Maybe it got cold in Etherspace?

"Yes, I don't know what happened when she helped us at the ranch but . . ." She sighed. "She's paler than she should be; her appetite is poor, and she was sick when we were looking for Urs. She could be sicker, she could get sicker if she keeps using her burdens." Not that Aeron would ever let on.

"An' you're scared she is gonna get under your skin and figure out what that heart of yours is hollering at her?" Nan twirled the empty needle with the kind of dexterity that Frei would have been proud of. *"She don't think a woman like you would look at her, let alone love her."* She paused and shook her head. *"Not something I thought I'd be saying."* She chuckled. *"Even old folks can learn new things, huh?"*

Renee beamed at her. "They would need someone as wonderful as you to thaw them."

"I'd more likely scare them out of the few white hairs they got left." She winked, then chuckled, sunshine flowing from her, white hair bobbing about.

"That would be good too." Renee leaned onto her fist. She'd missed talking to Nan, as crazy as it made her.

"Here's the thing, Blondie." Nan swooshed over and fussed with Renee's hair as she stood behind her. *"You have some senses lingering 'cause they're the ones you always had. It's just before, you ignored them."*

Renee looked up at her as Nan perched on the edge of the coffee table in front.

Nan tutted. *"Don't look at me like that, you know you did."*

"That was intuition." Intuition was different. It was experience, knowledge, and a subconscious narrowing of the options methodically. It was a process. It was logic.

"You knew somethin' weren't right when your papa . . ." Nan paused, squeezing Renee's arm. Renee tried not to think about her dad and brother being lost on the mountain. *"You knew something wasn't right when that Sam Casey went and drove you into a pole."* Nan wagged her finger. *"And you knew . . ."* She tapped Renee's chest. *"In there, that Shorty was innocent."*

"Maybe." It was intuition. "It was obvious and I *didn't* know it was Sam."

She didn't want to think about him. He was doing far too well in his trial. Aeron was better off out of the area with the papers sniffing around.

"You ignored it is why." Nan squeezed Renee's cheeks. *"You're gonna have to learn to trust yourself."*

"Easier said than done."

Nan nodded. *"Well, sure, but like Shorty, it's all about learnin' discernment."* She smiled. *"If it's something that helps others, makes you feel joy or peace, that's an indicator it's a good thing."*

"I was uneasy, scared when I thought about . . . him . . . when I thought about dad and Matt on that mountain." She pulled out her dad's medal from its hiding place in her holster. Years of service and the medal didn't even bear his name.

"Shorty gets them flashes sometimes, only she knows enough to understand what they mean." Nan sat beside her on the sofa. *"It ain't your fault. So what helped when you were goin' through it?"*

"I could see . . . well . . . I thought I could see dad and Matt when I was asleep . . . or maybe awake." Had it been a dream? "They were happy where they were. They were okay, safe."

"An' the other?" Nan seemed to know more than she was saying. Her reassuring smile made Renee think she could have been right, that they were okay.

"When Sam hit me, I wasn't sure what happened. My injuries from before must have made it worse." She felt the emotion bubble up as if it would burst from her either in laughter or tears. "Dad came and said he was proud of me. He told me that I needed to believe in love . . ."

Faith wasn't an easy concept for her. Her mother had no time for it, and she'd felt isolated from it before, not welcome, but being near Aeron, Frei, and Nan had stripped that hurt away. "He said . . . my best interests were always at heart . . . that . . . well . . . goodness wants what's best for me."

"An' what you learned about goodness, Blondie? What does my Shorty always do to you?" Nan patted her hand. *"What does she help you do?"*

"Be myself."

"You got it." Nan beamed. *"You just remember that. You're loved for who you are not what box you fit into."* She led Renee over to the window. Icy mist wrapped around the trees in the garden and made them twinkle with a silvery glow. *"Look at them trees, not one of them is the same . . . not really."* She held up a finger as Renee went to protest. *"Sure, we stick names on them 'cause folks like things neat but they all got different branches, different shapes sometimes. Some are tall, some are tiny but none of them gonna be elephants even if they tried."*

Renee chuckled. "True, but then their job isn't to look like an elephant."

"Ah." She waved it off. *"What I'm saying is the reason a tree is so beautiful is because it's a tree. It don't need to be anything in particular to be loved, it just is."* She wrapped an icy cold arm around Renee. *"But a tree, as different as it is from an elephant, still needs the same things to thrive."*

"Which are?" Renee could think of them in biology terms but she assumed Nan wasn't going for that.

"Nourishment, air and light." Nan held her gaze. *"You followin' or do I need Tiddles?"*

"Faith, hope, and love?" She was surprised at herself for saying it. Where had that come from?

Nan smiled at her. *"Good to see you been paying attention when Shorty is meditating."*

Renee shrugged. She paid far *too* much attention that was the problem. "I get the love . . . which is the light, right?" Nan nodded and Renee was certain she might get wrapped in a hug. She held up her hands, feeling better than she had in a while. "And the air?"

Nan winked, went over to a bookcase and tapped one of the books.

Renee followed. Cranial Osteopathy? She opened it and laughed.

"Enjoy reading, Blondie . . . An' you know . . ." Nan paused, holding her gaze. *"You're gonna need to talk to her, she's figuring things out on her own."*

"Things?" Renee mumbled, cuddling the book.

"She knows things are growin' between you even if she ain't twigged." Nan shook her head. *"An' you ain't gonna be able to keep sittin' on it . . . like a can of soda."*

Renee frowned. "Did you say soda?" She was sure Aeron had been muttering about that a lot when they were looking for Frei . . . right before her aura glowed with light and pinks. Hmmm . . .

Nan nodded. *"Like soda."* She faded and Renee looked down at the pages.

"Thank you," she whispered, feeling a breeze in response, and turned back to the book. She felt a glimmer of an idea and her intuition said it was a good one so, for once, she was going to listen.

Nourishment, light and air: faith, hope, and love . . .

Air—it made sense so much that it gave her goosebumps. She stared at the quote on how a cranial osteopath approached treatment and smiled, then laughed: Air.

She cleared her throat and focused on the line. "Every person has within them the breath of life."

RENEE STRETCHED OUT her legs and rolled her hips to shake off the twinge in her back. Sleeping on sofas wasn't as easy as it had been in her twenties. She stretched out her neck and arched her back, groaning at the crunch. It was worth it. A full night of reading and studying had given her the confidence she *could* help Aeron.

Energy prickled around her. She raised her eyebrow and glanced over her shoulder. Aeron was awake and she was trying to pretend she wasn't but the rosy cheeks gave her away.

"Quit staring," she whispered, trying to ignore the sleepy smile and deep color of her eyes.

"Frei still asleep, huh?" Aeron asked, her grin breaking out as she gave up pretending and sat up and plumped up the pillows. "You want to sleep now?"

Renee chuckled. "I did, for eight hours."

"Oh," Aeron mumbled, rubbing her hand over her face. "Guess I been out a while."

Renee stretched out her neck and energy prickled through her, again. She caught Aeron's gaze drifting lower than usual and cleared her throat.

Aeron snapped her eyes to Renee's, blush even more evident. "Guess . . . just . . . uh . . . wonderin' how you don't get chilly."

"Chilly?" She cocked her head but Aeron stared at her fingers like they'd give her an answer, her reddish-brown hair falling into her face, Nan had said to guide her. How to guide her without her realizing?

"You know, after my experience with my mom," she walked over to the bed and sat next to Aeron's feet, "when they caught me with that girl?" Did Aeron remember her talking about it?

"You mean when they made you answer like you were on trial?" Aeron's brow dipped, and she scrunched up her toes. "Mean, that's what they were."

"Yes, after that I retreated into my shell." She turned enough to focus on Aeron and gave her foot a squeeze. "I was very good at pretending to be someone else as you know."

Aeron nodded, and her big brown eyes filled with wonder like she was thrilled just to listen.

"When I protected Hartman . . ." She took a breath, meeting those beautiful brown eyes. "I was faced with an older woman who was *very* comfortable with her sexuality."

Aeron folded her arms and flexed her biceps. "She's mean and bitter."

Renee squeezed Aeron's toes—Neat cut nails, scars that Aeron had said were from running bare foot through the fields as a kid. She loved her feet being free. "Yes, but she was also successful, attractive, and confident."

Aeron's scowl deepened, and she scrunched her mouth to the side. "You think *she's* a looker?"

"Yes," she said, trying not to smile, "because she *is* attractive and knows how to dress."

"Please don't go telling me that's the woman you love 'cause I'm gonna have to carry you to a shrink." The scowl wrinkled Aeron's forehead until her long eyelashes touched her dark eyebrows when she blinked. Her tone was so gruff, so disgruntled, it made it even harder not to smile.

"Did you forget me telling you that the woman I love is the sweetest?" She studied the silk bedcovers between them. The covers caught the light from the lamp, the shadows cut in the fine, strong detail of Aeron's powerful legs. It felt good that Aeron had talked to her, that she wanted to know about her so much.

"Oh, yeah . . ." Aeron blew out a breath, and her floppy hair fluttered about. "Good."

"Anyway, when, as an adult not a hormone-addled teenager, I *was* attracted to Hartmann, it took me a good while to understand that was okay." She held up her hands. "Not okay as in I wanted anything more, but okay that I could be attracted to a woman."

"Your taste sucks." Aeron scrunched up her mouth, complete with unimpressed head jerk. "Fleming and her ain't appreciating you for who you really are."

"I'm guessing Owens didn't either?" She raised her eyebrows.

Aeron wagged her long finger. "No. You know she didn't. Hartmann is a chump." She wagged harder." Fleming . . . Well, she ain't a chump but she went off with that fella." She narrowed her eyes. "An' Owens, she was a chump too."

"No one is good enough, huh?" Renee squeezed Aeron's foot again in an attempt not to say too much, to give too much away. Baby steps.

Aeron shook her head, peering through her hair–still in her face. "None of them anyhow."

"So . . . who would be good enough?" She sat back against the bedpost at the foot of the bed, just to create space, some room to keep her emotions under control.

"Fine." Aeron grunted, sat up, and her strong shoulder muscles flexed. "I'll tell you." She closed her eyes, her lips pursed. "Somebody who wakes up thinkin' on you, who itches to tell you 'bout her day; somebody who'd stop by just to see how you're doin' and get mad when you ain't being yourself." She opened her eyes, eyelashes fluttering, and fixed on Renee. "Someone who loves you so much that you make their whole being sing with it." Her lips slid into a grin, and she tucked her hair behind her ear. "Yeah, she'd be there when you needed to cry or nurse you when you got sick; she'd back you up or step away and let you breathe, whatever you needed." She leaned onto her knees, eyes filled with enthusiasm. "A woman who would treat you as you should be: with love, dedication, and respect. The kind of love Nan got for my grandpa." She flicked her eyes to and fro then gave a curt nod. "Yeah, a woman who sees you for the incredible person you are."

Renee smiled. "Some woman."

"Yeah, but she'd be lucky to be with you." Aeron's eyes deepened, gentle, kind. Then she narrowed them and wagged her finger. "Hartmann ain't gonna make you feel that way."

"Definitely not," Renee said with a snort. "She is attractive but her temper makes mine look gentle."

Aeron winced.

"I'm not *that* bad." She poked her foot. "But what I'm saying is that when I realized I was attracted to her, it took a while to understand that's what it was and to know that was normal for me."

Aeron wiggled her toes like it tickled and sighed. "I'm being snippy, I know, it's just I feel . . . restless."

"Like your stomach flutters and you can't sleep, or eat, or think properly?" She leaned back on her hands, feeling those same feelings herself.

"Yeah, you know what it is?" Aeron whispered like she'd wanted to know for a while, peering from under her eyebrows.

"I do, but it means different things for everyone. Anyone in particular that makes you more restless?" she asked.

Aeron averted her gaze and her cheeks looked like she'd put blusher on. She flexed her long neck a few times and cleared her throat. "So . . . Hartmann wasn't mean to you all the time?"

"No, but I noticed that everyone we met was terrified of her. Not worried because she was some high-powered business woman, but terrified like she'd bite them." She shook her head and leaned back against the post at the foot of the bed. "Common sense told me she was nasty and to forget the job but Lilia said she'd be an ally."

"Mom has a habit of missing stuff." Aeron wiggled her toes, then grinned. "We were lucky that Frei took a shine to you."

How could she forget Frei breaking her out? "Yes, and that I thought she might be the unsub."

Aeron snorted out her laugh, shaking the bed with it.

"Hey, when you met her, you thought she was a bitch *with* burdens." She could feel herself chuckle too, hear how happy it sounded. "I was faced with the full-force of her cocky, stoic, pain-in-the-ass, front."

"You got a point there." Aeron smiled, a gentle smile, sheer affection in her eyes. They both loved Frei. They both needed to help her.

"Yes, I do. From what I *did* learn, Hartmann is way over Sven and Huber's heads." Which the dinner seemed to have proved. Just like when she'd known Hartmann, everyone was wary of her.

Aeron groaned and thunked her head against the headboard. "Like we needed any more crazy folks."

Renee winked at her. "Says you who was entertaining Megan earlier."

"She loves making Huber twitch." Aeron yawned, cheeks firing up once more. "Still don't get how she became his mistress. He don't even like her."

"He doesn't need to. He finds her attractive and she does her job." Renee held Aeron's gaze, hoping she was getting through. "Attraction doesn't always mean love."

"It don't?" Aeron blinked a few times, then screwed up her mouth. She furrowed her brow, then opened her mouth, and closed it. She held up her finger, then dropped it back down. Then she blinked again. "So . . . how'd you know when . . . well . . . it ain't . . . love?"

"Attraction is when you start gazing at physical attributes," she said, smiling no matter how hard she tried not to, "but love is seeing them as more than just trinkets to discover but part of someone who," she smiled at Aeron, "makes your heart sing."

"So you can be attracted *and* in love?" Aeron tucked her legs up to her chest. "Like it ain't . . . shallow . . . to notice stuff?"

"It's part of being in love," she said, squeezing Aeron's knee. "A good part but love, to me at least, is when you smile from the inside just because she's being herself."

"Like the stuff I said earlier?" Aeron's cheeks colored up again.

"Very much so." She held her gaze and squeezed her knee again, sending every bit of love she felt through the touch. "And then attraction is very much okay . . . and mutual."

Chapter 26

FREI STROLLED OUT of her room and stopped to lean on the banister. Huber had sent Megan away for a few days with Kevin. The pretense was as punishment for telling Jäger where he could attack Huber but it also kept Megan and Kevin too far away to overhear anything. It also helped so they could bring Aunt Bess, Stosur, and Jessie back without any questions.

Frei tried to keep her nonchalant air but it was harder to do since Caprock; like a wall had been shattered and she couldn't rebuild it. She was vulnerable, exposed, and freer. How did that work?

"Miss Locks?" Fahrer's gruff tone made her tense. She hadn't seen him since she'd been back, not really but even his voice made her memories bubble up.

"Yes?" Not nonchalant but edgy.

"Is it true?" he asked.

Was he really stopping to chat? "True?"

"About him." His deep eyes held a glint of anger, sorrow, or regret?

"If you mean Jäger, yes." She pushed back the flashes of what had happened and stared out from the balcony. Stosur was with Jessie in the main hallway and Jessie was learning how to rig a false surveillance loop. Aunt Bess sat chomping on a box of cookies, firing mock situations at them.

"I told you that they would hurt you if you pushed." Fahrer's voice held a helplessness that irritated her. "I told you it was better to know your place."

Frei glared at him. She'd loved him, looked up to him and his . . . acceptance stung. "I am entitled freedom. Everyone is." She wanted to hit him until he stopped acting like he didn't matter. "I want others to be free."

"Have you ever asked if they want to be?" He grunted. "You enforce what you want, the same as the owners."

"No. I give them the chance to have a choice," she snapped,

Jody Klaire

pushing back from the bannister, ready to charge him into the side table. "If you want to be pathetic and crawl back to them, that's your choice."

Fahrer scowled and faced her, like he was ready to do the same. "I do my job. I look after Mr. Huber. I'm not pathetic."

Frei grunted. "No, you are dependent on him."

Fahrer's eyes flicked to and fro—He didn't understand the word or what it meant—He could only just manage to read and write.

"It means that because this is your normal," she said, softening her tone. "You're scared of anything different."

He dipped his chin and she knew he agreed with her but then he raised his gaze, defiant. "I'm also scared he will hurt you again."

"Me too." She studied him. He still loved her, she could see that. In some way, she still loved him. They'd always share that but they had nothing in common. They'd both changed.

"Don't try and fight him." Fahrer gripped hold of her arms, desperation in his eyes. "You have your freedom."

"I also have her." She looked down at Jessie who was running rings around Stosur and taking every situation Aunt Bess threw at her in her stride. "Which means her safety comes first."

He looked at Jessie—agony rippled through his eyes, making them even more haunted than they usually appeared.

"She makes my heart fill with more love than I thought possible." She stroked her thumb over his stubble. He looked so much older than her, so tired, even though there were only a few years between them. "She's a blessing I didn't think I'd ever have."

His eyes swirled with affection. "It explains her attitude. You were as bossy."

"She's a lot like me, yes." She soaked in the joy of saying that, watching her mother and Jessie interact. Twenty minutes and Jessie was not only running the surveillance loop but doctoring it, causing Stosur and Aunt Bess to howl with laughter as the screen showed Huber strutting around in a tutu—she'd have done the same at her age given chance, she knew she would have.

"I'll make sure she stays safe." He leaned into her palm, drawing her attention back to him. "I couldn't help Suz . . . your sister . . . but I will help her."

"Hopefully she won't need it." She sucked in her worries, panic crunching up her stomach. How did being a mother make her worry so much?

"She is his." Fahrer's anger resurfaced. "He will try to stop his brother finding out."

She nodded.

"Then . . . you need all the help you can get." He pulled away, eyes filling with longing, with heartbreak. "It will ease the ache."

"I doubt it," she whispered.

Nothing would ease the rawness of their distance, the knowledge that it would only grow wider. Could they have been called lovers? Had they ever been close enough for that? Emotionally: yes, but Fahrer had never kissed her, never let her near. Could they really have ever been more when neither had ever dared whispered their feelings?

Fahrer turned as if he could no longer bear the truth of it but she grasped his hand. "Huber will always offer you a home. You understand that, don't you?"

She couldn't tell him why. She couldn't tell him that she was Huber's daughter. It was too risky.

Fahrer's broad shoulders slumped and he half-turned. "Mr. Huber keeps what is useful. He can't stand the sight of me."

She frowned, holding on, wanting to pull him back. "Why?"

"He has his reasons." The distance returned. He squeezed her hand, once, and walked away.

She watched him go, fighting the need to run after him. Huber took care of him. He had a name, good quarters. No matter how beaten, how angry a child he had been, Huber kept him close and he would always give him safety.

She turned back to Jessie, Stosur, and Aunt Bess giggling as they bantered back and forth. They had such a warm rapport, such a free way of communicating. Frei managed a few words if pushed but she was free with Aeron and Renee. She could talk to them and forget how much of a mess her past was. They were good like that.

If Aeron was beside her now, she would tell Frei to go down there and talk to the kid; Renee would fill her with confidence she could, and they'd drag her down there and show her how. Alone, she couldn't. Those scars just crept back at her and rubbed raw, reminding her that love meant distance . . . like Fahrer had distanced himself from her. It was the best way to guard the people she loved. That way, Jäger wouldn't see she cared and hurt them to hurt her.

Tears stung her eyes and she turned away, her whole body feeling so heavy, so tired. Every step labored along the balcony that had seen her sneak food up to her sister and Suz; watch Suz's battles with Megan; her fights with Huber over Suz being sold; how empty it felt without them; how small it felt as she grew; how claustrophobic it was with all her memories and worries swirling.

She glanced to the left as she headed down flared stairs of marble and lush carpet. The house had seen her grow and then outgrow it yet Fahrer remained in the same room, in the same mindset. Love to him meant distance. Yes, it would guard the people she loved yet she would guard them better by keeping them near. All but Fahrer who she knew now would never break free because he didn't want to. So she would grant him his distance but, somehow, it didn't stop her heart from breaking as she walked away.

RENEE AND I were in a sitting room with real uncomfortable chairs. I guess Huber wanted to make sure his guests didn't stay long. Sure, they weren't prison chairs but they felt like them. The back was too short and curved so one side of the seat dug into my spine; the seat weren't big enough to fit my butt on so I had to scrunch up my knees, and the fancy legs groaned under my weight. I was gonna focus on it though, 'cause if I fixed on the chair and not Renee, who was studying me, then maybe the wriggle would just quit wriggling.

"Megan is otherwise engaged," Huber said, striding in. "Kevin took to begging not to go with her."

"Which just made you say he was?" I asked. Kevin was creepy and sneaky but Megan selling slaves off to cretins like Crespo would get most begging.

"You think that's wise?" Stosur asked as she opened a piece of wall and nodded to Renee and I. "Jäger could get information off him."

I frowned. How'd the wall move like that?

"Grand houses often have doors concealed as panels," Renee whispered, a gentle, deep tone to her voice as she caught my eye.

"'Cause there's something wrong with doors just looking like doors?" I shook my head. Fancy prison chairs and doors that were walls? Rich folks confused me.

"Jäger doesn't want him," Huber said, giving me a pointed stare as he took a seat. He pulled his pants up to show his socks when he did it. "Kevin is far too much hard work."

"So you trust Megan with him?" Stosur asked, going to the tall window and leaning against the white painted shutter to the side.

"Yes." Huber crossed his legs, flashing some leg hair, and sat back.

Stosur narrowed her eyes but Frei wandered in, sadness coating her like a wet cloth.

"So, why are we in discussion?" Huber asked, checking his shirt cuffs.

"Jessie found a way in," Frei said, staring into space. She blinked a few times and looked at Huber. "She found a link. Sven's easiest asset to target is another school."

I tensed. Didn't think I could cope with more teenage hormones. I was like a kid with puppies when it came to helpless rejects, I'd want to adopt them all.

"We have to be fast, hard, and make it impressive." Frei looked to Stosur. "Sven has a lot of money invested in that school."

"But?" Renee leaned forward like she could read Frei better than me.

"Hartmann also has a lot of money invested in that school." Frei fiddled with the ring on her hand. "Which is why Sven thinks it's secure."

"Which it will be," Renee mumbled, picking at her short skirt. "What crazed idiot takes on a shark like Hartmann?"

Frei looked to Huber who smiled. Yes, they had stolen from her and Frei had broken out Renee.

"Harrison is there as the matron, Crespo is buying slaves that fail . . ." Frei whispered, those worry bees buzzing around her.

"Then it's guaranteed to be heavily guarded." Huber pursed his lips. "And worth ripping out from underneath them." He gave her a curt nod.

Frei looked to Stosur.

"I have plenty of willing helpers who would love to land a punch on Sven and Jäger." Stosur rolled from one shoulder to lean on the other and focused on Frei. The shutter clunked to the white wood panel behind it. She nodded, a quiet smile on her face.

Frei looked to me, more uncertain.

"Hey," I said, lifting up my paws. "I thought you were crazy taking on Caprock but you did it." I gave her my most confident grin. "Sweaty teens a specialty."

Frei's tension throbbed from her in waves as she looked to Renee.

Renee frowned, looking to each of us, exasperation in her gray eyes. "Do you realize how hard that would make you to keep safe?" She gave a dismissive flick of her hand. "You'll be in the open and they can shoot you on sight." She wagged a finger—long fingernails, felt scratchy looking at them. "The slaves there could turn and give them information . . . they could run." She flicked out her fingers. "And not to mention that I can't dodge Harrison in heels . . ." She kicked off her shoes and beamed at Frei, her nod certain. "So I want better equipment."

Frei let out a breath which deflated the balloon of worry floating around her. "We'll head back to mine and kit up." Determination and that defiance I knew so well shone through. "Two hundred kids, armed guards, snowy mountain range, and cameras . . ." She grinned. "Let's hit them."

Chapter 27

IT HAD BEEN one long flight to get to Europe and then we'd stopped only to eat, stow our gear onto a chopper a lot like Frei's, and head on back into the air. As always, I didn't get to know where we were, but the mountains were covered in snow which dusted the pine trees stretching as far as the eye could see. I spotted some cute looking chocolate box houses with lights twinkling away. Looked like St. Jude's in Colorado from that height.

Stosur lowered us down in a clearing as I tried to get over that it was evening back home but the early hours wherever we were—couldn't get my sizable skull around it.

"Team one is on the ground infiltrating through the main gate," Stosur said, turning in her seat. "Team two is scaling the north fence. The children will be led out through the main gate to the waiting trucks. That exit has to be clear."

Renee nodded, fixing some gadget to her special ops gear. She and Frei looked super cool. The suits hugged them tight, bullet vests over them, all manner of equipment and ammunition stashed in various places.

Renee's gray eyes met mine, like she'd heard my thoughts and she winked then turned back to Stosur. "I'll radio when we're ready for extraction."

Frei handed her a load of needles. "Quicker."

Renee eyed them. "I've got my CIG ones."

Frei smiled. "CIG used medically approved doses that are tested. After Caprock, they'll have rolled out immunization. And if you didn't notice, Jäger's men took longer to drop."

Renee took them. "Medically unapproved it is."

I winced—Didn't sound pleasant.

Frei loaded her pistol with bullets and flicked it back into her holster. "We're waiting on the signal?"

Stosur nodded, the lights from the console illuminating her latest disguise: Broken nose and facial hair. "Team one will let us know when they've cleared the guard house."

A flash hit me and I raised my eyebrows. "Oh, in that case, they need you guys."

All three looked to me.

"Guard ain't falling asleep and he's getting kinda cranky." I shrugged. "Good thing you got stuff that gets under the skin."

Renee sighed. "Immunization again?"

Frei shook her head. "Most likely his physiological response isn't textbook."

They looked to Stosur who was muttering away to herself. "They aren't in the guard house yet."

Renee tugged at my bulletproof vest and smiled up at me. "Any more flashes?"

I closed my eyes. "Yeah, Harrison will need a nap and the kid with the sniffles loves cops."

"Noted," Frei said and tapped my shoulder. "Move out."

Renee and Frei slipped out and into the dark of the forest. I rubbed my stomach, wanting to pull them back and keep them safe.

"Being part of the extraction team is nail-biting," Stosur said, flashing me a smile, "but we're essential. We make sure they get home."

I managed a nod. "Ain't a talent of mine . . . this action stuff."

Stosur smiled. "Not what I hear."

RENEE FOLLOWED FREI through the thick snow. Pine scent filled the crisp air. The stars twinkled overhead and they slowed as they crested a slope. The school, which looked like a converted fort or grand prison of some kind, sat below in darkness.

"Guard house at the front," Frei said, her voice filling Renee's earpiece.

"Team two?" She nodded to the group suited up to the left.

"Yes."

"Please tell me at least one of them is an adult?" she muttered. She understood that Stosur trained those she helped to help others but either everyone she dealt with was short or hadn't finished growing.

"You want a straight answer?" Frei picked up the pace. The group hadn't so much as glanced their way.

"Take that as a no." The fence was as tall as the school—

maybe five floors—barbed wire trailed over the top. She eyed it. "Electrified?"

"Don't get close enough to test that," Frei shot back. "Team one are surrounding the guard house."

"We're fast but we're not *that* fast." Renee yanked her rifle off her back, clicked on the scope, and dropped to one knee. "Guard is opening the door."

Frei dropped to her haunches. "Team one, come in."

"Miss Locks?" a sweet voice said.

Renee's heart skipped—They *were* just kids.

"Yes. Open the back window." Frei nodded to Renee. "Prove you still got it."

No pressure then. Renee loaded the dart. "Same weight as CIG?"

"Lighter by a milligram, flies straighter." Frei fiddled with something, scuffling about. "They've hit him with the dose. He's not dropping."

Renee adjusted. "On your order."

"Now."

Renee fired.

Zip.

Reloaded.

"Target down." Frei sounded impressed. Why? Hadn't she seen Renee hit twice that distance with ease?

"Guard at eleven o'clock," Frei shot. "Fire at will."

Renee swung to find him—his rifle was out—she fired.

Zip.

Reloaded.

"Target down." Frei tapped her shoulder. "Team one, clean up."

"Wow, thanks, Miss Locks," came the sweet reply.

"Any more?" Renee asked, flicking on the safety and dropping the rifle off her shoulder.

"Alex only told us about him. We get to Harrison." Frei was up and moving. Renee unclipped the scope and swung the rifle onto her back, mid-stride. "Sven's most valuable kids are together on the second floor. New kids. We get them out and leave the rest to Stosur's team."

"Yes, Miss Locks," she said in her best teasing tone. It was the only way she could think to stop from saluting. Mistresses weren't meant to salute.

"Does your English accent have to be so nasal?" Frei muttered as they ducked through the main gate, signaling to the kids tying up the guard. Renee looked at his chest—rising and falling—good.

"No, I just like irritating you and Alex," she said as they hurried up the main road and then frowned, seemed familiar. "You notice most of these places have the same set up?"

"We'll make an investigator out of you yet," Frei shot back, her tone laced with sarcasm.

"You want me to shoot you?" Renee muttered. "You were cuter when you were curled up in a ball. You get that you look innocent when you're dribbling?"

Frei glanced back at her, pressing the talk button on her throat. Why was she only talking to her? "You want me to tell Alex just why she gets so fidgety around you?" She laughed. "And then attraction is very much okay and mutual . . . Considering she's so receptive, she's dense."

Renee clicked her own talk button. "She can't see anything to do with herself . . . and bugging your friends is rude."

"Uh huh." Frei led them to the front doors. "You spelled it out for her and she's still clueless."

"Because she's not ready to deal with it." Renee sighed. "It'll click when she is."

Frei seemed to just touch the lock and the door opened. "Let's hope that isn't while we're at Sven's. Kid will be knocked sideways."

"I'm not *that* bad." Renee followed her in, raised her rifle.

Zip.

Zip.

One—two—guards dropped to the floor.

Frei opened fire.

Zip.

Zip.

Two more hit the deck.

Renee hurried over and dragged two guards to the reception room on the left. Frei grabbed a leg each of the other two and did the same.

"I didn't mean you. I knew what I felt when I realized I was in love." Frei grunted out a breath. "Can't say it was enjoyable."

"Yeah, first time floors you." Renee peeked out into the corridor. "Clear."

"You take the stairs at the back. Harrison will be in her quarters," Frei said. "I'll take the main stairs. Get rid of the guards. Extra patrols."

"You got it," Renee said. It was hard not to slip into default but inside they had to make sure they didn't appear too military, that's if anyone could hear through the muffler over her mouth.

Renee snuck along the corridor. Like Caprock, it had offices on the left and right, all in darkness and, if it was the same, the theatre for gala nights would be next to that. She paused outside the door, fed her optic-scope inside. One backstage complete with sets and scenery.

She moved on, around a corner, slid along the wall, watching the red beam sliding back and forth overhead. She switched her radio back to transmit to the whole team. "We have motion detectors. Back stairs."

"On it," Frei shot. Renee pulled back, why would there be motion detectors in a school? "Clear."

"Quick, even for you." She peeked around the corner. No red beam. "Impressive."

"As expected," Frei said in her cocky tone.

Renee rolled her eyes and crept up the back stairs but paused at the top. "Three guards, one sleeping hall monitor."

She crouched low, pulling her rifle around and loading it but before she could fire, one guard dropped, then the second, the third turned toward them—

Renee fired. *Zip.*

Third guard down and one hall monitor awake.

She fired again. *Zip.*

One hall monitor asleep.

"Clear," Frei said, slipped into view, and dragged the guards into the room with the monitor. "Harrison is on the right."

"On route." Renee headed into the hallway and put the optic scope through the keyhole.

Harrison was asleep in bed, snoring. Nice. She pulled out her picks and slid them into the lock. In seconds, the door clicked open and she pulled out her pistol and loaded it with a dart— Aeron said Harrison needed a nap.

Renee ducked in, fired. *Zip*—Harrison grunted and fell silent. She crept up and pulled out the pistol Harrison was holding under the sheet.

"Were they expecting us?"

"Shouldn't have been but she's a hawk," Frei said. "Plant the device and move."

Renee nodded . . . then paused. She cocked her head at the bracelet Harrison had on and leaned closer. Why was that familiar?

"Where are you?" Frei snapped.

Renee moved away, planted the stick in the port of the computer. It vibrated once and she headed out of the room, turned right, and stopped at the open door.

Frei was waiting. "Kids are huddled in the corner," she whispered.

"For us?" Renee holstered her pistol.

"Don't know. Keep close." Frei strode up to the bed and shook it.

The kids whimpered, and a boy shot up and stood in front of them. "You won't hurt . . ." His little voice trailed off as his gaze lighted on Frei in her gear.

Renee walked over. "I'm officer Worthington and this is Officer Locks, we're here to get you out." She hoped her Portuguese wasn't too rusty.

He turned to her. "Police?"

She nodded and dropped to one knee. "We're getting you all out."

He looked back at the girls. "They hurt them, I don't know what this place is but it isn't an orphanage."

"No, we need to get you to safety, okay?" She held out her hand. Frei nodded to her and strode out. "My commander has left you with me." She turned her palm up. We're a special task force. I'm going to take you to the roof and we'll get a ride in a helicopter."

His shoulders relaxed and he nodded to the girls. One of them sniffed and sobbed. Aeron had said sniffles loved the police so she smiled. "If you like, I'll show you my badge when we get in the air?"

The kid blinked up at her, then nodded, cuddling into the older girl. "Okay."

The boy took her hand, and the older girl took his and held the youngest close.

Renee nodded and led them out into the corridor but where was Frei?

FREI PAUSED BESIDE the smooth rendered wall and narrowed her eyes as she zoned in on the whimpering. Team two had emptied the place and all but Sven's three kids were out of the school and trailing, single file, down to the gate.

This floor had been cleared first so why could she hear movement in the room? The whimper sounded again followed by a harsh male voice. Muffled. She stopped outside the door and fed her scope in, then scowled as she fought the urge to pull her gun and use bullets.

"I told you, quiet," the man snapped as the kid cowered, hiding behind the bed from him. "You'll do as you're told."

Frei bit back her own memories, unlocked the door, and slipped inside. The kid's gaze tracked to hers—the thug hadn't gotten near him yet.

She nodded, putting her finger to her lips.

"Come here," the thug growled as the boy darted away from his grasp.

Frei stood up, pulled out the dart, and jabbed the thug in the most painful place she could think of, then covered his mouth as he yelped and dropped to the floor. "Kid, you want to get out of here?"

"Please," the boy whispered, wide-eyed and staring at the thug snoring. "But . . . I need my bear. I can't leave Ruffles behind."

Ugh, sucker punch. Frei held out her arms, and the kid climbed on her back. "Which room?"

"On that side," he said, waving across the hallway. "Are you a ninja?"

She smiled, she couldn't help herself. "Yes."

"Cool," he whispered.

She headed into the room and picked up the ruffled excuse for a bear. "This yours?" She scanned around the room, every other belonging had gone, beds made, wiped down, perfect training. Couldn't expect less from anyone trained by Stosur.

"That's him." The boy pulled him close, cuddling in. "It's okay, Ruffles, the ninja lady will help us."

He held out a paw for her to shake.

She got the feeling Aeron was grinning back at the chopper. "Nice to meet you."

"Ruffles," the boy said and looked at her.

"Right. Nice to meet you, Ruffles." She shook its paw and headed out into the corridor.

She was getting soft. Why was talking to a stuffed bear making her teary? Aeron, that's what it was, Aeron and Renee and their irritating, sentimental, sweet, kind, pain-in-her-ass hearts.

She headed into Harrison's room, retrieved the stick, and stowed it in her pocket then jogged up the stairs to the rooftop as the boy clung on. "Hold on, Ruffles."

Renee held the rope and cocked her head. "We adopting?"

"Straggler plus bear," she shot back.

"Ruffles," the boy said and, once again, held out the bear's paw.

Renee gave the bear a hug and grinned at the boy. "Welcome aboard, gentlemen," she said in Portuguese then held out her arms and the boy clambered to her as Aeron lowered down the harness. "You're going to come up with me," she once again said in Portuguese.

The boy looked back to Frei.

"Portuguese ninja," she mumbled in English and shrugged. "You're hitching a ride with her."

"Ruffles likes Portugal." He smiled.

Eh, kids were easier to please than people. Adults had a tendency to faff around, worrying about being hoisted until she just darted them.

Renee and the boy headed up and Frei scanned the rooftop and the grounds. The team was closing up the gate.

"We have anyone else we need to retrieve, Alex?" she said into her mic.

"Nope, glad you found this one though 'cause I was sending you back in," Aeron said, her rich tone full of a smile. How could she hear a smile? Didn't matter, she could. "Hey, Ruffles, good to meet you."

Frei sighed, took the harness, and slipped it on. Aeron made quick work of pulling her in, and she closed up. Renee pulled off her mask and she did the same, the kids gawping at them as they did so.

"You do kids," she mumbled at Renee and headed into the cockpit. "Enjoy."

Stosur swung them away with a smile. "Trucks on the move, school emptied, and one bear rescued . . . hello, Ruffles." She nodded over her shoulder to the bear. "Not a bad haul."

Frei pulled on her headset as Aeron launched into chatter with kids, and bear, and Renee mumble on about some badge. Wait—why did she have a badge?

"You're not meant to wear it in deep cover," Frei shot into the headset.

Renee looked up and shrugged. "Helps."

It was a medal, not a badge, and her father's. "Won't help if you get caught."

Renee sighed. "It stays in my holster and doesn't have a name on it."

Aeron leaned over across the gap. "Looks kinda shiny."

"Why do ninjas have badges?" the straggler asked as Renee scanned over the bear with the monitor and nodded. Good, clear. She didn't want to go pulling the stuffing out of Ruffles, he was cute. Cute? Ugh, she was getting too soft.

"Ninja?" Aeron raised her eyebrows.

Frei turned back to the front. "Don't ask."

She ignored the laughter from behind her and relaxed back into her seat. She smiled at the way Renee and Aeron interacted with the kids and glanced at her mom. Joy bubbled up, and she turned away so her mom didn't see it. Yeah, she was too soft.

Chapter 28

I HAD NO idea where Stosur was gonna stash two hundred kids but I was confident that she could. The flight back had been a real long one and even in a luxury plane like Frei's, it drained me. Most energy I felt was when Renee was near—it boosted me but then when she moved away, I realized how tired I was.

We'd moved camp back out to Frei's place and, while Renee, Frei, Jessie, Aunt Bess, and Stosur worked out tactics and trained, they let me rest. Aunt Bess had taken to feeding me cookies and Jessie stopped by a lot. She liked to tell me about the other kids from Caprock, who were at Aunt Bess's place. She'd tell me how Jed Jr. hadn't made a break for it just yet and Miroslav had taken to massaging Miranda's feet 'cause Jed had some weird phobia of swollen toes. The other girls were helping her with breathing exercises while Grimes had helped the boys make a cot for Jed Jr. . . . only the two cats were hogging it.

I wanted to send Jessie to them and knew Frei was feeling the same. I wanted her to be free, to celebrate it, but that wouldn't work, she was too set on helping.

"Gonna stick a bell on her," Aunt Bess muttered as she brought me food and tutted at Jessie who was in the yard taking on Stosur in snowball self-defense. "She don't help her by teaching her tricks."

"I guess she figures it could help her if she needs it." I took my plate of food. Some kind of chunky meat with a load of sauce. It smelled real good but I just weren't hungry.

"You're looking all kinds of pale," Aunt Bess said, touching the back of her hand to my forehead. "Nan talk to you 'bout it?"

I nodded.

"And?" She folded her arms. Her frilly sleeves were rolled up and they flapped as her arm flexed.

"If I rest up, I'll be fine." Stretching the truth but I didn't want her worrying.

"You ain't been fine since you were in the trough," She said, stroking my hair from my face. "You gotta listen to that body 'cause, take it from me, it'll nag you the more wrinkled you get."

"I share your genes," I said. "So I don't have to worry 'cause you look real good." I pushed my food around my plate. There was a load of green stuff mashed up in the middle of the meat. My mouth watered but my stomach weren't awake.

"Uh huh." She bellowed out her chuckle. "You got Lorelei charm alright."

"I ain't been feeling right since before my burdens got dimmed." I'd relived the hurt I'd displaced from folks and had been locked in a pillow prison for it. "Not sure it is my burdens though."

Aunt Bess eyed me. "An' it ain't gone when you sit in water?"

I shook my head. "I figure that if it's meant to be fixed, it will be."

"Helps if you tell somebody and they can check you out." She scowled at me. "You in pain, or sick or. . . What is it?"

"Nothing like that . . . not really." I chomped on my food. Black pepper and sour sauce, salty tender meat and the green creamy stuff. "Maybe it's just that I been busy since I got released."

She nodded but she weren't convinced. "Maybe you should help me and let the girls take on Jäger?"

I shook my head. "They need me. Jäger gets distracted by me."

She smiled, a big warm smile.

"What?" I asked.

She squeezed my shoulder and got to her feet. "You got a good heart. Definitely get that from Nan."

"And you, ain't got many folks who'd walk away from a guy in an apron, right?" I grinned at her.

"Good to know you were listening," she said and kissed me on the head. "Even if his beer clogs up my fridge."

I STEADIED MYSELF and headed down to the glass room to find everyone, Huber included, around the tree-table, pouring over papers.

"You taking a test?" I asked, looking around at them.

"We've got an invitation to Sven's," Frei said without looking up. "One we can't really turn down."

"But you wanted his attention?" I folded my arms. I didn't get it, again.

"Yes," Stosur mumbled, sketching away beside the window. "But he hasn't issued it, Hartmann has." She glanced at Renee.

"How come she is inviting folks to his place?" I weren't versed in social stuff but it seemed kinda rude.

"Because she's pushing Sven to prove his authority," Huber said, flicking through papers.

I picked up a sheet near me—a map of an estate with grounds. "How does he do that?"

"By doing what no one else has so far," Frei mumbled, rubbing her forehead, her eyes closed like it hurt to think. "Keep me from breaking in."

"But you don't have to, he—or Hartmann—has invited you." Why did she have so many pictures?

"Not breaking into his estate," Renee said, pulling me down to sit beside her. She squeezed my hand, flashing a gentle smile. "Hartmann has issued a challenge to them both. Sven has to prove he's clever by catching Frei."

Nope, I was still confused.

"Her challenge to Frei is to break into Cold Lock—his impenetrable security system," Renee said with a sigh and leaned her head on my shoulder.

"So she wants to see them both sweat?" I stared at a picture of the inside of the house. A small door in a wall. Something about it drew me to study it.

"Sven had to sell her more shares in Cold Lock to keep his head above water after we emptied the school." Stosur leaned over, placed a sketch down, and started another.

"Hartmann is dubious of the worth of Cold Lock," Huber said, tapping something on the picture and talking to Stosur in German. "Which means she wants him to prove it's impenetrable."

"Or disprove it so she can strike at Sven," Renee said, taking notes. "The shark is circling."

"So then why are we getting in the water?" I looked to Jessie but she had her headphones in and was tapping away at her laptop, then at Aunt Bess, set back from the others, who was busy talking to her papers.

"Because," Renee said, glancing up. "If Frei doesn't turn up,

Hartmann will assume she is the weak one worth focusing on."

She let out a weary sigh.

I looked to Frei. "Can you break in?"

She met my eyes. "Yes . . . if I can find it."

"Huh?"

"The main servers for Cold Lock are at his estate," she said, lifting up a wad of papers. "Think huge haystack and a lot of false needles . . . and Jäger, in his own home."

Renee's aura fizzed—She weren't looking for servers but for routes to keep Frei out of Jäger's reach and possible hazards; Aunt Bess was scoping out a nearby town to set up a base in; Huber was figuring out antidotes and medicine kits; Stosur was drawing out every detailed memory she had of the place—including possible extraction points; Jessie was learning how the Cold Lock system worked by playing with a dummy version on an offline laptop, and Frei was half-looking for possible locations and half-battling her fear that she was going to have to face Jäger again.

"Guess I'll make drinks and food?" I got to my feet only to get murmurs in response.

A locksmith taking on the guy who froze her to smash an impenetrable lock, prove she was strong to a lurking shark, and give her family freedom . . .?

If anyone could do it, Frei could.

Chapter 29

I WAS SICK of flying. We'd flown on the chopper into the next state and my ears had popped with all the turbulence. Everybody was busy revising every nook of Sven's place, and I'd sat staring out the window.

We'd landed some place in upstate Pennsylvania. Snow covered the ground and swirled through the air as the lights in the building of the small airport flickered on. We'd trudged from the hanger to a large van, a truck, a limo, and a sports car parked up in a row and Frei had told us that we would be in a convoy: Huber and Megan in a limo; Frei with Stosur in a van with our "slave" team—Stosur's guys; Aunt Bess and Jessie were in a truck; Renee and I would follow on.

I looked from the van to the sports car and sighed. I didn't know how I was gonna fold myself up small enough to fit in through the door.

"Don't look so rejected," Renee said with a smile as I hunched up enough to get inside, smacking my head for good measure. "We're at the back because we need to protect them."

"How can we when they're in a different vehicle?" The seat was kinda comfy, leather seats and a slick wood panel dash that twinkled in the dimming light. Hoped it came with snow tires too.

"We use it in close protection duty, if we hit any problems, Stosur will break twice and we'll block the road to give them space to get away." Renee pointed to the back seat. "Smoke canisters."

"So how'd *we* get out of trouble?" Sounded logical but maybe I was missing something.

"I have an assault rifle; stun grenades, knock out grenades, electrical scramblers, cold weather gear, survival kits, med kits, and a car that does zero to a hundred in under five seconds." She flashed me a dashing smile, pure confidence oozing from her. "And this is my comfort zone."

Okay, I was impressed; so impressed that I got shivers from it. Renee winked.

Again, energy rolled up through me and filled the car—Like when I'd broken my jaw and they'd tried to scan me. The room had been so potent with a magnetic field that it hummed. They'd said it would dislodge anything metal and I'd made the scanner throb so bad that it popped the lights. Yeah, the energy was like that, so present it hummed. Maybe there was a magnet in the car?

"We travel way more than normal," I mumbled, not sure what the energy was pulling me toward.

"Less than some," Renee said, leaning back in her seat and roaring us up the snowy road.

"You like Frei's cars more than you let on, huh?" I leaned into my seat. Doubted I looked that cool. Probably looked more like someone had tried to climb into a toy car. "How come she ain't the woman you're in love with?"

Renee rolled her eyes. "Are we back to that again?" She glanced at me and smiled. "Urs is like a sister and she likes rugged and wounded, or did you forget how stunned she was over that guard?"

"Yeah, how would anybody *want* to hang out with Hartmann?" Even if she had given him gadgets to play with. I stared out at the snowy fields. Places looked alike under blankets of white—like somebody had spread the icing on.

Renee raised an eyebrow. "Because she pays very well?"

I shrugged. Whatever, Hartmann was a chump. "She gets drawn to complicated. Fahrer's energy looks like I tried knitting it . . ." I shrugged as a wall of trees, dusted in white rose up from the horizon. "An' Nan would tell you I can't knit for Jell-O."

Renee chuckled but her energy tightened up, primed, like her focus heightened. There still weren't much but fields and hedgerows either side, frozen under snow. "Keep your senses alert."

"Why, the squirrels gonna throw things at us?" I was covering my own worry. I could feel we were getting closer to Sven's.

"Did you listen to the briefing at all?" She looked at me and blew out a breath that made her dusty blonde hair dance about. Thankfully I could look at her in pants and a sweater. Kinda. If the neckline wasn't so low that might have helped. "Owners often build estates in dense woodland."

I guessed that was supposed to make sense. Kinda like the

sweater. How was it supposed to keep her warm when I could see her bra again?

"Because they block prying eyes . . ." She cleared her throat and tapped me on the nose. "Cover noises . . . like gunshots?" She poked me. "You looked awake."

I shrugged. I had been but everything kept fuzzing in and out, like someone had stuck me in a glass jar.

We headed into the thick evergreen trees and I peered up. The forest was mature, the gray sky only peeking through in places. Our headlights lit the road in patches but I could make out the bare trunks, a carpet of brown needles below. It was so dense the snow had only managed to make the ground in patches. A wooden welcome sign perched on a tree stump: *Willkommen Kältedorf.*

"Welcome to cold town . . . or cold village," Renee said, slowing us. "I assume because the Eis family founded it."

"They made cars," I mumbled, seeing showrooms and factories in a flash. Felt queasy from the force of it.

"Yes, they were the ultimate luxury make. My dad had one he'd reconditioned from way back." She smiled, eyes filling with memories. "I used to help him work on her. Matt helped by handing us the tools."

The ache from losing them filled her and pressed on my chest so hard it twinged. "Your dad, Matt, they're like Nan I bet, watching over you, heckling you."

"Hope so," she whispered as the road led us through a white chocolate box village—at least it had been a long time ago. "I guess they all left when the family went missing."

I nodded, staring at the houses—old fashioned with nature covering them in snow dusted ivy but they looked almost like somebody would head out the front door or switch a light on. "So this lock thing freezes folks?"

Renee tapped the leather wheel as the convoy slowed. "Think of it this way. If you were trying to break into a car . . ."

I could see memories—were they memories?—of folks clearing their paths, chatting across fences, all in old fashioned clothes. "Why, I can't drive?"

"Theoretically." She poked me in the knee. "You try to break in but the car is prepared. It freezes you so you can't move, takes your picture, and runs it through a police system, takes your DNA, then steals your wallet." She shrugged and checked her rearview mirror. Aunt Bess and Jessie pulled off the road, cutting right, away from us. "The wallet bit doesn't seem to be common knowledge."

"If he's doing that, why is he so bothered about Frei stealing slaves?" I asked as the town disappeared and we headed toward a towering mountain.

"I don't know. I'm not sure how much he steals." Renee glanced up at a sign high above the road, a rusted up logo at the top.

I cocked my head. "I seen that before." But *where* had I seen it?

"It's the old logo. My dad's car had it." She smiled, glancing right as Aunt Bess's car headed toward an old factory. "Maybe you got it off me?"

Maybe. I shrugged off the feeling as we headed past the towering building, windows all still intact—as preserved and unused as the rest of the town—and followed the road twisting around the mountain. The trees huddled in on both sides again and I wiped my clammy hands on my jeans.

"Sneaky is his m.o.," Renee whispered, her grip tighter on the wheel—so much so I wiggled my fingers. "When he kisses someone's hand, he has a film on his lips that acts like a swab."

The trees got thicker, more intimidating, like they'd reach down and squash us. "You lost me."

"Did you actually pass boot camp?" She shook her head at me. "Because I read the report and it said you were one of the top in your class."

"I sucked." I held up my hand, trying not to look at the deepening shadows of the forest on either side. "File is just for show, I guess."

She shook her head. "Not those files."

"So why does he go swabbing folks?" I hadn't done that well. I mean, Frei had given me a badge or something when I escaped, but I thought everybody got one.

"He puts the DNA on file, searches every database . . ." She tapped the wheel again, like she was itching to take off her fake fingernails. "All he'll find on us is the dummy files Frei planted. Our real DNA is erased."

Phew.

We reached high enough my ears popped and I spotted two huge stone gateposts. "Guess that's the entrance."

Renee sighed, squeezed my knee then her energy flickered. "Yes, it is."

Fake English accent, fake nails, fused with my worry 'bout Frei, with the energy pounding at me until I gripped onto my knees. "I get bored easy, who am I gonna find to tease here?"

She smiled at me. "Good, read my energy." She glanced out of the window. Gate house was bigger than Caprock's had been. All slick with perfect walls and those windows you couldn't see in. "If I rub your stomach, that means keep talking."

"Ah, man, I can't remember stuff like this." I rubbed my hands over my face as the guards blocking the road talked through the window to Huber's limo.

"Focus. If I squeeze your knee I am asking you to concentrate on me; stroking your arm means stop talking; holding your gaze means we need to leave." She said it quick fire, military style as the guard checked the van.

"That's a lot of stuff to get mixed up." I cleared my throat, tensing as the guard eyed us through the window.

"I want them back at me," Renee shot—an order.

"Stomach: keep talking," I blurted as the guard waved us through. "Knee: concentrate on you." I could feel a load more guards lurking, watching, weapons loaded and ready to fire. "Arm: stop talking." There was a long stretch of white—a manicured lawn in summer. "Gaze: leave." I blinked. Had somebody switched on the lights? Huh? How'd I remember all that?

"And what do you do if our POI is being approached at three o'clock by an unsub?" Renee sounded every bit the commander as the convoy crawled its way up the long drive.

"I move to the unsub's three while you cut their direct line of sight, wait for the order, and distract their attention and keep it on me until our girl is at safe distance." All said like I had a clue. I grinned. How'd I learn that?

"If she's cut off from the exit?" Renee fired as the house—well it was as big as Serenity and then some—came into view.

"Place myself between her and the barrier and look for an alternate option," I fired back.

"If we're under fire and cannot reach our transport?" Renee slowed the car as we headed up an incline.

"Cover, conceal, and await instructions." Where was this coming from?

"If she hasn't been in contact for more than thirty minutes?" She tapped her nails, gazing out at the lights flooding the lawn and splashing yellowy light on the building.

"F.A.R and send status alerts." FAR? Find and . . . retrieve. I knew that one. Now, if I knew what a status alert would be that'd help.

Renee tapped her head like she could hear my thoughts . . . wait—Oh, hear my thoughts. I got it.

"If you're captured?" Her voice sounded more uncertain as she peered up at the countless windows staring down at us. House felt like it had puffed itself up, tilted to tower over us.

"I jab my finger with the weird plastic things in my pocket and shove it somewhere along my way." I shrugged. "I don't really think I could switch on a cellphone let alone type out a status message."

"You have something better," Renee whispered as Huber's limo stopped, Fahrer got out, and opened the back door. "And she usually makes me jump."

I chuckled. "I don't think Nan can fire off a status report to you." Megan looked Fahrer up and down before nestling into Huber's arm. "As cool as Nan is, she ain't meant to go helping too much."

"No, but she'll give me pointers." Renee smiled, watching Megan and Huber stroll up the dusty colored steps, talking to someone silhouetted in the large doorway. "But let's make sure we don't need that."

The van pulled up to the steps as the limo pulled away. The house was still chocolate box style like the town but heavily guarded gigantic chocolates. "What happens if I got to tell you we need to leave?"

Renee fluffed up her hair in the rearview mirror as we waited and put on that pale lipstick Worthington always wore. "You just tell me, Alex." She winked at me. "Your turn to order me around for a change."

I draped my arm over the back of her seat as a guard with shaved hair and one eye covered with a flesh-colored patch marched over and motioned for Renee to lower the window.

"Samson, Mr. Jäger is expecting you," he said, mouth turned down in a grimace as he flicked his gaze over Renee who flashed her thigh.

"If you want to keep those eyes, take 'em off what ain't yours," I snapped.

He was checking her for weapons, he weren't the kind of guy who'd dare drool over the owners. Like Fahrer, he felt his place was to shut up and follow orders.

"The attendant will park your car, Miss Worthington," the guard said, tilting his head in respect. The threat didn't so much as register. Guess he heard them a lot.

Renee slid up the window. "I know I don't like sharing but Samson takes it to a whole other level."

"Because Samson learned from inside what happens when somebody tries to go pickpocketing what's hers," I said as the guard went back to the van. Three of them were checking it over and trying to intimidate our team inside.

Renee stared at me.

I shrugged, watching Frei stroll up the steps. Her gaze defiant, her aura shaking. "Seen it once, these folks ain't got nothing on Lynn."

"I can only imagine." Renee studied me as a slave stood at distance waiting for us. Stosur—in a new disguise—had left the van and was at Frei's side. "You have more experience than you let on, don't you?"

"Remind me to tell you 'bout it sometime," I mumbled. Not that I wanted to talk it over. Guess that's kinda what Renee felt like sometimes. Things were harder to forget when you put them into words.

"How about now?" She leaned in, tilting her head like she really wanted me to see her collarbone.

"Ain't really the time," I mumbled, keeping my eyes on Frei talking to Huber.

"Work with me," she whispered, reaching up and stroking my cheek. "Psychology in action."

Didn't get how making folks wait was helpful and I was still keeping my eyes on Frei. "Lynn took care of me when I was first inside. She weren't easy to get on with if you didn't know her moods." Frei's aura prickled with fear as Huber disappeared inside. I dared to glance at Renee. "As nice as she was to me, she didn't like it all that much when some guards had their eyes on me."

Alarm filled Renee's eyes. "Lynn Thomas?" She sucked in a huge breath. "She should have been in solitary not sharing a cell."

Lynn had a reputation that most folks in Serenity shuddered at.

"Which is why ol' Bison stuck me in a cell with her." I smiled. We needed to get to Frei, Stosur was loitering but she couldn't stay there . . . and Renee had stuck a load of color across her eyelids. They were nice without it, with it they kinda caught the splashes of yellow light. "Drove him crazy she took a shine to me."

"How much of a shine?" Renee searched my eyes.

I waved her off. "What I'm saying is that I got to watch her in action. Nobody argued with me after she decided to take me under her wing."

"I can't believe they did that to you," she mumbled. I knew how many boxes shrinks had stuck Lynn into but to me, she'd been family, prison family and somebody who'd kept me safe.

"You never met her." I felt the tension from Renee's neck so placed my hand to her skin. Soft. Were necks normally as soft?

"I didn't have to, I read the reports." Renee smiled and her aura let out a sigh of relief as my hand warmed up.

"Then you know how effective she was when she wanted someone to quit looking at me." I smiled, enjoying the feeling of her taut muscles unwinding. "She didn't like sharing much either."

"We need a long conversation about this," she mumbled, her eyes sleepy.

"Relax, she thought of me like you think of Locks." I glared at the guy hovering to open our door. "She used to let me cuddle when I first got there and was lonely."

Renee stared at me.

"What?"

"Now I understand where you are getting your inspiration." She sighed as her energy calmed.

I shoved open my door, and the guy craned his neck as I stood up tall. "Learned from the best." I headed to her side and draped my arm over her shoulder. "Now get your pretty butt moving."

"What are you doing?" one of our slave team muttered to the guy gawping up at me. "Move inside. *I'll* park it."

"Er . . . sure . . ." He stumbled backward and scurried off.

Explained Renee delaying.

I turned to our team slave. "Bags to my room, don't even think about pilfering."

He nodded and got in the car. Frei stood in the entrance to the house, arms folded. I felt Jäger's energy near and Sven's, but I couldn't see them.

"Alex, you were late meeting us and then I had three police reports about a brawl?" She gave me an icy stare.

"Guy didn't take telling Roberta ain't worth his time." I folded my own arms and Renee rubbed my stomach. Right, keep talking. "Had to teach him manners."

"Five squad cars worth?" Her voice was close to a growl but her aura fired reassurance. Jäger and Sven were listening to every word.

"They bugged me." I shrugged.

Frei looked to Renee.

"She was in one of her moods." Renee rubbed at her arm like it was hurting her. "I shouldn't have talked to him. My fault."

"Alex, you need to cool it," Frei hissed, glancing back at the door like she was worried we'd be overheard. "Sven won't like mess." She blew out a breath. "It took a lot to cover your tracks."

I moved into her space and ran my thumb over her cheek. "You're good at it."

Frei lowered her gaze like she'd done to Jäger in front of me in Caprock. "Just keep your temper in check, please."

"Sure . . . if nobody bugs me." I glanced up as Jäger stood in the huge doorway. I held his gaze with my best "I'm cranky" stare.

Jäger smiled his shark smile: same black suit, same tie, same white shirt, and same boot-polish stubble on his square chin. "I'm sure I can find something to help you unwind."

His focus was zoned in on me like Renee and Frei weren't there. Good.

"Right now, I want to freshen up." I flexed my biceps and Renee stroked my arm. Yeah, I was happy to get moving. "Locks, you comin'?"

Frei nodded, her aura shuddering. "We need to talk business."

I shoved Renee into tottering up the steps but paused as we

got to Jäger and leaned against the stone beside him. "A girl got to keep busy."

His dark eyes flicked over me: rugged, ruthless, and like I was dinner. "Maybe you'll get time while you're here."

No, nope, no way. "Ah, Roberta got a temper of her own." I squeezed Renee whose aura was attempting to give him a knuckle sandwich. "Careful not to tread on her pretty little feet."

He laughed like she was a cute puppy. "Alex, you make things less dull."

How nice. "Wait till you catch me in a mood." I flashed a smile at Frei. "I got it . . . business."

We walked past Jäger into a cavernous entrance hall. Frei led us left as our footsteps clicked, thudded, and echoed back at us. The ceiling looked like it was miles above us, rustic furniture, marble statues, and tables with spindly legs. We turned another corner and Frei pushed open a small door—looked small compared to the huge surroundings but I could fit hunching over. Stone steps spiraled upward.

"Slave staircase," Frei whispered, pulling up the collar on her coat against the draft sweeping through. "Less likely to bump into admirers."

"You ain't a slave no more." I tried to fit my feet on the step but couldn't. It was only as wide as half my big flippers.

"I know." Frei tilted onto her toes and elegantly slid up the steps with ease. She could almost float the way she moved sometimes. "Our team is in place, the security chief is running our rooms." She smiled at me as I ducked. Good thing I'd never been a slave, I'd have had to wear a helmet. "They've given the bees honey but elsewhere they're buzzing."

Huh?

"She means we can talk in our rooms freely but out of them we're in cover." Renee smiled up at me. Even in heels she made little noise, gliding upward, much like Frei. Whereas Frei strolled with a stealth-like carefulness, Renee swayed her hips like a sleek lioness. Come to think of it, they could both be lionesses. They oozed enough confidence to be.

"As long as I can find a pillow, I'm good." I yawned. Being mean was hard work and I weren't no lioness, I lumbered along like a bear who was sleepwalking to the food store. "We getting bored by anyone else?"

Frei glanced over her shoulder at me. "No, good thing we have adjoining rooms."

Renee's eyebrows shot up, and she walked smack into the back of me. "Adjoining?"

Frei sighed. "Huber . . . or Megan . . . seems to have given Sven the impression I like to be . . . tucked in."

"I got to be in the mood for a bedtime story," my mouth fired off before I realized someone was lurking. Hey, my mouth was fast.

"I'll show you how I covered your tracks if you do," Frei said back, her aura firing a "well done" at me.

"That's what I like to hear," I said, pulling her into me as we came out into a tall corridor. This one had a carpet up the middle. Couldn't Sven afford to carpet the whole floor or something? I wrapped my other arm around Renee. "All we need is to toast s'mores and we got a vacation."

Their tense energy calmed as they chuckled but Jäger's energy prickled at me. I could feel him watching me—us—from behind. The hairs on my arms prickled in response and a sweeping blast of fear hit me from Frei.

Yeah, some vacation.

Chapter 30

LILIA PICKED AT her dinner with Eli and the girls, Ruth and Louise, chatting away but she was too centered on her thoughts to make out the topic. She hadn't had any flashes but her worries still probed at her, making it hard to surface from them. She'd nearly lost Aeron back in the boathouse when Jäger had fired at Frei; she'd nearly lost her to Sam in Oppidum; she could have lost her to the avalanche or Yannick in St. Jude's and several times in Serenity. Each worry, each time, probed at her, accused her, drained her.

"Girls, why don't you head on up and get ready for bed. I'll be up to read to you in a bit," Eli said, pulling a comical face at Aeron's half-sisters.

They howled with laughter, chiming a "yes, Daddy," before planting a kiss on his cheek, then Lilia's, and screeching off up the stairs.

"Now, I know you like to keep your stresses locked up behind those eyes," Eli said, leaning over his plate, full police chief hat on. "But you been so quiet, Ruth thought you were asleep."

Lilia smiled. It felt dazed and she was sure it looked the same. "I'll be fine after a good sleep."

"Load of raw rump," he shot back, furrowing his peppered furry brow.

She smiled wider, tickled at the expression. He had his own sayings, much like Nan, no wonder Aeron did. "Indeed it is."

"So, why are you worried about her now?" He glanced up the quirky wooden staircase, littered with toys including a range of swords and police chief hats.

"Can you remember if she had any problems as a child?" It hurt to ask, that she hadn't been there to know.

"You mean upstairs?" Eli tapped his receding hairline.

"No," she said, shaking her head at him. "Health-wise."

Eli pulled his mouth to the side—an expression Aeron wore when thinking—and stared down at his licked-clean plate—he loved fish and chips from the Welsh café in town. "She hit her head real hard once."

Lilia nodded. "I know about that. I mean sickness, that kind of thing."

Eli screwed his mouth up more. "She weren't phased by nothing. She was always out somewhere or she'd be with Nan." He smiled, his eyes tracking through some memory. "If I hadn't seen her in a while, I'd head to Nan's . . . she lived there more than at home." He rubbed a large hairy hand over his jaw. "Why?"

"No reason," she mumbled. "It's just she gets . . . drained . . . so quickly."

"Not surprising. Doubt there are many could fix up someone just by touching them." He scratched over the stubble on his chin. "Well . . . whatever it is she does."

"That's true." Lilia fiddled with her rings and leaned back in the wooden dining chair. "I just worry that it's tiring her."

"Me too." Eli smiled a quiet smile. "But she'll keep going. The girls will take care of her though." He wrinkled up his face like he was bracing himself. "And, no doubt that heckling mother of yours."

He jumped as Nan faded into view, giving him a good poke in the ribs. *"What you lookin' like a bee-chewer for now?"*

Lilia folded her arms as Eli shivered. "I do not look like a bee-chewer."

Eli sniggered. Lilia glared at him and he held up his hands. "Can see this is between mother and daughter?" He waved at the thin air beside him.

Nan raised her eyebrow and poked him in the side again.

He jumped, then scowled, then chuckled. "Some fine heckler." He shook his head. "Ain't nothin' but . . ." He grinned. "A Lorelei."

Nan grinned back and tapped him on the nose. *"She trainin' you better this time 'round."*

Lilia smiled as Eli furrowed his brow like he heard something. He collected up the plates and scurried off to the kitchen, muttering to himself.

"Quit the doe eyes an' spit out your stressin'." Nan swished to the seat next to Lilia.

"I'm worried about Aeron," Lilia whispered, watching Eli attempt to decipher the dishwasher—at least he thought it was.

In reality it was the wine cooler and he was a beer guy. Wine was for ladies.

"Sure you are, you gave birth to her." Nan leaned onto the table. *"You an' Bess keep making this white that bit whiter."* She tapped at the bouncing hair on her head.

"Thought Bess did that when she threatened to run off with . . ." Where had the boy been from? "That kid from . . ."

"Canada," Nan muttered. *"An' it helped a whole lot to get me white."* She tapped Lilia's hand. *"So what's Shorty done now?"*

"Nothing, it's just she's so tired and all the helping is . . ." She sighed; was it selfish to worry? "Draining her. She kept going when she was too sick when they needed to find Ursula."

Nan nodded.

"And . . . I worry that something is stopping her recharging." She leaned on her palm as Eli opened the freezer, dishes in hand then frowned down at it. "How did you cope for all those years?"

Nan let out a long sigh. *"I didn't. Not sure what mother does."* She smiled her brilliant beaming smile. *"But our Shorty got buddies as good and true in heart as her. They'll help."*

And Nan had avoided the question. "Nan?"

"You didn't ask nothin' but how I coped." Nan tutted, watching Eli try filling the sink with hand soap. *"She got friends, she got Bess, she got faith."*

"But there must be something more I can do to help?" Lilia picked at the sheen of the wood table as Eli picked up the oven brush to scrub at the plates.

"Blondie is working out a way to help," Nan said with a wink. *"She got the gray cells to work it out."*

Lilia clenched her jaw as the room faded in and out, and a flash flickered through her mind. "I'll tell Bess. She will get Renee to work on it . . . Yes . . . it'll help her to see it herself."

"Yup," Nan said like she was holding something back.

"Oh." Lilia got a flashed memory of Bess near a trough and her stomach lurched. "So Bess has already seen how it works."

Nan whistled like she hadn't said a word.

"I'll be as white as you if you keep this up," Lilia muttered, poking a finger through Nan's hand. "They need to sort Jäger out."

Nan nodded, chuckling as Eli started to sing to himself, badly.

"Now you're getting it. Best you go rescue the kitchen before he dries the dishes with a rug."

Lilia glanced at her laptop. "Sort Jäger out . . ." She hurried over to her laptop and turned it on. "They're going to need transport . . ."

Chapter 31

RENEE AND I were in a huge room with floor-to-ceiling windows with curtains the yuckiest color green I'd ever seen, a me-sized bed in burgundy, a desk in some dark wood with gold trims, dressing table to match, and a seating area in green leather with a glass-topped coffee table that made me think of Mrs. Stein back in Oppidum. Maybe it was 'cause it had an inset design of the Eis badge? Mrs. Stein had gone for Welsh on hers and I weren't sure she knew any. Did Sven know any German?

Renee wandered out of the bathroom as I tried unpacking the cases. I weren't the best at hanging delicate clothes, and Renee seemed to have left all her outerwear and just gone for thin and belt-length. Didn't she see the snow? And why all the heels that looked like they could hurt somebody? Sure, she was a shortstop but no matter how tall the spindles on her heels, she weren't gonna match my height.

"They're negligees," she said, popping her head around the doorframe.

"Er . . . right." Was that supposed to help me know where they went?

"Drawer," she said, toothbrush in her mouth. "And that's a corset."

"Why'd you got one of those?" I pulled it apart. Looked like torture equipment. "They stopped wearing them in the olden days."

Renee shook her head, methodically cleaning one tooth at a time. Why she had to clean her teeth different I didn't know. The Renee I knew clamped the brush between her teeth, buzzed away with electric, and made tunes when she gargled. Guess Roberta Snooty Worthington was too refined for gargle-songs.

"In the drawer," Renee said when I held it up to her.

I pulled out a load of tights with string attached like they were catapults. More weapons?

"Suspenders," she said, laughter in her eyes. "They go . . ."

"In the drawer," I muttered, shoving them in. If you asked me, the drawer resembled her weapons' case, not underwear. I wandered back to the case and pulled out one skimpy pair of pants. "If you couldn't afford ones that fit, I'd have got them."

Renee dabbed at her mouth with a flannel. "They're three-quarter length pants."

"Why?"

"They show off my calves," she said, throwing the flannel at me.

I caught it and looked down. She had real nice calves. "I don't get it."

"I know you don't." She walked over, pulled me away from the case, and over to a desk in the corner. "I need to test something out."

"If you're gonna try sticking me in a corset, I'll need a lot more material . . . maybe even a tent." I glanced back at the drawer. Yasmin, my friend back in Serenity, had tried dolling me up once. Makeup she'd "borrowed" from a guard didn't make me look anything but more crazy and, even if I weren't an expert, different colors on each eyelid weren't right.

Renee snorted. "You are perfect as you are," she said with a gentle smile. "You don't need torture equipment."

I frowned. "You read that off me?"

"Didn't need to, you looked like it would bite you." She sat on the desk in front of me and my gaze was drawn to her thighs. She'd ditched her pants in the bathroom and her skirt was all kinds of short again. "Eyes up, soldier," she whispered, tapping me on the nose.

I snapped my gaze to hers and sighed. "Then quit flashing. You can be a mistress *and* wear clothes."

"If I wandered around in my football jersey and shorts, I doubt they'd believe I was a mistress." She pulled a letter opener from inside her cleavage.

How'd she find space for it? There weren't much but lace.

"Alex, pay attention." She lifted my chin so I met her eyes— gray filled with energy and kindness. Yeah, she was used to me being dumb. "When you touch things, your mood swings, so I have been practicing how I can relax you."

"By flashing at me and making me open the mail?" Couldn't see how that'd work.

Renee took my hand and placed the letter opener on the desk. "By helping your body breathe."

Calmness flowed up from her touch and I stared down at our hands. Energy lapped at me in waves; cooling, stilling, easing my tension. "You get freaky?"

Renee smiled. "It's called cranial osteopathy. I've been teaching myself the technique. I'd like to road test."

I relaxed back into the chair. "You test all you like."

Renee placed the letter opener in my palm. "Glad you're on board."

"She blew up the center, boy. Have you no control over your own slaves." His father was angry? There was a surprise.

"Jäger stirred my anger, and hers. I'm sick of letting him do as he pleases to my property." He never stood up for himself, only for her and for the girls. Locks needed to be safe.

"Ah, so she wriggles into your affections. You know how that worked out for Sven." His father laughed. He hated it. "You got away with helping that locksmith escape only to wander into the same trap?"

"The girl is a locksmith." He pushed away the disgust in his gut. "I don't need a child to entertain me; I have the mistress you chose if you recall." His tone was so cold, so detached but it had to be. If his father knew why he loved Locks so much, if he understood why she was so gifted . . .

"So you grow a backbone." His father laughed again. "Nicely played, boy, and good to see a Jäger put in his place."

He raised an eyebrow. "You think it wise I take him on . . . after what happened to you?"

"You're not as blind. Love made me so." His father sighed. "He'll want her. He's always pilfered others' hard work."

I dropped the letter opener, tension burning through my arm. Renee placed her hand on mine and the tension soothed, faded, ebbed away.

"It's helping when you've finished touching the object," she said like she was making mental notes. "I'll try while you're holding it." She held up the letter opener.

I frowned and took it from her—

"Meet my locksmith, Huber," Sven said with a smug smile. He had been intolerable as a child and now, as a young man, he was more so.

"Sven, I have better things to do."

Sven wheezed then the puff of his inhaler sounded. Huber looked at him only to feel someone watching him. Next to Sven, a lady stood, white blonde hair flowing around her, brown eyes deep and kind, beauty shimmered from her tanned skin.

"I would say it's a pleasure but any poor slave stuck with him must feel little pleasure." He couldn't believe such a lady could ever be a slave.

"He is as witty as always," Sven said to her. The fact he acknowledged her said much of his sentiment toward her. "Perhaps I should send you to shake up what little assets he has?"

Huber laughed. He had no doubt the lady would run rings around him. Even the intelligence in her eyes held him to breathlessness. She'd more likely have him hand over what he had to see her smile.

"Now she has finished with her . . . distraction, I can show her off," Sven said, smiling at her like she was a toy.

The lady's eyes glinted with an empty sadness. Huber's heart squeezed with it. Sven turned to some other useless excuse for an owner and Huber moved closer to her.

"What pains you so much?" he whispered.

She rubbed her hand across her stomach. "They took her away. I cannot see her."

He looked down at her hand. "You have a child?"

She nodded.

"If Jäger's allowed you to have the pregnancy . . ." No, Sven's parents had their slaves "neutered." They were known for it, so how was she able to give birth? Unless . . . Sven had said distraction? The realization drilled fury through him and he balled his fists. "His?"

She looked away. Yes, his. Sven had no assets of yet and his parents controlled everything. As the eldest, they would have entrusted him to oversee her procedure. She was a locksmith; one of the rare few slaves that no owner with sense touched. They were too valuable. No, Sven's parents would have ripped his claim from him should they have known what he'd done to such a prize asset.

"She lives at the estate?" he asked.

She shook her head. "He took her away . . . for sale."

Huber didn't dare touch her but he wanted to, he wanted to comfort her. "I will see to it she has a good home."

She met his eyes. "I don't understand."

"If it soothes you that I do this?" He wanted her to see he wasn't like them. He wasn't faultless but he wasn't heartless either. His parents, for all their hard lessons, had taught him to be as much.

"It would. I cannot ask this . . ." She sighed. "It is not my place."

He moved close enough for her to feel his comfort, careful she didn't misunderstand it for attention. "You are a person. The only way they win is if you believe you are nothing." He held her gaze. "But you are free, in your heart, you are as free as any of us."

Her beautiful eyes glimmered with tears and, perhaps, hope. "You speak to me like I am an equal."

He smiled. "Because we are."

Renee took the letter opener from me and I rubbed at my throat. "You know, for a guy with steel in his eyes, he got a soft center."

She cocked her head.

I shrugged. "Nice to know where . . ." I glanced at the door. "Locks gets it."

"Someone listening?" Renee's thought filled my mind, and I nodded. She took my hand, dragged me to the door, ripped it open, and flashed a cheeky smile at Megan. "Oh, you need something?"

Megan looked her up and down. "Dinner is in an hour. Huber expects you to attend."

Renee rolled her gaze up Megan, just the same, and lingered on her chest like she was gonna wrestle her or her bra. "When we catch Locks, we'll tell her."

Megan narrowed her eyes, stepping back like Renee was poking at her. "She's not in her room."

I could feel she was.

"No, there's a lot of interesting scenery," Renee said like she'd rub her hands together any second. "With some prize architecture."

Megan studied Renee like she was trying to figure her out. If she did, hopefully, she could tell me 'cause I was lost. "Worth irritating Jäger for?"

"Oh, always," Renee responded with an odd smile I couldn't read. "When you've been close to Hartmann, you realize how he is but a minnow."

"And she still catches your eye?" Megan's aura tightened up like Renee had probed at her.

"Better not," I muttered. I didn't know what they were saying but she weren't going nowhere near Hartmann.

Renee kissed me on the cheek and shut our door behind her. "I have my hands full."

An urge fired through me, and I picked up Renee, making her wrap her legs around me as she giggled. I strode off down the corridor not able to see for her squirming until we headed around a corner, and she stopped.

"You can put me down now," she whispered into my ear. "Coast is clear."

"There's still cameras." I was sure there were. The long empty corridor had that weird carpet that only covered the middle. There were huge paintings of things that I couldn't make out and whoever sculpted the statues had been drinking.

"Not with the scrambler," Renee said, sliding from me to stand on her heels. "Our door is secure."

Her bra beeped.

"We just wait here till she goes?" I could feel Megan loitering outside Frei's door to check she wasn't inside. Frei had snuck into our room so she could spy all she liked.

"No, we carry on our tests." Renee led me through the weird display of kids' art and to a wide balcony leading to a grand set of stairs. Still only had half a carpet though.

"Did Sven paint the pictures or something?" I asked, frowning at more splashes on white.

"Modern art," Renee said with a chuckle. "Not a fan?"

"Looks like Mrs. Squirrel got caught in the paint can." I tapped one of the statues, getting a flash of some guy with an intense stare, making miniscule adjustments. "An' the girls in Serenity could have done better."

Renee led me down the stairs, her hand in mine, her energy full of confidence, of a sparkle. She was set on something, and

I'd learned it was just better to follow orders when she was in this mood.

"To the right is the billiard room—think pool; then there's a swimming pool, a sauna, two sitting rooms, one room he uses for poker games, a meeting room, a gym—doubt Sven's ever seen inside there—and some room that I can only guess what it's for." She shuddered. "To the right is the dining room, five sitting rooms, two day rooms, a sun room, three ballrooms, a three tiered library, and," she dragged me to the left and to a stop outside a mahogany door, "Sven's smoking room." She pulled out two prongs from her waistband, slid them into the lock, and double-checked up and down the corridor. She motioned to the tall-backed chair with dimpled leather. "Only he can't smoke with his asthma."

"I was kinda thinkin'," I said as she dragged me inside and shut the door. "You planning on smoking?"

She raised an eyebrow.

Guess not. "So what you want me to do?"

Renee walked over to a metal bucket with a load of ice in it. "Checking if I can still calm you here."

Road testing. I could work with that.

"And it would be useful to get some dirt." She winked.

I went to the ice bucket and touched it—

Locks is on her way. She must be taking on Sven. A real locksmith . . . a real one. She must be taking what's hers back.

"Why are you smiling? You know Mr. Jäger will start on you again if he catches you." The older woman's voice was exasperated as always, but she didn't understand.

"Locks took down Caprock. She took down his school in Europe. She could be ready to help us too." She was sure of it. She'd heard all about Locks when her sister had lived here. Yes, if anyone could get them out, Locks could.

"A few of the slaves are hoping Locks is going to help them escape too." Frei and Renee would be with me on wanting to get them out but I didn't think we could liberate an entire household. Schools were one thing but here? With all the guards? Older slaves seemed a lot like Fahrer: messed up, and I couldn't see them being happy for the help.

"Just don't tell her that or we'll be on overtime." Renee sat in Sven's chair. "Try something he might have touched." She smiled, picked the lock on the desk drawers, and pulled out an inhaler.

My chest felt tight just looking at it. I held out my hand, and she placed the metal top in my palm—

"You're a disappointment, Sven. You were something when I married you but what are you now?" Her voice jarred him. She wasn't anything compared to the locksmith but she had a name. The locksmith did as told. Yes, he'd find her.

"Two schools shut down. Your assets are dwindling," she snapped. "All you're interested in is finding a slave who's been gone for how many years?"

"What slave?" What did she know of him or his needs?

"You fool no one. Before she walked out of here we had prestige. We had a good name, now what?" She glared at him. She was so unattractive. Not fit like the locksmith. "Even your pathetic brother thinks he has a shot at you."

Jäger? He doubted that sniffling buffoon would dare look at him. Who even knew his first name? He wasn't important.

"You couldn't give me children, you waste what fortune you had. My father is demanding divorce," she snapped.

He sucked in the panic from the threat. He'd given the locksmith a child so it was her fault not his. "I'll get it back. Patience."

"Hah." She threw his inhaler at him. "You can't even breathe without this trash."

He'd get it back. Locks must be his. Only his child could be that clever, that beautiful. Yes, he'd prove she was his.

I swallowed so hard it felt like I'd grown an Adam's apple. *"We have a big problem."*

Renee nodded. "I had a feeling we did. What is it?" She glanced at the door.

Voices?

"Sven, he thinks Frei is his daughter. He's after her DNA." What did we do? Frei would try breaking into Cold Lock but what if Sven figured out that she wasn't his? What if he found out that Huber was Frei's dad, not him, and Stosur, his own missing locksmith, Frei's mom? Now I was sweating.

"Jäger, I don't have the patience for you. Where is your brother?" Harrison's voice filtered in. I tried to focus on her only for my knees to wobble.

Renee hurried to me. *"You can't do that here. Too many people, too many issues."* She met my eyes and placed her hands on mine, love and comfort pulsing over me. *"Keep quiet."*

"He's unavailable." Jäger sounded . . . humbled? Huh?

Renee cocked her head as if she was thinking the same.

"Then make him available," Harrison snapped. "Hartmann will be arriving shortly. I need to know what he wants."

"I can't, he's with his mistress." Jäger sounded like he was groveling. "Hartmann won't be here until dinner. Perhaps you could speak with him then?"

"Very well," Harrison muttered. "Show me to my room."

Jäger—or somebody—whistled.

"He's calling one of the servants." Renee shook her head. *"I don't know how they cope with being whistled at."*

"Says the woman who joined the army?" I moved her back from the door and a second later heard a click. I stared down at the lock. Uh oh.

"Relax, I can pick it." Renee gave me a confident smile.

"Follow me, Miss Harrison," a woman said.

"Get on with it," Harrison snapped.

I looked to Renee. *"Is it me or is she bossy, considering she ain't meant to be important?"*

She nodded. *"Why stay in a school all those years if you're someone with authority?"*

"Likes snotty kids?" I shrugged. I didn't think she liked teaching or if she'd ever actually taught.

Renee bumped my hip and knelt down next to the door, then sighed. *"She left the key in the lock."*

Great.

"Can you still pick it?" I looked at the window then remembered the prickly spikes Frei had been cut by. *"Don't want to try climbing out that way."*

Renee chewed on her lip, inserting her picks. *"Going to try poking it through . . . if it's lined up straight."* She scrunched up her face, then grinned. *"It's moving . . ."*

I huddled next to the door. *"Hallway is clear."*

Clunk.

I grinned. *"Commander Black kicks butt again."*

She looked up at me with teasing in her eyes. *"Got a bit of a fan, huh?"*

"Oh yeah!" I was about ready to high-five her.

She twiddled the picks about.

Click.

She blew out a breath, opened the door, and grabbed for the keys. "Hold onto these."

I put my hand out without thinking—

Harrison is here? Oh no, Sven will frame Lock's friends. He'll get them in trouble and then Locks won't help. Got to make sure they don't get in trouble.

Lock's friends?

"Harrison's here to try and fit us up for something." I sucked in a breath as it hit me. "The girl saw us go in the room. These are the keys to his wife's room. We need to go get her, now."

Renee stared at me.

"Move your butt." I grabbed her hand and dragged her to the slaves' staircase that Frei had showed us. We hurried up the narrow stairs, slaves peeking at us from safe distance. They were hoping we'd help too. I held onto the key, my hand heating up.

"Wait." Renee held up her hand to stop me. Pulled open the door. Ducked her head out, hand on gun. "Clear."

I hurried along, feeling from the keys the route the girl took every time she went to the wife's room. I dragged Renee to the left, down a long corridor, to the right. "There, her room."

Renee hurried ahead of me, took the key, opened the door. "She's on the floor." She checked the wife's pulse. "No marks on her."

I walked around the huge bed to the table beside the window. There were two glasses but one was still full. "Someone she was entertaining?"

I picked up the empty glass and touched the metal rim—

Why do I have to do this? Why can't he get his own hands dirty? He placed the tray on the table and poured the drink for her. He was sick of being treated like a slave.

"Jäger." I sighed, seeing a chopper land in the grounds. Hartmann had arrived. "Guess we got to wake her up enough."

Renee nodded, pulled something from her bra, and jabbed the wife's arm with it.

Mrs. Jäger gasped and opened her eyes.

"Do you want some help?" Renee asked in her fake accent, pulling Mrs. Jäger to lean against the bed. The swirly patterned carpet underneath was wet like she'd tipped some of the drink only why was the glass on the table?

"Please," Mrs. Jäger spluttered out.

I knelt next to her, and my hands roared into life the second I touched her. I looked to Renee. "Slave is outside, give her back the keys and get her to head to the kitchen to get some ice."

Renee nodded and hurried out of the door, and I winced as my hands prickled—

Why does Sven put up with the boy? He has been nothing but trouble. Surely he realizes that he wants his position? Why keep him close?

"Mrs. Jäger, I have your drink for you." He was always polite to her, like he was afraid of her. But then, she'd kept his greedy hands off the servants. If only she could catch him or they'd talk . . . then she could be rid of him.

Mrs. Jäger stared at me. Heat burned through to my fingertips, and she gasped, breathing clearly. I stumbled away from her, over to the dressing table. The room swayed as I gripped onto the wall. My heart wriggled, then skipped. Sweat gushed from me.

"What did you do?" she whispered, easing herself up onto the bed. "What was that?"

I gulped in my breaths, my chest tightened. "I had the right medicine in a gel. Quicker way to get it in you." That was kinda good. I'd use that again.

She nodded, then pulled out a case from under the bed, like it had been there a while. "Thank you."

"You guessing Sven ain't worth bothering with now?" I sounded more like Aeron than Alex and slumped into a spindly legged chair next to the dressing table.

"Yes. Most disappointing." She checked inside the case, then shut it.

"The chopper outside could take you to your parents." I glanced through the window. Couldn't see much further than the glass with my blurring vision but I could hear it there. "Be helpful if they knew Locks is an ally."

She studied me for a moment and picked up the case. "And Sven?"

"We got issues with the way he treats folks." I leaned onto my legs. Only made the wooziness worse. "By the way, that girl you're so nice to made sure we knew."

Renee came back in with the slave who'd left the keys and ice in a bucket. She showed the bucket to me and I shoved my hand in and grabbed a piece. I had no idea why I wanted to do it but I was happy to try anything not to pass out.

Renee pulled out a few pieces and handed them to Mrs. Jäger. "It'll help keep you awake long enough to get to the chopper."

She nodded, took it, and cast a glance over the pink-colored room. "Thank you."

Renee smiled but her gaze was on me. She wanted to know if I was okay, if helping had drained me. I gripped onto the ice which throbbed, sizzled in my palm, and dripped onto the floor in a puddle.

"Girl, you did me a service . . ." Mrs. Jäger said, smiling down at the slight girl and reached for her hand. "Why don't I give you a ride and we can get those papers discarded?"

The girl stared up at her. "Ma'am?"

"I've been trying to find reason to help for a while." She touched the girl's concaved cheeks. "You're too pretty to be safe around him."

"Where will I go?" The girl's croaky voice wobbled, her eyes full of wonder, her aura full of worry.

"Either stay with me—paid of course, or whatever you choose." Mrs. Jäger offered her hand again. "I need help to get me on the helicopter."

I nodded, she already felt sleepy. The girl went to her and held her by the elbow. She tried to take the case from her but Mrs. Jäger shook her head. "I'm capable of carrying my own things."

The girl nodded then held out a bunch of keys. "They might be useful, Miss Worthington."

Renee took them. "Thank you."

"Roberta will make sure nobody gives you a hard time on the way down." I went to the glass, careful not to touch the silver rim. *"Frei will need to run this."*

Renee nodded, handed me a set of plastic gloves and mask from her bra then led them out.

My hands trembled as I pulled on the stretchy gloves. They smelled of the perfume Renee was wearing. They were warm like her. I soaked up the energy from that and closed my eyes. I had a vague memory of cleaning up a scene in boot camp, or was it with Renee?

Ah well. I stuck the mask on and wobbled to my feet. Hopefully I'd remember as I went.

Chapter 32

I FINISHED CLEANING up the room, just, and tucked the glass in a clear bag in and hung it from my belt. I headed out into the corridor, not sure which way to go. Both ways looked identical with weird blob statues and Mrs. Squirrel paintings.

I blinked away the fuzz in my vision and wobbled to the left, feeling drawn that way, like I was following some trail. I hoped I was honing in on where Renee had gone and wandered along, then down a set of shiny white marble steps, then through some big gold-covered room that echoed with my footfalls, and down more white stone steps. My vision waned but my senses dragged me on. Down another set of grayer stone steps, around corners and down corridors more confined and with only bare stone all around. The quietness of dim lights and uneven floors almost felt like Serenity at nighttime when all the inmates were locked away and there was that silence, that intake of breath.

The smell of food tickled my nostrils and some kind of clattering filled my ears. I stopped, feeling more than seeing, a doorway in front, one to the left and one to the right.

The door in front filled my mind's eye. It was thinner than normal doors, like the kind I'd seen in books on ancient forts in Wales. Welsh people must have been real small back then or they had slaves? I'd go for the small thing, I liked Welsh folks.

"You remembered somethin' from your schoolin', Shorty?" Nan whooshed in with enough joy that I wanted to chuckle but was so tired I only managed a half-sob.

"Liked the bits about knights and castles," I whispered. I could feel slaves nearby but I didn't know if Sven could hear or see me down here.

"I know you drew them all out for a project." Nan swooshed to my side. *"You did real good in that one. We even got you some hay to stick on the paper."*

I nodded. "Would have worked out better if the teacher weren't allergic."

Nan chuckled. *"Sure, thing. So where you heading?"*

"I ain't sure. I just feel like I need to go that way." I motioned to the door and tried to follow her voice to find her. I didn't know if she was moving something around or cleaning but she kept making scraping noises.

"Ain't me shorty, think the spinner is having a hissy." I felt her over by the room on my left. I was close to the wall so I stepped away and the scraping sound stopped. *"You were always a bright spark."*

I rolled my eyes. "I got the urge to try and fit through this mini-people door." I'd have to duck and turn sideways if the picture in my head was accurate.

"Shorty, you ain't been able to use doors like that since you went to the funny farm." Nan tutted. *"You'll get wedged and then how will Blondie explain you?"*

"I'm not that wide." I folded my arms. "I got dragged to this door. I guess it's for a reason."

"Sure, but your brain is on vacation right now." Her voice was full of her laughter. *"And you got to wash away those ailments . . . your grandpa gets sidetracked sometimes he goes to pick me some flowers and finds himself hiking."*

Guess Etherspace had mountains. "Hopefully he don't take Tiddles then."

Nan laughed again. *"He does. Tiddles fits in his jacket real nice."*

A well-travelled cat.

"If you're gonna go exploring, you might want to sort your tip from your tail," Nan said, humming and then purring to someone . . . or maybe it was Tiddles purring.

"You talking to him or me?" I was pretty sure it had to be Tiddles.

"You, Shorty . . ." She tutted. *"Tiddles got his tail stuck on proper."*

She chuckled again and faded. I took a breath and squeezed my bulk through the door, wincing as I got wedged. I sucked in my breath and tried again, straining against the frame, holding the glass at safe distance to stop from cracking it. Come on . . . *Rip.* My shirt bust its buttons and I fell through, nutting the wall the other side. I held up the glass and sighed with relief. Yeah, some elite CIG agent, or soldier, or whatever I was. Didn't matter. Some folks did stealth, some folks did sharp-shooting but I did sniffing memories.

I could feel something stirring inside me, pulling me up the tiny steps to a bare stone dimly lit hallway; narrow and small with spaces off it. I didn't know how many slaves Sven had but I could feel so much energy: Worries, hurt, loneliness . . . and hope? Yeah, hope was glowing from some place.

I followed the feeling, through the corridors; past doors with nothing but a mattress on the floor and a slit for a window. Hope pulled me on, up another set of stairs to a little sitting area with make-shift furniture that had been mended up with care. There were oil heaters and lamps burning. Somebody had found some paint from somewhere and had given the stone a wash to brighten it up. There were hand-painted pictures hanging, showing the slaves were real good with pencil.

I sat in one of the chairs, feeling how the kids would gather around and listen to stories by the elder slaves; how they were taught to read and write and the adults made an effort to get them believing that they might have been slaves in the corridors but here, they were equal and loved.

I breathed it in. There was something special about that. So special that it filled my heart with the hope coating everything around me. I looked to the table and saw a battered, well-loved Bible and opened it up where somebody had stuck a bookmark in.

" . . . *the seed on good soil stands for those with a noble and good heart, who hear the word, retain it, and by persevering produce a crop.*"

I smiled down at it. I liked that. They might have been stuck here but they wanted to make sure they spread hope and light to each other. My kinda folks.

I placed the book back and noticed a pair of glasses on the side. Maybe they'd give me an idea why I was here—

" . . . *the children were held, had lost everything,*" a woman *with wrinkled up eyes said as the kids all sat on a cardboard carpet at her feet.* "*They became slaves to those their parents' trusted but they didn't give up.*" *She wagged a gnarled finger.* "*The boy took care of his sister, did as they told him, but made sure the others forced into service with him got comfort, got food and knew he wanted to free them."*

"But he couldn't," one child muttered. "We're still stuck here."

The woman nodded. "Yes, but one girl believed we could be free and worked hard until the owners couldn't do without her. Then she escaped and has been breaking slaves free since then."

"So why doesn't she come and get us?" another boy said.

"Because it's a story," a bigger boy muttered. "The locksmith isn't real. No one can escape. He has us chipped. She's just made up so you stop whining."

"It is true. She was here. She was a slave. I heard wheezy talking about her." A teenage girl leaned forward and tickled one of the younger kids. "He gets mad that she walked out under his nose."

"Yeah, and there was that other girl, the one who looked like her; she was here too," a teenage boy said. "I remember her giving me her sandwich." He nodded. "It was a nice sandwich."

"That's only two," one of the small kids said. "Two isn't a lot."

"How'd you know," a kid next to her said. "You can't count."

"I know how to get to three, so there." She screwed up her face.

The old woman smiled. "The locksmith is a wonderful woman with a good heart. If she can help, she'll help." She smiled at the kids around her. She remembered the locksmith well, she saw her grow, blossom, and break free.

I turned and the old woman, far more bent and battered than in the memory, smiled at me.

"You're a little tall for a thief, girl," she said with a gapped smile.

"I work for Locks, for . . . the locksmith you knew." I felt that surge of need, need to help, to break these people free. "We're getting you out."

She tutted. "Don't say things you can't mean."

I could feel a load of people watching and smiled. "I ain't. I was locked up in a place like this, locked up inside and out." I held out my hand to her. "They busted me out and I want to do the same for you."

"I'm a little old to climb fences." She took my hand with her gnarled one.

A flash hit me so hard I stumbled.

"You won't need to but you got to keep everyone together. Make sure they all are ready to get going." I nodded. "We're already doing it slowly."

"They are, I seen two go . . . Mrs. Jäger took one and the security lady took the other," a young woman said. She'd been the kid in the memory who knew how to get to three. She wasn't a whole lot taller.

"You know why?" I said as faces appeared from their hiding places.

The old woman shook her head.

"Take a good hard look in her eyes next time you see her," I said. "She looks a whole lot different without her disguise."

The woman studied me. "This is true?"

I nodded. "You seen Locks, right?"

That earned me a lot of nodding and murmuring.

"White blonde hair and a gift for lifting objects?" I smiled as the old woman's eyes flickered with recognition. "Yeah, she ain't forgot you . . . and who better than to break you out, than *two* locksmiths?"

Chapter 33

FREI SLIPPED BACK into Aeron and Renee's room through the internal door. She'd gone for a shower and they still weren't back. She pulled out her cellphone, blinked at the backlit screen, and scrolled to Renee's contact card. Her pulse and blood pressure readings from a few minutes before were good, her location . . . was in the corridor outside. If only she could do the same for Aeron. She'd be with Renee though, Renee wouldn't let her out of her sight.

"Sneaking out *before* dinner?" Frei said, folding her arms as Renee slipped in. "Isn't it supposed to be more of a buzz after curfew?"

"Age," Renee mumbled scanning the room. "Need to sleep after curfew these days." She went to the bathroom. "She's not here?"

"I thought she was with you?" Frei tracked through her phone, knowing full well it wasn't going to give her any answers.

Renee sighed. "Sven sent Jäger to get rid of his wife. We had to get her out."

"That was who was on the chopper?" She'd noticed the chopper waiting and someone get on it but assumed it was one of Hartmann's entourage. She fiddled with the ring on her finger. "Sven wouldn't be that stupid."

"He's desperate," Renee said, peering out through the windows. "*Alex* had to help her."

"Room is scrambled, you can talk freely," Frei said, double checking on her phone. "Wait—help?"

Renee held her gaze.

Frei pressed speed dial. "Jessie, you have a location on Aeron?"

Jessie answered by chomping away on something. At least she was eating. "Came out of Mrs. Jäger's room . . . um . . . went on a walkabout . . ." She munched away. "Blew the camera near the kitchens." She sighed. "No other footage after that."

"Mousey, why you at that computer? You got your apple

crumble to finish." Aunt Bess sounded like a mom. Frei wasn't sure she ever would.

"Mom is looking for Aeron," Jessie said all sweet and innocent. "I'm helping . . . I am . . . ask Mom."

"Icy?" Aunt Bess rustled the mouthpiece. "You disturbing your girl's dinner? She ain't gonna sprout if she don't get fed and watered."

"Only way to make sure she's not sneaking off?" Frei asked, nodding to Renee. They hurried out of the room and checked the corridors.

"So Shorty?" Aunt Bess asked, the hint of worry in her voice.

Frei lingered next to a fifty-thousand-dollar bust of some woman. She'd stolen it three times. Huber must have lost it in cards, again. Why he'd kept sending her to get it she didn't know. Wasn't worth fifty thousand. It looked like something the kitchen would throw out.

"Shorty is fine. She's just exploring without a spotter," she said, hoping it eased Aunt Bess's worries. She'd been shaken after they were attacked by Jäger. She glossed over it with her laidback style but Frei saw through it.

Renee checked around a corner, shook her head at Frei. So she waved toward the direction of the kitchens. Best they start there.

"Well, if her nose is twitchin' best you catch her before she goes fixin' folks up and faintin'." Aunt Bess let out a long weary sigh. "You can keep the earpiece in, Mousey, but you got to eat your dessert."

"Yes, Miss Lorelei," Jessie chimed.

Renee hurried to join Frei, and they turned toward the balcony over the main stairs.

"I ain't been a miss in a *long* time, kid." Aunt Bess chuckled.

Renee picked the lock to a room on the right and hurried in. "Not at the landing site," she said in a hushed whisper.

Frei hurried down the stairs, Renee catching up to her as they reached the first floor. "Let's hope the kitchen staff are open to bribery if she's passed out there."

Some slaves were too scarred, too beaten to do anything other than report such things to the owners—Fahrer was like that, her classmates in Caprock, Jones and Sawyer, had been. Some would ignore anything they hadn't been asked to see but could still spill the truth if pushed and then some, some like her, like Suz, they'd been happy to keep their mouths shut and help.

"Looks like I'm going on alone," Renee muttered, ducking into a room on the left. "You've got a fan club."

Frei lifted her gaze from her phone and groaned. Theo. Wonderful. He strolled along the corridor toward her, his heat trace device in hand. She steeled herself. He couldn't follow any trails if he was distracted.

RENEE HID BEHIND the door and sighed. What did she do? Leave one protectee to go find the other? What if Jäger caught Frei?

She stuck the flesh-colored earpiece in and punched in Jessie's number. "Jessie, do you copy?"

"I copy," Jessie said, bouncing with energy as always. "Yes, Aunt Bess, I promise . . . I'm eating it all . . . Renee is on the phone."

"What Blondie want? She ain't with your mom?" Aunt Bess muttered. "They only been there five minutes."

Renee glanced through the gap in the door.

"Miss Locks?" Theo said, pulling his shoulders back, device forgotten. "You have much on your mind?" His eyes tracked over Frei, intelligent eyes, kindness in them. His low brow cast shadow over them but not in a threatening way, nothing about him was threatening. Strong, yes, but kind.

"Yes?" Frei mumbled. Was she flustered?

"Hmm . . ." He rubbed over his stubbled chin; The hairs thick and dark. "I would perhaps surmise that you may be suffering from heartbreak."

Frei blinked at him. "Sweeping assessment."

He wagged his finger. "You did not eat much at the dinner party and you talked to no one, looked at no one and now walk the corridors alone." He nodded a curt nod. "Thus, you seem to be exhibiting signs of heartbreak."

Frei's lips twitched in a smile, her icy blue eyes showed a flash of something . . . attraction? "I'm exhibiting signs that I was once a slave."

Theo scowled. "A what?"

Frei rolled her eyes. "If your aunt hasn't let it slip what her field of expertise is, then you really should have checked it out."

Renee glanced at the other side of the room. Only one door. "Jessie," she whispered into her earpiece, as she and Aunt Bess bickered. "Jessie, do you have a location for Jäger?"

"Which one?" Jessie chomped away.

"All of them, please." She peered out of the door.

"You were really a slave?" Theo leaned in, his attention solely on Frei. "I didn't think that went on anymore."

Frei gave him the kind of withering look recruits suffered. "You think all those people follow her around for fun?" She put her hands on her hips, drawing her coat back until it looked like she had wings. "You think all the staff in the house scuttle around because they are paid?"

Theo shook his head, wagging his device at her. "I . . ." He rubbed at his chin again. "My mother said . . ." He shook his head. "You're playing with me."

Renee winced. He was going to get it.

"Playing? You think I had a great big chunk of metal rammed through each ear for fun?" Frei narrowed her eyes.

Theo held up his hands, waving them about. "You did?" He peered at Frei's ears. "That's terrible." He scowled. "Who did this to you. I will . . . I will . . ."

"I have the locations," Jessie piped up into Renee's ear. "Scumbag Jäger is in his bedroom . . . practicing fighting . . . dweeb." Jessie muttered to herself. "Sven is on his way to dinner with his mistress." She muttered in Dutch. "Mrs. Jäger isn't on any of my screens and . . ." She muttered more in Dutch. "Harrison is there?"

"No digging, Mousey," Aunt Bess muttered. Good thing she was supervising.

"And . . ." If Theo was wandering around, where was his boss? "Where is Hartmann?"

Frei moved to the side, drawing Theo's gaze with her and giving Renee a free route out.

"Hartmann is arguing with Grandpa and Megan over cards," Jessie said with a sigh. "And Megan is cheating."

"Knowing Huber and Hartmann, so are they," she whispered,

slipping out into the corridor and hurrying toward the stairs to the kitchen. "If Theo leaves *Locks*, I want to know."

"Got it. Want me to tell Grandma? She'll keep an eye on her." Jessie sounded delighted that she could say grandma.

"Yes, please." Renee slipped out, hurried down the corridor, and snuck down a set of back stairs. She'd memorized the layout but it was always different when she got to a location. Pictures didn't show how a place felt. Not that she felt like Aeron did, but they had an energy?

"Kitchen on the right," she mumbled, ducking her head through the door. Steam and activity greeted her. Dinner smelled good. "Laundry on the left." She hurried across to check but there were only piles of laundry. "In front is a slave staircase . . ." She let out a sigh as Aeron squeezed out the doorway, shirt ripped open at the buttons and the glass in a bag dangling from her belt. "And one Alex Riley."

"You got her?" Jessie whooped and she heard a slap. "Mini-five!"

Aunt Bess chuckled. "Mousey-five!"

Renee rolled her eyes, cut the call, and hurried to Aeron. "Where have you been?"

"Sorry. Followed my freaky side," Aeron mumbled, rubbing her neck.

Renee took her hand and dragged her up the stairs. She looked ashen. "We need to get you back to the room."

They reached the top of the stairs, and Frei turned Theo, doing the same. "Alex, you have to wait for meals to be served. Scaring the staff doesn't help."

Aeron laughed. "Sure, but it gives me a buzz." She glared at Theo who looked at her with disgust. "Ain't you got work to do?"

Theo nodded and hurried off.

Renee grabbed Frei's elbow as they reached her. "Then let's get you both to your rooms." She blew out a breath. Two protectees accounted for and hopefully Jessie had finished her dessert. Blondie-five.

Chapter 34

WE GOT TO the corridor to our room only for Huber and Megan to be coming our way. I glanced at Renee who let out a long sigh.

"Dinner," she muttered. "We need to get you back to the room."

"You can't," Frei whispered, worry in her eyes. "Hartmann will be expecting us all to show."

I clattered into one of the blob statues, Renee dived for it and stopped it from toppling to the floor. "I can just sit there, then go back to the room."

Renee and Frei exchanged a glance.

"What? You don't think I can?" I steadied myself with the plinth, only for it to wobble and Frei to move me away as Renee replaced the statue.

"No," Renee said, catching my elbow and holding me steady as Huber and Megan reached us. "But we don't have a lot of choice."

"Alex?" Huber said, his tone impatient but his aura wiggling like he wanted to help keep me upright. He'd guessed just why I was wobbling. "Drinking before dinner is impolite."

Drinking? He was helping me. I could do that. I'd felt plenty of drunk folks. "Needed to liven things up a bit." I let out a shuddering yawn. "Ain't much happening to amuse me."

Renee exchanged another glance with Frei who was trying to hand something to her behind my back.

"And being locked in a cell was amusement?" Huber said, his tone full of disgust. All show for Megan. He wanted her to think he didn't rate me much.

"Yeah, especially when somebody got locked in with me." I winked at Megan who batted her eyelashes at me. "We eating or am I taking room service?"

"Try and be respectful to Hartmann," Frei muttered at me as we headed back toward the stairs. I could see her aura more than I could see her.

Renee tightened her grip on my elbow, steering me. "She could be useful."

"How?" I snapped as I stumbled my way down the steps. The main door had some kind of window above it and soft moonlight shone through it. At least I thought it was moonlight, felt like it the way it stirred my heart.

"Good tailoring for a start," Megan purred from behind me.

Moonlight Sonata twinkled into life inside me, the soft thrumming of notes filtering through me. Renee's hand on my skin echoed with it.

"If clothes are all it takes to sway you, you're a lot easier to please than Roberta," I said, slapping Renee on her butt. Oh yeah, was she gonna sock me one.

"I am an expensive companion," Renee said through a false giggle like her aura was planning on poking me, hard.

"Now that I can vouch for," Frei said, striding ahead, her aura fizzing like static on a TV; looked like it too. "Worth the money."

"I'll take that compliment," Renee said like she was genuinely touched. Her aura wasn't showing nothing. I could see Megan's which was all twitchy like she was up to something; Frei's was like static; Huber's skulked behind him like it wanted to mope about losing the card game but Renee's . . . I couldn't even see it.

Huber's energy primed like it was ready for action. "You should have played cards with us, Alex," he said like it was for someone else's benefit. "That would have kept you entertained."

She looks distracted. If she's not careful, she'll miss something. Do I stop Ursula going to dinner? his thoughts rattled through me like he was speaking out loud. He wasn't, and it wasn't a flash but it wasn't the same as when I heard Renee either. Whatever it was, my knees wobbled 'and my whole body flushed with sweat.

"Yeah, guess," I mumbled. I sucked at cards. Sure, I could read everybody around the table but I wouldn't know one card from another.

What is she doing? Can't she follow my lead? Huber's feelings rattled through me again and I swayed with it. I was gonna pass out.

I scowled at his aura 'cause it was all I could see. "What you eying me for. If I wanted to tell you where I was, I would."

His aura smiled. Guess he was happy.

"Best not to annoy her," Megan purred. Her aura snuck a peek as if it was checking the coast was clear. *I don't want to take her on. She'd floor me.*

Oh no. I could hear Megan too? My heart sped up, laboring as it did so. I felt sick. It weren't right. I needed to block it out.

"Glad someone got some sense." I smiled at her in a way I hope creeped her out as much as it did me.

Oh, she's got some fight. I could do with someone who knows how to handle themselves. Megan's thought shot through. "And Locks does?"

"Sure," I grunted and my knees buckled. Renee held me upright, helping me into the dining room. "Roberta too."

"Are you seriously flirting with her?" Renee's thought was like I normally heard it and her energy poked me, hard. "I like to keep you happy, Alex."

Now the blonde has potential too. How does she keep them both so amused? Locks doesn't warm to people easily. Megan's energy focused on Renee like it'd pulled out a spyglass and examined her then moved over to Frei. *Never shows any emotion. Hard to know what she thinks.* "So only certain people get to call you Alex?"

"Yeah." Why were we just standing about? I could see the energy of the slaves, leaving jet washes of worry; Sven whose aura jingled about with smugness; Hartmann whose energy looked more shark-like than her reputation; Theo's aura was pink and sparkly; and Jäger's was a dirty mush of meanness. "Locks taught me that folks needed to know their place."

"Willing students are always a joy to teach," Frei said in her bored monotone. "Move."

Renee flinched like she'd salute. I clamped her arm to her side in case.

The blonde is scared of her? Interesting. Megan's energy scoured Renee. She was fascinated.

Her legs are more toned than before. Always good to have a view. Hartmann's voice hit me and I growled. I knew exactly who she was drooling over, and I was gonna throw pickle juice at her.

"Calm. Why are you trying to relocate my ribs?" Renee bumped my hip. Still couldn't see her energy. I really needed to. I needed help. I wanted to go back out to the hallway and hear music.

"She's drooling over your legs." I tried to relax my grip but she felt like a life raft. Why couldn't I see anybody? *"You're distracting."*

"That's the point. You want her distracted." Renee squeezed my arm.

"Well, if it isn't Locks and her . . . strays." Hartmann's aura shot out at me like it wanted to slap me.

I flexed my bicep. I was twice her size and shark or not, she weren't touching Renee. "Shame you lost so much money on the European school," shot out of my mouth before I could shut it.

How did she know that? Hartmann's energy had its hackles up.

"Aeron. Do not bait her. She is high risk." Renee was using Serenity speak. Inmates who were locked up in solitary, who were so dangerous that the staff needed to strap them down and sedate them. Well, *I'd* been high risk once.

"Shame you decided to let scud in your pond," I said through gritted teeth, glancing over at Sven. I didn't know why but Frei had told me to trust it when it happened. It was training.

"Not bad for a common criminal," Hartmann muttered as Theo launched into conversation with Megan about how buffed up the wood floor was. I couldn't see the floor.

"Common?" I shook my head. "Common is for wimps who can't look after their own business."

"Aeron, quit it." Renee pinched my arm.

"And you think I can't?" Hartmann took a step toward me. Energy poised to launch an attack.

Huber, Megan, Theo, Renee, the entire room stopped, tensed, watching.

"I *know* you can't." I took a step forward and glared down at her energy, hoping it covered my blindness. "And you're getting too old to go picking fights you can't win."

"And who says I can't?" Hartmann stepped forward again. *She thinks she can talk to me this way?*

I shrugged off Renee and moved into Hartmann's space until I towered over her. "The fact I can bench press your skinny ass one handed."

She means it. Crazy or knows something? Hartmann's confidence shuddered and insecurity wriggled up and wrapped around her. "I'll take skinny as a complement."

"Good." I motioned for her to get moving.

Hartmann's aura smiled, an unsure smile. "Let's not keep Sven waiting, dear."

Must have been talking to Theo with the gentle tone. Why was she so nice to him?

She even takes on Hartmann? Megan was reeling. She wasn't sure if she was impressed or thought I was crazy.

Huber pulled her to walk after Hartmann and Theo, their auras unsteady. Frei's energy calmed like I'd helped her feel more secure but Renee's flicked up at me like she'd boot me in the shins.

"Are you nuts?" Her aura wagged at me. If I could see her, her eyes would have been rolling with that stormy look, her hands on her hips. *"She could hurt you, I can't cope with that. Don't you get that yet?"*

"She's too scared to even look at me." I yanked Renee in close and shoved her toward the table. *"You're a lady and nobody should go lookin' at you with such . . . disrespect."*

Renee leaned up and kissed me on the cheek. She moved Frei to my right and stopped me as we must have reached the table.

"When did I marry her?" I felt Frei take my hand and place it on the back of the chair. Could she tell I couldn't see?

"You didn't, but if she's on my left, she'll be next to Jäger." Renee's aura shot out like it wanted to knock him clean off his chair. *"I'll deal with him."*

"Yes, ma'am." I pulled out both their chairs, waited for them to sit, then lifted them both under, much to the delight of Sven who wheezed out a chuckle.

"Manly but impressive none the less," he said from my left someplace. *Now that old bag is out of my way, I can start a fresh. I need her share.*

He didn't know his wife had left? Explained his happy mood.

"Yes," Jäger said with a grunt. "Samson has fine physical attributes." *What does she see in the thief? Why did she get in the way?*

"Perfect for a skill captain. Shame to lose her really," Harrison said from behind me. *Where is the body? What is Sven doing? I didn't come here to socialize.*

"She was never yours," Frei said in a bored tone. *Why is she still here? She is a house matron. What does Sven want with her? Does he have more schools?*

I rubbed at my forehead. Why could I hear everyone? Why couldn't I see? My head throbbed from it. Block it out . . . needed to block it out.

"Oh, of course, the ex-student becomes a businesswoman," Harrison said with arrogance. "You were always good at stealing things." *I don't want her greedy eyes on me. I worked hard to get myself out of one mess. I am not getting into another one.*

I gripped my head. I wasn't sure which conversation was going on out loud and which was in their heads.

"Yes, locksmiths are valuable, aren't they?" Huber said, his aura giving a smug nod. *And you won't get your hands on her. She's never been a slave.*

"And what is this?" Theo asked, his tone sharp like he'd been waiting for the opportunity. *Was Miss Locks telling the truth? Why would Aunt Sabine act like this?*

"Calm, Theo, it's a polite word for her . . . hobby." Hartmann's aura prickled. *Yes, Locks would be useful to get on board. The muscle would be too and the blonde . . . I could do with the company.*

I leaned forward. "I'd call it a profession seeming as she's proved her skill." My hands were drenched. I needed to avoid the cutlery but how could I when I couldn't see it? I didn't need to read any more. I needed to shut off. Why couldn't I shut off?

"Quite," Sven said like he wanted to throw his fork at me. "She is quite the asset."

"She ain't nobody's asset," I snapped.

"Are you touching something?" Renee leaned around me as if going to talk to Frei. *"Maybe under your elbow?"*

Frei leaned in as if to talk to Renee back. They started talking in German too fast for me to understand. Theo, across from us, smiled right through his aura. He missed home.

Hartmann's aura wriggled with amusement. *So he's into the muscle? Perhaps he can distract her? He could do with some fun.*

"I'm getting bored." I sat back, hoping I wouldn't touch anything only I wasn't sure if I had in the first place.

"Calm, Alex, we'll eat soon." Frei leaned in and squeezed my knee like Renee did a lot.

She might be worth paying more attention to. Jäger's thought hit me and I glanced over, his aura snaked toward Renee.

"Move," I said, getting to my feet and pulling Renee's chair back, and her to boot.

"Aeron, what are you doing now?" She sat there and I guessed was staring up at me. I knew everybody else was, even if I couldn't see them.

"You want to make me say it twice?" I snapped.

Renee didn't move. Guess she was too stunned so I picked her up, seat and all, and shoved her in my place and took a seat next to Jäger. "You look more interesting right now."

His shark smile glimmered through his energy. Yeah, crazy attracted crazy. *How fitting if I could take her attention away from Locks.*

"You know, you didn't finish telling me about your trophies," I said, hoping I managed to be as slimy as Megan.

"Aeron!" Renee sounded ready to slap me. Her aura tried to.

Jäger laughed. "Oh, I'll be more than happy to reconvene."

And then the blonde may find she needs attention. "I'm surprised Locks hasn't stolen them," Hartmann said.

Renee laughed, fake and full of irritation. "Locks doesn't need to, she has enough trophies of her own."

Who cares. I want her DNA. Sven cleared his throat. "I'm glad that she took a break from stealing and collecting trophies to come here."

I could feel he was reaching out his hand. Had to do something. I leaned forward to block it only for my skin to touch metal cutlery on the table—

Lay the table? What does he think I am, a slave?

Oh no. Jäger had laid the table. Fury rocketed through me, the room, and everybody in it came into focus. I shot to my feet, making the table jump.

"I'm bored." I yanked my chair back. "I been waiting around for food. What are you trying to do, starve us?" I picked up the chair and hurled it at Harrison who ducked. It swept over her head, and hit the window with a crash. "It ain't polite." I picked up the centerpiece with some vase and threw it Sven's way. His mistress shoved him out of the way in time for it to zip past and smash on the floor.

"Okay, okay," Renee muttered. "We'll find something fun . . ."

"Shame," Hartmann said with a smile. "You were entertaining us."

I picked up the empty plate and threw it. Hartmann ducked and Theo covered her. I had a spoon in my grip. I scowled at it, then glared at her.

"No." Renee stepped in front of me, yanked my face down, and pressed her lips to mine. The room faded, music crashed through me, energy, light, warmth, thudding, fuzzing, ding, ding, ding, body, pores, heart pounded. Fury evaporated, sparks, light, tingles.

She pulled back. Frei had her hands on my waistband. Renee had the spoon.

I stumbled backward. Turned. Fled from the room. Too much noise, too much energy. Sobs broke free. Shuddered from me, loud in my ears.

"We're here," Frei said, catching up, walking close but not touching.

"Deep breaths," Renee said, her tone uncertain.

I clattered into the wall, smacking my shoulder. They righted me but my balance dipped, and I dropped to my knees.

"Nearly there," Frei said, pulling me back up. "Nearly to the room."

Renee had hold of my belt, and they dragged me down the corridor. Too much noise, emotion, hurt. Couldn't breathe. Crushing me.

"Nan," Renee whispered. "Nan, please help."

"Blondie, you hollering—ah," Nan said like she knew what was up.

"How do we help?" Renee asked as Frei opened the door to the room with her lock-shaped key. I gripped my head and scrabbled away as noise screeched through my ears. "She couldn't wash before and now she's sick."

"Shower." Nan swooshed around me. *"Shorty, you need to keep your shield up."*

"Can't . . ." I managed, clutching my head. My head swirled as the memory of Mrs. Jäger taking the drink filled my head. No, I couldn't relive it in full, I needed to get rid of it.

Frei picked me up, strong, calm and lifted me into the shower as Renee turned on the jets. Warmth hit me and I collapsed to my knees.

"Focus on it washing away," Nan said. *"Too much energy fizzles your circuits."*

I leaned on the wall, my head throbbing. It fought back the pending memory, and the water sucked me in, sucking the pain from me.

"We need to find a barrier," Renee said as Frei headed over to the towels. "What else can help?"

"Exercise always helped her before," Nan said, her voice calm, warm, loving and calm.

I relived Mrs. Jäger collapsing to the floor, the pain shot through me as she clutched her throat, then the throbbing eased. I gasped for breath but it didn't seem like they noticed.

"She can't use a gym here," Renee whispered. "It's too risky."

"'cause of touching?" Nan asked and I felt cold on my shoulder. It soothed me, her voice soothed me. *"Keep under the water. You got to help yourself too."*

I lay my palms flat to the wall, forcing back the panic. Had to keep awake.

"Jäger uses the gym," Frei said like she was answering Renee more than Nan. "I'm guessing he laid the table too?"

"Cranial didn't help a lot," Renee mumbled. "Should we pull her out?"

"Not yet. And you helped her keep present enough to get out of there." Nan tutted like she always did when I'd worried her as a kid. *"Best you don't get so close again."*

The water eased the tension in my muscles, sapped at the ache in my chest, and I could feel the cold of the tiles.

"I'll talk to my mom," Frei whispered, worry in her voice. "We'll see if there's anything we can do to help."

"Pull her out of the jet but keep workin' on her," Nan said, cold washing over my shoulder once more. *"Soothe her like you know best to."*

I closed my eyes and felt a swell of sadness as Renee pulled me back to sit on the floor. Sadness I knew was my own. I missed Nan. I missed cuddling up on her lap and listening to the waterwheel churn. I missed that sense of security. She'd always soothed me. She'd always been there.

"That's it. You just got to let the steam out some place." Nan faded as she said it. *"Just let off steam."*

I shuddered out a breath. The feelings, the thoughts, the fury of Jäger rattled through then music. I leaned my head back against the wall.

Real music, light, warmth. Renee. She'd pulled me up when I was drowning in the feelings. How? I couldn't place it, it was too fuzzy.

"Hey, I'm here," she whispered, her touch soft against my tense neck. "You just needed to calm."

I heard my own sobbing, felt my tears on my cheeks. Like I had climbed ashore, storm beaten and exhausted. Renee sat beside me and rested my head on her shoulder. The sadness from Nan eased with the comfort, and I closed my eyes, thinking of the waterwheel back home.

Chapter 35

RENEE HELPED AERON from the shower and moved her to the bathroom chair. She'd started sobbing when Nan faded and hadn't stopped. Not an anguished cry but a whimper that hurt to hear.

"Hey, I'm here," she said in her own accent. It would take her being herself to reach Aeron. "Can I towel you off?"

Aeron nodded, staring at the tiles.

Renee pulled off Aeron's top, seeing goosebumps all over her skin. "You cold?"

Aeron shrugged.

Renee toweled her down and tapped her lip. Nan had said that love helped. She looked at Aeron. It might work? She hurried into the bedroom to their wardrobes and pulled out her favorite bed shirt. She always wore her football jersey and Aeron always smiled at her, shook her head, and said how it looked like a dress.

"Arms up," she whispered, slid away the towel, and slid on the jersey.

Aeron closed her eyes like she'd been wrapped in a hug. "It smells like you," she mumbled.

Renee nodded and pulled her to stand. "You know why it's my favorite scent?"

Aeron shook her head but she was less distant.

"It reminds me of you." She pulled off Aeron's pants and wrapped the towel around her. "I was wearing it when we met."

"Did the same with Fleming," Aeron grunted.

"I did but I actually *like* this scent." Renee pulled out the bed shorts she'd set out and handed them to Aeron. "Change and I'll tell you why."

Aeron nodded but her movements were robotic. Maybe she'd been wrong to kiss her but it was the only way to break through, the only thing she could think of to break Aeron from the overload. It had been enough, just enough to get her to the room. Nan had said so.

"After I was hurt, when I was recovering, I kept smelling this unique mix of flowers and soap. I had no idea what it was." She took the discarded towel and helped Aeron tuck the football jersey in. "But whenever I felt down, I could smell it."

She took Aeron's hand, led her into the bedroom, and urged her to sit on the bed. "I searched every shop, everywhere I could to find something similar."

"Why?" Aeron asked, her deep brown eyes starting to show that twinkle she loved so much.

"When you walked into my office, the smell filled the air like I was standing in a windswept field." She smiled to herself, changing into her own t-shirt and shorts. Roberta Worthington would have to have a night off. "It was the exact same smell . . ."

Aeron studied her, face drawn, dark circles under her eyes. "You think I smell of flowers?"

"Sort of . . ." She felt raw telling her. She wanted to but it felt so . . . exposing. "But I've never found the flower that matches it or the soap but . . . it's comforting."

She pulled back the bedsheets, helped Aeron in, and tucked her in. She went around to her side to get in.

"You smell of mountain air and something soft and sweet." Aeron shivered, and Renee shifted until she could wrap herself around her. "You smell good though."

"I smell of hairspray." Renee grunted. "And FYI, I do not like hairspray."

"You don't?" Aeron rolled her head to look at her.

"No. It makes me gag." She slid her hand under Aeron's top, to her diaphragm, and placed her palm at the point needed to release the tension there. "False nails drive me nuts, high heels hurt my feet, and the mini-skirt is *not* enjoyable to wear."

"It ain't?" There was the soft tone, the curiosity, the smile.

"No, you make me *want* to be myself." She felt Aeron's muscles release.

Aeron groaned. "That works real good," she mumbled with a half-yawn. "Don't get why I lost it so bad."

"Because it's an intense situation," Renee whispered back. "Felt like being back in Caprock during the mid-terms."

It had. Yes, back in Caprock she'd found different coping mechanisms when she'd had some of Aeron's burdens. They weren't great ones . . . but maybe they could help.

Aeron murmured. "You got a point."

"I do and I did some breathing exercises which helped." She moved closer, hoping Aeron could feel every bit of love and comfort she could send her way. "I'd like to teach you them."

Aeron smiled, a tired, wrung-out smile. "You kinda teach me stuff a lot."

"Older woman," she said with a wink.

"I like it," Aeron whispered, her brown eyes deeper, holding her gaze, studying her, questions and uncertainty in her eyes. "I don't get why."

"You will." Renee adjusted to ease a spot of tension on Aeron's ribcage. Best she broke eye contact. Her own energy needed to be calm and ignore how her lips still tingled. "Breathe in and focus on calm energy filling your core."

Aeron did as told, broad shoulders, her chest expanding.

"Hold it." She shone every bit of love she could. "Release it back with love."

Aeron wheezed out her breath, her taut muscles relaxed further. "Feels nice."

Renee leaned up and kissed her on the cheek. "Good."

Aeron pulled her in closer still until she had to wrap her leg over not to hit knees. "I'm sorry I got overloaded."

"Don't be. If anything, you made sure no one was in doubt you're a mean criminal with a temper." She shook her head, shaking off her own worries as Aeron's calm soothed her. She forced the feel of Aeron's lips out of her mind, of the jolt of feeling that pulse through the contact. No peck on the lips should ever feel *that* good. Wow.

"I ain't been battered like that since Serenity," Aeron said, kissing her on the forehead. "Should have known better."

Renee looked up and met her eyes. Energy rippled up like a current, over her, through her; her senses pulling her to lean in . . .

"We'll figure it out," she mumbled, clearing her throat.

Aeron studied her, like she could feel the energy, her feelings, innocent curiosity flickered across then something more magnetic. "You think?"

Show her? Guide her? Nan had said to do that. Renee smiled, leaned up, and pecked Aeron on the chin. "Hey, I'm good at my job."

Aeron blinked a few times, mouth inches from hers—like she wanted to lean in but wasn't sure why.

There went her heart speeding up. Breathe. Pull back.

Aeron dropped her gaze to her lips.

"Quit staring, dimwit," she whispered and forced herself to pull back. She clamped her head to Aeron's shoulder just to break eye contact. Instead she sent every bit of feeling through her touch, every bit of comfort and relaxed into warmth and that flowery, soapy smell that was Aeron. A smell that filled her with ease, with nervousness, with hope. It wasn't logic or sensible but something told her the scent was love.

Chapter 36

FREI CREPT ALONG the corridor from Huber's room. Stosur had been in there with the glass Aeron had retrieved from Mrs. Jäger's room. They had enough of a sample to run a test and hopefully find an anti-venom.

"Miss Locks?" Theo called from behind her, and she sighed, stopped next to a bust of Sven in his twenties, and turned.

"*Wie gehts?*" She spotted the device in his hands. No doubt it would lead to questions about being in Huber's room.

"*Gut, danke.*" He glanced at Huber's door. "*Und du?*" said more like "why were you in there?"

"He had something I wanted," she said, folding her arms.

"But he is at dinner?" Theo frowned, his deep brow furrowing.

"Yes, it's harder to acquire something when you are being watched." But not impossible. She bowed low. "The wonder of being a locksmith."

"You're proud you're a thief?" He searched her eyes like it hurt him she could be that way.

"You can only steal if they owned it in the first place." She held up her phone. "When it is yours, I would say it is merely retrieving."

Theo cocked his head. "So you break in?"

"Yes," she said, holding up her hands. "That way I avoid Megan."

He gave her a lopsided smile, and her stomach fluttered.

"Is there something more I may help you with?" she asked. It was better that she avoided him. He was far too easy to like.

"I wished to know if your friend needs help." He shrugged, lifting up the device. "She was in distress."

Did he really want to know how she was? "Alex is a complex character."

Theo nodded. "And has a lot of pain?" He rubbed at the back of his neck. "I have a brother with . . ." He sighed. "Complex needs."

"I know." She met his eyes. She'd researched him . . . more than was necessary. "You think your aunt influences him?"

Theo's eyebrows shot up.

She smiled. Yes, he may be able to find out something about her but he wasn't in her league and he didn't have Aeron and Lilia. "Why else would a man who was tipped to be head of police become a servant for his slave owner of an aunt." She held up her hand. "And don't bother saying you were unaware. You are far more intelligent than that."

Theo's shoulder's slumped. "I had my suspicions . . . and I have my reasons for joining her company."

"It's called an integrated cardiac defibrillator." She smiled at him. "But your wish to help your baby brother is your real reason."

"You say this like you know me." He said it as if he wanted her to.

"I do, at least your file. You have been covering up for him most of your life." She sighed. "And, take it from me, it never works."

"You have brothers . . . sisters?" His eyes filled with sympathy. Something that he hadn't found out about her?

"I *had* two." She swallowed back the pain, the flashes of Suz, the cries from her sister.

"What happened?" He shifted on his feet as if he wanted to come to her, to squeeze the hurt from her.

"Jäger did," she whispered, not sure why she said it aloud.

"He hurt her?" Theo glanced over his shoulder and moved closer.

"He shot her . . ." She rubbed at her throat. The words still caught there, threatened to draw tears. "My younger sister, he . . . she was taken here . . . now . . . I don't know where she is."

"If he has done this, I will talk to Aunt Sabine. She will help," Theo mumbled, leaning closer still.

"She only wants what is Sven's." She shook her head. How could he think she had a shred of kindness in her?

"She is ruthless in business, yes, but it is legal." His broad jaw jutted out.

"Nothing about your aunt is legal. A thief in a business suit is still a thief." She laughed at his shocked expression. "Do not take it so personally. You are not the first she has fooled into thinking she is . . ." She laughed again, breathing in his aftershave, then pulling away. "Legal."

She turned and left him, knowing he was staring after her. He pulled her out of herself. She smiled. Wasn't that what Renee said Aeron did to her? She glanced over her shoulder and felt that flutter he was watching. Best to steer clear.

Chapter 37

STARK WHITE DAYLIGHT bathed the room in stripes as I sat with Renee, Stosur, and Frei in Frei's large bedroom. The leather sofa was only big enough to perch on so Renee was opposite on a tall-backed fancy chair, Frei was perched on the coffee table, laptop on her knees, and Stosur sat on the windowsill, staring out.

They hadn't said a word since I told them about the slaves and how, if Stosur was the locksmith they'd talked about, that she could have had a brother.

"It's common," Stosur said, standing near the window, her eyes held a tint of blue through the brown. "Many slaves don't know who they are related to . . . the owners like to separate families."

"Do you remember anyone like that?" Renee asked. The light glowed against her soft skin, her warm blonde eyelashes fluttering.

"Yes, there was an older boy. He was very sick." She smiled with a fondness. "He worked away from me, from everyone. They said he was one of those who worked on Cold Lock."

"What sickness?" Frei asked, her pale skin washed out by the light, making her eyes so much more piercing.

"I'm not sure exactly but he used a cane at first and then by the time I left . . ." She sighed. "He could barely speak or move . . . he needed help." She gazed out of the window at the white-coated grounds, pink-tinted clouds above and forest dusted with snow hats. Memories flicked around her, some made her ache, some lifted her. The boy, if he had been her brother had been a good memory.

"Then he *was* your brother," Frei whispered, looking up from her laptop. "I had the same sickness."

"Jessie had it too," I said with a shrug. Renee glared at me but I held up my hands. "I didn't know 'til I started helping her asthma . . . and she asked. She'd read your file."

Renee looked from Frei to me and folded her arms. "No wonder you were so out of it."

I shrugged again, studying my toes. I preferred walking around without shoes on. Somehow it helped drain energy away but I kinda liked the feeling of scrunching up my toes too.

"Thank you," Frei said with such emotion that it hit me like a gunshot.

"Yes, thank you," Stosur whispered, and I shuddered from another shot of feeling.

Renee got up, walked over, and squeezed me so tight I thought she was trying to crack my neck before perching on my knees. "Next time, just tell me."

I rubbed my neck. Didn't know why everybody was getting so emotional, it was mini-Frankenfrei. I couldn't just let her get sick now, could I?

"So anyhow, I told them all that we'd get them out." I looked up to Frei whose eyes misted, the unshed tears glimmering in the light. "I don't know how but I know we can." I bit my lip. "We can, right?"

Frei looked to Stosur who beamed at me—made her broken nose scrunch up. "You want us to get over three hundred slaves out from under the nose of a man who no one breaks free from?"

"And under the nose of a creep who is lurking in wait," Renee added, hanging back from my shoulders and gazing up at me.

"And heat tracking technology . . ." Frei's lips twitched in a smile.

"Not to mention that we have to prove to Hartmann that Cold Lock can be broken into." Stosur raised her wonky eyebrows. Her disguise had a wart with several hairs sprouting out of her cheek. Reminded me of some of the guards in Serenity.

"Er . . . yeah?" It didn't sound so easy when they said it like that.

Renee wheezed out a breath, grinned, then rolled her head to look at Frei. "Well, I'm up for it."

Frei stared at her, shock in her eyes and aura. "You are?"

"Urs, I enjoyed breaking a certain prisoner free. It gave me a buzz." Renee rubbed my shoulder, flashing a confident smile at me. "We took down Caprock, took down the European school . . . Why not swipe his own slaves out from under him while we're at it?"

"We can use the old warehouse in town," Stosur said, energy firing into life. "My team could move them out a few at a time."

"And the guards?" Frei asked, looking from Renee to Stosur.

"You have darts, don't you?" Stosur said. "It's a way to throw him off balance. A perfect way to show Hartmann he's weak . . ." She beamed at Renee. "And there is quite a buzz to freeing slaves."

Frei's aura prickled around her. She wanted to help but she was worried about Stosur, about Jessie, about Jäger. "I have to concentrate on finding Cold Lock . . ."

"But this is like when we were looking for you," I said, leaning forward with Renee still perched, the sofa tilting with us. "I had this urge to save two kittens, an urge to help a guy in an airport . . ."

"And I gave a drug store owner a whole load of money," Renee said, rubbing the bridge of her nose.

Frei nodded, hugging her laptop, eyes filled with exasperation. "That goes without saying that you both love to help."

"Detours sometimes show you shortcuts," I said with a smile, enjoying Renee doing more of that cranial stuff on my neck. "My freaky side dragged my sizable butt through that door for a reason."

Frei's eyes twinkled. "I trust your freaky butt."

I nodded and gave Renee a squeeze of thanks. I felt stronger, calmer. "Good. So . . . any ideas how we smuggle out folks?"

Frei turned her laptop around. "Way ahead of you."

Chapter 38

SVEN INVITED EVERYBODY for dinner again but somehow missed Renee and I out. Now, I couldn't figure how that was, when my table manners were so good. Maybe he hadn't enjoyed me testing his mistress's reflexes or something?

"We are starting with the youngest and one of them is deaf," Renee said to me as we snuck along the corridor. She had her earpiece in, which was buzzing at me. "Jessie, you copy."

I heard Jessie's sweet voice chirp back and tried relaxing my shoulders as we squeezed in through a slave door and up a set of steps.

"Stosur conferred with the oldest slave. She is organizing them, and they will be on the fifth floor." Renee checked her watch on her wrist. "Stosur is going to rappel down to the window and pull them up. From there they are zip-lining down into the trees to the north where Aunt Bess is waiting to take them back to the factory."

Was she talking to me or Jessie? I concentrated on not tumbling down the steps.

"I'll need confirmation that the spikes on the window have been disarmed," Renee said, Commander Black creeping to the surface. Man, I got goosebumps when she did that. "Only that window?"

I pulled myself onto the landing and took a breath. My calves were burning from stomping up on my tiptoes.

"Guards?" she asked, leading me down the corridor, nodding to the slaves watching us from their rooms. "Two patrols . . ." She sighed and met my eyes. "And Jäger is on the prowl."

Great. "Mousey, you keep where you are. I don't want to have to go tearing across the lawn to come save you." I hoped I said it loud enough she could hear.

Renee placed her finger over my lips. "No, no, if I see you, I'll dart you, twice."

I nodded. She would. I could hear Jessie muttering something in response and it sounded "grunting teenager." Even Frei's genes could get hormonal it seemed.

"Huber is with her. He's not going to let her out of his sight." Renee led me into the sitting room where the older slave sat in her chair, waiting for us. Renee held out her hand. "Pleasure to meet you. We're your rescue team for this evening. If you could get everyone to listen to us and follow our instructions, I hope we'll have a smooth escape."

I chuckled.

The older woman did too. "Some of the younger ones are wriggly but they'll listen."

"So we got five here," I said, counting the ones lined up in coats. "So where's the others?" I was sure Stosur said there were more.

"Five are at dinner," she said with a sigh. "Two are tending to Hartmann's room as she disliked the lumpy mattress."

"And the other eight?" Renee asked, all humor gone.

"Are downstairs in the kitchens." She nodded to the five waiting. "Best we work as we go."

Sounded fair. I looked to Renee who nodded.

"Which window?" she asked.

The woman shook her head, confusion trailing through the motion. "Window?"

Tapping filled the awkward silence, and I grinned at Stosur who was on a rope outside the window. I headed over and opened it up, shivering with the flurry of snow that hit my face. "Guessing this window is the one we're using?"

Stosur nodded. "Evening, Lindsey."

"It really is you." The woman got to her feet, hobbled over, and gripped Stosur by the cheeks. "Can't say you've aged well, girl."

Stosur squeezed her gnarled hand and kissed it. "And changed my hair."

The woman let out a hoarse chuckle then motioned to the kids lined up. "You go now. Our locksmith will break you out."

The first kid, taller than the others, took a big breath and lifted her arms. Renee hoisted her up into Stosur's waiting grasp, and she clipped them to her. She nodded to Renee who let go and started her climb upward.

"You mind if we call you Lindsey?" I asked, smiling at the old woman.

"Of course, Miss Samson," she fired back.

I took her hand in mine. "To you, I'm Aeron."

Renee stared at me for a moment, then relaxed. "And I'm Renee."

Lindsey looked from Renee to me. "You are not who you say you are?"

"Who is?" I said as a small person zipped down a line high overhead and disappeared into the trees. I nodded to Renee. "First mini-person is shaking but in good hands."

Stosur appeared in the window. Smooth and slow did it.

ALL FIVE OF the slaves had gotten into the trees without a problem and five more were lined up and ready to go zip-lining. We had the kitchen staff and two of the slaves in Hartmann's room to go.

"Lindsey," one slave said, hurrying in. Her long hair scraggly. "Jäger is following her again."

"Come and wait with the others," Lindsey said, her wrinkled hand trembled as she urged the girl forward. "He may find something else more interesting."

She didn't believe a word of it.

I looked to Renee. "That's me." I held up my finger as she opened her mouth. "If I keep standing still like this, folks are gonna think I'm one of the dumb busts out in the hall."

The kids snorted. Glad they were with me.

"You get the girl, you come back. If I have to come looking for you, I'll be mad." She furrowed her blonde brow. "Really mad."

I saluted. "Yes, ma'am." Hey, I was sure I did it right.

"Get going." She waved me off and lifted up the next child to Stosur.

I hurried out and up the stairs. I didn't need an earpiece or Jessie. I could feel Jäger's intentions, and I could feel the kid's fear. Distraction. I could give him a distraction alright.

RENEE WAITED PATIENTLY as the girl with disheveled hair clambered up onto the ledge. The girl's body shook, her breathing in gulps.

"You don't like heights?" Renee asked, holding her tightly.

"I . . . I'm not sure." She shook harder as Stosur dropped down in front of her. "I think I'll go back in . . ."

"No, no . . ." Stosur held onto her, eyes dropping to the spikes below her. "Keep your feet up."

The girl shook her head. "I want to go back in."

Renee held her steady. "You can't. You're up there now. Just a quick climb and you'll be free."

Stosur took the girl from her and nodded. Renee let go and the girl clung on to Stosur as she tried to fumble with the clasp. "That's it, just take slow breaths." Stosur pulled herself up, slower than before. "I've got you."

Renee looked back to Lindsey who watched on with worry in her eyes. "She gets scared?"

Lindsey nodded. "She got pushed from the stairs as a child. Jäger in one of his tempers." She gazed up as Stosur headed up the wall. "I thought it was only stairs."

"No . . . no . . . calm . . ." Stosur's voice held panic. "Calm down."

"I can't, I need to get down." The girl's voice rose.

Renee glanced at the door. They could be heard. She leaned out, the girl was wriggling, her voice rising.

"I can't risk her alerting them," Renee whispered. She pulled out her dart gun. "You have her secure?"

"No . . ." Stosur scrambled as the girl kicked away from her, dropped.

Renee threw her gun in, shoved her arms out . . . caught her. Her elbow hit the spike and pain shot through it. "Thought you said they were disarmed." She strained to keep the girl off the spike.

"They are, but they're still coated in venom." Stosur muttered to the rope. "Jammed."

Renee grunted with the effort. She could feel Lindsey trying to pull her in.

"Got you," Frei said, pulling her in and placing the girl on the floor. She pulled out something from her pants and injected it into Renee's spasmed arm. "Take a few breaths."

Renee nodded as Frei injected the girl with a sedative. The girl fell asleep, and Frei handed her up to Stosur.

"Dinner was boring?" Renee asked, panting as the anti-venom worked through her system.

"Without you two, yes," Frei said, smiling at Lindsey who watched on with relief and awe in her wrinkled eyes. "Now, let's free some slaves."

Chapter 39

THE HALLWAYS WERE empty as I followed my senses toward Jäger. Some of it looked forgotten like nobody had been there for years. One corridor on my left felt so much like it that I expected to see cobwebs concealing the entrance but it looked as neat and furnished with kids' art as the others.

The kid running from Jäger had started to sob and I could hear her even though I shouldn't be able to—an echoing cry that wasn't a flash or a thought. I shuddered and tried to focus on my armor. Sooner I got to her, sooner it would stop.

"Shorty, you need to rest up. You can't keep on tuning in when you ain't got the legs to stand it," Nan whispered to me as I picked up my pace.

"I can't let him catch her, Nan." I glanced to my left where I could feel her. "You know what he did to . . ." I glanced over my shoulder. "Locks."

"Sure, an' I get why you want to help but if you keep pushing your own body, you ain't gonna be a lot of help to nobody." Nan prodded me in the ribs as I ducked around a corner. *"I know you ain't gone deaf."*

I broke into a trot. The cries were getting louder. "It's my job. I didn't want it . . . remember? I wanted to find some peace and quiet." I looked around, knowing the kid was hiding some place near, but where? "But I'm here so I'm helping."

Nan sighed. *"Then use those wiles of yours and not your brawn."*

She faded, and I shook off the need to ask her to come back, to spend time with her, to sit someplace and rest. Instead I wiped my sweaty hands on my jeans and pulled open a door on my left. The kid cowered from me, hands above her head like I'd beat her.

"Kid, it's okay." I knelt beside her. "Lindsey sent me to get you."

She peered between her fingers. "She did?"

I nodded. "You got to hurry. They're waiting for you."

She huddled down again. "He's following me. If I run there, he'll find them."

I touched her shoulder. "He won't."

She took a few breaths, then sprinted out of the room and down the corridor. I shut the door, pulled myself up to my full height, then Nan's words prickled at me. Wiles. *Did* I have any wiles? I leaned against the wall, hoping my smile was a sure one as Jäger limped around the corner.

"You know," I said, folding my arms. "You're getting kinda slow."

His dark eyes trailed over me, then narrowed.

"You looking for anybody in particular?" I cocked my head like it was funny.

"No," he said, his aura buttoning its lip—truthful as always. "Are you?"

"Well, you see, it's kinda funny. I saw this kid who caught my eye and I needed some entertainment." I shrugged, hoping I sounded mean. "Then she goes and whines at me saying I was worse than Mr. Jäger."

He scowled, bushy black eyebrows almost touching his nose. "She was lying."

I wagged my finger. "Nope. I made real sure of it." I looked him up and down. Same suit, again. Did he have a wardrobe full? "Guess you're losing your touch."

He pulled his boot-polish stubble chin in. "I have other things on my mind."

I laughed, making sure it was clear that I was laughing at him. "You mean the pathetic attempt to get Locks?"

"Pathetic?" He narrowed his eyes further, a glint in them I hadn't seen as potent since Sam pointed a gun at me.

"Yeah, I mean, there was me thinking you were all that . . ." I shook my head. "Only for you to lose her in Caprock, limp away in Baltimore, and now even the slaves ain't scared of you." I wagged my finger. "An' I noticed that your brother ain't got no looks on you."

"Don't count me out yet, Alex," he said, a slow, creepy smile touching his lips. "She's proven before that she can't resist being a hero."

She *was* a hero through and through. "And you think she'll fall for more of your tricks?"

"Count on it." His smile was shark-like again. He was up to something and my gut twisted. I needed to know just what, so I pushed off the wall and strolled toward him.

"So there's still some fight in you then," I purred, hoping I was doing a great Megan impression. "Don't like being disappointed."

I tidied the buttons on his shirt collar. Renee sometimes did that when in cover. Must be wile-like. Renee could charm most folks.

Jäger gripped hold of my hand. "I wouldn't like to disappoint you, Alex."

"Lure her out, boy," Sven snapped, brandishing his inhaler at him. "I've cleaned up enough of your messes."

"Yes, Sven." He gripped onto his belt to stop from throttling him. Was it his fault his wife had seen the attack coming? Was it his fault she'd made herself immune? No. Sven wasn't as clever as he liked to think. Messes? It was Sven's mess.

"I want her DNA." Sven glared at him with watery eyes. "Then I want you to get rid of the others." He flicked his inhaler at the door. "Harrison is lurking and I don't want her feeding any of this back."

Jäger stared at him. "You want me to take Harrison out?"

"And Hartmann, Theo, Huber . . . the lot of them." Sven laughed, his double chin wobbling.

He'd lost it. There was no way he was taking on Hartmann or Harrison. The others, perhaps, but he wasn't stupid. Sven wouldn't back him up if they caught him.

"Why are you still standing there?" Sven glared at him. "I have things to do, boy."

Jäger turned and strode out. He shut the door and stared at the handle. He wouldn't do it. Hartmann was too well guarded and Harrison . . . ? No chance.

I blinked away the memory, hoping my smile covered the sweat dribbling down my neck.

"Why haven't you just taken the place for yourself?" I asked, running my hands over his shoulders. Yeah, the suit was identical, cotton with a sheen? Maybe he never changed his clothes. Maybe that's why he tried suffocating everyone with his aftershave.

"I learned from childhood it was better to let the fly find the web by itself." He stroked my cheek—

"Boy, you lost. Why did you lose?" His father smacked him with the trophy. The metal stung his side. "What kind of pathetic idiot are you?"
   Lose? He was nine. He came second out of hundreds. "Sorry, Mr. Jäger."
   "Sorry?" His father laughed, anger in his eyes. "I'll show you sorry."

I jumped as the blow landed. No wonder the guy was deranged. "Why the loyalty to Sven when he cares nothing for you?"
   "You may see it as weakness," Jäger whispered. "But you don't know me."

"Hit him again and I'll shoot," Sven spat, wheezing hard, pistol in his shaking hand.
   Their father turned and laughed. "Shoot?" He laughed harder. He stank of drink. He always stank. "You are too weak to pull the trigger."
   Bam.
   Their father gripped his shoulder, hunched over.
   Bam.
   Their father's leg buckled. He dropped to one knee.
   "We've put up with you long enough," Sven snapped. "I want the locksmith and I want control of the household."
   Bam.
   Their father slumped to the floor. Jäger stared down at him.
   "Get rid of the evidence," Sven said, placing the gun on the table. "If mother doesn't co-operate, you know what to do."
   Jäger nodded. "Yes, Sven." He didn't know how to get rid of evidence. "Won't they know?"
   "No," Sven said, strolling to the door. He stopped and turned. "Don't disappoint me."

I pulled back from him, trembling. "So brotherly loyalty?"
   Jäger grabbed hold of my shoulders. "You think I'm sentimental enough to care?"

I shoved him off balance, buckling his bad knee with mine. "No, just don't get why you can't own up to your issues." I smiled at him as he winced. "At least I don't go hiding mine."

He lunged at me, I stepped to the side, caught his hand, quicker than it took to blink—

"Relax, I'll lure her out." He eyed Harrison, lifting onto the balls of his feet. She made him feel like his mother had, like he was worthless.

"Lure her out?" Harrison glared down her nose at him. "Boy, I warned you not to stir Huber's temper; I warned you to leave the slave alone." She picked up the phone. "She cost us millions. I have to deal with my employers."

Jäger pressed the receiver down. "You don't need to tell anyone."

Harrison smacked him across the head with the receiver. "You need me to teach you manners?"

Jäger blinked, stepped back. First the doctor looking after the slave had hurt him—she moved too fast; then Harrison? No. They were useless, like slaves. His father told him so. He'd warned not to trust them. They were all vermin.

"You've tested my patience enough, boy. Get out of my sight and stay away from that slave." She looked him up and down with disgust. "I have to break it to your brother that, not only have we missed a locksmith, but she's halved his assets."

"He still has the other girl," he mumbled, rubbing at his head. Sven wanted that child desperately. He couldn't see why. So she bore some resemblance to the slave who ran. Who cared? What was so important about one slave? "I lured her out once."

"You were lucky." Harrison clicked her fingers at him. "Go, or I'll fill him in on your behavior."

He hunched his shoulders, hung his head. "Yes, Ms. Harrison."

"Like I said, you're slow." I dropped his hand and let him right himself against the wall. "An' I ain't got the patience to wait around for you." I turned and strolled away from him, feeling his frustration, that swirling rage that bubbled around him but I kept on walking. I needed to get back to Renee.

RENEE NODDED TO Frei as the slaves from the dining hall zipped, one by one, down the rope. Her hand ached but the medication had kicked in, leaving her with a razor like gash on her arm but the venom was gone.

"Can I still go?" A voluptuous teenager hurried in, cheeks rosy. "Got delayed."

Lindsey smiled and placed a kiss on her cheek. "Of course. Did . . ." she glanced at Renee and Frei. "Miss Samson find you?"

The teenager nodded. "She was laughing at Mr. Jäger when I left." She hurried over to the window. Lindsey wrestled to help her into a coat and placed the drawstring bag over her shoulder. "Sounded like he was scared of her."

"He is," Frei whispered, holding out her hand to help the girl onto the window sill.

The teenager raised her eyebrows. "Glad she wasn't mad at me then."

Stosur dropped down and held out her hands. The girl was confident as she held on. She looked ready to leave the estate behind.

Renee turned to Frei and held up her hand but Frei pushed it away and hugged her.

"Did *you* get hit by the venom?" Renee mumbled, enjoying the hug.

"No, I just love you." Frei pulled back, shook herself off, and turned to Lindsey. "We'll try for more with the next batch."

Lindsey nodded. "And the wire?"

Frei pointed to the window. Stosur zipped along it. "She's detached it and will reel it in."

Renee leaned on the window sill. Frei had helped her across from Hartmann's roof top in the same manner . . . with one side detached? Why did that make her queasy?

"Relax, it's locksmith practice," Frei shot at her, a cocky grin on her face.

"It's insane." She rubbed her hand over her face, the snow from the window cold against her cheeks. Stosur must have landed because the zip-line snapped through the air and disappeared into the trees.

"Only if you fall." Frei shut the window and wiped the

snowflakes from it. "If Jäger is lurking, it's best we're in our rooms." She smiled at Lindsey. "Pleasure to meet you."

"*Ebenfalls,*" Lindsey said back.

Renee nodded, pushed Frei into motion, and followed her down the staircase. "Considering she's been here a while, you'd think she'd have asked to leave first."

Frei shook her head. "She looks like she wants to get all the children out first." She tucked her hands in her pockets. "I think we could find it hard to get her to leave at all."

"Institutionalized?" Renee paused to raise her eyebrows at a nude sculpture of a man guarding one of the hallways. "Sven doesn't have a six-pack."

"Not in reality." Frei cast a bored glance at the sculpture. "But in his head, who knows."

They turned the corner, and Aeron was bent at the waist, panting like she'd done drills.

"Kid find you?" Aeron said, looking up from hunching over.

Renee nodded, fighting every urge to run over and check she was okay. "Did you decide to work out?"

"Out of breath walking," Aeron managed. "Ain't sure why but I got speckles in my eyes."

Renee exchanged a glance with Frei.

"Quit worryin' 'bout me and get me someplace I can sit," Aeron muttered, her ear-length redwood-tint hair falling into her tanned face. "I don't want to keep gawping at this freaky statue."

"It's a hat stand," Frei said, helping Aeron straighten up. "There was a phase when every owner had a hat stand that looked like it was a dummy."

Aeron frowned at it. "But it's metal."

"Platinum," Frei said, tapping it.

"Whatever, it's freaky." Aeron reached out for Renee and she couldn't hold back. No, she hurried to her side and wrapped an arm around her strong waist. "You get the kids out?"

Renee nodded, trying to conceal the worry building inside. Aeron was too pale, those dark circles re-emerging under her eyes. "Locks couldn't resist the fun."

Aeron managed a tired grin. "Good to hear." She held up a fist. "Go, Team Locks."

Frei snorted with laughter, and Renee shook her head. Go, Team Locks indeed.

Chapter 40

THE SNOW PICKED up outside the windows as I crawled out of bed. Misty white made it hard to see further than the flowerbeds below. Renee was busy humming to herself, checking over her weapons and wandering around in the catapult tights and a corset. I didn't know where she was gonna cram all her kit but I thought better not to ask. Just looking at her made me feel . . . flustered? Was that the right word? I wasn't sure if it was but either way, I couldn't look at her.

The more she hummed the worse I felt so I headed to the internal door to Frei's like it would give me some air. How could being around Renee make me feel like I was drowning?

I pushed open the door and heard the shower going but Stosur was at Frei's desk, hunched over a laptop.

"You look worried," she said without turning around. "You shouldn't be. You did well at dinner."

"How did hurling stuff make you think that?" I asked, shoving my hands in my pockets. Renee was humming *Moonlight Sonata* to herself so I wandered toward Stosur, just to find space to breathe.

"It made it clear you weren't to be targeted." She tapped away, her furry chin catching the light. I'd seen in Huber's memories how breathtaking she was. Maybe the disguises were like Frei's hair, a statement that she wasn't just about looks.

"How?" I leaned against the post of Frei's bed. She loved long hot showers by the relief rolling from the bathroom in waves.

Stosur shut the laptop and turned to examine me. "Even rich, ruthless criminals don't know what to do with someone so unstable."

"I can't get that overloaded again." She knew that and I didn't know why I was saying it but it was something to drown out the music rolling through my head.

"No." She turned and pulled out, what looked like, skin from her pocket. "Gloves, they feel and look like your own skin."

I took them off her. They felt stretchy and matched my skin color exactly.

"They are breathable so they'll allow your sweat out, along with your heat but should give you some barrier." Stosur perched on the stool like we were discussing flower arranging. "It's not much."

"It's something." I tucked them safe in my pocket. "Any closer to finding where Cold Lock is?"

Stosur sighed and shook her head. "There's nothing. All the newer additions have no facility that would suit what a system like that needs and there's no extra security."

I glanced at the bathroom. "It's been here awhile, been here since Sven was young."

"How do you know?" Stosur leaned forward onto her legs, clasping her hands together.

"I can feel it off you. Huber broke the band from you . . . and you escaped." I shoved my hands in my pockets and held the gloves. I needed the barrier. "It was the same system then."

"An older version, perhaps." She nodded like it made sense to her. "But I didn't know where it was housed."

I sat on the edge of the bed and hovered my hand over her arm—

"You have to leave. The security system is down." Huber knelt, knife in hand, and placed the blade to the band holding it in place.

"That can't be. You'll be hurt if you try that—"

He cut the band.

She waited for him to be shocked, for an alarm to sound but nothing. Huber threw the band into the trash and held his hand out. "I've done the same to the girls."

"What about you?" She couldn't go without him too. Her heart ached too much.

"I will follow on when you're settled." He was lying, and they both knew it. He'd cover her tracks, make sure she got away and risk all he had to do so.

"He's a good man," she said with a quiet smile.

"Like he told you, he ain't faultless but he ain't heartless either." I shook off the woozy feeling. Renee's humming got louder in my head.

"You know," Stosur whispered, glancing at the doorway behind me. "With her fitness, tone, her beauty and the way she carries herself, I'm not surprised Hartmann has trouble forgetting her." Her eyes twinkled.

"I don't need to be thinking about Hartmann drooling over her. I read enough of her slimy thoughts about Renee." I shook my head, Hartmann grinning at Renee flitting through my mind. "It's hard enough to concentrate as it is." I rubbed my hand over my face—it was hard enough to breathe with it, like her perfume was circling me.

"That sounds less like reading and more like feeling." Stosur shook her head with a breathy chuckle.

"I don't feel stuff like that." I shrugged, feeling like a dumb kid. How could I explain it in a way normal folks would understand? They felt their own feelings and, if they were like Renee, figured themselves out real quick. "I only get what everybody else feels."

Stosur pulled down the sleeve of her sweater and placed her hand over mine. A gesture much like Nan used when I was young. Somehow it gave me a glimmer of that feeling too. "You keep telling yourself that."

"What you mean?"

"What I said." She smiled at me. "You're a wonderful young woman with a big heart. You're entitled to feel it beat."

"That's . . ." I couldn't help but smile back even if it did hurt. "Thank you, but I'm pretty sure I'm just getting what everybody else feels."

"Or perhaps you're not." Stosur gave my hand a squeeze and pulled back as Frei strolled into the room, dressed and with a determined look in her eyes.

"You have the gloves? Good." She straightened a hair that wasn't precise. "I'm hoping that we can follow Theo after lunch. Maybe he will give us a clue where the main hub is."

I cocked my head. "He ain't part of Sven's household though."

"No, but he's got that heat-tracking device for a reason." Frei nodded to Stosur. "Hartmann wants that system if she's circling Sven."

"You could be right but why is she spending her time playing cards with Huber and Megan?" Stosur got up and straightened out her back. "She's happy to sit back and watch."

"Or she just wants us to think that," Renee said, striding in. She wore a short skirt, low top with no straps showing her shoulders. She'd made up her face in a way that made it impossible to tear my gaze away—lips shiny, eyes enhanced somehow, and hair that made me cough looking at it.

I swallowed. It weren't the Renee I knew but her energy smashed into me.

"So you're going to keep her distracted?" Frei asked, amusement in her voice. I wanted to look at her instead but couldn't.

"And the rest of the table," Stosur said with a gentle laugh. I felt someone touch my wrist. "Sven will be impressed, that much I know."

Renee raised an eyebrow at Stosur, and my gut rolled. "Then maybe I'll get some answers off him while I'm at it."

Frei poked me in the cheek—I got a flash of Theo checking up on her. Explained her confident mood. "You need to move for us to go to lunch."

I blinked a few times. My legs had gone on vacation.

Renee met my gaze, her eyes swirling, the rims catching the wintery glow from the window. "Move it, dimwit."

Frei helped me up and I stumbled around to face the door, feeling like somebody had thrown ice cold water over me. Again, I didn't get how not looking at Renee could make me feel so cold.

LUNCH WASN'T GOING well. I could feel everyone so much that I was suffocating; flashes from Serenity pummeled me; the emotions of everyone present swirled above me, slapping me with random bursts. I was next to Jäger again, Renee to my right, Frei next to her. No one would meet my eyes, and I didn't want to meet theirs. I focused on my armor, trying to block every probing feeling but when I did, I just got drawn to Renee until everything else dimmed out.

Renee had Hartmann's attention and didn't seem to notice me at all. Hartmann's gaze was glued to her, so much so, Sven asked her questions, twice, and she didn't so much as murmur at him; Theo kept smiling at Frei, who was doing her best to shove down how much she liked him; Sven's confidence was growing because he thought Frei couldn't beat his system; his mistress had a cold, and her feet ached; Jäger was shaken by me being so close after our discussion in the hallway; Huber had lost a load of money to Hartmann and was plotting how to get it back; Megan was enjoying watching Huber stew, and Harrison was watching it all like she was taking notes. I wanted to hold my head in my hands and go find somewhere quiet to curl up.

Renee leaned back in her chair, a lazy smile on her face, flicked her gaze over Hartmann, and winked at her.

I glared at my empty bowl. I wanted to hurl it but I wasn't sure if it was at Renee or Hartmann.

"You have strong hands, Samson," Sven said. "You work out?"

I looked up and stared at him. He was after my DNA I guessed but asking someone as built as me if they worked out was just dumb.

"Sure," I muttered and went back to glaring at my bowl. It had the Eis logo in the middle. Not the new one but the one we'd seen on the rusted-up sign back in the town. I cocked my head. I'd seen that before? Where? It bugged me or maybe that was Hartmann's smug mood? She loved Renee's attention. Didn't know what Renee found attractive. Beating people wasn't nice, being a slave owner was worth pickle juice in the eye.

I looked over at the sauces and stuff in the middle of the table. You pickled stuff in vinegar, maybe I could use that.

"I thought you'd like to come on the hunt with me," Sven said. I didn't know who to but I tried not to think about poor furries getting shot at. "Samson?"

"Not much challenge to go shooting at creatures." I smiled my meanest smile. "More fun when they're on two legs." I glared at Hartmann for good measure. My mood gave my words enough of an edge, all the hairs on the back of my neck stood up. Yeah, I'd freaked myself out again.

"Alex, you can't do that here," Frei said like she was exasperated.

I eyed her, making every effort not to look at Renee, her legs, or the sleepy smile on her face. "Why not?"

Jäger leaned forward. "I ask that question myself."

Bet he did. Chump.

"You'd more likely shoot yourself," Sven spat at him, dark veins bulging, then he smiled a watery smile. "Perhaps that is more appealing."

Oh nice guy, shoot his deranged brother? He'd shot his father so it wasn't too much bother.

Jäger smiled a forced smile.

"Guess you know how to handle a gun?" I said it with sarcasm. The guy would need his inhaler to stand let alone traipse after somebody with a heavy rifle.

"Of course," Sven said with a smarmy grin. "I often clay shoot."

I got the picture of him with the rifle on a stand while one of his slaves did the shooting and he took the credit.

"Nice." Said like I was bored.

Hartmann did something that Renee was trying her best to ignore. A rush of feeling pounded through me, and I slammed my chair back. Hartmann shot a smug smile at me. I picked up my bowl, and the smile vanished.

"Alex, calm," Frei said, her tone rippling with concern.

"Calm?" I glared at Hartmann. "Not the best person to irritate." I dropped the bowl back onto the table, stalked off to the bathroom, and slammed the door behind me.

I went to the faucet and ripped off my gloves. Had to be some kind of ailment. Nan had gotten Renee to put me in the shower. It had to help.

Ugh. Renee.

My mood sliced through me, making my gut ache and flutter so I turned on the faucet. Shouldn't really heal on my own, I'd promised Renee.

I scowled. Why would she notice, she was too busy batting her eyelids at Hartmann. I shoved my mitts under, not caring if it concussed me. Maybe it'd knock out the stupid wriggling too. The water was cool, nice on my warm hands but it didn't bite.

"Come on," I muttered, shoving my hands in further.

Cool, refreshing, but no bites.

Frei strode in, leaned against the door, and let out a long, heavy sigh. "Sooner we break the lock, the sooner we can go home."

"Yeah, hurry up and break it already," I said, focusing on the water. Why wasn't it helping?

"Washing something away?" She asked, studying me.

"Trying to." My hands were getting colder and stung so I ran the hot water and put one under that—maybe that'd work?

"Who was hurt?" She leaned against the counter beside me.

"Nobody, I'm trying to heal myself." One hand was warm the other was cold and there was no healing but now I *did* need the bathroom.

Frei touched my arm. "Did you injure yourself? The food? What?"

"No, nope and didn't." I shrugged. "Why ain't it working?"

"Flashes?" Her tone showed her worry, and it filtered through her touch.

"No, but Theo got hollered at for checking on you earlier." I stuck the plug in the sink. Still water had worked before. "He don't much care. Guy is head over hind for you."

Frei cleared her throat. "He's using me to get information on Huber."

"No, he really did just want to know how you were." I plunged my hands in—warm—and it still weren't biting.

"That's not helpful," she muttered, picking at the edge of the marble top. "I don't need you to remind me how . . . pleasant he is."

"Sorry." I threw the water onto my face. Did I need to sit in it or something?

"This isn't like the other night," she said, her voice soft.

I shook my head.

"So?" She took my hand to stop me sticking my head in the sink and raised her white blonde eyebrows.

"Worthington," I muttered. "I . . . she . . . Why can't she wear pants like a normal person?"

I was mad 'cause she wasn't wearing pants? Huh?

Frei's energy filled with laughter and her icy blues sparkled. "It would be easier to talk to her in pants?"

"Yes, no . . . I ain't sure but if Hartmann stares at her much more, I might just throw her through the window." I shook my head. *Had* to be someone else's feelings. I didn't get mad. Hartmann wasn't doing anything unexpected. She was a creep. Creeps did creepy things.

"Renee is keeping her distracted to help me." Frei's voice was soft. "I just stole her room key." She lifted up her cellphone and inserted the card into it.

"Why didn't she just tell me?" Didn't help my mood much. I

still wanted to dunk Renee in the sink until she quit flashing eyes at crazy people. "She never tells me nothin'."

"No, she's a terrible . . . team worker." Frei meant commander— Yeah, and the unspoken, "she was my commander and she didn't have to tell me zip," filled the silence.

"If you want the team to stay strong, helps if we all know what the play is," I snapped. The water wasn't biting so I ducked my face in.

Nothing.

"Sometimes," Frei said with a smile running through her voice. "So apart from her sultry attire, and Hartmann appreciating it, is there any other reason why you're so desperate to bathe in the sink?"

"Not funny." I dunked my face again—Nothing. I yanked my head out. "Can't focus. Can't concentrate. She's driving me nuts." I dunked my head again—Nothing. "Must be an ailment." I held my face under the water until my lungs protested. "Got to wash it off."

"I can see that's working out for you." She handed me a towel. "Ever thought you just don't like other people fawning over her?"

I ripped the plug out. "It ain't that. I get annoyed when folks do that, sure, but this is like I'm so mad I want to yell at her."

"Because she told you she found Hartmann attractive?" Frei took the towel and handed me another.

"You ain't meant to bug your friends." I rubbed at my wet hair.

"Oddly, Renee said the same." She cocked her head. "I didn't bug either of you. I could just hear you. The door was ajar."

I leaned over the empty sink. White bowl, gold faucet inset in marble. Went with the marble floor and marble walls. "You were sleeping?"

"I thought you'd be able to read I was dozing?" Frei leaned against the sink. "I'm used to sleeping light . . . Suz." She stared up at the ceiling like she was trying to hide the swell of hurt.

I squeezed her shoulder. "When folks are sleeping or resting, I guess it's private. I can't feel them then."

"Really?" She took the second towel off me like she didn't feel a thing and handed me a third.

My top was soaked. Great. How'd I explain that? "Yeah. If I touch them sometimes and they need help, I can feel it." I rubbed at my shirt. Didn't know why I couldn't have buttons all the way up. Renee was showing enough cleavage for the both of us. "Nora once had trouble in Serenity and she was slipping unconscious . . . I could feel where she was then."

"Safety clause." Frei placed the towels all neat and folded on the counter. "What sparked you getting this bad?"

I sighed. "Been getting worse for a while but since . . ." When was it? It hurt to think. My brain was too fuzzed. "Since dinner maybe?"

"Because you got overloaded or . . . because she *kissed* you?" Frei peered up at me from under her eyebrows. Her aura looked like she wanted to laugh, smile, and not show any emotion all at once so it just wriggled about.

"She did?" The memory roared up from inside—

Renee stepped in front of me, yanked my face down, and pressed her lips to mine. The room faded, music crashed through me, energy, light, warmth, thudding, fuzzing, ding, ding, ding, body, pores, heart pounded. Fury evaporated, sparks, light, tingles.

I touched my fingers to my lips. She'd kissed me? My hands trembled like I was on a flume ride with no restraints.

"You didn't remember . . . interesting . . ." Frei sounded like a doctor or a shrink, and I didn't much like either.

"What?" I turned on the faucet. My gut was wriggling, rolling, and aching.

"You remember now though . . ." She leaned in, her smile gentle. "Thought you were too calm about it."

"I am." Which sounded squeaky and unhinged.

"You just need to know if what you're feeling right now," Frei held my shoulders like she knew I wanted to climb into the sink, "are your feelings."

I nodded. Sounded like a great way to get rid of them. "How?"

Frei chewed on her lip. "You won't like it."

"I can't feel like this . . ." I shook my head. "I don't feel like this. I never feel like this . . ." I shook my head harder, maybe that would rattle sense into my brain? "She loves somebody . . . really loves them."

Frei nodded. "She does . . ." She pursed her lips. "Maybe you could test it out when she's asleep?" She shook her head as if picturing Renee punching her for it. "That way, you'll know if you feel . . . what you feel . . . genuinely."

"Are you telling me to drool on her when she's prone 'cause I've been one on one with her and it hurts." I rubbed at my shoulder. She was a mean fighter. No shortstop should be that strong.

"I am telling you that . . ." Frei squeezed my shoulders. "Even if she wakes up, she won't be angry. She'll understand."

"Fine for you to say, you wouldn't be the one thrown through a window." I shuddered. Didn't like to think how fiery she'd get with that.

"She won't get angry. She'll help you as best she can." Frei smiled at me. "And you'll know if it is you or if it's her."

"Guess that ain't gonna help you with Theo?" I could hear movement—or feel it—from the dining room. "You really like him, don't you?"

She leaned against the sink next to me, and we stared at the swirly marble wall. "Yes." She shook her head. "So if you are feeling things . . . you're in good company."

I bumped her shoulder. "He's a nice guy." I smiled. "But if he upsets you, I'll knock his teeth out."

Frei laughed and pushed off the counter. "Thank you, Alex. Good to know you approve."

I squeezed her hand. "I do. I want to see you happy."

She nodded and let go. "Back at you."

Chapter 41

FREI FOLLOWED THEO from the table, careful to keep her distance as he headed outside to the grounds. Aeron had skulked off up to her room from the bathroom, and Renee hadn't missed it but Frei had said nothing, only slipped Hartmann's key back into her pocket. Instead she focused on Theo. She was sure he was looking for Cold Lock and she wanted to ask him, to talk to him. Theo disappeared around a corner, and she stopped next to the garden wall and leaned against it, closing her eyes. The cold bathed her face, sharpened her breaths, and that unmistakable and indescribable smell of snow filled her stinging nostrils.

She didn't know how Aeron was coping because she felt overloaded with her own feelings. Theo moved her, drew her to him, made her want to share but how? She didn't know him; they hadn't talked much but . . . something . . . buzzed in the space between them when he looked at her.

"You are not succeeding with relaxation?" Theo asked from in front of her.

Frei peeked open an eye, and Theo smiled like he wasn't going anywhere. "For personal security, you are not much good," she muttered, opening both eyes. He was far too attractive, it wasn't fair. "What if Hartmann needs her nose wiped?"

Theo laughed a joy-filled laugh. "Then she can get her own tissue. It was bad enough that her ex-girlfriend did everything for her." He shook his head. "I'd have left the first time she was so demanding."

"Really?" Maybe this was a glitch in his demeanor? Something she could cling to and discard her feelings over. "You are not a man to stay?"

"Not what I said," Theo said with his charming smile. "I think a relationship should always be equal. You are a team."

Ugh. Great, now he sounded like Aeron. "And your parents are?"

He nodded. "Yes, my mother owns the bakery my father works

in." His eyes twinkled. "Along with the farm and a good few businesses in the nearby village."

He said it all in German, his accent filling her with some kind of yearning that made her want to sigh.

She *did not* sigh. "So not just a farmer?"

Theo shrugged. "She bought them when they were under threat of closing. She wanted to maintain our traditions."

Fantastic, even his parents were noble.

"My sisters are all still in school." He beamed like he adored them. "When I go home, they like to tell me how they are doing. They're all like my mother, all forthright and take no prisoners."

"And yet your brother is different?" She studied his kind face, his gentle eyes. Goodness seemed to shine from him.

Theo looked up at the house. "He left when he was sixteen to work for Aunt Sabine . . . and like I said . . . he has complex needs."

"Because he knows she's a slave owner?" She folded her arms, hoping it would act like a barrier but felt more like she'd just hugged herself.

He wagged his finger. "So you say. I am not here to investigate her business."

"No, you're here to stop me breaking into Cold Lock," she said, wanting to make it clear where they stood.

Theo furrowed his brow, genuine shock in his eyes. "Why would you do that?" He shook his head. "I'm here to find an heirloom."

"If you're on about the trinket she's trying to win off Huber," Frei rolled her eyes and pushed off the wall and strode toward the orangery, "it's just a prize she won in a card game."

"Yes," Theo said, striding to catch up. "She did. It took her years to find out who had it."

"Nothing to do with how much it's worth?" A hundred million. Some price for a load of compressed minerals.

"More to do with who it was valuable to." He kept up with her, like he'd walked alongside her for years. Why did it feel . . . normal? "My grandmother, you know of her?"

"Why would I?"

"The reason I came was for my mother. She doesn't like my

aunt but they both adored my grandmother." He held out his hand as they reached the steps.

Frei stared at it.

"They're icy. It makes me feel like I'm useful if I can stop you falling." He shrugged and offered his hand again.

"If I couldn't climb down icy steps, I'd be terrible at my job." And why did she really *want* to hold his hand?

"Indulge me?" He offered a sweet smile.

"Don't squeal if *you* fall." She took his hand and pulled him to keep up. "So why did they tell you it was important to your grandmother?"

"It is the Eis family jewel." He studied her like he expected her to know it. "It was meant to sit in the main hallway, but when the family went missing, it was removed."

"So *your* family is the mysterious Eis?" How was that mysterious? They hadn't gone anywhere.

"No," Theo said with a chuckle. "My grandmother was engaged to the brother, Theo Eis . . ." He smiled. "Why I was named it." He held her hand, seeming happy to let her lead him yet he felt like a steady presence, ready to be there should she need him. "The brother died but the Eis family took great care of her."

"Let me guess, it is sentimental and good old Aunty Sabine wants to return it?" She laughed. Sounded like a tale Hartmann would spin.

"She was nanny to their children," Theo said, tutting at her. "They were close even when my grandmother remarried . . . she was one of the few who knew of their children." He held open the door to the orangery.

"Didn't they like them?" Frei muttered, striding through.

"The children went missing when the parents did," Theo said, shutting the door. "My grandmother tried to tell the authorities but they wouldn't listen."

"And the big priceless jewel?" Frei folded her arms.

"My grandmother spent so long trying to find the children. She was certain that they had been taken and wished to return their heritage to them." His eyes filled with passion, with a focus she understood more than she liked. "She filled my mother and Aunt Sabine with her thoughts on what happened; they both want to help the family that once helped her."

Frei put her hands on her hips. "Again, I don't see where the jewel comes in?"

"It's an heirloom." Theo mirrored her gesture. "Aunt Sabine has been collecting them all since she built her own estate." He shrugged. "She is genuine in her desire to give the Eis family back what is theirs . . . she seals it away, unlike her other assets which she flaunts."

She knew. She'd stolen it from there.

"You know nothing of the history?" He cocked his head.

"I was a slave. Why bother to teach me such things?" She stuck out her chin.

His eyes glinted with annoyance. "You were never a slave, not inside. You have strength."

"And others do not?" She turned away but he reached for her hand.

"What I mean is that they can only make you a prisoner in body but your mind . . . I cannot believe you have ever allowed them to imprison it." His voice was soft, kind. "You are free in your heart."

"Says the expert?" He sounded so much like Stosur had when they'd met, the belief that if she wasn't chained inside, she wasn't really a slave.

"I may not know anything of slavery in this sense but I have seen many enslaved by their love of money or by addiction." He shrugged when she turned back to him. "It is far harder to find release from those prisons."

Something rippled through her with his words. She leaned in and kissed him on the cheek.

He beamed at her. "I say something you like?"

She nodded. Why had she done that? Why was it wriggling through her stomach and why, just why did she want to do it again? "So who were these friends?"

His smile grew and he rubbed at his cheek, awe in his eyes. "Three prominent men, Hartmann—who my grandmother married; Jäger—who was asked to take over the family business in an attempt to save it when they could not be found."

"And?" Why was he pausing?

"And his best friend but the man who left abruptly, refused to talk about what had happened and . . ." He sighed, holding onto her hand like she'd run. "And a man who everyone is sure turned on them."

She turned to face him. "And this would bother me . . . ?"

"Because the man's name was Huber." He held on.

"He's not old enough." She tried to pull away. "He is not like that."

"His father," Theo whispered, glancing at the doorway. "Which is why no one can stand to deal with Huber now."

It made too much sense; the owners who couldn't stand to look at him before she made him money; why he never took on anyone directly even when it meant something to him; why he'd had to scrabble for money. Megan had always said she put up with him when others wouldn't have . . .

"My aunt believes that the jewel incriminates Huber's father somehow. She was close to proving her theory when it was stolen." He gave her a lopsided smile. "By a locksmith . . . so I am told."

"And she needs to think about what you've said." Frei pulled her hand away. "I need to talk to him."

She didn't wait for Theo to answer but hurried out of the back door, up another set of steps, and froze. Jäger stood a few feet from her, his smile sharp. Fear sucked at her. Stopped her feet from moving.

"If it isn't the slave . . ." He limped toward her. His hand dropped to his back.

Panic shot through her, she turned and sprinted. No thoughts in her mind but to run.

Chapter 42

RENEE KEPT HER pace steady as she headed back to the room. Frei had snuck away before she could see where she'd gone, Jessie wasn't answering her radio, and Aeron hadn't come back from the bathroom. How could she protect people when they kept running off?

She stomped into the room, saw Aeron slumped on the sofa, and kicked it. "Explain."

Aeron got up. Her front was soaked, showing off every inch of muscle, every curve she had. She didn't so much as look at Renee but headed to the bathroom.

Renee pulled her around by the arm. "Not a request." She sounded like a soldier.

Aeron saluted with a grunt and turned back around.

Renee narrowed her eyes. Cheeky. "About turn."

Aeron stopped but stayed with her back to her.

Oh no, she was *not* disrespecting her. "Drop and give me a hundred. Now." She put her hands on her hips. Nan had said she needed barriers. Fine. She'd get those muscles doing something useful.

Aeron got into position and hammered them out.

"I want an explanation." She was glad there were no cameras because Renee Black had roared to the surface and she wasn't going anywhere.

"Ain't in the mood to talk," Aeron muttered.

"Then you'll give me another hundred." She went to the dressing table and flicked off her heels.

Aeron's shoulders flexed, her back pulsed with strength, and she tried not to groan. Maybe she should have scolded Aeron after she'd made her change.

"Why the insubordination?" She rubbed at her feet, glad of the relief. Why any woman in her right mind would choose to wear them every day, she didn't know.

Aeron remained in position.

"I asked you a question." It had been difficult to cover both Frei and Aeron in the bathroom. When Aeron disappeared, and Frei had avoided eye contact, it had raised eyebrows. It had taken a lot of logic for her not to jump to the same conclusion. "You forget my rank?"

Aeron said nothing.

"I want another hundred. One arm." She folded her arms. What was with her? "I can do this all night."

Aeron pushed out, powerful arms hard at work.

"You put me in a difficult position. I don't like losing sight of either of you. Losing sight of both of you is *not* acceptable." She watched Aeron's steady motion, her biceps rippling, her back muscles pulsing. "You think it is?"

"No." Aeron finished her set.

"No?" Did she want to see her in boot camp mode? "No, what?"

"Can't say that here." Aeron held her position.

"Room is scrambled. You *can* say it." Why was she avoiding her? "Again."

Aeron dipped and fired out another set.

"I want to hear you say it." She pulled off her blouse and wandered past Aeron to the bathroom. How did people wear makeup every day? Her skin was sore and she had spots. She hadn't had this many spots since she was a teenager.

"No," Aeron grunted.

Renee stopped and turned in the doorway. Aeron's gaze was on her chest. *"No?"*

Aeron flicked her gaze to the floor. "I'm not at liberty to say."

She laughed. She couldn't help it. There was the woman she met in the institution. The attitude, the defensive wit, the tough inmate. "Then we'll keep going until you decide you are."

Aeron grunted out another set, and Renee walked into the bathroom, scrubbing her face. She pulled off her skirt and unstrapped her gun from her thigh, making sure she was in Aeron's line of sight, and Aeron pushed out her set faster, like she was desperate to get rid of something.

"Did Frei dunk you?" Renee stood in the doorway, hands on hips.

Aeron stared at the ground, sweat dripping off her.

"Did she?"

Aeron shook her head.

"So why are you soaked?" She rolled down the stockings and stood right in front of her. "Next I'll make you bench-press me, you want that?"

Aeron spluttered out a breath.

"Didn't think so," she said, leaning over. Aeron was wobbling just with her this close. "So?"

"Hartmann wants the jewel so bad it hurts; Harrison is there to clean up because Sven wants Jäger to get rid of Hartmann, Theo, Huber." Aeron pushed out another set.

"Not what I asked." Renee ran her foot up Aeron's shoulder. "Why did you walk off?"

"I'm entitled to use the bathroom," Aeron muttered, panting.

"To bathe?" Renee flicked her foot out and knocked Aeron's elbows.

Aeron slumped to the floor with a grunt. "Yeah." Attitude.

"You got a problem with me?" Renee lifted Aeron's chin with her foot. "Have you?"

Aeron's gaze tracked over her, and her eyes deepened then flickered with panic. "Yeah."

Renee laughed. "Really? You'd prefer I go sleep in Hartmann's room."

Aeron's eyes pulsed with anger.

"She was paying me more attention." Renee held her gaze. "She *is* attractive."

"Don't you dare." Aeron's growl was so low that it rumbled from her. Not a nasty order but panic. "She'll hurt you."

"Yes, but then my job is to stop you two getting hurt." She stooped and flipped Aeron onto her back. "And I get really irritated when I have no one to protect because they aren't in sight."

Aeron shrugged. "I was gonna get mad. I didn't want to get mad."

"You were already there," Renee muttered, standing over her. "You never let a POI slip from sight." She scowled. "You need me to drill it into you?"

"No, ma'am." Aeron's attitude shattered, and she huffed out her breaths. "Didn't mean to make you worry."

Renee held out her hand. "Accepted."

Aeron gripped it, and she swore she could see the frustration, the insecurity, that restless energy she remembered herself the first time she fell in love. She cocked her head. Was Aeron falling in love? Nice thought. She sighed. Too nice.

"I'm not interested in Hartmann," she said, forcing her tone to be gentle. "I did what was needed for Frei to get the key."

"I know. Don't care. She's smarmy." Aeron stomped into the bathroom. "Don't like her."

"You said the same about Owens," Renee whispered, staring after her, fighting the urge to follow her.

Aeron poked her head around the door. Why was she changing in there? "I did. She was."

"So then you know the response." Renee shook her head as Aeron came out in a t-shirt, scowled out the window then yanked a sweater on. "She isn't my type."

"Yeah, 'cause your ex-fiancé was such a jock?" Aeron threw her some pants. "Need to dress for the cold."

She caught them and pulled them on. Thick pants. "Not everyone is as ridged as you."

"No they ain't." There was the attitude again as Aeron pulled out two bullet vests and two jackets.

"But then if I was only interested in what attracted me, I'd be very shallow." She frowned and pulled on a sweater, put her bullet vest on, and took the jacket. "I see more than just your pecs."

Aeron flexed them in response and pulled boots out from under the bed. "Hartmann ain't looking further with you."

"Stop pouting." Renee put her boots on and looked up to hold Aeron's gaze. "She didn't see me in my underwear, did she?"

Aeron cleared her throat.

"So why are we kitting up?" she asked, picking her gun up and sliding it inside her jacket.

"Jäger," Aeron said, pointing to the window. "Just saw him limp by."

"And?" Renee checked her darts, still full.

"Frei was ahead of him." Aeron motioned to the door. "An' our POI is out of sight with an unsub on her tail."

Adrenaline fired through her, she ripped open the door, and checked her earpiece. "So where's Jessie?"

Aeron sighed, locked the door behind them, and stretched out her legs to match Renee's trot. "Jäger specialty . . . luring out heroes."

Renee checked her earpiece again, she couldn't get a response from anyone.

"Some folks can do more than just bake cookies," Aeron whispered as they headed down the stairs.

"Hope so. I don't want to give him the chance to hurt her again." Renee pulled out her secondary pistol and loaded it with bullets.

Chapter 43

FREI GLANCED OVER her shoulder and checked her watch again. She'd keep running if she had to, if Jessie didn't know where she was going, she couldn't follow.

"Found her yet?" she said into her mouthpiece. Stosur was frantic, trying to locate where Jessie could be, and Aunt Bess was trying to keep her calm.

"No, she's not on any camera," Stosur said, her voice thin. "Bess has driven up in the car."

Frei tried to control her jaw trembling. It was too cold to be out without gear for long, the snow was falling too fast, the mist too thick. She felt her feet slide and managed to right herself before she slipped. Lake, she was on the boating lake. She could feel the ice creak under her feet. She glanced over her shoulder again, Jäger was limping along behind. He was fast, even on one good leg.

"Where's Aeron?" She could see Renee making good headway to reach her position.

"She's stopped in the snow, she's shouting something to Renee and has turned," Stosur said. "Looks like she's talking to someone."

"Nan," Frei wheezed out. "Send Bess to Aeron. She'll find Jessie."

"And you?" Stosur sounded like she was ready to forget breaking into Cold Lock and just take on Jäger.

"I have the best protection." She crouched low on the ice. "And I want to see how well he skates."

She paused in the middle of the lake, turned, and pulled her pistol from her holster.

"Slave, you need to rest?" Jäger laughed, mist bellowing from his mouth, low brow, shark eyes glinting. "Your injuries bothering you?"

Frei smiled, suppressing the shiver through her spine. "Not as much as yours. Did they keep the bullet for you or just leave it in?"

Jäger scowled. He stomped forward, pulling his gun.

"We both know you won't shoot," she said, backing up further.

He eyed the ground beneath him. "What makes you think that, slave?"

"There's no point playing with the bait when you're looking for a fish." She glanced to the side. The water beneath would be far below icy. Her clothes were heavy.

"And who says you aren't the fish?" He raised his gun.

Bam. Bam. Frei fired at the ice, rolled, the crack split through the air, ice sheets tipping. Jäger plunged into the water, fired. *Bam.*

She dived to the right, sucking in her breath as her body hit the water. She pulled the trigger. *Bam, bam.*

Jäger rolled away, onto the ice.

Zip.

He gripped his wounded thigh, yanked a dart from it. "So the blonde comes to the rescue again."

He raised his gun.

Zip.

His arm dropped limp to his side. Renee sprinted into view. Frei gripped onto the ice, trying to pull herself up. Too heavy. She strained against the weight but her grip kept slipping.

Jäger grabbed at his radio with his free hand, muttered something into it, picked up his pistol. Renee raised her gun again. He holstered his and staggered off toward the house, laughing.

She scurried around, gaze tracking over ice.

"Here!" Frei gasped for air, the cold sucking at her, freezing up her lungs.

Renee lay on the ice, spread out, and scurried toward her. She held out her hand. "If you run off again, I'll shoot you."

Frei gripped her warm hand, yanked herself out of the water, and spread herself on the creaking ice. "Why did he leave?"

Renee crawled with her to the side as Aeron hurried into view with a foil blanket.

"Don't know." Renee wheezed like she was either out of breath or had panicked herself.

"Aunt Bess got her," Aeron managed between pants. "Jessie was heading through the forest." She wrapped Frei in the blanket and hugged her. "She got her."

Frei let herself be hugged, soaking in the warmth. "He just left."

"He got hollered at for something," Aeron said, like she had teased him for it. "Ain't sure why but he was worried 'bout it."

Frei stayed close to Aeron as Renee led the way toward the house. She spotted Theo as they reached the grounds, and he scowled.

"He saw Jäger . . . he's about ready to punch him," Aeron whispered.

"I don't want him anywhere near." Frei shivered through her words. "Don't want him to get hurt."

Renee broke from her intense focus to raise an eyebrow. "Sounds serious."

Frei burrowed into Aeron. "Jäger is faster than he looks."

"I pulled a move on him," Aeron said as they led Frei through the back door and around the swimming pool. She was tempted to sit in the sauna to warm up. "A real move like you guys."

Renee smiled at her. "Good to see you pay some attention."

They headed out of the swimming pool into the hallways and Aeron frowned. "Hey, I pay a load of attention."

"To the training," Renee said, teasing in her voice, pausing them as she scanned over the main staircase.

"I meant that," Aeron muttered, pulling Frei in close as they headed up the stairs.

"Uh huh," Renee shot at her, dragging them into motion, eyes scouring every inch.

"I did." Aeron looked down at Frei. "You got that, right?"

"You're warm. I don't care." She held on, thawing enough that the relief Aunt Bess had found Jessie hit her, making her throat ache.

Aeron laughed, and Renee opened the door to Frei's room and ushered them inside. Stosur hurried over, gripped Frei to her, and squeezed.

She smiled and squeezed back. "Please tie her to something."

Stosur laughed, holding her like they'd never been separated, like only moms could. "Oh, Bess is ahead of you even if Jessie was trying to help."

Frei glanced at Aeron and Renee who were still bickering. "If they'd break for breath, I'd thank them."

Stosur tutted. "Better you don't slip away again and give them a headache."

Frei looked up and chuckled. "Did you just tell me off?"

Stosur nodded. "I think I did."

Frei shivered, then turned and headed to the bathroom. Why did that make her throat ache more? Long hot shower. She cleared her throat. She just needed a shower.

Chapter 44

EVENING DREW IN as the swirling snow outside covered every inch in deep drifts. The lights had flickered on and off a couple of times, the pipes groaned to fight off the cold and spread warmth through the drafty hallways. Stosur had alerted us to Jäger and Sven leaving the house to trudge across the grounds somewhere. They'd had guards with them so whatever they were up to, it was sneaky.

Frei, ignoring my glare, had sent Renee down to the card game with Hartmann. She wanted Renee to find out about the families who'd been friends with the missing Eis family. Frei was bothered by it, like it rubbed at her conscience. I chose to avoid reading too much; if she needed me to know, she'd tell me.

Stosur and Aunt Bess were back in position to rescue more slaves. This time Stosur would do it alone and send them down the zip-line to Aunt Bess. Stosur wanted us to draw attention away from it by being visible elsewhere . . . and Aunt Bess had tied Jessie to the chair in their base so she couldn't go charging in.

I rubbed my cold hands as I joined Frei in the corridor. We were going lock hunting. Frei would have had an easier time just sneaking around on her own but, Renee's orders, she had me lumbering along behind her as protection. If Jäger did try a sneak attack, I was gonna flatten him. I didn't care what grade of crazy he was. If I had to heal anyone else he'd gone and hurt, I'd need a battery charger myself.

"You need to let me work," Frei said as she studied her phone. "I don't want you feeling anything, okay?"

I shivered. "Why? Be quicker if I just sniffed it out."

"Or you'll blow something . . . their circuits or your own." She smiled up at me, her collar turned up, showing she hadn't thawed out as much as she was pretending. "Jessie has noticed he keeps going off camera on the third floor."

"You mean Theo?" I grinned, enjoying the blush on her pale cheeks.

"Yes." She looked at me from under her blonde eyebrows. "I can play that game too, you know."

I shoved my hands in my pockets. "Not funny."

Frei grinned a lopsided grin as we reached the stairs up to the third floor. "No?"

"No." I wagged my finger at her. "Don't think I won't flatten your hair."

Frei turned on the carpeted step, teasing in her eyes. "Don't think I won't steal your cookies."

Ooh, low. I darted at her, and she danced out of reach.

"You're slower than Megan," she shot at me.

"Okay, now you're getting it." I trotted after her as she jogged backward, then stopped—the forgotten corridor called to me again, and I searched it, trying to figure out why it was pulling at me. There was some dumb bust of a fat guy, blobs on canvas, half-carpeted floor but the carpet was deeper in color, like no one ever used it.

"What are you looking at?" Frei wandered back to my side, looking down at her watch. "There's no heat traces down there."

"Don't know. I know there ain't no one down there . . . I just . . ." I shrugged. "There's something about it."

Frei pulled something out of her back pocket and turned it on. The screen fuzzed so I stepped to the side, and Frei shook her head. "Worse than usual."

I leaned against the wall, hearing children laughing, running, happy and carefree. "Think I'm more receptive."

"What did she do when she kissed you?" Frei gave me a half smile and studied her screen. "No machines running. Not even heating."

I placed my hand to the stone. I could feel the happiness, the love, faded like a black-and-white photograph.

"It's original," Frei said, walking over to the pillar and scouring it. "Most of the place had new render and a lot of marble."

"So why didn't they do the same with this place?" I could feel emotions, feel the memories but I wasn't sure whose they were. The odd echo of laughter grew, and Frei stepped back, like she could feel it, and shivered.

"Don't think it's where they're hiding the main hub," she mumbled, rubbing her arms, confused why she was so uneasy.

"Stone holds energy," I said, pulling myself away and moving her with me. "If it's a lot of energy, it coats it somehow." I heard a scurrying of mini-feet and turned to see a slave hurrying along, carrying a pack on her back. She looked up at me with awe in her eyes, then concern as she studied my face.

"Miss Samson, Miss Locks, you are on the wrong floor," she whispered, glancing over her shoulder down the corridor.

"We're having a tour," Frei said with a cheeky smile. "You never know what we might find."

The slave's smile was a shy one, and she gazed up at me again. "Shouldn't you be resting?"

I raised an eyebrow. "Should I?"

Frei nodded to her, and the girl hurried off. I watched her go. Resting?

"You look like crap," Frei said with a shrug. "Not as bad as you did when you found me in the boathouse . . . but close."

"Worthington pumped me with a load of stuff to get me looking *that* good." I rubbed my hand over my face. Maybe that's why I felt so clammy? Cold sweats.

"We still are." Frei strode on ahead and paused at the corner. "No cameras . . . or he's scrambling them."

I lumbered up behind her. I could feel Theo and whatever was shooting sparks through his heart. I winced and rubbed my chest.

Frei glanced back at me. "He has a defibrillator in his chest." She tapped my hand. "No cuddling him."

I saluted. "Ma'am."

She pursed her lips at me, then turned back to watched Theo who was following the device in his hand and wandering up a corridor, ignoring the guards eying him like they were gonna pull their guns . . . big guns.

"Looks promising," I whispered, pulling back. With my stealth skills they'd spot us easily.

"It is." Frei tapped something into her phone, then eyed the door next to us. "Detour?"

She knelt down and inserted her prongs in the lock.

"Why not?" I followed her inside and shut the door. One big bare room with nothing but mirrors on one side. "Unless you're gonna teach me ballet?"

Frei snorted and motioned for me to move. "Never know. I might take it back to boot camp."

"Glad I graduated then," I mumbled. Ballet *and* boot camp. No thanks.

Chapter 45

IN ONE OF the large sitting rooms, Renee scanned a bored eye over her cards. Snow swirled outside the wall of windows, some ivy-like plant crawling up the inside like it was trying to break free. She didn't blame it, cards were boring on a good day; with Hartmann, Megan, Huber, Sven's mistress and Harrison, they were the height of tedium.

"So, he is too busy to entertain his own guests?" Hartmann said, flicking a card off the top of the pack. "Or is he just scared we'll take his house off him in cards?"

Harrison, Megan, and the mistress all laughed an edgy laugh.

"I believe he is spending time with his brother," the mistress said, her nails too long for her to hold her cards properly.

"Now there's a pathetic excuse," Huber said with a grunt. His glare was on his hand and he scratched at his cheek. A tell. The hand wasn't good then. How did he win at all in cards? He had countless tells.

"Now, now, Huber. No need to treat the lady like that." Hartmann eyed him across the polished wood table. She, on the other hand, had very little tells, just that smug smile, that intensity in her blue eyes.

"I'll treat her as I please," Huber said back, holding her stare.

Harrison looked from one to the other, her hawk-like eyes glinted with irritation, then she slammed her cards down with a thunk. "And I have better things to do."

Hartmann held up her hand, thick gold rings catching the light. "You do?"

Megan slipped an extra card from her skirt, caught Renee looking and winked. She didn't blame her. Perhaps all mistresses tired of cards.

"Some of us work for a living, Sabine," Harrison snapped, wrinkled up her pointy nose like she was disgusted, and got to her feet—guess her hand had been as bad as Huber's. "You," she said to the mistress. "You come with me. We're finding those useless buffoons."

The mistress nodded, downed her cards, and hurried after Harrison.

Huber raised an eyebrow. "And you let her get away with that?"

Hartmann waved it off. "I have less on her these days."

Renee focused on her cards. Harrison? Odd when she was a school matron, then someone called in to clean up after Jäger. Now she was using Hartmann's first name. Renee tapped her nails to her cards. Investigation wasn't her strong point but her nose pulled her to look deeper into Harrison.

"Now . . ." Hartmann turned her gaze to Renee and she twitched her lips. "What are you calling yourself at the moment?"

Huber raised an eyebrow and scratched his cheek again, glaring at Harrison's discarded hand. "Whatever Locks tells her to."

Hartmann laughed, a husky laugh, and tapped her finger to her wine glass. Her silk shirt accentuated her sculpted face, her blonde hair. It fascinated her how, although they shared pale skin, hair, and blue eyes, how different Hartmann and Frei looked. Hartmann was . . . rugged? Not quite, but it was the closest she could describe her.

"What were you when you crawled into my house?" Hartmann rolled her finger around the glass rim.

"I've been a lot of people," Renee said with a sigh. She needed one of Harrison's cards. "Some I like to . . . forget."

Hartmann laughed, her finger still tracing the rim until the glass let out a squeaky whine. "But you remember me."

Huber clapped his hands, another glare at Harrison's cards. "And I would like my dinner to stay down, thank you."

Renee gave him a cutting stare. "Because you are so sophisticated?" She tapped the half-empty glass beside him. "You're a common thief, or so I'm told."

She looked to Megan who smiled a satisfied smile.

"Common?" He sat back and eyed her. "I'm not the one who offers a service to get what she wants."

Renee narrowed her eyes. Frei wanted to know about the Eis family, it was one way to get an answer. "But I hear your parents were happy to sell out friends to get it."

Huber's face drained of color, pain, anger circled in his eyes. Sore spot and then some.

Hartmann tapped her glass again. "Why the silence? Everyone knows your lack of pedigree."

Huber glared at her. "There were *three* friends," he spat. "Two profited from their disappearance. Who else would know where the children were than their nanny?"

Hartmann leaned in, a nasty glint in her eyes. "Says the boy whose family skulked away with half the property."

"Hah." Huber slammed down his cards, covering them like Megan would steal them from under him—wise man. "And yet no one looks at the man who steals the family's own home from underneath him."

Megan exchanged a glance with Hartmann who flicked her finger in dismissal. "You don't believe he steps in to help?"

Huber blew out a breath. "The man made a fortune selling off every piece Eis had."

"What *were* their first names?" Renee muttered. It really got under her skin. "And why can't any of you use Jäger's?"

"Jacob and Lindsey," Hartmann snapped, glare focused on Huber. "Their brother was—"

"Theo, yes, I got that bit," Renee said as Megan pushed back her chair. "And Jäger?"

Huber and Hartmann exchanged a glance like neither knew.

Renee looked to Megan who shrugged, threw her cards down, and rose to her feet. "If they don't know, I'm not going to."

"I didn't say you could leave," Huber's focus was riveted to Hartmann like he'd dive across the table and tackle her.

"But I did," Hartmann said with a smug grin and ran her finger over the rim of her glass once more.

Renee was helpless but to watch Megan leave. What if she tried attacking Frei on Jäger's behalf? She could stumble on the slaves escaping. Renee ran her hand inside her blouse and covered it with her cards, pressing the button to call Jessie. "So either way, Megan has left to fix her hair and that leaves me thin on good company."

Huber blurted out a laugh and knocked back the rest of his drink. "If you consider Megan good company then you are more vacant than you appear."

Hartmann looked Renee up and down, her smile sure. "You don't think I am good company?"

Renee shrugged and waved her cards around like she was ready to throw them down herself. Maybe she could still catch Megan? Or . . . she could give Huber the chance to catch her. "I have a short memory."

Hartmann leaned forward, blue eyes igniting with her usual confidence. "Huber, this card game is private."

"And that's what I'll say to Alex should she ask." He gave Renee a pointed stare and threw down his cards. Why was he getting snippy? She'd saved him having to give Hartmann the shirt off his back.

"I know how to handle her." Renee said it like she did know, but if Aeron's attitude after lunch was anything to go by, Hartmann would need to hide inside Cold Lock . . . for a while.

Huber glared at her, nodded to Hartmann and strode off. Renee could only hope it was after Megan.

"You intrigue me," Hartmann said, her full charming smile as disarming as always. "You know, I have an opening for a mistress."

"I heard your most recent one fell short," Renee said, plastering a fake smile on her face. "Which duty was she so bad at?"

"The slaves," Hartmann said with a sigh. "It's so hard to find a woman with all three qualities." She wagged a finger at Renee. "Now, if I'd known you were more . . . experienced . . . than you looked, I would have been happy to employ you."

"You weren't very open about your position," Renee said, with a smug smile. "Fortunately Locks is more forthright."

"Yes, I see she has you entertaining that criminal." Hartmann flicked her hand, only it was half-hearted like Aeron impressed her. "If one is to be a successful mistress, starting off with a slave hardly seems fitting."

"Which is why I work with a locksmith." In cover or not, she wanted it clear her loyalty to Frei was a partnership.

"We'll see how good a locksmith she is." Hartmann smiled and placed her cards down. It was a strong hand. "But Sven is on the ropes, and it takes experience to complete the task."

Renee stroked her hand along Hartmann's finger. "So that's why you're here? It seems far more personal than that."

"What has my dear nephew been telling you?" She smiled, a dashing smile. "He can get so intense about things."

"Oh, he tells me nothing," Renee said, not sure if Hartmann

would hurt Theo if she said otherwise. "But everyone knows about the Eis family."

Hartmann grabbed her hand, laced their fingers together. "Such tales are not my concern. Perhaps I'll just prefer to bankrupt owners and then do as I please?" Said in a cordial manner like it was just fine to enslave people.

"And what has Sven done that bothers you so?" Renee gave her a sultry smile. "You have always had a lot of passion."

Hartmann smiled like she was enjoying the flattery but there was no hiding the shark-like hunger glinting in her blue eyes. "If you were closer or in my employment, I may be inclined to tell you."

Renee laughed. She doubted it. "Or discipline me for asking."

Hartmann nodded, those steely eyes twinkling with challenge. "You have a good memory."

"Yes, a broken cheekbone will help the process." Renee pulled her hand away and placed her cards down. Hartmann's hand had been good but hers was far better . . . and she had *no* tells. "Being treated well is the best incentive to do a good job . . ." She stood up and winked at her. "Might be worth remembering."

She could feel Hartmann staring after her but didn't look over her shoulder. No, she wanted to keep Hartmann intrigued—they needed to keep her onside. She pressed call again on her phone and turned on her earpiece.

"Jessie, did you get all that?" she whispered, heading out into the corridor. For all the people that lived and worked there, it felt empty.

"Yep. Aeron needed to cut Megan off," Jessie mumbled, chomping on something again. At the rate Bess kept feeding her, she'd be tall and wide to match. "Mom is talking to Theo . . . again."

Renee held in her laugh. Jessie's grunt showed how perceptive she was. "Keep me updated on their position."

"You got it." Jessie chomped some more. "Good thing Aeron couldn't hear any of the slimy lady, huh?"

Renee laughed, making a slave cleaning the bust of Sven with a six-pack jump. "Now why do you say that?"

"Well . . . you know . . . 'cause you two are . . ." Jessie's voice trailed off. "I mean . . . it's obvious."

"What's obvious, Mousey?" Bess said, like she'd just walked into the room.

"Er . . . Aeron?" Jessie said it like she was unsure how Bess would react.

"With Blondie?" Bess breathed out a sigh. "It's so obvious, kid, even an old wrinkly like me can see it in flashing lights."

"Hey, I try not to let it show," Renee muttered, climbing the stairs to the third floor. "I can't help it."

"You mean she *doesn't* know?" Jessie said, and a full teenage giggle erupted.

"Now, Mousey, don't go giggling at your elders." Bess was chuckling herself.

Renee cut the line. She was *not* getting heckled by the support team. She slowed, catching sight of Frei talking to Theo up ahead. Megan was nowhere to be seen but then neither was Aeron, again.

Chapter 46

FREI TOLD ME that Megan had left the card game, and I got the urge to head her off. I couldn't feel Jäger anywhere near and Theo's feelings for her were genuine so I left Frei and strolled back the way we came. The lights were dimmer like the generator was struggling to keep up, and they flickered as I lumbered my way past more crazy artwork—for some reason, there was a sculpture of an inhaler which looked melted in the middle. I didn't get it. The light overhead dimmed and flickered, and I stared up at it. I blew computers but I didn't usually blow lights unless I was touching the switch. Huh?

The light flickered again, and then a shot of sneakiness wriggled through me, followed by Megan tottering into view. Guess my freaky side was working hard.

"Ain't you meant to be losing money?" I said, making sure I took up enough space that she'd need to work hard to get around me.

Megan laughed like she was genuinely tickled. "Cards are so very boring."

"Then why you play them all the time?" I weren't a big fan but Nan loved them, or maybe that was just because she was playing with my grandpa and they weren't betting.

"Huber likes to be penniless?" She looked me up and down, her thick lipstick shimmering at me. "And you have more sense."

"Ain't hard." I shrugged, then wobbled as the corridor to my right shimmered. I glanced that way—that same forgotten corridor. "I been thinkin," my mouth fired off. "How is it that there are different size doors for the slaves?"

"Keeps the girls away from boys' attentions." Megan looked over at the nearest slave door.

"Don't want them pregnant?" I asked, and my knees started wobbling. The light overhead flickered again. Maybe it took energy for my training to kick in.

"Makes them harder to sell." She said it much like I'd seen

in all the memories but something was false about it. Her aura wriggled like she was lying.

"And you like to make good money?" I focused on her, picking up on her energy. She was hiding something. Was Jäger around? I tried to feel for him, my knees wobbled more, and the lights flickered like they'd pop. He wasn't near. She wasn't distracting me. So what was she hiding?

"Yes. What other use do they have?" She smiled but her aura wriggled again.

"Don't know, entertainment for guys like Jäger?" I said, hoping she couldn't see my hands getting the wobbles too.

"He's most disappointing." Her anger was genuine and her eyes flickered with pain, her aura drooping . . . regret?

"Yet you still helped him come after Locks," I said. She opened her mouth but I wagged my finger. "Don't think I didn't notice that pretty little hind."

She smiled like I'd paid her a compliment. "Glad to see someone appreciates it."

"Sure, you got a lot to appreciate but I like Locks and," I leaned against the wall beside her, "I get real hurt when folks go upsetting her."

Megan's energy tensed like she wasn't sure if it was a threat or if I wanted something from her.

I went for a charming smile. "You ain't as fixed on hurting her as you make out, are you?"

Megan tensed again and pursed her shiny lips. "Locks has every reason to detest the sight of me." She shrugged, and her aura ached.

"Yeah, shooting her sister makes it hard to like a person." I held her gaze. She knew Suz had been Sven's, it shot from her like she was desperate to tell someone, to be rid of it.

"Her sister escaped so I recall," she said, trying to cover it up. She wasn't sure if she could trust me.

"Uh huh, and how would it look if Sven found out his own brother shot his girl?" I smiled. "Don't think I ain't watching him try collecting DNA neither."

She glanced back up the corridor. "How do you know all this?"

"Same way I know you ain't what you appear." I leaned in closer. "And you ain't the cretin you're trying hard to be."

She stepped back. "You don't know me."

I grabbed her by the elbow and the lights dimmed once more—

Smoky air, cold night, gunfire cracked through panicked cries. She sprinted from the car, gun raised. Where was it? Who was firing? She pressed her earpiece. "Fahrer, where are you?" She scrambled through a river, waded, not caring. Had to move. "They trust you. If they keep firing, Jäger will fire back."

Crack. Crack.

She ducked behind a nearby fence. Was it Suz? Was she firing? Or was it the police? She'd seen lights.

"He had Sven's men with him. Had to fight my way through," Fahrer muttered. His voice gruff yet she could hear the sheer panic. Yes, they needed to get there. They had to reach the girls. "Why does he have Sven's men?"

"Must be after Suz," Megan whispered and primed her gun, She'd take him out. She didn't care. They hadn't kept her safe this long for Jäger to cart her off.

"No," Fahrer whispered, just one word but filled with devastation.

Her skin prickled with the sound. Her stomach clenched with it, and she fumbled for her binoculars. Jäger had the younger sister over his shoulder. She kicked and screamed. Not panic but pain. Where were the other girls? Where? Frantic, she scanned for them only for Jäger to laugh once more. He half-turned. Crack. *She tracked his line of fire . . .*

Agony ripped through her, squeezed her, crushed her heart and her lungs until she bent double with the pain. "No."

Suz. On her knees, bullet wounds riddled her. She raised her gun, trying to hit Jäger but the gun fell from her hand.

Jäger raised his gun, and Megan opened fire. She didn't care if she got caught. How could he? Why would he shoot a child? *"Fahrer, move. Get to her. Now."*

Fahrer sprinted into the clearing. Jäger turned.

"Not straight at him!" She winced. What was he doing? He knew Jäger was fast.

Crack.

Fahrer dropped to one knee.

"Just get to her," she snapped, yanked the rifle off her back and fired.

Crack, crack. *Had to aim for his feet, his legs. Didn't dare hit the youngest girl.*

Jäger ducked and sprinted, laughing as he went. He handed the girl to Sven's men, got in his car, and screeched off.

Megan bolted over the fence, sprinted to Suz who clutched her stomach, eyes locked on the retreating car.

Too much blood. Too many wounds. "Keep the pressure on them," she said, hearing her tears fill her voice. "Stay with me."

Suz frowned, confusion in her glassy eyes. Sad now, tired. "Why are you here?"

"Girl, you aren't the only one who cares." *She tasted the salty tears in her throat, pulled Suz's coat off—that stupid jacket that she paraded—and placed it under her head.* "What are you doing here?"

Suz gasped in her breaths. Shaved blonde hair, cut features, peaches and cream complexion and full lips. She'd been such a beautiful child, an angry one, but beautiful. So many scars now, all over her trembling blood soaked hands. Tired eyes, beaten eyes.

"Car," *Fahrer muttered, as he pressed his hands to the pulsing wound on her chest. A helpless gesture.*

"It's Locks. Slow her down." *She shuddered out her tears, not caring that he saw. She was meant to be hard but she couldn't, she couldn't lock this away.* "Don't let her see this."

He nodded, a helpless glance at Suz, and limped away. Megan turned back. Felt the blood slow under her hands. Suz's eyes drooped, blood pooled on her dry, cracked lips as the mist billowed up from her gasps.

"You aren't the bitch you pretend to be," *she managed, shuddering, shaking. So very brave. Who took on a Jäger?*

Megan smiled, maybe the first time she'd ever done so for her. "Oh, I am but you get attached. That's the problem." *Attached like they were her own children. She adored the three of them. She never expected that. She was there to do a job, but oh, how she loved them.*

"Yeah . . . I . . . miss . . . our fights." *Suz coughed. More blood. Her throat flexed as she strained to breathe. No fear, no more anger, just acceptance.*

Megan pulled her close, hugged her. Showed her everything

she couldn't before. Such a brave girl, brave young woman. The pride of it ripped at her. It hurt. It tore through her and she gripped on not willing to let go. "Me too."

"Look after her . . ." Suz lifted a shaking hand and wiped away Megan's tears with a tired smile. Misty breaths puffed out, weaker, weaker. She glanced at the clearing Fahrer had run to. "She'll get weepy."

Megan nodded, gripping onto her shoulders, desperate. No. She couldn't let go. She couldn't.

Suz let through one more smile and fluttered her eyes closed. "Glad . . . you're . . . here."

She fell limp and mist disappeared from her mouth, her nose. The light from the clear sky bathed her in white, like she was sleeping.

"No." She clung on, gripped Suz's slender shoulders, stroked dirt covered cheeks and stubbled short hair. Her head pounded with the pain, body shuddered with it. Her chest squeezed. "No."

"Please . . . don't let them hurt you," Fahrer pleaded close by. No. Must be Locks. She couldn't be seen here, Locks would never understand. She lay Suz down. Kissed her forehead. Swallowed the agony. She had to get back to Huber. She had to get the younger sister back.

Lock's whimper of pain from behind seared through her heart as she stumbled across the field, hurried through the river, out of sight. The pain in Lock's sobbing howl clawed through her. Tears dripped from her chin as she clambered up the banking and climbed into her car.

Shaking, shivering, numb with the grief. She turned the ignition, screeched away. Shoved her tears down. She needed to compose herself. The girls needed her to. She gripped the wheel with shaking hands. It wasn't her place to comfort Locks. She'd never take it anyway.

The lights flickered, buzzing overhead. I stared at Megan as she rubbed her hand. She'd been trying to take care of them?

"You were selling the girls, you gave them stuff." I glared at her.

She narrowed her eyes. "I can't stop men getting to them;

there's too many to watch." She shook her head. "They're contraceptives."

"Locks never took them." I sighed. She hadn't taken them because she thought they were to keep the girls young.

"No, hence why we have a massive problem." She met my eyes. "I am not letting him get to the girl, you understand?" She shook her head, truth shimmering around her lips. "I was close to getting her to safety . . ."

"I took the bullet for Locks," I whispered. "He tried to shoot her."

Megan scowled. "He would. Jäger skates on his own thin ice yet Sven ignores that it will see him submerged too."

"Why?" I leaned in closer. "Why would he do that?"

"He needs him. Without Jäger, who would fear him?" She took my hand from her elbow with an unsure smile. "I'm not the only one who isn't what she seems."

"All you need to know is I care as much as you do and he's not getting anywhere near Locks or the girl." I held her gaze. "An' . . . you know what? I might just keep an eye on you too."

"I need no help." She shook her head then primped her long hair. "I deserve what I get. I let Suz get hurt."

"No, you gave her comfort and let her know you cared." I wanted her to see that. "You were there, it counts."

Megan smiled a sad smile, tilted up, and kissed me on the cheek. "My heart will always disagree."

I watched her totter off, watched her slam back down her shields and the lights faded back up. She'd been watching me to make sure I wasn't hurting Frei. I could see now why she'd stayed with Huber when he was so mean. I didn't know who had sent her there in the first place or who she really worked for but she loved the kids in her care. I stared at the gold sculpture. She loved Frei and her sisters more than most. The clicking of her heels faded, and I wiped the tears from my eyes. Whatever reason she'd started out with, right now, she was ready to take on Jäger herself to protect Frei.

Not such a scumbag.

Chapter 47

FREI HELD HER distance, peeking through the doorways from darkened rooms as she followed Theo. The corridor he strolled down, gaze on his device, was packed with security; Bare marble walls, cameras groaning as they pivoted on their mounts. Guards patrolled each offshoot, all with semi-automatic weapons and hyper-alert body language.

Sven was waiting for her to strike, she knew he was, but if he was worried enough to ramp up the security, why leave the house and take Jäger?

"Miss Locks?" Theo whispered, peeking his head through the doorway she was holding ajar. If he wasn't so cute, she'd have to dart him—cute? What?

"Theo," she said with a sigh and held open the door. "*Wie gehts?*"

"Very well, thank you," he said with his usual easy charm. "May I ask the same of you?"

In other words, why are you spying on me? She smiled. "Highly tuned, as always."

His lovely eyes twinkled. "And to what are we tuning into?"

Lovely? Ugh.

"You." She nodded like she always followed handsome men around. Handsome? Lovely? Cute? Was she Renee now? "I wanted to thank you for stalking me in the garden."

He laughed, soft, low. His smile broad and genuine. "Pleasure. So you wanted to return the favor?"

Wanted? She *wanted* to tell him about Jessie, about why they were here; she *wanted* to ask him to understand, to offer his support. "Yes, you are very impolite. You wandered off down corridors that are . . ." She thumbed to the heavy white paneled door. "Clicky."

"Clicky?" He cocked his head, a half smile sliding into place.

"Yes, I don't have a semi-automatic, and they aren't going to let me down there without one." And darts, binds, shutting off the cameras, possibly dodging traps, and finding a door that looked like a wall without Aeron.

"Nothing interesting down there," he said like there was. "My aunt doesn't trust Sven to do his job."

As in look after Cold Lock? "Considering he's supposed to be such an honorable man from a family who strived so hard to take over all their late friend's properties and business, he can't be trusted?" She put her hand over her chest. "Shocking."

Theo narrowed his eyes.

"Yes, I talked to Huber. Ever thought everyone was mistaken?" She didn't need any CIG or locksmith training to figure it out. "Two families earned a lot of money because the family disappeared and one removed themselves from society and didn't press for a claim."

He moved in closer to her, like he either wanted to quieten her or pull her to him and ask for more information. "You think my aunt is untruthful?"

The gentle scent of his aftershave dazed her. How? Was it venom? "Yes. She's not telling you the whole story."

Theo was a good man, at least from what she could tell, and he must have known Hartmann was sly.

He glanced over his shoulder and closed the door. He motioned for her to walk and stopped to glance back as they crept through the empty darkened rooms. The snow seemed to glow outside the window under the clear night sky, peaceful. "Because Huber said so?"

"Because I think so." She paused. She wanted to reach him, needed to. So she strode through what must be a guest sitting room and knelt beside its thick white door. She motioned for Theo to look through it before daring to lean in and do the same. Three guards with sneers and more bulk than looked comfortable came out of a room. "Why guard a corridor with no interest?"

"There was enough feeling that the Huber family retreated, yes." Theo studied her, his long eyelashes fluttering, his face only inches from hers. "Why would an innocent man leave his fortune behind and let guilty parties walk away?"

Avoiding the question. "My guess would be that either he was devastated by losing his friend or he retreated in order to consider his options." Maybe Huber's father had been as affected as she had losing Suz. It had looked like a retreat to most back then, but she'd been withdrawing for a reason. She placed her hand to the door, to steady herself, to quell the surge of pain from even the memory.

"Or he killed the family and put their children into service," Theo muttered, then his eyes flickered with something.

Ah, so he wasn't meant to tell her that much. "Odd thing to do when everyone knew about these children."

Theo sighed, straightened up, and backed away from the door. He reached for her hand and pulled her through the room, then stopped beside the window. "They didn't. Either the family knew they were under threat or wanted to give their children privacy but only the friends . . ." His eyes caught the moonlight, shimmered with it, shimmered with . . . something deeper. Then he glanced over his shoulder. "Only the friends knew they existed."

"Why hide your own children?" she whispered, caught by the pull to him. The need to move closer to him. Instead she turned and hurried into the mirrored studio.

"I don't know," he whispered, clasping her hand and slowing her. He turned her, pulling her closer, his gaze locked with hers. "But we want to return their inheritance."

"Yes, well, Huber has never been much good at cards," Hartmann said outside the door and laughed her arrogant laugh.

Frei tensed. Pulled her hand free. What was she doing? "I think Sven might have something to say about that." She moved to a polite distance, missing his closeness, his aftershave still swirling around her.

He reached for her hand again but she opened the door as Hartmann strolled toward them, a smug smile on her face.

"Not if it isn't his any longer," Theo whispered, then turned to Hartmann. "You look wonderful this evening."

Hartmann laughed but it sounded razor sharp. "Theo, you talk such nonsense." She eyed them both, a glint in her eyes. "But it seems someone likes to listen."

Frei folded her arms. "No, it seems someone likes to have me followed."

Hartmann laughed that razor laugh again, this time edged with irritation. Yes, Frei was no longer a slave to talk at but someone who'd happily return the jibe. "Theo has more pressing things to do than follow a thief."

"A locksmith, Frau Hartmann," she looked Hartmann up and down, making sure it was a challenge, "and one who he feels is eying your own prize." She gave her a smug smile, turned, and strode away.

They had a location to target. A heavily guarded corridor . . . could be easily remedied with some help from the kitchen staff. Perfect.

Chapter 48

FREI KNOCKED ON the door halfway through the night, and Renee was up and dressed in seconds while I stumbled out of bed, clipped my toe on the post, and, hopped around, as she let Frei in.

"I want to hit that corridor before Hartmann has the chance to change the code." Frei handed Renee a vial and cast an amused glance at me. "If you need to get out, use it."

Renee shook her head at me still hopping around, and clutched the vial. "What about you two?"

"I can sneak out of anywhere." Frei looked to me, holding out a gun as Renee started pulling out vests from under the bed. "If you need to use it, aim for the biggest surface."

"I don't do weapons." I was not shooting nobody.

"It's a dart gun." She shoved it toward me. "If you need to dart a guard and drag him into the nearest room." Her icy blues narrowed and she gave me a full Frankenfrei stare. "They *will* open fire if they catch you."

I took the plastic contraption and shoved it in my pocket. I didn't care, I still weren't shooting. It was too small for my paws anyhow.

Renee tutted, pulled it out of my pocket, and helped me into a vest before fighting to get me into the holster. She wheezed out a breath, an exasperated smile on her face. "Vest secure."

"Ain't folks gonna wonder why I'm lumbering around with a dart gun and bullet-proof vest on?" I looked conspicuous enough already.

"No, if we have an issue, our team set off a distraction, and you're out looking for intruders. Helpful as Jäger and Sven aren't back." Frei nodded to me, tapped my vest, and took a breath. "Hopefully there was enough sedative in everyone's drink that they're sleeping heavily."

"How'd you do that?" I rubbed at my stomach. I didn't much like sneaky.

"Our dear security chief and Huber." Frei offered a smile and strode out. She tapped her ear. "On route. Status?"

I winced as a load of bees rattled around in my skull—Whatever contraptions Renee had on, she had a lot of them.

The house was quiet, that sense of waiting, the feeling of being watched by hopeful slaves from each door we passed; the buzz of Frei and Renee's equipment, the twist in my gut that Sven was lurking, ready for us to move, Jäger ready to spring a trap. Each marble corridor, each statue felt almost alive with the tension thrumming all around. My top was soaked with sweat as we reached a huge marble corridor on the other side of the house with a load of smaller corridors jutting off it. Same carpet, same blob sculptures but this corridor throbbed with electricity, crackling as I followed Renee and Frei.

I was sure that if Sven caught us, we'd have to escape, and I didn't like the idea of trying to slip out of a house full of guards with automatic rifles, bad attitudes, and heat sensors.

"Guards are still lurking." Renee held up her hand and halted us next to a narrow corridor then and looked up at me. She made some kind of signal with her hand. I was pretty sure it was a military one I was supposed to know so I kept in tight to Renee, hoping that was what she meant.

"Aeron, I said hold back, I'm going to recon." Renee's exasperated thought fizzled through my head. She raised her eyebrow and held up her hand. *"Focus, Captain."*

I nodded and tucked in next to Frei as Renee snuck ahead. *"Why'd I have to be a captain anyway? I only seen the sea once."*

Renee's shoulders shook with laughter and she stopped, glancing over her shoulder. *"Quit it."*

Frei looked to me and raised her eyebrows.

I shrugged.

Frei shook her head. "Freaky and weird, the pair of you."

Couldn't argue with that.

Renee made some other hand gesture, and Frei pulled out her gun. My gut twisted again but my vest was in the way so I couldn't rub it. Felt queasy and ready to turn back and go wait in the room.

"Relax, we're darting them," Renee mouthed, nonchalant, like Frei was going for popsicles.

Frei crept past her, ducked across the narrow space, and

pressed herself to the opposite wall next to some huge picture of multicolored splodges. She met my gaze like I was meant to do something.

"You're our recon." Renee nodded to me, confidence, calm.

Recon, I could do that. I closed my eyes to feel the guards and the lights buzzed at me. *"Ain't seen a peep."*

Frei held up three fingers and raised her pistol.

They both fired.

Frei flicked her hand about, and Renee and her hurried into the corridor. Guess that meant move? I'd sucked at operation practice.

Renee and Frei carried the guards to a door as I tried to sneak after them. Frei flicked a card in the lock, and it opened.

She stood in the doorway. Her eyes widened. She ducked—a blade shot into the space where her head had just been.

I covered my face with my hands and peered through my fingers. I couldn't cope.

Frei shook her head, stood up, and dragged the guy inside; then reappeared, taking the second guy off Renee who watched the corridor like blades always shot at folks' heads. Then Frei dragged the guy in, then hurried out, smiled up at me, and touched my hand.

"Jack-knives are installed in most secure places, girl. Step on the pressure plate and you'll get steel shooting at you." Huber *stood on a plate in the floor and pointed to the dummy set up against the wall.*

Crack.

The knife speared through with enough force that foam plumed out of the other side.

She winced. She didn't want to get acquainted with them.

I winced too. Some childhood.

Frei made some kind of flappy hand gesture to Renee who pulled me behind her, gun at the ready. Tension rippled through me and I tried to breathe through it. Lots of armed guards, only one way out. They could outrun them . . . I weren't real sure I could.

We reached a crossing of corridors, and Frei smiled back at us.

Guess she was asking which way? I closed my eyes . . . I waved in my best attempt at straight on.

"You look more like you're doing 'Row Your Boat.'" Renee shook her head and pulled me behind her.

"Theo's room on right." I tapped her on the shoulder.

She stopped, crouched, and Frei did the same. Renee did the hand dance again, and Frei nodded.

"Military folks are kinda freaky too, huh?" I smiled. It was like they could read each other's minds.

"That's because we're the best." Renee furrowed her brow like she was set on proving it. *"She knows every move."*

I was glad of it as we crept down the corridor. Then I glared at a door on our right: Hartmann's room. Didn't want to tell Renee she was in there. It was bad enough they'd played cards.

Renee turned and rolled her eyes. *"I'll use vials."* She shook her head as Frei halted at a split corridor.

I rubbed my neck. *"I think you can get in both ways?"*

Renee waved to Frei who waved back, and I stood there like a chump.

"She wants us to take the left." Renee stood up and holstered her gun. She wrapped her arm around me and pulled me down the corridor.

"Um . . . why ain't you being sneaky no more?" I peeked at Frei before the wall cut my line of sight. *She* was sneaking.

"Because, with the two of us, it's more convincing if we're just being adventurous," Renee whispered and strolled down the corridor like we were on vacation.

I tapped the holster. "But I'm wearing a load of stuff that gives me the jitters."

She smiled. "Won't need it. You're with me."

I glanced back up the hallway. What if Frei stepped on one of them plates, or I did?

"Calm." Renee's thoughts fired reassurance at me. *"We plant the first device."* She smiled up at me, pulled me toward her until I was half-cwtching her, half-cwtching the wall. How could she breathe? *"Tracks whoever comes up and down the corridor."*

She pulled something out of her blouse, snapped it to the wall, and grinned up at me. She placed her finger to my lips, pulled me over to the opposite wall. Why was she trying to judo throw me?

She reached in her blouse again. Did she have an entire tool kit in there? Her gray eyes twinkled with laughter as she looked up at me. "Perks of being a woman."

I raised my eyebrows. "Nobody gave me that kind of bra."

Her pale shiny lips slid into a smile. "You'd electrocute someone, that's why." She placed the device to the wall. "*Camera.*"

A light slid from the ceiling above us.

Flashed red.

Uh oh.

Renee's face drained. She glanced down the corridor.

"No chance, they're already heading our way." One way in and guards were sprinting along it toward us.

Renee grabbed my hand, dragged me along the bland corridor. Tried each door handle. Locked. I let go of her and tried some. All locked.

We reached where the corridor became a glass-box sitting area and Renee hurried to the windows. "*No fire escape.*"

"Call Mr. Jäger," a guard shouted out as Renee heaved to try and open the window. It didn't budge.

He knew they'd fall for it. Now Mr. Jäger can have fun with the locksmith. He grinned to the others and checked his rifle. Yeah, this will be good.

Rifles ratcheting, my heart pounded. I looked from the chair to the window. Maybe I could throw it through?

"*Won't work, it's bullet proof.*" Renee held out her hand to me. "*How many?*"

"*Twenty, maybe more. Frei is inside the room.*" She was safe in there. The guards were in our corridor.

"Check the rooms in case they came back this way," one guy shouted.

"Sir."

Shame that we'll catch the locksmith. She could have brought him down. Maybe she'd have freed us too. Don't really want to shoot them.

I met Renee's eyes. "*They're getting closer.*"

"They can't get out. They'll have to go through us." Said like the guard was ready to pull the trigger.

Hope he gives us time with them. I'd love to see how the locksmith squirms.

Cold sweat trickled down the back of my neck.

Renee gave me a calm look like we weren't in a pickle. *"It'll take too long to pick the lock."*

I glared at the door nearest me

He'll drag it out with them. No, I'll just shoot. Can't bear hearing them cry.

I barged into the door and the handle buckled. Cracked at the side. I fell into the room. A slave's room: bed, chair, desk, lamp. Bland.

Renee hurried in. Over to the window. I shut the door. Leaned against it.

Where are they? I can't be bothered to search the rooms. Maybe we could just fire at them?

I held it closed. If they opened fire at least I could shield Renee.

"Mr. Jäger is on his way," he said with a grin. Oh yeah, he was gonna be real pleased with their haul.

"Any ideas?" I held onto the door handle, I'd have to keep it in place.

"Too far up." Her eyes tracked over the room. "We can't risk the venom in the spikes."

The guards grew closer.

"Something is on this wall." He shook his head, looking at the monitor in his hands. "Can't find it."

"Who cares. They must have come this way. Search the rooms."

I met Renee's eyes. She was trying for calm, for controlled, for agent, but fear was prickling all over her.

Yeah, we were in a big pickle.

FREI STOPPED, AND her stomach lurched as her wristwatch flashed in the dark. She looked up at the monitor. She was close, so close to finding where the main hub was. Logic told her she may not get another chance to get into the system; nagged at her that Jessie's safety, Huber's and Stosur's safety was in her hands . . .

Her heart told logic to get stuffed. She yanked the USB from the drive, pulled out her pistol, and slid open the door. If they got in once, they would again.

She pressed herself to the wall and crept to peek around to the other corridor. Aeron and Renee weren't there but the alert light was on, hanging from the ceiling. There were at least twenty guards heading down the corridor toward a boxy windowed area.

"Get to safety," Theo said from beside her.

She jumped and turned only to see him nod.

"I can't, they're down there." She would take him, the guards, and everyone else on if she had to.

He nodded and held up his device. "I know." He motioned with his head. "Best you get back to your room."

Did she trust him?

She searched his eyes, finding honesty there. She trusted him. Her heart trusted him. She turned and hurried along the corridor, then broke into a sprint. "Bess, cut the connections. Jäger is on the prowl."

"You got it," Bess said and the line cut.

Frei sprinted down the stairs to the second floor. Stosur was waiting for her and ushered her inside.

"You triggered the alarm?" Stosur bolted the door, looking ready to zip-line her out.

"No, Aeron and Renee did." She was panting but not from the sprint; her heart was pounding in her chest.

"You left them?" Stosur stared at her.

"No. Theo . . ." She met her eyes. She'd *never* leave them and run. "He said he'd help them. I have to trust him."

Stosur took the USB off her. "I'll get this to Bess . . . see what we can find." She glanced around the room. "Jäger is scared of Aeron . . . use it." Stosur yanked up the window, climbed out, and disappeared from sight.

Frei looked around the room, desperate to go back, to go rescue them. Use it? She pushed open the internal door. It could work.

RENEE PULLED ME behind her as the guards pooled in the area outside the door. I didn't know where Frei was but I couldn't feel her through the nasty intentions of the guards outside.

"Clear!" He slammed shut the door. Why didn't they just shoot through them?

"Clear!" Each room empty, so where were they? They must be hiding in a room. They couldn't have gotten out.

"You keep low." Renee pulled a smoke canister from under her blouse.

I looked to the bed. Maybe we could use it as cover. Could a mattress stop bullets . . . or slow them down?

"Not the time for a nap, Lorelei." Renee sounded calm but her aura was firing up like she was ready to fight. *"The noise will attract them this close."*

Only a couple of rooms left to search. They were getting closer. He licked his lips. Oh, yeah. Mr. Jäger was gonna be pleased.

He reached for the door handle.

"You are going the wrong way," Theo snapped outside the door. "Why are you going to the sitting area?"

"They can't have gotten out," the guard muttered. "We'd have seen them."

"You are blind." Theo sounded like he was ready to punch them. "This says they go straight around you and head away."

Mr. Jäger told us not to argue with Hartmann and her slaves. He said he'd deal with them. He looked down at the door handle. Maybe the guy was right. Hartmann probably wanted the locksmith too.

"Mr. Jäger will go nuts," another guard muttered. "Follow the security chief."

"He know we were in here?" Renee held her breath. Her pistol steady even though I could see the pulse in her neck thudding.

It felt like Theo knew. He did know. I wheezed out a breath and squeezed Renee's shoulder. "Love will do that to a guy, I guess," I whispered.

Renee shuddered out her breath, aura and eyes filling with relief. "Hostiles?"

"All heading down the corridor Frei went down." I yanked her into motion and pulled her up the corridor. "He ain't gonna be able to hold them off long."

Renee held me back as she reached the corner. The guards were arguing, yanking open doors.

We've lost them? How could we lose them? Mr. Jäger is gonna go nuts.

Renee shoved me forward and sped up into a run as we got halfway.

"The trace says they went this way, into this room," he said tapping his screen, and nodded, stepping away.

The guards burst in to an open window. They needed to buy it. Would they buy it? Didn't matter, Miss Locks was worth it.

"They're gone." The guard turned with a growl. "We need to catch them. Move out."

"Guards are heading back our way now." I slowed, panic making it hard to breathe. Felt woozy. Corridor swayed. Renee held onto my arm, pulled me to the right as we hit the main hallway.

"Return to the room. Guards out in force. I repeat. Get back to your room," Aunt Bess said, sounding calm, controlled. I could hear her even through the crackling.

"Find me a slave passage," Renee ordered, pushing me against the wall.

"Search every room. They must have come this way." He waved to the others. They needed to find them. He didn't want to

see Mr. Jäger in a mood.

"Heading our way." I glanced back. The corridor swayed but I closed my eyes and tried to feel only for my knees to buckle.

"Here," a sweet voice called from behind me.

Renee dragged me over to the small, trembling girl holding the door, and we snuck through. The kid only just managed to shut it as the corridor filled with voices; one voice in particular: Jäger.

"You lost her?" He glared at the idiot. "How could you lose her?" He took out his pistol, fired, and turned to the others. "Incentive enough?"

They nodded, scurried off. He caught sight of Hartmann watching from her doorway and bowed his head. Sven wanted him to get rid of her but he needed to get rid of Locks. It had to be her. Who else would fall for the trap?

"We got to get back to the room," I whispered. "Jäger can't argue if we are there."

"This way," the slave said, tucking her bushy brown hair behind her ears with trembling hands. "We can take a shortcut."

Renee looked to me with a smile. Yeah, it was good to have allies.

"Where's Jäger?" Renee whispered, holding onto me as I stumbled along.

I closed my eyes.

"Mr. Jäger, the intruder left through the window," Theo said. If Jäger went near her, he'd shoot. He didn't care what Aunt Sabine wanted.

"The intruder was Locks," Jäger snapped back. His nostrils flared, finger playing with the trigger on his pistol.

Theo made a point of staring at it with disgust. He'd heard the gunshot, sent a medical team. "Miss Locks?" He laughed as Aunt Sabine wandered toward them in her dressing gown. "Mr. Jäger thinks Miss Locks has fallen for his bait."

Jäger glared at him.

"Locks?" Hartmann cocked her head. "We have some sport?"

Sport? Theo glared at her.

"Relax, Theo. I don't think it's her for one second." Hartmann looked Jäger up and down. *"If she'd broken in, she wouldn't have been so silly as to set off an alarm."*

"I told him this and asked how someone could trigger two corridors at once." He shook his head, hoping Aunt Sabine couldn't see through it. *"And the cameras show nothing."*

"Theo is trying to slow him down. They're on the main corridor." I opened my eyes and ducked under a low beam. "He'll know someone helped us."

Renee glanced at the girl leading us over and under through the cramped space. The girl was shaking so hard my knees shook with her.

"Yeah. Sven is on his way back to the house," I whispered, hoping the girl didn't hear. Fear was already squeezing at her.

Renee clicked her talk button. "We need an extraction for a helper."

"Following your signal, keep the girl with you in the room," Stosur said, her voice clear even through the crackling. "I'm on my way back as we speak."

The girl scurried down a steep set of steps. Bruises littered her skinny arms as she held the wall to steady herself.

Renee held out her hand and nodded to me, firing confidence, calm. *"You're with me. Focus on the steps."*

"Made for short folks," I muttered, scrambling behind, trying not to trip and squish them both.

The girl stopped, took a breath so big she looked like she was trying to shove her bony shoulders in her ears, and met my eyes. "Here," she managed with a trembling voice and pointed to the doorway. "You just need to get across the corridor."

I smiled at her. Like I was letting her get hurt. "You get a passport out, kid."

"I didn't help for that." She took another huge breath and shook her head. Would have looked more convincing if her whole body wasn't shaking. "It's safer for you if I'm not there."

"Kid, if you think I'm gonna let that creep get his hands on you, you're drinkin' way more than a kid should." I picked her up, under one arm, and the girl clung to me. I nodded to Renee.

"Clear."

Renee's aura fired with some emotion I couldn't read, she pushed open the door, pistol readied, and nodded to Frei who opened our bedroom door. "Clear."

I darted across with the kid into the bedroom and over to the window where Stosur was waiting. Snow swirled around me as I lifted up the kid who clung on to Stosur.

"Hold on," Stosur said and zipped down the wire. I closed up the window, yanked shut the curtains, and dragged the sofa over to cover the snow.

Frei hung out the doorway, gesturing like she was gonna throw something. "Move."

"Why is there so much noise?" Huber strode up the corridor, clasping Megan's hand in case she thought about going back to the room. Ursula would need space to get them back and in position.

"Mr. Huber," Theo said in his stiff manner. "I have requested they stop the alarm. The intruder has left the premises."

"The intruder is Locks!" Jäger stepped into Theo's space.

Theo puffed himself up. Brave boy. "Nonsense. I have camera feed that Miss Locks, Miss Worthington, and Miss Samson went into Miss Samson's room." Theo held up the screen. Jessie had doctored it to appear that way.

"It does look convincing," Hartmann said, her amusement curling her lips. "Perhaps I will count it as Sven's failure?"

Theo nodded. "So much for impenetrable when the intruder gets away without being seen."

Jäger didn't look so confident now. "It was Locks."

Renee pulled her pistol as Jäger and the others drew nearer and tugged at something out of sight.

"You got to get in here," I muttered, striding to the doorway. Renee was fiddling with something, like she was caught. "Come on."

Renee yanked harder, something snapped and she picked up her heels, one broken. She glanced up the corridor. Voices, footfalls, closer.

"Move your ass or I'll come get you," Frei snapped.

Renee sprinted across barefoot and dived into the room.

Frei shut the door and locked it as Renee ripped off her
vest, her gun, her equipment, and threw them in the case. Frei
wrestled off my vest and gun, threw them and the heels in, and
slid it under the bed, then met my eyes. "You need to make this
convincing."

"Me?" Convince them of what?

"Open it," Jäger snapped outside the door. "Now."

"Mr. Jäger," Theo snapped back. "This is not where the trail
leads. We are wasting our efforts here. The intruder has left."

"It is her, I will show you it is." Jäger sounded more shark-like
than usual. He was ready to drag us out.

I glanced at Renee who was yanking off her blouse and dived
into bed. Frei nodded to me and did the same.

"I will not allow you to do this," Theo snapped. "Aunt Sabine,
this is disrespectful."

"Quite, but I'm not against checking." Hartmann sounded like
she really wanted to check too.

Huber grunted. "Very well, but if they are . . . otherwise
engaged . . . and you are wrong, I will expect compensation."

"You don't own her, Huber," Jäger shot back.

"But I have been woken up. I dislike being woken up." Huber
sounded close to laughing but I could feel his panic.

"Quite," Hartmann said. "I will expect it too. Theo, if you
will."

Theo's tension hit me even through the door. "But—"

"Don't argue, there's a good boy," she said in her patronizing
tone.

I glanced back at the bed again. Convincing. Right. I ripped
off my shirt, I went to the bed, yanked out the first pistol I could
find—Renee's spare by the wriggle through my gut—and stormed
to the door and yanked it open with my best, "Oh, I'm real mad,"
face on.

"I don't recall giving you a key," I snarled at Theo who had the
key in his hand.

Hartmann, Huber, Theo, and Megan all stared at me slack-
jawed. Then Hartmann cocked her head, Theo stared at the floor,
and Huber looked at Megan who was eyeing me like I was a
cookie.

Jäger stepped forward, his eyes shark like, his stubbled chin shoved out as he sneered. His whole body and aura tensed like he'd shoot me anyway.

"Who is it?" Renee asked in a purr.

"Whoever it is, tell them you'll shoot them if they don't go away," Frei added in a tone just as burring.

Yeah, didn't that earn me a load of raised eyebrows from the group in the hall. Jäger's energy flicked at me, and I forced myself not to move back. I couldn't give him the opening he was searching for. If I buckled, he'd know, they'd know so I sneered right back at him. "I'm thinkin' of just shooting anyway."

Theo peered around me, cleared his throat, and averted his eyes again. "I told you, the intruder was not in there."

Hartmann ran her gaze up and down me, a smile on her face. "Maybe we should check?"

"Huber, if I'd wanted to put on a show, I would have charged for it." Frei strolled out of bed, picked up her shirt from the floor, and placed her hand to my back. "Alex, calm."

Jäger flicked his gaze to her, and his hand dropped to his gun.

"I will not calm." I stepped into Jäger's space, nose to nose, and rammed my pistol to his chin, forcing him to focus on me. "I didn't request an audience neither."

"Well, now I've seen more of these ladies than is respectful, I will go to bed." Huber yawned, yanked at Megan who was gawping at me, and led her off toward his room. "Theo, less noise next time, if you please."

Jäger narrowed his eyes, a nasty glint in them as he scoured for a weakness. I narrowed mine back. He was *not* getting to Frei. I didn't care what kind of crazy he was.

Theo nodded, his cheeks rosy. "I am sorry we disturbed you . . . very sorry."

Jäger flexed his hand on his gun.

"I ain't impressed," I snarled, pressing the gun harder into his square chin.

Hartmann looked me up and down with a smarmy grin on her face. "Oh, but I am . . . Come, Theo, we have an actual intruder to find." She glared up at Jäger and elbowed him in the back. "Move."

He didn't. He wanted to get to Frei. His aura circled with it, flicked out at me.

I smoothed my finger along the trigger.

His eyes flickered with recognition. His aura pulsed with confusion, a hesitation. I rammed my free hand into his shoulder and shoved him away. He stared at me as he stumbled backward.

I pointed the pistol at him, hoping he couldn't see that I was shaking so hard I had the shivers.

He flexed his hand near his gun, his thoughts battling. Would he shoot anyway? Would I?

I smoothed my finger over the trigger again. I could feel Renee's energy through the metal, her control. I soaked it in and forced back my tensed up shoulders.

Jäger's aura wobbled. He dropped his gaze to the gun, then turned and skulked off.

Hartmann looked me up and down again, then tucked her hand through Theo's elbow and strolled along behind. "Well worth being woken up for, wouldn't you say?" she said with a chuckle.

Theo glanced over his shoulder, relief in his eyes. "It's disrespectful."

"Quite, but still worth it." Hartmann yawned then leaned in to look at Theo's device. "And the intruder . . . ?"

Theo held the heat tracker up. "Climbed through the window like I said . . ."

I shut the door and leaned against it. It rattled with each slow, shuddering breath as Renee slumped back onto the bed.

Frei took the pistol from my trembling hand. "Good thing you didn't wave this around too much. Safety is off."

"I know." I took long, slow breaths. "So did he."

She met my eyes, studied me, and her icy eyes shimmered with tears like I'd made her proud. She cleared her throat. "I need to check on Jessie," she mumbled and turned toward her room.

"Oh no, you stay in here," Renee said, getting out of bed, her chest rising and falling as she pulled on her blouse. "Jäger could be lurking, and Aunt Bess is sitting on her, we're good." She tapped her ear.

"Jäger won't be good when Sven gets hold of him," Frei mumbled like she was trying to hide the fact her eyes had sprung a leak. "I'll be fine."

Renee grabbed hold of her arm and pushed her toward the sofa. "Just because I haven't got a Bavarian accent, there's no need to be picky." She closed the internal door and smiled like she wanted to cwtch her. "Follow orders."

"Who made you general?" Frei muttered, rubbed her eyes with the back of her sleeve and did as told, plumping up cushions.

"You're a POI and that means I outrank you right now," Renee said, poking out her tongue. She lifted her eyes to me, her gray eyes full and intense with some thought. "And you . . ." her aura danced and sparkled, "you were fantastic."

Frei nodded, still sniffing. "Good job."

Renee walked over and kissed me on the chin. "I'm not sure where that came from but I'm impressed, Lorelei." She tapped me on the nose and strolled to the bathroom, casting a smile over her shoulder. "*Really* impressed."

Chapter 49

WEAK SUNLIGHT BATHED the room with washed-out color as I cuddled up under the covers. It had taken longer to get my body moving, so I huddled for warmth as Renee puttered around Frei who tapped away on her laptop.

Stosur strode in through the internal door before Renee had her pistol halfway to pointing and smiled. "Stand down."

Renee lowered her gun, blowing a strand of hair from her face. "Sorry, edgy."

"Not surprised." Stosur squeezed her shoulder and looked to Frei. "Aunt Bess had to move the base and the slaves. Sven and Jäger were looking for locations we could be getting help from." She sighed, straightening out her back. "Which will make it too hard to get more slaves out the way we have been."

"The drive showed that Cold Lock is somewhere in the building but that's a periphery hub." Frei glared at her laptop. "There are half-copied files that show it does have the location on it." She showed the screen to Stosur, her eyes wide like she needed approval, or help.

Stosur leaned over her and read the screen. "You did well to get that much."

I felt Huber before he tapped on the door and nodded to Renee, hoping it would calm her. Renee smiled but it was tight. She'd not slept but kept watch on Frei, paced, checked on me, and paced some more. She pulled open the door and scoured the corridor as Huber strode in.

"That was too close," Huber muttered, nodding to Stosur. His sharp eyes looked as worn as Renee's. Guess he hadn't slept a whole lot either. "Hartmann is pushing me at cards. I can't keep playing her, or she'll bankrupt me."

"She's cheating," I said, hugging my knees. The room was buzzing with worry bees to the point I felt like plugging my ears. "Megan is showing your hand to her."

Huber narrowed his eyes. "Is she?" He played with his cufflinks. "Maybe I'll offer to sell her to Hartmann?"

"No," I said, not sure how much to say. "Keep her close . . . just don't go losing that jewel Hartmann wants so much."

Huber sighed. "Already did." He pulled out his phone. "Fahrer will bring it . . . but I'm planning on winning it back first."

"You can't. They're playing you," I mumbled, gripping my knees tighter. Still felt cold.

"Yes, but if I don't play, Hartmann's entire focus will be on you." He glanced at Stosur and Frei busy muttering in German over the laptop. "Better you find the system, quickly."

Frei looked up at him from under her eyebrows but it was less cutting and more seeking reassurance. "I'm planning to."

Huber gave a curt nod, and his energy fired pure confidence at her. It drifted around her, and Frei's shoulders relaxed. "I have no doubt."

He turned, straightened his cuff links again, and strode out.

"We need to move the slaves at the same time," Stosur said, rubbing her thumb over Frei's shoulder. Her energy was as confident but swirled from her in a wave of calm. "Perhaps cut the power, get them out . . ." She looked to Frei. "Give you the time to hack that hub."

Frei nodded, confidence echoing in her aura. "It runs on its own generator. If the power is out, then we can find what is still running far better."

"They'll know you're striking," Renee said, chewing on her lip.

"Not if most of them are asleep." Stosur squeezed Frei's shoulder then met Renee's gaze, firing confidence across at her. "I'll set up distractions, cover the slaves and your location."

"Jessie needs to help," I said, huddling up for warmth. I could see all the energy but it weren't helping my nerves. "Get Aunt Bess to tie them together but we'll need Jessie."

Stosur nodded and her smile was sure, calm. "On it." She patted Frei on the shoulder, squeezed Renee's hand as she strode by, and disappeared out into the corridor.

I shivered.

"Aeron, you look . . ." Renee sighed, wandered to the bed, and wagged my foot with her hand. "You don't look well enough to help."

I shrugged, enjoying the warmth easing through the silk covers into my toes. "You need me too."

Frei shut her laptop and ran her hand over the lid. "Maybe you could both leave and—"

"No chance," Renee and I shot at her.

Frei held up her hands and turned to us. "So then, we wait until Stosur has got everyone in place and smash the lock."

Chapter 50

FREI COULDN'T FACE her lunch, and she'd excused herself, not bothered that Jäger had been beaten enough his eye was swollen closed. He could still fire a pistol and would if he got the chance, and she didn't want it aimed at Renee or Aeron.

She strode down the corridor on the second floor, passing a statue of a woman holding picks. She slowed, had she seen it before? She didn't think so, at least it had never caught her eye. The woman was beautiful, the smooth white flawless.

"Miss Locks?" Theo called from behind her.

Her stomach wriggled. So inconvenient. "Yes, Theo?"

"You were fortunate." He sighed, joining her and running his gaze over the statue. "What if they had found you?" He shook his head and turned to her. "I have not seen men so intent on using their guns."

He should have seen them in boot camp. That was the one bit where she had everyone's attention. She turned, not in the mood to offer explanations. "Thank you for your assistance."

Theo hurried around to stand in front of her. "You are foolish if you decide to try again." He held up his hands. "Sven wants you to do it, and Jäger . . ." He shuddered. "The man was focused on you being at fault."

"Yes, Jäger and I have a very long and boring history," she said and walked around. She didn't want to tell Theo and she did. She wanted to tell him to leave her alone and yet she felt so much better when he didn't. Irritating.

"How badly has he hurt you?" Theo reached for her hand.

Frei gripped his wrist, then sighed, and let go. "More than you wish to know."

Theo searched her eyes. "I will arrest him, have him face court." He held his hand out to her. "I will see him jailed for hurting you."

She smiled. "And Sven will pay whatever judge or court to find him innocent." She took his hand and squeezed it. "But I have more important things to protect."

Theo dropped his gaze to her stomach. Was she rubbing her hand across it? Silly mistake. She turned to leave but Theo caught up to her again. "He is after your DNA?"

She nodded.

"And Jäger wishes to hide it . . ." Theo glanced down the corridor. "It would not matter if you erased it. You are both around to take a sample."

"True, which is what he tries to remedy." She felt her cellphone buzz and turned away once more. "The only way she is safe is if I remove the base file and prove to Hartmann that I can break in."

"My aunt wishes to take his business, his property. She may be more respectful." Theo hurried along behind her. "She may help."

"Your aunt wants a jewel which somehow has made its way to the house. The only thing she is interested in is money." She sighed. "And she'll do what it takes to get it back, including letting Sven and Jäger sort out their mess."

"You're wrong," Theo whispered, his clear eyes full of honesty, of affection and concern. "Let me help you."

"The best way you can do that is to stay away from me." She went to him, pressed her lips to his. Every pore tingled, confirming what had been so obvious from first seeing him. "It is hard enough on my heart as it is."

She turned, ducked into the slaves' hallway, and blew out a breath. Love was inconvenient. Like Fahrer—she and Theo were too distant in standpoint; she could never be with him, he would always be Hartmann's nephew and that would put Jessie in danger. Of all the roles she had been, whether slave, locksmith or general, none compared to a role she was set on excelling in: motherhood.

Chapter 51

I COULDN'T FIND the energy to get out of bed, glad that Renee let me sleep for a while. I woke up to see swirling snow in the misty night sky and turned to find Renee asleep, propped up against the pillows, her book on her chest. It wasn't the kind of book she normally read but she'd been smiling a lot so I guessed she liked it. Her glasses had slanted to the side and I frowned—I'd fixed her eyes and there were no lenses in them but maybe Roberta "Snooty" Worthington wouldn't look so snooty without spectacles.

I didn't know what had stirred me but I was wide awake. Renee had left the lamp on so maybe it was that? I took the book off her, careful to place the bookmark in. Renee's books were always dogged-eared with turned down corners. Some of them were so battered, I swore she used them as weapons. Not so much for Worthington.

I placed the book on the table and went to switch off the lamp only for Frei's idea to pop into my head: kiss her while she was asleep . . .

Nope, not going there. Renee could wake up and throw me through the window. I didn't want to get acquainted with the spikes.

Her aura was sleeping, like she was; colors calm and peaceful. So maybe Frei was right, and I would know if I was feeling a feeling or sensing a feeling then? Renee was older, experienced, and maybe she had more hormones than I did. She thought I was just feeling what she did. Just her hormones 'cause she was normal.

I didn't feel slushy stuff. I'd only ever had that pull with her. Why? If I kissed her and didn't feel nothing and she woke up, how would I explain it? It would hurt her feelings. Not that she'd ever look at me but I didn't think being told I didn't get nothing from kissing her would make her feel good.

I pulled off her glasses and placed them on the bedside table.

She'd had a sneaky bar of chocolate before drifting off even though good ol' Worthington was allergic. Hah.

Her eyelids fluttered like she was off tearing around some dreamscape, most likely with mud in her hair and maybe a chopper. Her face was soft in the lamplight; her lips in a gentle smile. The wriggle in my stomach made me shudder.

Nope, no. Kissing folks who were sleeping was . . . well . . . kinda not right. I wouldn't be happy with somebody just puckering up while I was prone, no way. Besides, what if I did feel something? What if I was staring at her because I was attracted? And what if she didn't mind me kissing her?

Even if she did, she wouldn't like it as much as kissing the woman she loved. And she'd made it real clear how much she was in love. Some folks were real blessed.

How didn't they know? Why couldn't they see how incredible she was? Renee murmured in her sleep, her smile grew then she let out a wistful sigh. Why hadn't she told them? Who wouldn't love her? And . . . if I stayed staring at her and she woke up, it was just as bad as kissing her anyway.

I took a deep breath and leaned closer. I could feel warmth from her without even touching her but not an aura or energy like normal. She smelled of that scent, that mix of fresh mountain air, warm wood, flowers, and her fruity shampoo. Yeah, soft and sweet. It filled my nostrils, fuzzed up my head. I hovered, in case she stirred and her energy flowed into life . . . Nope, still fast asleep.

Maybe I should just check with my hand first? That way I could say she had a hair or something. Still on the crazy side but she might not get so violent with that.

I ran my finger down her soft cheek. Warm, the ridge of her cheekbone under supple skin. It looked flawless in the light from the lamp, and my fingertips tingled but not from energy. It was dormant like her snoozing away. I looked down at my fingers. So why were they tingling?

My shoulder protested at my position, and I shifted, trying to stop the pins and needles, only to bump my nose to hers. I tensed. She'd wake up; I'd be on my butt . . .

Renee fiddled with her face like she was taking off her glasses and placed thin air on the nightstand. Then she turned toward me and burrowed closer.

Phew.

Her warm breath tickled my chin. The soft skin on her neck flexed when she swallowed; her collar bone was strong, perfect. The pulse running up the side of her neck thudded, rhythmical, steady. The wriggle rippled up again as I focused on the pulse. The deep purple of the silk pillow, the light tan on her pale skin. The soft feel of the silk under my hand, the prickle of the fine golden hairs on her arm tickled mine as I leaned over

It was just a kiss, right? That way, if they weren't my feelings, I could stop worrying about staring at her.

My hands trembled—didn't know why I was so nervous. It was Renee. She'd seen me locked inside myself, hurling palettes off a roof, half ready to pass out, mad, upset, lonely, and full of joy. She knew me. She knew I didn't do nothing the easy way.

I . . .

Ah, just kiss her already.

I leaned in, hovered then swallowed. Felt like a magnet was pulling me in, easing me down. I planted my lips ready to snap back but caught her bottom lip. Fruity balm, soft. Electric pinged through the touch, my lips, my face, my head, my neck, my body.

Ding, it jolted through me. My body buzzed into life, reverberated, every pore, every part thrummed. The wriggle rolled through like I was heading down the mountain with no brakes, wind in my hair, carefree, and that magnet pulled me down.

I moved to her top lip and the current heightened. Energy screamed through. Ding, ding, ding, like lights illuminating, every system switching on, firing into life, firing tickles right to my fingertips and pinging around in my chest. Intense. More intense than water. Snapped around me, pulled me in. Locked me there. Locked me to her. Under waves, the current, I was pulled under. Pulled into her.

I needed to stop.

I couldn't.

How did I stop?

Renee murmured against my mouth. Low, burring, rolling up from her to me, into me, around me, and I sank deeper. I brushed my lips over hers, savored the fruity taste, the warmth, the feeling, the rolling, rumbling feeling soaring through me. Energy fired through the contact. Music pulsed into life . . . and her lips moved.

Uh oh.

The wave sucked me under. The current too strong. I got pulled in, losing myself below the surface. Emotion smashed through me, over me, into me. Waves stronger than me.

I needed to stop. She was waking up. I could feel her energy. I couldn't stop. I . . . didn't *want* to stop. I really didn't want to stop.

Uh oh, and then some.

I shut my eyes, trying to find enough sense to break the kiss but it felt good . . . really good. Oh, wow, did it feel good.

Renee's hand slid up the middle of my chest and she eased me up, breaking the contact, drenching me in cold again. My lungs heaved like I'd been pressing weights, my body felt so . . . wired.

Couldn't open my eyes. Couldn't breathe. How? How did it feel so good?

Renee stroked my cheek, gentle, calm. "You'll have to open them eventually."

"Yeah." My voice sounded lower, breathy. "Um . . ." I peeked them open.

Gray eyes swirled with energy, with something, with energy so fierce that it stole my breath. I needed to kiss her all over again. Yeah, need. I didn't care if she kicked my butt. I focused on her lips, shimmering, but she slid her finger up over my lips and raised an eyebrow.

Yeah, explain this.

"I . . ." My voice still sounded funny so I cleared my throat. "It's just . . ." I looked down at her lips. Shiny. Had I made them shiny? Fruity. Hint of chocolate. "Seemed . . . like . . . er . . . a good idea?"

"Seemed?" Her aura swirled around me, her eyes swirled with amusement and that energy clamped me in place, music filling my head.

"Yeah . . . I mean . . . It *was* . . . a good idea . . ." I tried to move my arms but I couldn't. Her free hand was on my side and even her touch fired ripples through me. "You know . . . you're wow . . . and yeah . . ." My brain cells had been fried and I just wanted to lean in. "It's just . . . well . . . Frei . . . thought it'd . . . er . . . help."

"Oh, we're blaming this on Urs?" She wet her lips, gaze on mine. Energy hurtled through me, and I leaned in but she held me away from her, amusement and exasperation pulsing from her. "Aeron?"

Had I lost my mind? Panic broke through the haze and I pushed up. "I . . . Sorry . . ."

Renee cocked her head, not angry one bit. "Sorry?"

My stomach about-turned—No, I weren't sorry; I weren't sorry one bit. Ah man. That wasn't her . . . that was me? It really was me. I wheezed out a breath. They were my own feelings. They really were my feelings.

"You keep . . . you make me . . . feel funny." I held up my hands, hoping she wouldn't sock me one. I couldn't read her or her aura at all and it sounded like I was blaming her. I touched my lips. Fruity. Chocolate. Her lips were so soft.

Her eyes twinkled. "I make you feel . . . funny?"

I cleared my throat, trying to break from the weird haze. "Yeah, you just look so . . . It's you flashing all the time." I nodded. Yeah, it was just that. I wagged my finger, sitting up. "You keep showing your legs."

She raised an eyebrow and turned onto her side, her hair fell into her face, her eyes, onto her lips. "Uh huh."

I rubbed my face. "I tried washing it away . . . but it didn't work." My lips were buzzing like I'd kissed a socket. "You weren't meant to wake up."

Renee laughed, gentle, breathy. "You shot enough emotion into me, you could have jump-started a chopper."

"I did?" I held up my shaking hands. She was being so kind. It didn't help. She needed to be mad, or yell at me . . . something to stop the buzzing. "I didn't mean to . . . I just . . . I didn't mean to do that?"

She took my hand. "It's okay." She sat up beside me. "I'm not mad."

"You should be." I could feel tears on my cheeks. Why was I upset? "Thought it'd help."

Renee stroked my tears away with the pad of her thumb. "Did it?"

I shook my head. "Energy is worse than before. I fried my head." I tapped it, only to get drawn back to her lips. "I . . . it's too . . . how?"

She smiled at me, and she kissed my hand. "It's okay, I—"

Frei slammed open the door that joined our rooms. "Up, dress. We're moving."

I scrambled off the bed and scrubbed the tears away. "You got it."

Frei raised an eyebrow.

"Don't ask," I mumbled, grabbing my vest from under the bed. "We taking on Jäger or not?"

Renee was studying me but I couldn't read her, and I couldn't think.

"Yes," Frei said, nodding to Renee as she kitted up. "You take Hartmann."

That hurt so much all the breath sucked from my gut.

Renee nodded, cocking her head at me. "I'll use vials."

I tore my gaze from her. "What you need me to do?"

"First, I need you to dart Theo, then . . . follow your nose," Frei said, her eyes glimmering with a fusion of worry and confidence. "If anyone can find it, it'll be you."

Chapter 52

THE CASE WAS discarded on the bed, the silk sheets scrunched up as Renee perched on the edge, put her earpiece in and tested the signal. She pulled her hair down enough to cover it. The piece was flesh colored and could only be seen if touched but she wanted to make sure. Playing cards with Hartmann was one thing but keeping her occupied enough not to notice the electricity going out would take some doing.

"Aeron, I need you to monitor the slave passages until the power is out," Frei said near the door, double checking the kit in her leather roll. Locksmith tools. "Just don't forget to dart Theo. If he spots us, he'll try to help."

"Er . . . sure?" Aeron mumbled, half in the bathroom like she wanted to hide in there. She dangled her holster from one hand and poked out her tongue.

"What's the location on our unsubs?" Renee asked, trying to ignore Aeron fumbling with her dart gun. She wanted to help, and Frei raised her eyebrows as if asking why she wasn't but what could she say? Her own brain was scrambling to push Aeron and her kiss aside and focus.

"Huber is going to curtail Harrison and is taking Megan with him. He'll slip them the sedatives when they are in one of the first floor sitting rooms." Frei studied her, then kinked her brow and looked from Aeron to her and back, a half smile on her face. "Sven and Jäger are in Sven's smoking room attempting to avoid Hartmann." She smiled wider, shook her head, and looked back to her tools. "Wouldn't be surprised if he's packed just in case."

Aeron loaded the gun with the safety off, dropped the dart pack, twice, and her holster was on upside down. Renee checked her own gun. Aeron needed space that was clear, crowding her wasn't going to help calm her.

"You think Hartmann would accept Jäger knocking on our door as failure?" She checked the secondary pistol and lifted her skirt to strap it to holster there. That one had bullets.

"No, she wants entertainment and more so the jewel," Frei muttered and shook her head. "Don't see how it could prove my grandfather was guilty of anything."

She heard something as Hartmann fell asleep and stilled. The thief moved without effort; slid open the portrait and reappeared with a large gem.

"Who are you?" Renee said, her pistol raised at the thief.

"I will ask the same of you," Frei said. She had been so much more hardened back then. Her eyes glinted with arrogance but she was thinner, like she hadn't yet filled her tall frame.

"I'm the one with the gun, I ask the questions." Something about her was different to any of the people she'd met getting close to Hartmann. There was an intensity about her, a fire that somehow echoed her own.

"I didn't think she was into blondes." Frei flashed a grin and nodded to the snoring lump in the bed. "You look a little too . . . high class for her."

It didn't feel like an insult the way Frei said it. How could she think that about Hartmann? Everyone else seemed in awe of her . . . or maybe intimidated. "Who are you?"

"Who's to say I'm not another of her friends?" Frei wrinkled her nose with disgust.

"She told me there's no one," Renee snapped. Why did that look hurt so much? Why did it matter what this thief thought?

"You believe a criminal like her?" Frei's expression changed when she looked back to Renee. Not disgust now but curiosity. So it was Hartmann *who repulsed her?*

"A what?" She stared at Frei. There was no way that Lilia would send her to protect anyone illegal . . . would she? "What evidence do you have?"

"Evidence?" Frei frowned. "Sind Sie Polizistin?"

Renee flinched before she could clamp the reaction down.

Frei wrinkled up her face like she'd smack her palm to her head. "You are *a police officer?"*

"Not exactly." Renee's grip on the gun wobbled. How had the thief seen through her so quickly? Wait, was she using her own accent? Why? She never did this.

"Take some advice. No one will arrest her and, even if they

did, no one would convict her." Frei sounded so certain of it that it was hard not to believe her. "Do yourself a favor and run before your . . . charm . . . wears off. You don't want to see her hidden depths."

Renee shook her head. No, she couldn't just leave, even if her instincts told her to. "Lilia said I'd find a true ally in the heart . . . or her heart . . ." She couldn't go back. How could she explain that she'd left a POI to run on a hunch? "It's important. She saw her. I have to stay."

Frei raised her eyebrows like Renee was crazy. "Good luck. Hartmann has nothing close to a heart."

Renee put her hand on her hip and wagged the gun at Frei. "Who are you and was sind sie?"

"Freut mich." Frei bowed low and flashed a charming grin. "I am a locksmith. Locks to my many admirers."

"A what?"

Hartmann stopped snoring. Uh oh.

Renee glanced back, only to see that Hartmann had shifted onto her side. Renee turned back. The thief was gone and the rope she'd used to climb in was reeling up. "Hey!"

"Would love to stay and chat but I don't do group bonding," Frei shot at her from the air duct.

Renee put her hands on her hips and looked over at the portrait still ajar. She walked inside, pulled open the drawers. Hundreds and hundreds of "ownership papers" for the house staff, for children. Countless jewels and a whole collection of statues. She picked up a rusted plaque of a logo and cocked her head. Hartmann didn't look like the kind of woman to collect classic car memorabilia. The thief was telling the truth but who could she talk to? Renee walked back out, shut the portrait, and took it in. Some blonde woman hoisting her hair above her head ready to place two hairpins in.

Renee opened her mouth, then closed it.

"Fish impression?" Frei said, pulling on the rest of her special ops gear.

"No . . ." She looked at the leather roll Frei carried. "The Heart of a Woman."

Frei stopped and raised her eyebrows. "Did you dart yourself?"

Renee walked over to Aeron, took the gun from her, and loaded it correctly, then put the safety on. "She's a locksmith."

"Who, Aeron?" Frei snorted out a laugh.

"I ain't that bad," Aeron mumbled, brown puppy-dog eyes on show.

Frei grinned at her. "I'd rather you be the sniffer dog and leave fitting through small spaces to me."

Aeron perked up, her gaze anywhere but Renee. "Yeah, I'd get stuck real good."

Renee pulled Aeron's vest together, zipped it properly, and checked the straps. She turned the holster around and slid the gun in. "The Heart of a Woman was the painting, right?"

Frei nodded. "Yes?"

"And you got the Heart of a Woman from inside it?" Renee checked over Aeron's belt, holster correct and on the left, med kit at the back, pen knife, energy sachets. Good.

"Yes?" Frei put her hands on her hips but it didn't quite look the same without the jacket.

"That's why it incriminates Huber." Renee held her gaze. "The portrait wasn't of you, and it was painted in the twenties so it's not your mom yet that woman looked a *lot* like you . . . and she had hairpins."

Frei cocked her head like she was scanning it over in her brain, and her eyes widened. "Or lock picks."

Renee nodded. "Or lock picks."

Aeron rubbed her hand over the back of her neck. "I don't get it."

"The portrait was of Frei's grandmother," Renee said, making sure to catch Aeron's eye and send as much reassurance as she could her way. "Who was also a locksmith."

"Makes sense, so why is it so . . . ah hah!" Aeron held up her hands. "'Cause Huber only met Stosur in Sven's."

"Because . . ." Renee looked to Frei who nodded, shock in her eyes. "There aren't many people who could afford a jewel, let alone have it named after them, and Theo said Hartmann collected Eis property."

Aeron looked to Frei. "Then we need to figure out what happened . . . fast."

Frei scowled. "I have other things to do than chase ghosts."

"It won't matter if you hack that lock if we don't prove your grandfather didn't go making your sneaky thief of a grandmother disappear." Aeron hurried to the door and pulled back the handle. "'Cause Hartmann is set on getting her own kind of justice for it."

Renee looked to Frei. "I'll keep her out cold. You break that lock . . ." She looked at them both. "And then we need to make slaves . . . and that jewel . . . disappear."

Chapter 53

MY HEAD, MY heart and my whole body shuddered and shook as we headed down the corridor. Renee was set to head downstairs to Hartmann, Frei was set to head to the third floor, and I was set to wobble like Jell-O.

Frei glanced down the corridor as her earpiece crackled. "The others are in place. Jessie will cut the power when she gets your signal," she said to Renee then eyed us both with her full "general Frankenfrei" look. "If you're in danger, you retreat. No heroics."

Renee saluted, and it didn't take burdens to know she was ignoring that order. I shrugged. I didn't have the energy to salute.

Frei sighed. "I love you both to the point it hurts but if you make me mess my hair up, I'll shoot you."

"Same goes to you if I break a nail," Renee shot back, in a more nasal English tone than normal. "If I think you're in trouble, I'm coming to get you."

I nodded. "Same here."

Frei pulled us both into a hug. "Then let's make sure no one breaks nails or messes hair up."

I put my hand through mine, wasn't sure my hair was ever tidy anyhow and I didn't have no nails. Frei shook her head at me, turned, strode off, and slipped into one of the slave doors.

We stood there, in silence, but I could feel Renee holding her breath just like I was. We had to get Frei out. We had to keep her family safe.

Renee turned to me, and I stared at the bust of a blob person opposite. I needed her reassurance, but I didn't know how to ask. I should tell her I was sorry but I wasn't and, I didn't want to lie.

"I'm trained, I have vials and I can floor her with one punch," she said in her soft gentle tone, her real accent then pulled me 'round by the cheeks to look at her. Gray eyes filled with kindness and some swirling thought I couldn't read. "You keep yourself safe, please."

"Sure," I mumbled, getting blasted by a tide of wriggles. The lights flickered overhead. I looked up at them.

Renee tutted and dropped her hands to my vest. She checked it over like she hadn't already and then checked my dart gun. "If you need it, use it. It won't hurt anyone."

I nodded, if it was to keep them both safe.

She smiled, leaned up, and kissed me on the tip of my nose. "If you need me, Nan is at the ready."

She was so kind, even though I'd messed up, she sounded like she cared. How could I ever have thought she didn't. The wriggle rolled up again, the lights groaned like they'd pop, and I cleared my throat.

She pulled back and turned away.

I couldn't let her walk away without saying something . . . anything. I pulled her back by the hand and into a hug. The lights buzzed louder. I didn't care. I needed the hug and I didn't want to let go. "She's stashed swords in her bedroom . . . behind her bed."

Renee squeezed and smiled up at me. "You got it."

I pushed her back before I did anything dumb again, and she sighed, tapped me on the chin, and strode away. Her hips swayed as she slunk along the marble corridor, looking a whole lot more like art than any of the dumb sculptures. Looking the way she did, Hartmann wasn't gonna take long to succumb and follow her. I swallowed back the sick feeling in my gut and turned toward the stairs up to the third floor. Heart of a Woman? A Locksmith . . . An Eis . . . My heart skipped, and I rubbed over my chest, ignoring the trembling in my knees. I had memories to sniff out.

Chapter 54

FREI SNUCK THROUGH the lonely, dark passages until she reached Lindsey and Stosur in the makeshift living room. The oil lamps flickered, low, as slaves huddled around with whatever scrap of belongings they owned. Each face showed fear yet a glimmer of hope filled their eyes. Just like the kids back in Caprock, just like she must have once looked herself. No pressure.

"If you get the signal, you blow the distraction," Stosur, in special ops gear, told one kid, handing them a device. "Security cameras looping."

"Jessie, have the kitchen staff shut up after dinner?" Frei asked, testing her earpiece again. She didn't want Jessie anywhere but at least Aunt Bess was with her.

"Hey, Mom, they put the vials in the guards' food. Most of them are out," Jessie said in her jolly tone.

Frei swallowed back the way her heart filled just with the word "mom."

Stosur smiled at her like she knew the feeling well and clicked her earpiece. "Most?"

"You heard Mousey. Some of them ain't snoozing like a squirrel so you'll have to zip their butts with sleeping juice," Aunt Bess said with a chuckle as Frei looked at the long line of slaves ready to go. "An' I'm sitting on Mousey . . . and I run out of sweets . . . could have sworn I put some somewhere . . . now where'd they go?"

Stosur shook her head and turned to her team. They were in the same uniform as Sven's slaves but each one was kitted up and would get them out. "One at a time, slow, steady. Your contact is ready with the truck."

The kids saluted and hurried down the stairs.

"Slaves will wait in the laundry room. I'll be down there guarding them." Stosur walked to her, checked over her radio, and tidied the strap of her holster. "When you find the location of the main hub, I'll make my way there."

Frei shook her head, not sure why it helped that Stosur was fussing, but it did. "I need you to escort the slaves to Aunt Bess . . . help Jessie . . ."

Stosur gave her shoulder a quick squeeze. "As brave and noble as that is, you can't do this alone and two locksmiths are a lot harder to catch."

Frei sighed. "If I dart you, will it work?"

"No, I'm your mother. Who do you think gave Huber the immunizations in the first place?" Stosur beamed at her.

Frei shrugged it off but it felt good to hear Stosur say so. She checked her watch, trying not to show how much it meant. "So now we wait while Renee lures away a shark."

Chapter 55

RENEE NODDED TO Huber as he distracted Megan and Harrison with some line about matrons and mistresses learning from each other. Their backs were turned so Renee slipped into the sitting room, slid shut the door, locked it and smiled up at Hartmann who turned from making her drink.

Hartmann's gaze went to the door, the lock and then ran up Renee. "I called for a slave." A determined smile touched her lips. "Who do I pay to get you?"

Renee leaned against the door. "Who says you need to pay?"

"Experience." Hartmann picked up her glass.

Renee spotted the odd sheen as it caught the light and strode over, took Hartmann's glass, and ran her hand up and over her shoulder.

Hartmann caught her hand, her smile surer. "What are you buttering me up for?"

"Maybe I remember more than I let on." Renee looked her up and down, trying to push down the sudden surge of guilt. Aeron Lorelei and her kiss, how was she supposed to seduce people with her in her head?

Hartmann smiled as though whatever look Renee had in her eyes, it was compelling. "Maybe we should talk about this more in my room?"

Already? Wow, the woman was easy. "So quick?"

Hartmann laughed. "I lost my patience years ago." She took Renee's hand, dragged her to the door, unlocked it, and strode toward the stairs.

"Miss Hartmann," Jäger called from outside Sven's smoking room. "Sven would like you to join us for drinks."

Hartmann waved him off. "I'm busy, boy, go bother someone who cares."

Renee raised her eyebrows.

"If he thinks I trust him to serve me anything, he is more of an idiot than he looks." Hartmann pulled her up the stairs and along the main corridor, through the seating area. Renee glanced to her right. Theo was walking along a smaller corridor running parallel to them. He disappeared behind walls then reappeared in the gaps. Renee tensed. He had his heat tracker out again. Must be on the trail. Had to cut him off.

"Where *is* she?" Frei's voice filled her earpiece.

"Aeron?" Stosur asked. "She's meant to be watching the passages."

"*After* she darted Theo," Frei muttered back. "I told her no sniffing until she darts him."

Renee looked at Hartmann who was too set on the stairs ahead. Someone needed to dart him before they met at the bottom of the stairs. If Theo saw her with Hartmann, he'd know something was up, and if he was anything like she assumed, he'd try helping. She had enough people to worry about.

"Wait, I see her." Frei mumbled something in German to herself which sounded a bit like, "holding gun backward," to Renee. She fought the urge to groan. Aeron may have not liked guns but she *was* trained. Why did she keep forgetting the basics? "Lorelei, zap his ass."

Hartmann continued to pull them on, they'd be at the landing where the corridors met in seconds. Renee heard Theo yelp and winced but Hartmann kept striding like she didn't notice.

"Miss Samson?" Theo grunted—Frei must be near to have seen Aeron. "What are you . . . ? Are you shooting at something?"

"Can't touch you . . . hold still . . . I don't want to fry your batteries," Aeron mumbled.

Theo yelped again.

"The wall bother you, Lorelei?" Frei muttered.

"Hey, I missed my foot by inches with the first shot." Aeron blew out a breath. "It's a lot harder when folks move. Renee must have super skills."

Renee grinned to herself as Hartmann pulled her up the set of stairs.

"Maybe." Frei sounded like she agreed but wasn't going to let Renee know that. "Now you can go back to whatever you were up to."

"Who says I was?" Aeron sounded like she was folding her arms.

"Me." Frei let out a breath and cut the line.

Hartmann pulled her onto the third floor, and Renee slowed her, spun her around and pushed her off. "If I remember correctly, yanking me around means you are not in the best of moods?"

Hartmann looked her up and down. "I'm not."

Renee backed off a few steps. "I got a broken cheek. I'd rather not repeat it."

Hartmann nodded. "Your assumption is fair." She tided her blouse collar. "I got word that Sven's wife is filing for divorce."

Good on her. "And this bothers you . . . because?"

"Her family will be after half of his estate and I've spent years trying to secure it." Her pale eyes glinted.

"Years?" Renee strolled closer. "As I also remember, your place was bigger."

Hartmann smiled. "Oh, it is, but it's personal." She held out her hand. "Perhaps I'll be in a better mood to talk with entertainment."

Because that didn't make her feel cheap at all, did it? "You will be." Renee caught sight of Aeron reaching the top of the stairs and rolled her finger at Hartmann, strolling backward.

Hartmann smiled and closed the gap, forcing Renee to back up faster to keep from being tackled. She tried to ignore the way Aeron's shoulders slumped, and turned, strode ahead and made sure her hips were Hartmann's full focus.

"Down here," Hartmann said, grabbing her elbow and ushering her past the two guards glaring at them from their post at the corridor entrance.

"You need extra security?" Renee asked, hoping it sounded and looked like she'd never been down the corridor before.

"Perhaps." Hartmann stopped outside her room and pushed open the door.

Renee smiled and strolled in, trailing her finger under Hartmann's chin as she passed. As Hartmann followed her in and focused on locking the door, Renee touched her earpiece.

"Your room is bigger too," she said, taking out the earpiece and placing it in her bra. Hartmann liked to whisper in her ear so she hoped Frei had heard the cue. "Why don't we forget the lights and try some lamps?"

Hartmann went to the table and turned the oil lamp up so Renee went to the switch and shut off the lights. Entertainment

. . . She rubbed her hand over her chest, making a show of it for Hartmann but checking her vial was there. Entertainment. She got all the fun jobs.

Chapter 56

I WATCHED RENEE lead Hartmann off and slices of cold wriggled through my gut. It weren't about the kiss or how she found Hartmann attractive but that I was worried, real worried. She'd been through so much with Yannick, been crushed in every way, and I just didn't want to see her get hurt again.

"Nan, keep an eye on her, please?" I asked, turning to the empty hallway.

"You got it, Shorty," Nan said in a distant voice.

I took a long breath and walked to the edge of the corridor. Energy bounced from it, feelings from folks who had gone up and down there a long time ago. I closed my eyes only for my head to fuzz. Gushing filled my ears and I held onto the pillar just to calm myself—

"They are stealing from you, Tomas," she said with worry in her eyes. They had spent so many years breaking people free without anyone noticing but money was disappearing from the accounts and if they dug deep enough, they'd find out the truth. "You can't trust them."

"I have to, you said yourself how he treated slaves," he told her, his eyes icy blue. His family had known nothing of the slave trade before they met. Tomas Eis, his handsome face and huge heart, he'd adored her. It mattered nothing to him that she'd broken into his house, that she had cost him so much to buy her out. He never cared. His only concern was her, was loving her and hoping she would do the same in return. It had taken her so long but . . . she did. Years of marriage, children, and as she looked at him, in that moment, she realized what she felt was so much love.

"And what of our own children?" She glanced at them. One in the cot, sound asleep, and the eldest playing with his toys like he couldn't hear. He could. She knew he could.

"No one knows about them," Tomas said with a beaming smile. He adored their children as much as he adored her. "We

have good friends." He smiled at her, squeezed her cheek, and pulled on his coat. "I won't be long."

She watched him go and hugged herself. She didn't dare say that she loved him, dare ask him not to go again. He was right. There were other slaves to save like her . . . she turned and headed to the office. She needed to catch the thief before they found out too much.

I frowned and pushed back off the pillar, pulling out the metal embedded in the stone. I stared down at it. I had no idea what it was. It didn't look like a breadcrumb. I walked into the corridor, a swirl of moments, of memories, swept around me like the snow outside. I forced myself to walk, even though my legs felt like I was wading through a raging river. I gripped onto the side to help myself, then winced as I felt the metal picture frame beneath my hand—

"He hasn't returned?" Huber asked, a pained look in his eyes. "Why?"

"He went on a business trip," she said, thrusting the accounts into his hands. "Now explain why you have been draining his money."

Huber frowned down at the sheets. "What would I want his money for?"

I grunted and tried to peel my fingers off the metal only to feel something else. I pulled it out, another metal thing like the piece from the pillar. I placed them both in my pocket then turned and waded through the energy to what had caught my eye. The bust of a woman with two picks in her hand.

"The Heart of a Woman," I whispered and steadied my trembling hand. I reached out and touched it—

"I need you to hide the children," she held back her tears. It was better Hartmann didn't see her cry. They'd been friends for so long that she would ask questions.

"Hide them?" Hartmann shook her head. "Why?"

"Tomas hasn't come home . . . I think he's been hurt." How did she explain? Huber had been perplexed by the missing money

and had been happy to look into it. She hadn't let him. No, instead she'd sent him away, warned him she would call the authorities.

"Hurt . . . by who?" Hartmann played with her wedding ring. "The same as . . . ?"

She nodded. "Yes, I think they targeted them both." She took Hartmann by the shoulders. "Please."

"Of course. I will tell Fredrick. He will help." Hartmann fell silent and scowled. "What?"

"I need it to be just you and me." She rubbed at the tears brimming.

"Fredrick won't hurt them," Hartmann said, her tone blunt. "Explain."

She backed up, hurried to the door. "It's better I go . . . I can't . . . please."

I pulled out another part from the back of the statue and smiled as I pulled out the other pieces. A lock. I looked at the door in front, drawing me to it.

"The lock is the key," a familiar voice said.

Click, a pistol loaded behind me.

I turned to Lindsey and smiled. "I have to help them . . . and that means I have to figure out just what happened."

She glanced over her shoulder, the pistol wobbling in her hand. "I don't want them to get hurt."

"I get that." I smiled at her. "So help us follow the tradition you started and free some slaves . . ." I thumbed to the door. "And make sure your own family gets to be free too."

Lindsey tucked the gun behind her back and straightened up to stand exactly like her daughter and granddaughter did. She took the lock off me and strode to the door. "In that case, you'll need my help."

Chapter 57

THE OIL LAMP flickered light through the large bedroom, making the glass in her hand shimmer as Renee stood at the drinks cabinet. The room was much like the one she shared with Aeron—huge bed, two high-backed chairs around a fireplace, a large window, and dressing table beside it.

Hartmann had lit the fire and sat in her chair, watching. "I'm intrigued as to why you changed your mind."

"Your fascination with the gem we liberated is curious," Renee said. Slowly, keep her busy. She poured two large glasses, slipped the vial in, and swilled it around.

"Huber tell you as much?" Hartmann held out her hand for the drink, thick gold sovereign ring on her finger. "Whatever you say, Locks does as he asks."

"Once a slave . . . ?" Renee took a seat, crossing her legs to show her thigh.

"Quite. Besides, he would get rid of it, the moment he realized." Hartmann knocked back the glass, gaze on her legs.

"You really think so?" She smiled, took the glass back, and perched it on her knee. "Another?"

Hartmann nodded, a smile touching her lips. "Yes, he doesn't want his sordid family history being exposed."

Was she on about Frei? Stosur? She refilled Hartmann's glass. "He's *more* sordid?"

Hartmann laughed, reclining back in her chair, smug. "Oh yes, the both of them are. Both got away with their families' crimes."

Renee walked back and handed her the glass. "Locks won't be happy if you target him."

"That's where you come in." She smiled a charming smile, taking Renee's hand, along with the glass and pulled her closer. "Megan has been useful, she's kept at least one of them safe but best we don't leave it to her and Fahrer to keep Locks out of the way."

"Megan?"

Hartmann laced their fingers together then knocked back the glass with her other hand. "Yes, she's always been an asset." She sighed. "She'll see to Huber while we leave."

Renee held her calm. She needed to tell Frei, she needed to get someone to Huber. "I'm still unsure why you have such a distaste for him."

"His father betrayed the Eis family. It's known how he stole their children." She leaned forward, a glint in her eyes, and eased Renee closer still, forcing her to perch on her knee. "My mother thought they had gone but . . . then first that girl breaks out of Caprock, then her sister, then Locks. Good genes show."

"I don't follow." Renee smiled but why wasn't Hartmann out cold yet? Any closer and she'd need to pull her darts.

"Eis were geniuses, at least Lindsey was. My mother never said how Lindsey met Tomas but she was beautiful . . . Who asks questions of a beautiful woman?" She smiled. "Tomas made so many things but he particularly excelled in locks . . . and . . ." She eyed Renee, her hand on her exposed thigh. "My mother always said there were tales Lindsey excelled in breaking them."

Panic hit her but she placed the glass on the table, stood up, and offered her hand to Hartmann. "And you think Locks is their . . . ?"

"Grandchild," Hartmann said, following her to the bed. "I promised my mother I would continue her search and give them back their household."

"Very sweet of you." Renee leaned against the bedpost. Why wasn't the vial kicking in? She had to do . . . something.

Chapter 58

JÄGER LIMPED OUT of Sven's office, touching his hand to his swollen cheek. Why was he at fault because Hartmann didn't drink the stupid drink? He smiled as he spotted Harrison and primed his pistol. She turned and glared at him.

"Don't be more of a fool than you already are," she snapped, pulling on her coat. "He'll find out that you shot the girl." She picked up her bag. "And when he gets Locks' DNA, he'll know you shot his girl."

Jäger glared down at her. "Not if I get to her first."

Harrison looked him up and down. "She's no child now, boy." She held his gaze, making him hunch. "And she's not alone."

"So you flee?" He laughed. "Worried that they'll take offense?"

"Yes," Harrison said, pulling open the front door. "I don't want to be in their crosshairs."

She slammed the door shut, and snow swirled around him, landing on the floor. She'd risk leaving in blizzard conditions? Coward.

His phone beeped. He pulled it out and smiled down at it. The trap was set. Perfect. The lights went out, heating groaned, and he smiled, pulling his gun. Now to get rid of the evidence.

GRAND ROOM, LARGE bed with posts and a canopy above it but every surface coated in dust as thick as the snow outside. Cobwebs hung from angles, covered the desk and elegant chair in front of the shuttered window. Two bed tables, one with a clean, dustless picture and the other with some kind of leather roll. I guessed that's where Frei got the idea for her tool kit from.

Lindsey tracked her gaze over the room she'd loved. It was clear that she snuck in occasionally to look at the picture of Tomas Eis. His blonde hair was styled, smart suit in place and a dashing smile that Frei produced if you could tickle her enough.

"So the eyes are from him?" I asked as she picked up the picture and ran her fingers over his face.

"Yes, mine are brown." She smiled, wistful. "It's such a strong gene that they used it as the family name when they came to America."

"But the thieving comes from you?" I leaned against the chest of drawers, making some mini-legged critter scurry away.

"Yes. Our . . . profession goes back generations." She met my eyes, hers so beaten on the surface but something swirled below, a fire, a fight . . . a steel. "Made us . . . valuable." She sighed. "Too valuable, which is why we became slaves."

"To?"

She shook her head. "It doesn't matter now." She placed the picture down, walked to the bed, and pulled back the headboard with a click. The bed shrank and the headboard flapped down showing a pretty ancient looking computer.

"That's it?"

Lindsey laughed. "Yes. That's it. I come in to update the circuits, change running capabilities now and again, block Sven's attempts to find it . . ." She rolled her misty eyes. "But sometimes older is better."

I didn't have one iota but it was better I didn't go near it. The lights cut, and Lindsey sighed. "The generator knocks out the heating too. It takes hours to get it back running."

"Sorry, Locks thought it'd help her break the slaves out." I shrugged and nodded to Stosur as she strode in, pistol raised, then lowered it and stared at Lindsey and the computer.

"It needs you and Locks," Lindsey said with a cheeky smile. "To unlock it."

Stosur strode over, then did a double take at the picture on the bedside table, then looked at Lindsey, then looked back at it, and shook her head. "Does not telling people you're related to them run in the family?"

"Yes," Lindsey said in a Frei-like bored tone. "That way, you stop them being forced into stealing things."

"You turned that into freeing people," Stosur said, tapping into the computer. "Or so I hear."

Lindsey chuckled. "Yes."

"The story was about you?" I asked as Stosur inserted a USB like Frei used a lot.

"No." Lindsey went back to the picture then held it up and smiled at Stosur. "It was about you."

I felt my knees wobble and clattered into the chest of drawers, grabbing onto the handle to stop myself falling. Metal—

"I need to get her out, to get her children out," Huber whispered to her son but he was too ill to hear. "Please."

She heard the tone like it was an echo of her own memory. Love. He loved her. She slunk back and hurried through the house. Her son hadn't been able to work anything for years, she'd watched, learned, kept him looking useful to Sven. She snuck into the corridor, retrieved the pieces, and unlocked the door. She needed to pause the program long enough . . . she looked at the picture on the bedside table. Then she'd make sure the only way in was with two Eis working together. Yes, then he wouldn't know how or who helped her girls escape.

I glanced at the door. "If you figured that out," I mumbled to Stosur. "Then it wouldn't take much for Jessie to."

"What do you mean?"

I reached for the door handle, missing it the first time as my head throbbed and my vision wobbled. "She thinks you need two locksmiths to get in . . ." I found the handle and pulled. Why'd it feel so heavy? "She thinks that means where Frei is."

"No," Lindsey said, panic in her voice. "If anyone else goes in there at the same time, it will set off the trap."

"What trap?" Stosur said, looking to me.

"Jäger will know . . ." Lindsey said as I stumbled into the corridor.

"On it," I managed, hoping I was heading in a straight line. "You stay put."

The energy fuzzed at me, throbbed, and crackled. Without the lights I couldn't see nothing. I had to rely on feeling. My heart skipped. Only I didn't think I had a lot of battery left.

Chapter 59

DARK ROOM, MONITOR flickered. Silence, other than the sound of Frei's frantic tapping on the keyboard. She crouched low, checking her earpiece and sighed as she got no response. She would have to wait and hope Aeron had led Stosur to the main hub.

"Come on," she muttered, looking at the monitor. She'd got through to the system but she needed Stosur to activate her side.

Door slid open to her left, she tensed.

"Mom?"

No. "You need to get out."

Jessie slipped inside and held the door open. "I came to get you." She glanced into the corridor then motioned to her. "Mom, Jäger's system just fired up and Sven and a few of his guys nearly took out grandma's team and Aunt Bess had to take them on."

"No one radioed." Frei tapped her earpiece. Her watch hadn't activated. There'd been no indication.

Jessie sighed in true teenage fashion. "I just sprinted through a gunfight, and up three flights of stairs, down a corridor filling with guards to get to you." She scowled and shifted on her feet. "So move before we set off any—"

The door slammed shut. A red light flickered above them.

"Traps," Jessie finished with a sigh, and she looked down at the pressure plate. "Great."

Frei looked at the light. Slight complication. "I didn't hear any gunfire." She hurried to the door and tried to force it open. Too heavy.

"Aunt Bess kicks ass, that's why." Jessie shook her head. "Should have seen her dart the suckers." She sounded like a Lorelei.

"Window?" Frei went to it. Red lasers shined outside it. A trap.

"Vent has a trigger, Door has a second pressure plate." Jessie chewed on her lip. "We need help from outside."

Frei nodded. "Radio?"

"Jäger's blocking the signal." Jessie gave her a glare. "Which is why I just performed CIG-style moves."

Okay, when they got out, she was cutting down on her time with Bess. Even her accent held a hint of the Lorelei lilt.

Frei re-checked her radio, it squealed back at her. Panic squirmed its way through her stomach, and she went to the computer. "Maybe there's a way to unlock it from here."

Otherwise they were trapped. Well and truly trapped.

Chapter 60

I FOUGHT MY way blind through the corridor and broke free of its pull only to hear gunfire somewhere distant. I felt along in the dark then saw something on the floor.

Fahrer.

I knelt next to him, touched him—Nothing. He was gone. I pulled his sleeves, looking for something metal—Nothing. Tears filled my eyes, and I rubbed my face on my shoulder, forcing myself to focus. "Come on."

I needed to read him. Was Frei out of the room? Who'd hit him? I lifted up his pant legs. No gun. Someone had stripped it. My breaths shuddered in and out, loud to my ears. Think . . .

Slaves, Frei said older slaves had metal in their ears. I reached out—

"You're not getting to her," Fahrer snapped, throwing himself out of the door at Jäger. He'd tried to stop the girl but she was too fast, too much like Locks had been. He'd called after her but she was focused, her only thought getting to Locks. He drove with his legs and tackled Jäger to the ground. "You won't hurt her again!"

Jäger laughed and kicked him off. He wrenched up his shoulder, flipped him onto his back. Too quick. He reached for his gun—

Bam.

I hung my head. What a waste. Jäger was skilled. How else would he have scared so many people? You needed reflexes like a locksmith to beat him—

"Stay still." Theo hurried over. Good man. He loved her. She seemed to smile when he was around. He was good for her.

"Jäger has . . . a gun . . ." Breathing was too hard. He was too tired. "The girl . . . it's a trap . . . She needs you."

Theo looked down the corridor and back to him.

Fahrer nodded. "Go."

He watched Theo run and lay his head back, the corridor slowly fading from view.

I threw myself to my feet, stumbling, clattering into one of the ornaments on the side as I tried to keep my feet moving down the dark corridor. *"Renee!"*

Jessie needed her, Frei needed her. I ducked around the corner and clattered into two guards—Move.

I Rolled. Pulled my dart gun. Fired.

Zip.

Zip.

They dropped.

I stared at the gun. Huh?

"Don't think, move!" I yelled at myself. Up on my feet, heart pounding. Guards were alert and ready to fire. Where was Frei? Couldn't feel her.

My feet wouldn't work properly, like they were switching off. Had to keep going. Closed my eyes. Where was Frei?

Trapped. We have to get out. How do we get out?

My gut dropped.

She was still in the room and . . . Jessie was with her.

"Renee!"

Three guards stepped out in front of me, goggles on their heads. I fired.

Zip.

Zip.

Zip.

The three of them dropped and I broke into a sprint, hurdling the darted guards. *"Renee!"*

Why couldn't I use a radio like normal folks?

Chapter 61

RENEE LAY BACK against the pillows, giving Hartmann a confident smile, even if she wasn't. Hartmann didn't even look dozy.

"Expecting me to fall asleep?" Hartmann asked with a sly smile. "Oh, I caught onto that eventually."

"Took you a while." What did she do now? She glanced at the door.

"Thinking of going somewhere?" Hartmann tapped her on the tip of the nose, climbing up the bed.

"Maybe . . ." She smiled. "Maybe I just wanted to see if you could keep up?"

Hartmann laughed. "Oh, I doubt that." She leaned over her to hold the headboard.

Bed—Aeron had said she had swords behind the bed—move.

Renee rolled to the side. Hartmann attacked with a long thin sword.

Swipe.

Renee dodged. Rolled. Grabbed for the chair. "I don't want to have to shoot you."

Hartmann laughed then pointed to the floor. Her dart gun. Helpful.

Swipe—Hartmann went for the torso.

She ducked backward. Blocked with the chair. Swiveled, hurdled onto the bed, and sprinted to the headboard. She threw a pillow behind her. Hartmann swiped. Feathers plumed into the air. Renee reached over—second sword—Perfect. She swiveled, parried. Slammed the blade to the bed.

Clang.

Blocked the attack.

"Now why haven't we done this before?" Hartmann said, swishing her sword about. "Much more entertaining than being knocked out."

"You're not really much of a challenge." She jumped sideward onto the floor, stooped to pick up her gun. Raised her sword.

Clang.

She blocked an overhead attack.

Clang.

And another.

"As if I wouldn't know you'd try stealing the evidence back," Hartmann said with a laugh. "What do you care as long as you get your jewels."

Clang.

"Me?" Showed how little Hartmann knew. "I have no interest in some glittery gem." She ducked a swipe to her head. "And, however much I enjoy a touch of fencing. I have things to do."

Clang.

She parried another attack. "And, I have friends to rescue."

"Hah." Hartmann stabbed forward. Renee jumped to the side. "You only want the money. I'm *not* letting you steal the evidence."

Clang.

"I worked hard to find it, to get it back." Hartmann stabbed at her. Renee blocked.

Clang.

"So as pleasing as you are, you're in my way." Hartmann swiped.

Clang.

Renee blocked the attack. Kneed Hartmann in the stomach. Ripped the sword from her hand. Kicked her to the floor. "I couldn't care a less about a chunk of mineral. We're trying to protect her family."

Hartmann frowned. "What do you mean?"

"Jäger is sick." She threw the swords along the floor into the bathroom and raised her dart gun. "And he wants to cover up hurting her."

"Explain." Hartmann touched her fingers to her bleeding lip.

"She and her *daughter* are on his radar." Renee waited for her to catch up.

Hartmann's eyes widened.

"And right now I need to make sure she's safe." Renee glanced at the door.

"He covers his tracks . . . ?" Hartmann got to her feet, raising her hands. "He targets her?"

Renee nodded. "Yes. I gave him the limp when he tried shooting her."

Hartmann studied her. "How do I believe you?"

Renee holstered the gun and went to the door. "Because if I wasn't telling the truth. I'd have just shot you."

Hartmann followed her out, frowning at the darkened corridor. "I want her safe to prove who is guilty. No idiot is getting in the way."

"Renee!" Renee heard Aeron's thought, saw the guards on the floor. "We need to move."

Chapter 62

BESS LORELEI HAD a lot of tinnitus. Firing an automatic gun converted to fire darts in rapid succession would do that. Maybe it was the blizzard? It had frozen her chin and given her the aches, she should have brought ear muffs. They would have helped.

She ushered the remaining slaves onto the truck, hit three guards with one burst of fire, pressed the button to close the door, and tapped on the truck.

"Get movin'," she called and hit another two guards.

The truck slid into motion, snow-chains crunching and clunking before gripping. Bess ducked away from it and over to the guard hut she'd cleared and checked on the sleeping occupants. A car sped down the road from the house toward her and she set herself to fire, then stopped as it overtook the truck and hurtled on out.

Was that . . . ? Couldn't be. Maybe it was the snow sticking to her eyelashes or maybe it had frozen her brain but she cocked her head. Must be seeing things. She turned back to the road, hurried along it, and felt in her pockets for her sweets. A good sweet would calm the ringing, always did.

She darted another five guards bursting out of the front door, and a breeze tickled her. "Momma, you know where my sweets are?"

The breeze hit her harder like she was being scolded.

"Hey, I'm heading in, I just need a sweet." She shrugged. Now the slaves were out, she should go in and get Aeron.

The breeze hit her again.

"I'm cold enough as it is. Just tell me already," she muttered, and maybe tell her where her sweets were too.

The sudden urge to head to the roof and find the winch Stosur had used before filled her mind.

"I ain't sure I got the bulk to lift Shorty up on that." She looked up, into the snow-thick air and tried to figure out how many sets of stairs she was going to have to punish her knee on.

The breeze hit her again.

"Alright, already." She snuck through the front door and darted three more guards. Guess she'd just do what her momma told her to.

Chapter 63

FREI PULLED JESSIE behind the desk as the door opened. She knew it would be Jäger but even so, her body trembled. Fear prickled all the way through her as Jessie gripped her hand tight. Jessie didn't have a bullet-proof vest on.

"Well . . . what a pleasant surprise," Jäger purred as he limped in, and the door slid shut behind him. "Nice family reunion."

Frei raised her pistol. "If you move closer, I'll fire."

"If you fire, I'll press this and that floor you're standing on becomes a pressure plate." He grinned. "You maybe fast, Slave, but how good is she?"

Jessie gripped on tighter.

Frei squeezed back and narrowed her eyes. "She's faster than you think."

He laughed. "Would you like to try it?"

He pulled out his gun. Frei's hand trembled, and she tried to override the way her body shut down. She was a sharp shooter but she wasn't Renee. She'd back herself normally. Jäger threw her off. If she missed, he'd press the button. She squeezed Jessie's hand. No, it was too risky.

"Yes, not so clever now." Jäger smiled and slid his finger to the trigger—

The door slid open.

"No!" Theo threw himself at Jäger.

Frei threw Jessie in front of her, rolled, Jäger hit the button. Spikes shot out of the wall both sides.

Theo yelped.

Frei shoved Jessie out of the door. Couldn't stop. Had to get her out. She glanced at Theo—Spike through the shoulder. Her heart ached. Couldn't help him. Had to leave.

Jäger kicked Theo, sending him clattering to the floor, and picked up his pistol.

"Go!" Theo dived for him.

Frei sprinted out of the room—half carrying Jessie—her heart torn. He needed help. He needed her.

Bam.

She whimpered with the sound. Didn't dare turn back. Had to keep running. Had to keep Jessie safe.

Bam.

She grabbed Jessie, rolled—splinters flew at them. No. Her heart ached. Jäger had the gun. She yanked open the door to the slave stairs. They scrambled inside.

Bam.

Bullet kicked off the wall beside her.

"Run." She guided Jessie up the stairs. "Don't think, don't look back. Just run."

Jessie sped up as they navigated the stairs, and Frei blinked back the tears. Theo had been there, again. He'd given her and Jessie the chance to get away, and she'd had to leave him there.

Bam.

Shut it away. Need to keep Jessie safe. She pushed off the stair and threw herself out of the way, rolling into a sprint. Where did she run when Jäger knew the house better than she did?

Chapter 64

SHADOWED PATCHES IN the narrow corridor, broken up by moonlight from tall windows. I reached the turn. Where the two corridors split. Frei was on the right hand side.

A breeze hit me.

I dived to my left. Clattered into the wall opposite and turned. *Bam*—Jäger's bullet chipped off the wall next to my head.

"Thanks, Nan," I wheezed and fired.

Zip—Dart hit him in the butt as he limp-ran down the corridor. He turned. Raised his pistol. I rolled, threw myself behind the wall.

Bam.

Pain ripped through my shoulder as dust kicked up at me. I staggered to my feet. The pain made it even harder to see straight and I ducked my head out. Just an empty corridor, moonlight bathing sections. Must be following Frei. I couldn't feel her in the room, couldn't feel Jessie. I started to run after him but a whimper hit my ears. I turned.

"Theo!" I sprinted to him. He lay in a pool of moonlight, clutched at his chest. Blood poured from it. His shoulder was gashed too. I couldn't touch him. What did I do?

"Locks . . . he's . . . girl . . ." He managed and his eyes rolled.

Oh no.

I couldn't touch him. *"Renee!"*

"Here!" Renee sprinted over, flashlight out, beam washed over us. Hartmann hurried after her, and they dropped down beside me.

"Theo, oh . . . please . . . Wake up." Hartmann clung to him but Renee pushed her away, scanned the wounds, glanced at me.

"He's still there," I said, wincing from the light, or maybe the pain in my shoulder, or both. "I need to wake him up enough."

Hartmann furrowed her brow but Renee shoved something from her bra up his nose. He spluttered.

"You need help?" I glared at Hartmann. "He's got to ask."

"Theo . . ." She spouted off something in German. I got the help bit but that was it.

Theo nodded. "*Bitte . . . bitte.*"

I looked to Renee. "Good enough for you?"

She nodded.

I placed my hands on his chest. The flashlight buzzed, flickered. Sparks shot at me. His chest jolted. There went his defibrillator. "You might want to move back."

"What are you doing?" Hartmann mumbled.

"Her job," Renee said, switched off her flashlight, and handed it to Hartmann. "You stay back, you listen. She helps."

His chest warmed, my hands warmed. His heart sped up. He gasped, and his eyes snapped open. "Locks . . ."

He tried to move. I pushed him down. "Ain't done."

Hartmann stared at me. The pale light cut deep shadows under her furrowed brow.

My hands heated up. I winced as the bullet hit his chest, then the venom hit his system, then the spike ploughed into his shoulder.

"Jäger, he's after her . . ." I looked to Renee. "Go. Go find her."

Renee nodded and sprinted off as Theo rubbed his hand over his chest, then collapsed into Hartmann's arms with a snore.

"What did you do?" Hartmann looked at where the wound had been. "How?"

"Doesn't matter," I managed. Pain in my hands, in my shoulder, vision wobbled. "We just need to get him to the dining room . . . where you got Megan holding Huber."

"And Sven," Hartmann said with a curt nod.

"No, Sven is in the slave corridors." I glanced at the doorway to the slave stairway. Renee could get there. She'd help.

"Nan," I whispered as I pulled myself up and clung to the wall. "Frei and Jessie need your help."

Chapter 65

NARROW CORRIDORS, IN deep shadow, empty, winding, and cluttered. Frei hurdled a beam across the floor, trying to get her training to kick in, to calm down but her heart pounded too hard. Jessie stumbled ahead of her.

Frei stooped to catch her before she clattered into the wall. "Up, you can do this."

"My legs are burning, Mom," Jessie mumbled, tucking her bushy hair back as she stumbled to regain her balance. "They won't work properly."

Frei tried her radio again. "Still nothing."

"Hopefully Grandma could get into the system." Jessie puffed as they squeezed through a narrow gap and ran up another set of stairs.

"Me too." She hoisted Jessie up into her arms. It wasn't as easy as in Caprock, she was growing. She'd be her height or more. "Hold on."

Jessie pulled the pistol from Frei's holster and flicked off the safety. She turned to look over Frei's shoulder.

Bam—Jessie fired.

Bam—Jäger was fast even with a limp.

Frei ducked around the wall, back into a sprint. Should she take the main corridor? No, it was narrower here, he couldn't get a clean shot.

"You hit him?" Frei asked, dodging around a divot in the stone floor.

"No, I'd have cheered." Jessie wheezed. "It put him off."

"Keep it up." Frei reached a set of stairs to go up or down . . . up.

Bam—Jessie muttered.

Bam.

Frei swerved to the left. Bullet pinged off the stone next to her cheek. Dust hit her eye. Pain. Sharp stinging pain.

Bam—"Nearly," Jessie muttered.

Bam.

Frei leapt off the step, bullet hit the wall next to her. She sprinted down the corridor. A room straight ahead. A door to the corridor on the right. She tried it. Locked.

"Shoot the lock," she could hear the worry in her voice.

Jessie aimed.

Bam.

Frei yanked the door open. Bricked up.

No.

"Mom, we got to move." Jessie gripped onto her shoulder.

Room straight ahead. Would have to do. She charged at the door. Clattered through into the room. Bed. Desk. Lamp. Chair. Window.

Bam—Bullet pinged off the wall.

Jessie fired around it—*Bam.*

Jäger's laugh rang out through the echoing space. "Oh dear . . . How do you get out of this one, slave?"

Frei pulled Jessie to the side of her. Shut the door. Grabbed the iron cast bed, rammed it up against it, and went to the window.

Aunt Bess's face looked back. "I got the feeling you needed a hand?"

Frei whimpered with relief. "Yes . . . please." She picked Jessie up before she could argue.

"Careful of them spikes. I ain't got the buzz like Shorty has," Aunt Bess said. She was suspended from some kind of rope.

"Don't know where my mom is," Frei whispered. "Don't know if she hacked the system."

"I'll keep trying her radio," Bess said like she hung from ropes all the time.

Crash—Jäger smashed the door open.

She shoved Jessie out of the window. Drew her knife. Threw it.

Jäger grunted as it dinged off the wall next to his head.

Jessie scrambled through. Aunt Bess drew her gun—*Bam—Bam—Bam.*

Jäger darted behind the wall.

"Get her out. Please," she whispered.

Aunt Bess nodded, zipped upward.

Frei sprinted forward. Picked up her blade. Swiped and caught him across the arm as he raised his gun. She booted him in the stomach and smashed his gun to the wall. "I'm sick and tired of you."

She smacked him in the face.

He laughed and threw her backward. She clattered into the wall, head inches from the stone. "It's mutual."

He drew his blade.

She lifted hers.

No more running.

Chapter 66

RENEE HURRIED THROUGH the passageways, night-vision on. The gunfire was distant and she didn't know where it was coming from.

"Blondie, I ain't meant to say nothin' in these situations," Nan said appearing beside her. *"But sometimes you got to watch them wheezes 'cause they can be downright sneaky."*

Renee smiled. She turned right and headed down the stairs. Wheezes? Had to mean Sven. "Thanks, Nan."

"Just get your sharp shooting eyes on. He can load a sentence that one." Nan nodded to her and faded. Renee scrambled down the steps. She glanced out of the door—corridor, decorated, three sofas in a sitting area. She shut her eyes. Second floor sitting area, directly above the dining room.

"Renee, you copy?" Stosur sounded frantic.

"I copy." She fished her earpiece out of her bra and rammed it in her ear. "Status?"

"Slaves are freed; Jessie is on the roof with Bess; I'm in the system but I need help," Stosur answered. "And I don't know where Ursula is."

"Grandma, Aunt Bess is taking me in," Jessie fired off, panting. "I don't want hassle, you need me."

"Corridor should be clear." Renee steadied herself. Jessie was out but where was Frei?

"Mom is kicking Jäger's . . . um . . . butt," Jessie said.

"He probably messed her hair up," Renee said, hoping she sounded confident, and slowed as she spotted Sven lurking in the corridor as if waiting for someone. No doubt Jäger had been meant to send Frei his way only Jäger wanted to keep her from him.

She checked her pistol. One dart left and then it would have to be bullets. She took aim.

Zip.

Sven slumped forward. Renee walked over to him and took his pistol off him.

She touched her earpiece. "I have Sven. I want to get him to Hartmann."

"Why?" Jessie sounded worried.

"Because, if I'm right, she'll know exactly what to do with him." Renee pulled over one of the tipped-over ornaments: An old Eis car, the gold wheels worked enough to save her back and she huffed Sven onto it and headed to the stairs.

Dining room it was.

Chapter 67

BESS HELD JESSIE tight to her as they crept down the dark corridors. The sculptures took on odd shapes, and it held an eerie sense of quiet. It reminded her of blazing combat zones where she'd find refuge only a short distance from the fighting yet somehow it would hold an oppressive anticipation. Gave her the jitters, and she pulled out her cross and gave it a kiss.

"Corridor is on the left," Jessie whispered, glancing over her shoulder. "Feels like someone is crawling up my spine."

"Yeah," Bess said, making sure she sounded unbothered. "Live action for you."

"How did you do this for so long?" Jessie peered up at her as they stepped over a load of guards sprawled out and snoozing.

"Crazy juice." She winked at Jessie. Some things were better left in her head.

"And then some," Jessie wheezed and pointed to the right as they reached a split path. "Just down there."

"Okay, Mousey." Bess slowed her as they reached the room. "I'm gonna wait out here but if you ain't slinking your butt out here when I call, I'm gonna lasso you."

Jessie gave her an unimpressed look. "I don't slink."

"Yeah, you do." She grinned at her. "I can lasso."

Jessie poked her tongue out and headed inside. She doubted that the radio link would work so wedged the door open with some sticky device on the floor. Dried blood. Nice.

"Grandma Mousey, this is Aunt Shorty, mini-paws are on the wheel." She chuckled to herself. She used to make Ol' Willie laugh with her status updates. He'd been a good commander, shame he was only a name on the memorial wall. Guy would have made some woman real happy.

"She needs to access the system the same time as I do," Stosur said like she was smiling.

"Mini-paws, you get that? You got to snaffle the cheese in unison," She called through the door. The lighter she kept Jessie feeling, the less she'd think about the fact she *had* to unlock the system for her family.

"Why mini-paws?" Jessie muttered. "I don't even like cheese."

"All mice like cheese," Bess said with a wink. She was sure they didn't, one critter that had kept her company through a long imprisonment always turned its nose up. Boot camp food was cheap and nasty . . . or had been. Doubted they gave recruits plastic cheese and burgers now.

"Ready to chomp the cheese," Jessie fired with the touch of hysterical giggle.

"Mini-paws is ready," Bess said into her radio.

"On three," Stosur said.

"Three," Bess called.

The lights came on, the pipes clunked, and she looked to Jessie who was hitting a button and pulling sheets of paper out of a printer.

"Mini-paws has found a whole load of DNA traces related to us," Jessie said, eyes on the screen. "Copying and printing."

"Print off the finances of the Eis family too," Bess said like someone had taken over her tongue.

She sighed. She thought she'd left that behind when she'd retired. It was bad enough when she told the CIG shrink once and got sectioned for a month . . . Charles Black had sure been fun to be confined with. Once you'd cut through the stiff exterior, he was as fiery and funny as his daughter. She grinned. Yeah, Charlie would be real proud of Renee.

"You got it, Freaky Senior," Jessie called out, winking at her as she scurried from screen to printer and back.

"I'm sending files from Caprock to print," Stosur said like she wanted to print off the whole system. "Anything else we need, Lindsey?"

"No," Lindsey, whoever she was, said. "Why don't you leave the papers with me, get to safety. With the three of them present, you could be in danger."

Bess cocked her head. "She got backup . . . you locksmiths may be useful but you got Lorelei ladies on your side, and I'm pretty sure our Blondie could shoot a hair off a centipede."

"I trust them," Stosur said. "Implicitly."

Bess grinned and nodded to Jessie who gave her the thumbs

up, carrying half a tree trunk her way. "I do the heavy lifting, kid, your paws might fall off."

"You sound like Aeron," Jessie muttered then grinned up at her as she handed over the papers. "I like that."

Bess whipped the rope around Jessie's waist before she could react and smiled. "Good. 'Cause you ain't going nowhere unless it's with me in tow."

Jessie sighed. "Sneaky."

"Guess your skills are catching," she said, bumping Jessie's hip. "Commander, we're on our way to Huber's location."

"So I gather," Renee said in a dry tone. "This is what Aeron would sound like if she could wear a radio."

"Sure thing. Now scoot, Blondie, Nan ain't breezing your butt for nothing." She winked at Jessie who stared up at her. "What?"

"I thought only Aeron was . . . um . . . Freaky?" Jessie studied her, her posture more confident now the lights were back on, and she beamed at Stosur and an older lady who joined them from a side corridor.

"Kid, I don't need freaky skills. I just know my momma." She nodded to Stosur and the older lady. "If I was freaky, I'd sniff out my sweets . . ." Now where were they?

Chapter 68

MY VISION STARTED to wane as I fumbled my way down the main fanned staircase and toward the dining room. Hartmann had gone on ahead as I'd asked. I didn't want her to get distracted if I passed out. We had to clear Huber's family of guilt.

I gripped hold of my shoulder, feeling trickling warmth trace down my shoulder blade inside my vest. Just had to keep moving, make sure I could protect Frei if Huber's family was guilty. I knew she'd try to stop Hartmann from hurting him, Jäger would take advantage.

"Shorty, you ain't fit enough to keep going. You got to find your aunt. You need help." Nan sounded all kinds of worried, and I stopped, seeing her in front of me.

"Guess I really am hurt, huh?" I asked, my heart skipping as I took her in. I'd missed her face, I'd missed her smile.

"You know you are." Nan sighed.

"I got to help. I know I got to." I stared at Sven out cold on top of a model car.

"An' you got that boy's hurt stored up in your hands . . . you took more than he asked." Nan wagged her finger at me, hair bobbing as she did so.

"Yes, I did." I wrapped my arms around her, feeling the cold and not caring. "If I hadn't, that device was fried and he'd drop anyhow."

I felt Nan squeeze, the cold more intense. *"Then, I guess I'll keep you company."*

"Thank you," I whispered and lifted a shaking leg to boot Sven on his model car through the double doors to the dining room.

Hartmann smiled down at Sven as Megan hurried over and dragged him around the other side, halfway along the shiny dining table next to Huber. She tied Sven up as Huber glared at her. Theo was across two dining room chairs on the door to the right of me. Hartmann was at the foot of the table near Theo, her position so she could watch the slave door to her right, the opposite slave door, and everybody seated.

"Now all three families are represented," Hartmann said, glancing back at Theo. "I will state why we are here."

"This is nonsense," Huber snapped as Sven started to wake up. "For all we know, the Eis family could be alive; or all three families were to blame . . . What does it matter?"

"My mother spent her life trying to solve the crime, even estrangement from her own husband didn't stop her." Hartmann held his stare and intensified her own. "We grew up with nothing, he disowned us but she wanted to find the children."

"Why?" Huber frowned. "What were they to her?"

"She was attached to them," Hartmann said as I slumped next to Theo. Felt like Blackbear mountain was sitting on my chest. "The boy was ill . . . she nursed them."

"And?" Huber said it like he didn't care.

"And, sometimes that makes you feel maternal even when they aren't yours," Megan whispered. "It makes you feel like your duty is to help them."

"And she felt guilty," I managed. Was I out of breath? I was sweating, cold sweat, woozy.

Hartmann eyed me. "Nonsense."

"It ain't." I looked to Huber who nodded, reassurance in his aura. He knew I was hit. Must have looked all kinds of pale. "Lindsey Eis went to her for help but your mom wanted to go to her husband. Lindsey was too scared to say nothing more so left."

"How do you know this?" Hartmann asked. She didn't know what to think of me. Her aura waved and wiggled in confusion.

"Same way Theo is only sleeping." I tried to catch my breath. Must have been getting blood on the fancy chair.

"Then we continue." She waved to the large football-sized jewel in the middle of the table.

Megan went to Huber, pricked his finger with something then placed it on some plastic, or glass, stick. She went to a laptop set up at the head of the table and inserted the stick in a device beside it.

"Huber's DNA confirmed," Megan said, nodding to Hartmann.

I looked up at the slave door opposite, then at Sven who fluttered open his watery eyes as Megan strode toward him.

Chapter 69

FREI TOOK A blow to the jaw and crumpled to the ground, her head buzzing from the impact. She rolled to her left. Jäger's knife hit the stone floor.

Clash.

She kicked out and booted him in his wounded leg, causing it to buckle. Jäger swiped. Caught her across the stomach. Flesh wound. Panic gripped her. Why couldn't she calm?

"Slave, you still trying to prove something?" Jäger spat at her, taller somehow in the dim light, imposing. His brow cast shadow over his eyes, shark eyes, cold glint. "You know you're worthless."

"*I'm* worthless?" She shivered but managed to wheeze out a laugh. Fear squeezed her.

Renee swept her leg out. Frei smashed forward and landed face first beside her. "That's because he scares you. It tenses you up, narrows your attentional field and you miss the cues."

Her brain wouldn't quiet, wouldn't let her worries go and let her body react on instinct.

"Relaxation, visualization, picking a point nearby." She flipped up onto her feet. "Confidence . . . you just have to find a way to unlock it." She picked up the stick and smashed the dummy with a swing attack. The stick split, bamboo splinters spraying out as the dummy slammed to the mat. "You're not alone anymore."

Jäger's constant jibes threw her off, every time. She knew what he was doing but she couldn't focus.

"You have no bank balance. Mine is bigger than your ego," she managed. Didn't sound cocky, sounded terrified. Breathe.

Clang.

She only just blocked the jab to her throat, smacking her head to the wall. Dazed. "Touchy."

Jäger booted her in the stomach. "You think I care what trinkets you steal?"

She rolled but he booted her side. There went a rib. Get off the floor. She needed to get up. Jäger booted her back down.

"In your place, slave." He snarled, raising his blade.

"And again . . ." She watched the recruits push out another set. They were mud-soaked, rain dripping from them into the sodden dirt. She stood over them, watching each one for any sign of weakness. "Again."

One by one they dropped, battered, beaten, the best way to break them down. Most wouldn't cope for longer than a week.

"Again. You think you're worthy of CIG?" She stood there, she cared nothing of the rain. They thought she was a machine, and she did her best to prove it. "What are you doing here? You think you deserve a place?" She laughed. "You can't even do basics." She focused, not sure if she was seeing things when one recruit kept going. Everyone else had gone in. The rain beat down on her as she walked over.

"Lorelei, you call that a push-up?" She sneered down at the kid. If she broke her, she could go home. The kid had been through enough. Why force her into the line of fire again?

Aeron glared up at her through the rain.

"You think you can keep going?" She laughed, hating that she sounded so much like Huber but if she broke her, Aeron could go home.

"Yes," Aeron grunted and pushed up. Then Frei saw it, that steel, that defiance in her brown eyes, that pain from being a slave. Different prison, same pain.

"You think you are good enough to be here?" She glared down at her, masking the swell of feeling for the kid.

"And then some." Aeron dropped an arm, using only one.

"Why?" She heard the curiosity in her own voice, rain dripping from her onto Aeron's face.

"'Cause you ain't no better than me." She narrowed her eyes. "Everybody gotta pee."

Frei laughed, not sure how delirious she must be.

Clang.

"You're not alone anymore."

Aeron, Renee, her parents, Jessie, Aunt Bess. No, she wasn't alone. She could do this. They believed she could.

Jäger went for her shoulder.

Clang.

She smacked his blade away from him. He'd go for her throat next.

"I'm going to remind you of your place, slave," he spat.

"Everybody gotta pee," she shot at him, laughing. Yeah, she'd lost it.

He lunged.

She parried with ease, rammed his head into the wall, and was on her feet before he groaned. He had a dart in his ass, and she dragged it downward as she pulled it out. Aeron's darts? Good shot that soldier.

Jäger kicked his leg out, she caught it, slammed him back into the wall, and rolled her shoulders out. Her head shut up heckling and her focus flooded into place. "You're disappointing."

Jäger flipped, swiped with his right. She caught it, rammed his elbow straight until it crunched, and hurled him into the wall behind her.

"I spent years being scared of you." She shook her head. Not seeing him, not really, just another opponent. No harder than training. Armor, guess her armor was love. "And this is all you have?"

Jäger growled, slashed at her. She caught his hand. Stamped on it and booted him in the stomach. "It isn't so pleasant when I do it to you, is it?"

She booted him in the side. Grabbed his leg, yanked him upward as he scrambled to find his balance, and threw him backward. He stumbled down the stairs, battering his arms on the wall as he stopped himself rolling. She strolled down the stairs. He righted himself at the bottom and met her eyes. Not so confident now.

"Attentional field," Frei said as she headed toward him. "When you're over aroused, your body tightens and your focus gets too narrow." She flicked her leg up, caught him across the cheek with her foot, and he smashed into the wall. "And you miss things."

Jäger touched his split lip.

She dodged the uppercut and punched him in the stomach. "That's for my sister." She straightened him up and smashed her fist into his nose. "That's for Suz." She punched him in the stomach again. "That's for trying to hurt my baby girl." She brought her knee up and stared, hard, into his watering eyes. "And that's for me."

He slumped back to the floor, his eyes dazed as he gripped himself. "You are a slave. A pathetic slave."

He drew his gun. She ducked her head to the side.

Bam.

Hit the wall behind her.

"And you talk too much." She fired her dart gun.

Zip. Zip. Zip.

Jäger laughed. "I'm immune, slave . . ." His eyes flickered.

Frei held up the dart. "Not to this dose. Turns out Jessie and her friends have a talent for it." She looked at it. Miroslav in particular. "Won't hurt you . . . but the test subject did get a headache." Poor Grimes.

Jäger's eyelids drooped, and Frei smiled at him, yanked him up by the collar, and pointed to the door in front. "That's the dining room. Now be a gentleman and open the door."

She hurled him at it. He smashed through it and crashed to the floor, out cold. Frei strolled through and nodded to Huber and Hartmann. "Sorry, I had to teach him some manners. Did I miss anything?"

Huber beamed at her, all sense of reserve forgotten. "Well done, girl. Well done."

Chapter 70

BESS HELD ONTO Jessie as they neared the dining room. She didn't want any of them to go charging in until they knew what was going on.

Lindsey stepped in front of them, desperation in her eyes. "Please, I don't know who's responsible. I can't bear to lose any more family."

Stosur squeezed her shoulder, like she so often did to Frei. "How don't they know who you are?" She motioned to the artwork, the sculptures all around. "How did you hide yourself?"

Lindsey tapped Stosur's cheek. "Same way you do, although I can imagine your version is far less itchy."

"You have a disguise on?" Jessie looked up at her. "So how do we know it's really you?"

Lindsey pulled a lighter from her pocket, ignited it, and placed it next to her ear. The skin melted, peeled, and she rolled it off. Her face was far more wrinkled but she matched the beauty of the portraits still. She took one step back and bowed. "Convinced enough?"

Bess looked to Jessie.

"How'd we know you haven't got a disguise under the disguise?" Jessie mumbled, awe in her eyes.

"Can't do that," Stosur said, taking the lighter and doing the same to her disguise. Bess's jaw dropped at the stunning woman who emerged: white blonde hair, brown eyes with flickers of blue, tanned skin but as though it had been cut from ice. Frei had some genes. "It would stop the pores breathing."

Lindsey nodded, her eyes tracking over Stosur's face. "You're so much like him." She scratched her own cheek with her fingernail and blood dribbled out. "But so you can be convinced."

Jessie winced. "I'd have just taken your word for it." She looked to Bess. "Guess that's were mom gets her dramatic side from."

Bess nodded.

"I stayed in the hope I could find out who hurt them," Lindsey said. "I never got close but hiding here was the best way I could keep them safe."

"It worked." Stosur sighed. "I'm sorry you didn't tell me so I could get you, the both of you out."

"He was too ill by then. I'm surprised none of you have shown symptoms. Many of the Eis family were lost to it." She hugged herself. "I think his brother had symptoms but I can't be sure."

"Oh we had it," Jessie said with a shrug. "But we have Aeron." Lindsey stared at her.

Jessie shrugged. "Seriously, she's super cool."

Bess hugged Jessie in close. "You got that right."

Crash.

Bess pulled Jessie over to peek in through the gap in the doors. Jäger was out on the floor looking like he'd gone swimming with a croc.

"Sorry, I had to teach him some manners. Did I miss anything?" Frei said as she strolled into the dining room.

"Oh, mom is so cool too." Jessie looked up to Stosur and Lindsey who nodded.

"Yes, well, now that you are here . . . Megan, if you will," Hartmann said to Megan who moved into view and strode over to Frei and hesitated.

"I need your hand," Megan snapped.

"No." Frei glared at her. "I did as you asked, Hartmann. I broke into Cold Lock and now we're leaving."

Hartmann raised her pistol at Huber who was tied to a chair. "If you don't, I shoot, and I don't think your friend is in a fit state to help anyone."

Frei's gaze moved to something on the right, and her face drained. "You'd do that to her when she helped you . . ." Her eyes tracked over something else. "She helped Theo."

"Yes." Hartmann sounded unmoved. "Now hand it over or I shoot."

Jessie looked up at Stosur.

"A slight problem," Lindsey muttered. "She'll assume guilt."

"I should go in, tell her," Jessie said, moving for the door. Bess picked her up as she squirmed.

"You ain't going nowhere near. Your mom will figure something out—"

"Fine." Frei held out her finger, and Megan jabbed her. She looked to Huber. "I love you. I love her too much to see you hurt."

Huber smiled at her. "You assume that Sabine has some semblance of honor."

"Go to your friend," Hartmann said like she was doing it in spite of Huber. "Megan, run the DNA."

Bess shifted, trying to see who was hurt. Renee maybe? Her stomach plummeted to her knees. Or Aeron. She could only see Sven sitting there next to Huber, tied up. His finger had been jabbed too by the look of it.

Megan sighed a heavy sigh. "Eis . . ." Her voice faded.

"Megan." Hartmann warned.

"And Huber," Megan mumbled.

Sven's face lit up. "Hah, so the tales are true."

Jessie looked to Stosur. "We can't let him get hurt."

"If Sven finds out, he'll be a slave," Stosur whispered back. "Sven will own him."

Jessie shrugged. "So we'll break him out. It's better than Hartmann shooting him."

Stosur sighed. "You're right . . . you're right." She looked to Lindsey. "Your DNA isn't going to help much, is it?"

Lindsey shook her head. "Unless you want to prove why you can pick locks."

Stosur looked to Bess. "Keep her out of this."

Bess saluted, and Stosur headed in.

"Frau Hartmann, I would like to prove Huber's family is innocent in this matter." Stosur sounded like she was ready to take her on. Bess looked at Lindsey. Maybe she should get them both to safety?

"The locksmith," Sven said with a gasp. His eyes filled with water, and he wheezed out his breath. Huber's eyes filled with adoration as he gazed at her. Bess didn't blame him, the woman was some looker.

"You think you can?" Hartmann asked, amusement in her voice. Guess she enjoyed seeing Sven wheeze.

Stosur held out her hand. "If you will, Megan."

Megan pricked her finger and headed back out of sight, and Bess held onto Jessie.

"I'm not moving," Jessie muttered.

"Hey, I'm wrinkly, it ain't good for me to get all stressed," Bess mumbled not sure why she wanted to hide her face and maybe peer between her fingers. She knew Huber and Stosur were Frei's parents.

"Eis," Megan said, sounding like someone had smacked her. "And . . . this gene . . . it's familiar. It's in a few files but nothing that's relevant."

"And you'll find that those are some of my genes in Locks," Stosur said with pride, flexing her back as she did so. "She's done wonders with them."

"And mine," Huber whispered, love in his eyes, in his smile.

"You stole her?" Sven spat and glared at him, shunting around in his chair like he was trying to kick him.

"She is not a toy," Huber shot back. "I was only happy to help her be free." He looked to the right. "Satisfied?"

"No." Hartmann sounded confused. "How does this prove your innocence? All it does is show that you owe Sven more than you are worth."

Huber shrugged. "Couldn't care less. He tries coming near me, and I'll remove his inhaler."

"Your entire household," Hartmann said with a grunt. "Not just you."

Bess looked to Lindsey. "What does that mean?"

"That he, his slaves, and . . . Frei are now Sven's." Lindsey rubbed her hands over her face. "What do we do now?"

Chapter 71

FREI WAS OVER me somewhere but all I could see was her aura. The room had faded from view long ago, and I could only hear snippets of voices above me and the loud pounding of my heart. Among the auras, odd camera rolls of memories played out, dinners and laughter.

Tomas Eis was strongest in them. He'd loved the estate and working with his brother. Theo was shorter than him with an awkward way of standing, but still dashing. I'd watched them as kids, sword fighting; watched them as teenagers, hurrying in with baseball gear on; as adults with ladies in tow, and then alone. The energy had changed between them. There was no longer that bond but some kind of barrier.

"I cannot let you do this," Theo said, his gait more unsteady. "She is a thief. You cannot marry her."

"I love her," Tomas said, his gaze full of pain as he looked at Theo. "No one has ever made me feel that way."

"Find a better woman. A woman who won't steal your money from under you." Theo jerked and twitched.

"You say such things but you don't know her." Tomas sighed. "However you feel, she has agreed to marry me."

"Then I will tell our parents." Theo nodded, his worry turning down his mouth. "I love you too much to see you do this."

The scene faded, and Tomas appeared, more worn now. He was alone, pouring over something laid out on the table.

"There is no word?" Lindsey asked, her stomach blooming with their unborn child.

"None," Tomas muttered. "I know he went there but I cannot see how he got in."

She peered over her shoulder, and fear filled her eyes. "Why would he go there?"

"He is unwell." Tomas rubbed his forehead. "I need to find him."

"You will," she said, moving away from him, rubbing her hand over her stomach. "Or I will," she whispered as she hurried away.

My heart slowed, and I searched for air. Frei was saying something to me but she was too far away. Instead Lindsey appeared with Theo.

"You like the look of the silverware," Theo snapped as he walked in.

Lindsey placed the candlestick down, frowning at him. "I wondered who had made it, why?"

"So you can steal it?" Theo glared at her. "Thief."

Lindsey sighed. "You think so little of me."

"Yes. You work for him. You steal things from others for him." *He took the candlestick, and she cowered like he would beat her. He stopped. "I am removing it. I would never raise a hand to you."*

"Why? If you think I am but a slave to scold." She glared up at him, agony in her eyes.

"A slave?" Theo twitched, then shook his head. "Why would I say such a thing?"

"Because you are no better than him," she snapped, backing up. "Your disgust is clear."

Theo put down the candlestick. "Then talk to me and change my mind."

"I can't," she blurted, tears in her eyes. "You are too kind, too much like Tomas . . . you will get hurt."

"You have to keep awake," Frei said, and I felt her shake me. "Please, stay awake."

I opened my eyes enough to see Jessie holding her hand out to Megan. " . . . I can prove he did."

I looked up at Hartmann, seeing more of her aura. Frei held my hand. She didn't know what to do. Her emotions smashed into each other as she glared up at Megan.

"Eis and Huber grandparents as known," Megan said, tapping away. "And . . ." She paused. "One of her parents was a Jäger."

Hartmann glanced at the doorway like she wondered who else was lurking outside. Her face faded in and out. "Then that cancels the debt."

Sven growled under his breath.

"Yet, we still have no answer on what happened." Hartmann sighed. "Even though he stored the DNA inside the jewel, it was for nothing."

"Help me up," I said to Frei.

She shook her head. "You can't. I need to keep pressure on the wound."

I met her eyes, they looked much bluer in my fading vision. "I can solve it. Help me up."

"I don't care who did what," Frei muttered.

"I do." Hartmann came over to me. "You think you can tell us more?"

She hauled me up. The room swayed. My legs buckled, and Frei held me steady. Aunt Bess was outside, peeking through the door like she'd dart everybody. I stumbled to the table, dragging my feet along, and slumped next to the jewel. I took a breath and placed my hands on it—

Tomas ran through the tunnels, he was close to the location. Theo was being held there, he knew he was.

"Tomas, no!" Theo yelled.

Bam.

Tomas skidded around the corner. Theo slumped to the floor. He'd been cold before he hit the ground. "Why?"

Tears engulfed him, spluttering from him as he gripped Theo's body close. He'd been fading, that much they knew so why hold him here? Why shoot him?

"Use what's precious to draw out the treasure," a voice behind him said. "And a fitting treasure it is too."

Tomas turned and faced Jäger head on. "Why? Why would you do this?"

He wagged his gun. "Now, no pretending you aren't stealing slaves." He primed the pistol. "Besides, you have my locksmith and I want her back."

Bam.

I gasped for breath—only auras around, energy, my heartbeat pounding, thumping, straining. "Jäger. It was Jäger." I clung onto Frei. "Shot them both . . . Lured . . . like with Suz . . . Treasure."

I collapsed backward, and Frei lay me on the floor.

"How do you know?" Hartmann snapped. "How?"

"Check . . . accounts . . . motive . . ." I gripped my chest, my heart skipped. Pain shot down my left arm, and I felt my head hit the floor.

Chapter 72

FREI STARTED CPR, not sure how long she could keep Aeron alive. The bullet wound was too deep. They needed to get her to water.

"Megan?" Hartmann strode to Megan as she shook her head at the screen.

"I can't find anything, it's all been wiped," Megan said, looking up at Huber, her eyes wide with pleading. "It will prove you're innocent."

Aunt Bess and Lindsey strode in. Frei turned her focus back to Aeron. "I need to move her."

Aunt Bess hurried over. "Shorty, come on, don't freak your aunt out."

Hartmann raised her eyebrows at Bess then eyed Lindsey, shock in her eyes. "You were here all along?"

"Yes." Lindsey put a load of papers on the table. "Finances of the three friends. Tomas must have looked into them when Theo went missing."

Hartmann strode over, Megan too. Huber and Sven looked at each other but Jessie and Stosur hurried to Frei and knelt beside Aeron.

"Gunshot?" Stosur asked, compressing the wound.

Frei kept pumping as Aunt Bess gave Aeron mouth-to-mouth. "Yes."

"How?" Jessie's voice wobbled. She took Aeron's hand.

"Saving us," Frei muttered. "Caught Jäger in the thigh with a dart."

"It's conclusive," Hartmann said, glaring at Sven. "Your family was bankrupt when they took over the estate. Huber and my father were not but I can't do anything about it because there's no free member of the family."

"Surely we can," Megan muttered. "He can't just get away with it."

"Yes, Locks has seen to that. She broke into the system, and that means I am taking the rest of your assets," Hartmann said, glared at Sven then turned to Jessie. "Perhaps your family will accept it back as a gift."

Jessie squeezed Aeron's hand. "I've always been free."

Aunt Bess met Frei's gaze. "She ain't sparking."

"We need help," Frei muttered to Hartmann. "We have to get her to the pool."

Hartmann stared at Jessie. "You've always been free?"

Frei nodded to Aunt Bess, and they lifted Aeron up with Stosur.

"Yes, Grandma faked my papers. I was adopted instead." Jessie held up Aeron's hand like she was desperate to help. "Even tricked Jäger into paying for my education. Check the papers."

They carried Aeron to the doorway as Hartmann scrabbled through the papers.

"She's right . . ." Hartmann blurted out. "She's always been free."

"Who cares," Jessie muttered.

"You should." Megan peered over Hartmann's shoulders. "You claim the debt. All the estate, the slaves, the money . . . they go to you."

"And I doubt you can pay that back, Sven," Hartmann said. "Which means your household belongs to her."

"No," Sven snapped.

Bam.

Frei looked up. Sven held his bleeding hand as Renee sprinted in and over to Aeron. "Had to wait. Nan."

Frei nodded to her. "Pool."

"No, won't work." Renee met her eyes. "But snow might."

Chapter 73

RENEE HURRIED IN front of the others and pushed open the doors as Hartmann and Megan followed. "Sabine, what was wrong with Theo, exactly."

Hartmann hurried to catch up. "Heart attack. It damaged his AV Node, why?"

"How did he survive?" Renee met her eyes.

"I was with him. I kept pumping until the ambulance arrived." Hartmann looked at Aeron, limp, fading.

"How many heart attacks?" Renee shoved open the main doors, gasping as the icy flurry of snow swept through her. The snow was up to the top of the steps already.

"Two." Hartmann frowned at her. "The second one did the most damage."

Renee met Frei's eyes. "How many?"

"Just the one." Frei nodded to Aunt Bess, and they put Aeron in the snow.

"I don't understand?" Hartmann looked to Megan.

Renee dropped to her knees and sank into the snow. She placed her hands to Aeron's stomach. Normally she felt a swirl of energy, of vibrant vitality but all that was left was a faint fading pulse.

Frei dropped to her knees and placed her hands over Aeron's chest. "Come on, don't quit. Fight."

Aunt Bess cradled Aeron's head, cooing to her, tears dribbling off her nose. Jessie was still attached to her hand, holding it to her face. "Please wake up."

Renee felt the pulse strain. She glanced up at Hartmann, Megan. "Go get Huber. Now." She looked to Stosur as Megan ran off. "It took two of us in the river in Baltimore. She needs more energy. We have to give her energy."

Stosur nodded and placed her hands on Aeron's wounded shoulder. "What do you need me to do?"

"Ask." Renee met her eyes. "Pray."

Stosur bowed her head and the pulse picked up, then strained again. They had to help her, to reach her before she relived Theo's second heart attack. She didn't have the energy.

Huber hurried out, pulling Megan with him. He dropped down next to Stosur and put his hands on Aeron's exposed stomach. "I know . . . I'm asking."

Megan followed his lead and bowed her head.

Renee searched for the pulse. It jumped, then strained. She looked up at Hartmann. "Help us."

"Who am I to ask for help?" She shook her head. "I'm not worthy."

Renee smiled at her. "Worth a shot."

Hartmann nodded and lowered to her knees the opposite side to Megan and Huber. Renee moved her hand up. The pulse strained, picked up, then Aeron's body tensed. Faster, faster, tripled, too fast, pounding. She grunted. Strained. Gasped. Heart Stopped.

"No!" Renee pushed out CPR. Blood stained the snow under Aeron's shoulder. Moonlight bathed her face. Pale. Lifeless. "Please."

She pumped, tears dripping from her. She had to come back. She had to.

Frei leaned in, mouth to mouth. Tears pulsed from her onto Aeron's cheeks. Aunt Bess gripped Aeron's head, like she was willing her to keep going. Willing her to fight.

"Please," she whispered. "Please, you gotta keep going."

Silence.

Renee kept pumping. Frei kept giving breaths. One glance. They couldn't lose her. They couldn't. Not Aeron.

"Nan!" Renee yelled it to the starry sky. "Nan!"

"Jump start," Nan whispered.

Aunt Bess met her eyes. "You heard her. Do it."

"You shot enough emotion into me, you could have jump-started a chopper."

Renee scrambled up to Aeron's face, swapping places with Frei who scurried to her chest.

"What do you want us to do?" Stosur whispered.

"Keep praying," Frei sobbed. "Keep praying."

Renee focused on Aeron's cooling face. Jump start. She gripped her cool cheeks. "Get your butt back here."

She pressed her lips to Aeron's, firing every bit of feeling, of love, of light she could.

Pulse—*"So who are you?" Maybe she would lower the shield if Renee got her talking about how she felt, about who she—*
"Aeron Lorelei, but then I thought you'd read it on the notes."

"Nothing," Jessie blurted. "There's no pulse."

"Keep going," Aunt Bess whispered, nodding to Renee. "You can do this."

"I love you, you get that?" she whispered, stroking Aeron's hair from her brow. Getting colder. Drifting away. No. "I loved you since I saw you. Do you get that?" She leaned in and kissed her again.

Pulse—*Aeron met her eyes as if she understood how locked up she'd been and she got pulled into a soggy hug. "I can't argue with that. I reckon you've proved beyond doubt that you're good at your job."*

"Nothing," Huber grunted. "She has to wake up."

"She will," Frei said, pumping. Sweat dribbling from her. "Renee can reach her."

"I'm meant to keep you safe." Renee fought back her tears. The energy was faint, only a glimmer and fading, fast. She pressed her lips to Aeron's again.

Pulse—*"I found it hard readjusting to people not seeing inside me."*
Aeron took the steaming offering and drained it in one gulp so she handed her the other cup. "Maybe that's 'cause you didn't want them to?"
Renee smiled. "Not everyone wants to, like you, Aeron."

"Still nothing," Frei shuddered out.

"It will work," Stosur said, her tone calm, resolute. "I believe it will work." She met Huber's eyes, and he nodded.

"Yes. I've seen it myself. She can," he whispered.

"She helped me," Jessie said, sobbing, sniffling. "Come on, Aeron. Please."

"Keep going," Renee blurted. "Please . . . keep going." She pressed her lips to Aeron's again.

Pulse—*Renee sighed. "I'm horrible. There's no excuse. I say things I don't mean but please, please, don't ever think I don't care about you." She touched Aeron's bruised forehead. "I mean it, I adore you, you great big dimwit."*
Aeron peered down at her with the biggest set of puppy dog eyes. "You do?"
"Guaranteed. Even if I yell at you, act like I don't, or we argue." Renee smiled, stroking her thumb over her cheek. Music floated from her to Aeron, energy wrapped around them. "You're a part of me."

"Don't you get that," Renee whispered. "I love you . . . we all love you." She looked at everyone helping.
"Yes. You can do this, girl." Huber's eyes shone with tears, with steel.
"You can." Stosur nodded. "You can."
"Come on, Shorty." Aunt Bess stroked Aeron's hair. "You quit lying 'round."
"Yes," Frei wheezed it out. "Fight."
"You showed us how to stand up and be strong," Jessie whispered. "You can do it."
"Even I know you can," Megan whispered, so quiet, yet the sheer belief shone from her. It flowed, Renee could feel it flow. Gentle, quiet.
Huber sobbed, then shook his head. "I don't know why I'm crying, I can't stop it."
Hartmann sniffed, tears bursting free, and nodded. "Me either . . . I really care." She stared at Aeron in shock. "I care."
Renee looked to Frei. It had to be working.
"Keep going." Frei nodded, pumping, fighting. "You can reach her."
Renee pressed her lips to Aeron's again.

Pulse—*"Yeah, you are." Aeron held her hands there; they warmed. "Can't you feel it?"*
"All I can feel is heat and tingling." Her voice wobbled, and she bit her lip.

"You really believe that, doc?" Aeron whispered.

She spread her hands out and focused on Aeron's stomach. "You're sicker than you're letting on."

"You didn't need to touch me to figure that one out." Aeron smiled at her, trying to reassure her. "Relax, I got you to keep an eye on me."

"I'm not helping you. I can feel that." She shut her eyes, her tears spilled down her cheeks. "All I can do is feel how much damage you're taking on."

"You're easing it. That helps." Aeron smiled at her, a tired smile.

"I can't stand it that you're in pain." She shook her head, voice cracking. "I can't."

"Believe it's for a reason." Aeron met her eyes. She'd keep going, keep trying to help Frei.

Renee felt something flicker, some energy fade in. She pressed her lips again.

Pulse—*"Tell me . . . what?" Her whisper was raw with the need to know.*

"You really want to know?" Aeron had such a cheeky grin on her face, such a twinkle in her eyes that it was hard not to get pulled in. Hope fluttered through her, daring her to think, to wonder if Aeron felt something in return. "Yes."

Aeron leaned in and shook her head, her face so serious. "You got a cappuccino moustache."

Renee's heart groaned, and she narrowed her eyes at her. Yeah, Aeron didn't need to be an empath to know she was going to smack her with the napkin.

From one, to the other, tears, prayers, energy. Just a whisper, just a faint flicker. Renee smiled against Aeron's lips. Steady and slow, that music had filtered in. "You make me hear music," she murmured against her lips.

Pulse—*Renee slid her hand up Aeron's chest and pushed her up, breaking the contact. She tried to calm her breathing. A kiss should not feel that potent. Wow. She opened her eyes to see Aeron clamping hers shut, panting, and stroked her soft cheek. "You'll have to open them eventually."*

"Yeah." Aeron's soft husky voice sent a shudder through her. "Um . . ." Aeron peeked open her eyes, her cheeks glowing. Her gaze ran over Renee's face, her eyes deeper, like she wanted to kiss her. Renee slid her finger up over Aeron's lips and raised an eyebrow.

"I . . ." Aeron squeaked then cleared her throat. "It's just . . ." She looked down at Renee's lips, "Seemed . . . like . . . er . . . a good idea?"

"It was," Renee whispered. "You're starting to get it. So quit lying around and get your butt back here, dimwit."

Nothing.

"Please."

Nothing.

"I think she's gone," Stosur whispered, sobbing.

"No!" Renee gripped Aeron by the collar and yanked her upward. "I love you. You get that. Get. Your. Butt. Back. Here." She pulled Aeron to her, focused every single ounce of love she had, of music, of laughter, of joy, and pressed her lips to Aeron's.

Jolt.

Renee looked up. The others lay sprawled, rubbing hands, shock in their eyes.

"What happened?" Hartmann muttered.

"Static shock and then some," Frei said, shaking her hand off.

Aeron's lips parted.

"We've got her," Renee looked to Frei. "Shower, pool, whatever is close."

"Pool," Stosur muttered, scrambling to her feet and taking Aeron's shoulder. Aunt Bess, Frei, Renee, hoisted her up as the others followed on. Hartmann hurried ahead and pulled open the doors to the pool.

They hurried in, and Frei dived in, Renee too, and Aunt Bess lowered Aeron down.

"Get ready to pull us out," Renee called, focused on holding Aeron's head up.

"Water's not pulling," Frei muttered.

"It will." Renee met her gaze. "This could really hurt."

Frei nodded, complete faith in her icy blues. "Worth it."

Renee took Aeron's face, closed her eyes, and placed every ounce of feeling into the kiss.

Jolt.

Renee held her lips there, and Frei groaned. "I'm not kissing you too but I will drown you."

Jolt. Lights flickered.

Renee held on.

"Can feel a pulse," Frei called out. "Got a pulse."

Jolt. Lights buzzed.

Renee felt her heart skip, she held Aeron's hand and squeezed it.

Jolt. Pop. Crash. Lights popped. Glass shattered, and Aeron gasped.

Renee pulled back. "Got her!"

The water gripped on. Swirled. Sucked them under the surface. She gripped onto Aeron, air crushed from her lungs. Frei grimaced, her face contorted even under the water.

Air. She needed air. Couldn't breathe. Not giving up.

Frei met her eyes, neither of them could breathe.

Air . . . needed '. . . couldn't . . . breathe . . . air. Her vision fuzzed . . .

Aeron snapped her eyes open. Reached up her hand. Yanked them upward. They broke through to the surface. "Now!"

Huber, Stosur, Jessie, Aunt Bess, Megan, Hartmann, Lindsey heaved to drag them to safety, the current strong, swirling.

Aeron hauled them upward with one powerful arm, onto the side, free of the water's pull, and Renee collapsed onto her back with a grunt, sucked in the air, coughing, spluttering.

"Why is it," Frei muttered, panting, gasping. "That since I've known you, I've been half-drowned more than is normal?"

"What happened?" Aeron sounded groggy at best.

"My thoughts exactly," Hartmann muttered.

Renee sucked in her breaths. She couldn't find the air to speak.

"Did we free folks?" Aeron mumbled.

Renee reached out and took Aeron's trembling hand, soaking in her rosy cheeks, her bright brown eyes, her breathing and very much alive. "Yes," she whispered, treasuring the feel of Aeron's warmth, of her. "Yes, we did."

Chapter 74

LILIA PULLED OUT yet another batch of cookies and slid them onto the rack. Eli would be twice the size of the cabin if she kept making them but it was something to do, anything to calm the panic swirling in her stomach.

Her phone rang, juddering across the counter, and she grabbed for it. "Bess, tell me they are fine."

"Twig, you know if they weren't I'd have called you sooner." Bess tutted, sounding so much like Nan. "I still can't find my sweets."

"In your sock," Lilia said, feeling relief gush from her. "Don't ask me why because I'd have to understand you for that."

Bess chuckled. "Knew you'd help." She heard rustling. "Helps with the popping."

Lilia wiggled her jaw at the thought. "So what aren't you saying?"

"Nothing."

"You need me to send Momma?" Lilia said, knowing she sounded like she had when they were kids.

Bess wheezed out a breath. "Snitch. Fine." Bess took a big breath. "The slaves got freed but the alarm went off, Mousey had to help her grandma break a lock; Icy kicked Jäger's hind, and he'll sure be walking funny for a while . . ." She took another breath. "Turns out Jäger's family stole Icy's family estate from them so Mousey got it all back because some woman named Hartmann said so." She took another breath. "But don't ask me how cause I needed my sweets at that point. Anyhow . . . Icy's guy got hurt so Shorty had to help him but her own circuits were fried so Blondie got us to put her in snow and tried mouth to mouth . . ."

"Not what I saw in my vision," Lilia mumbled.

"Seriously, Twig. I seen more steam in a freezer." Bess chuckled. "So then we drowned them in the pool until Shorty quit lying about but I ain't sure why you need it off me 'cause I'm pretty sure you saw it anyhow."

"How is Aeron now . . . ?" Lilia chewed on her lip. Like Eli, Aeron was incapable of seeing love until it smacked her with a shovel. He'd been the same. She'd had to spell it out and even then he'd wandered off and taken a week to speak to her.

"Sleeping but either she don't remember or she ain't getting the hint that Blondie loves her." Aunt Bess roared with laughter. "She don't get that from our side."

"It's not funny," she said, laughing herself. "Not all of us are so adept at wooing people."

Bess laughed harder. "Ah, Twig, you knock me out. Wooing?"

"Yes, well . . . whatever you did to poor Grimes." She shook her head. "I hope there are medical facilities for Miranda there?"

"Sure, I'm staying till Mousey and Icy got the hang of it. Their grandpa and grandma are too. Oh and a great-grandma who got some mean card skills." She clicked her tongue. "Well, got to go rustle up breakfast."

"Bess?"

"Yeah?" Bess sounded like she was looking for something again.

"In your sock." She shook her head. Bess could do so many complex tasks then forget where she'd put her sweets.

"Ah, thanks . . ." She hummed. "Oh an' Mousey turned Jäger and his brother over to the authorities, only the authorities happen to be sleeping off Shorty's help."

Lilia raised her eyebrows. "Sounds like you all need some sleep."

"You'd think in a big ol' kitchen like this, there'd be something to rustle up," Bess muttered away to herself.

"I'm sure one of the many locksmiths in attendance could help you."

She heard a cupboard crack. "Don't need no attending."

Lilia felt a breeze and smiled. "So you listened to momma for once, huh?"

"Ain't got one iota what you're hollering 'bout." Bess tutted, but Lilia could hear her smile. "Now where'd they keep the meat . . ."

Lilia rolled her eyes. "I'll send cookies."

Bess cut the line, and Lilia leaned on the counter, sending up prayers of thanks.

"How is she?" Eli whispered from the second floor landing. "How are they?"

"If Bess was anything to go by . . . they pulled it off . . . and I'm assuming the can of pop just got shaken." She smiled. "She did great."

He beamed and snuck down in his eclectic underwear. "Calls for a cookie in my book."

Lilia picked up two and handed him one. "I heartily agree."

•

Chapter 75

FREI LEANED AGAINST the doorjamb and watched Huber, Stosur, Lindsey, Hartmann, Theo, and Jessie deep in conversation. She smiled as Jessie shook her head at something Hartmann said and pointed to whatever she had on her piece of paper.

"No, they aren't owned by anyone. They just have normal employment contracts and they can have leave so they can use any of the other houses to vacation in." Jessie looked to Theo. "And they need help to adjust so they don't get upset."

Hartmann smiled, a genuine smile. "I think we can manage that but you risk them leaking out information about Cold Lock."

"They don't really know anything. Sven didn't. He relied on using the periphery hub." Jessie looked to Lindsey. "I have someone who is awesome at computers and would love to get the chance to learn from you."

Lindsey smiled. "Of course."

"Can we guarantee that they are going to get a fair trial?" Jessie said to Theo. "I mean it, no influence from anyone. I want them to go through it properly."

Theo nodded. "A secure court. There is a judge I know who is fair but this will have to be an international court, without public access."

Hartmann patted him on the hand. "Why bother? We know what their crimes are. They're guilty."

Jessie sighed a real teenage sigh. "Because, it's justice." She glanced up and met Frei's eyes. "The right way." She wagged her finger. "Nowhere that has nasty penalties. Confined is one thing but we're better than that."

"We are, are we?" Huber said, his eyes filling with amusement.

"Yes. Mom, Aeron, and Renee didn't work so hard for us to revert to barbarianism." She held Hartmann's stare with the kind of steel Huber would be proud of. "And, if we are to remain business partners, I'd like you to try and adapt to equality too . . . please."

Hartmann laughed and tapped the table. "I like that you're forthright . . ." She smiled at Theo. "I will leave that *adaption* to Theo."

Theo raised his eyebrows.

"Unless you would like to explain to your former employers how your heart has healed itself?" Hartmann shook her head. "The surgeon will be hard enough."

"Surgeon?" Stosur asked, concern in her eyes.

"Yes, the small matter of removing his ICD." Hartmann got to her feet. "You know, you are a curious family." She gathered up her papers and snapped her fingers. Her servants hurried to her—Jessie had already made her employ them and break their ownership papers—and slid on her long coat. "When someone targets you, enslaves generations of your family, and kills members . . . you are set only on confining them to prevent hurt to others."

Jessie nodded. "I am working on forgiving them too." She looked to Frei once more. "Aeron taught me that."

Hartmann sighed. "Yes, she does seem to have a way about her." She looked to Theo. "I'll meet you at the helicopter."

She strode past Frei, then stopped. "Such a kind heart in a child." She looked Frei up and down. "Much like her mother."

"I wasn't so kind," Frei said, her gaze drifting to Theo. "Or did you miss the injuries?"

"No, I didn't." Hartmann smiled at her. "But I think most would have shot him."

"Maybe." Frei shrugged. "But I don't want him on my conscience. I'm happier just to let it go." She let out a long weary breath.

Hartmann nodded and strode off, and Frei rolled to lean her back against the wall, and looked up and down the corridors. It was all Jessie's now.

"You are quite a lady," Theo said as he walked into the hallway, smart in his tailored suit. His face more healthy now Aeron had healed him . . . and yes, more handsome. "I can't say that I've ever met anyone like you, your family, or your . . . friends."

Frei laughed. "I'll take that as a compliment."

He smiled his broad joy-filled smile. "I'm not sure how she helped me but . . . ." He sighed and scrunched his lips to the side. "She doesn't appear to be as violent as she depicts."

Frei raised her eyebrow. "You don't say."

He tutted and wagged his finger at her, his clear eyes twinkling. "You are a puzzle, Miss Locks." He looked down the long corridor, out of the pool room windows as the chopper started up. "But one I would very much like to get to solve."

"That could take a while," she whispered, wanting to check him over, to make sure he was healed, to hold him.

"I very much feel that you are worth every effort." He stooped, took her hand, and kissed it.

She held his hand, pulled him to her, and sank into his lips. "Love always is."

His smile filled his eyes. "Yes, I believe it is."

Frei let his hand go and watched him stride off. She knew it was as hard for him to get on the chopper as it was for her to watch him go.

Some journey. From a slave, to locksmith, to general, to having parents who could marry; a daughter with a fortune and successful business; friends who she adored more than was natural . . . and Theo.

She shook her head and wandered up the main fanned staircase. The family crest caught her eye set into the marble overhead. A Eis? Explained why she'd always loved fast cars.

Chapter 76

RENEE PULLED HER coat around her as Huber hurried over to the chopper, catching Megan's hand as she tottered toward it.

"You tied me up," he said, yanking her to him. "You think you can scuttle off without reprimand."

Megan raised an eyebrow. "Huber, if you try reprimanding me, I'll flatten you."

Huber laughed. "Good thing I don't have need of your services anymore."

"I'm glad I didn't have to shoot you," she said, kissing him on the cheek and wiping off her lipstick, a nervous glance at Frei as she strode out. "I'm glad Locks has her freedom."

Frei halted in front of her and looked Huber up and down. "Aeron told me what you did for Suz, for us."

"Part of the job, don't get emotional about it," Megan shot back.

Frei held out her hand. "You're the sneakiest woman I've ever set eyes on."

Megan took her hand, gave it a brief shake and turned back to the helicopter, tears in her eyes. "You had to pick something up from me."

Renee snuggled into her coat with a smile as Theo helped Megan aboard. Somewhere inside were Sven and Jäger, bound and gagged.

"Renee Black," Hartmann said from next to her ear.

Renee turned and raised an eyebrow at her. "Took you long enough."

Hartmann laughed and wagged her finger. "I had no idea you had such passion." She smiled at her. "And that vacancy for a mistress is still open."

Renee chuckled. "Unless you want to see Alex mad, probably best I keep to my day job."

Hartmann glanced up at the house. "Yes. I'm a lot like my mother." She pursed her lips like she wasn't sure if that bothered her or pleased her. "And she was loyal to the Eis family because they were so kind to her." She met Renee's eyes. "You took care of my family, and you didn't shoot me." She smiled. "Which means, you have my loyalty should you ever wish to stop by."

"Do I need to bring sleeping vials?" Renee raised her eyebrow.

Hartmann laughed, strode toward the chopper, and stopped to look over her shoulder. "It's always a pleasure to have you run rings around me."

Renee nodded and watched her board the chopper. She pulled Frei to her as the rotors roared and lifted the machine free of the ground.

"I'm staying for a while," Frei said, waving. "I want to make sure Miroslav and the others get here safely and Jessie is set."

"And then?" Renee took in the spiky hair, the icy eyes, somehow softer in the snowy light.

"I will head back to CIG, gracefully let them know I have better things to do." Frei met her eyes. "But I'll be on speed-dial, always."

Renee squeezed her arm. "You earned a long vacation."

Frei nodded. "I'll be working with Bess, Lilia for a while." She looked back at the house. "Sam is doing too well in his trial. He's causing doubt over Aeron's innocence." She sighed. "Best she doesn't recuperate at home."

"I owe her a road trip anyhow." Renee rested her head on Frei's shoulder. "Besides, she seems to think you told her to kiss me."

Frei tensed. "Ah." She held up her hands, a half grin on her face. "Did she?"

"Oh, yeah." Renee shook her head. "How else do you think I knew it would fire enough energy into her?"

Frei chuckled. "So . . . ?"

Renee poked her. "Now she can't even meet my eyes." She frowned. "She thought I'd beat her, I swear."

"She did think that." Frei poked her back. "What did you do to her?"

"Me?" Renee put her hands on her hips. "I'm not the one telling her to kiss me while I'm asleep."

"Thought you'd thank me." Frei put her hands on her hips, pulling the sides of her jacket back like wings. "Not like you haven't been hoping for it."

Renee wagged her finger. "But she wasn't ready, and now she's freaked. How am I supposed to fly her anywhere for hours when she can barely make a sentence around me?"

"You'll think of something." Frei patted her on the shoulder.

Renee lunged into a hug. "Thank you."

Frei squeezed her, every word they never uttered seemed to hang there. Why say it, when they already knew? "Whatever, Black. Just don't expect flowers."

Chapter 77

I WATCHED THE chopper roar away through the bedroom window, not quite sure how we'd pulled it off. I ran my hand over my chest and winced. It still hurt, a lot.

"Shorty, you make me want to shake you sometimes," Nan said, breezing in to sit beside me. I could see her clearly, her eyes filled with worry.

"Everybody gets sick, least I did something useful to get that way." I shrugged. I was a protection officer. I doubted any were free of scars.

"Your momma ain't gonna be so calm about it." Nan sighed, pulling out her knitting. *"I got to figure out how to unpickle things again."*

"You don't have to." I sat next to her, enjoying taking her in. Her eyes that I knew were like mine; her fluffy white hair; her kind smile. "I'm gonna rest up for a while anyhow . . . I'll take a load of showers."

Nan tutted at me. *"It'll take that and more . . ."* She smiled at me. *"But, sure . . . if you rest, if you take care of yourself . . ."* She ran a cold finger down my cheek. *"You did good, Shorty. Real good."*

She faded, and I turned and wobbled to my feet as Aunt Bess strolled in.

"Shorty, you was a big peanut." She wagged her finger at me. "And now you're a great hulking one who's real heavy to carry around." She smiled. "So quit it."

Had she been talking to Nan? I saluted. "Yes, ma'am."

Aunt Bess chuckled. "You ain't got a clue how to do that have you?"

"Nope." I shrugged and went to pick up my bags but she tutted at me. "I do the heavy lifting."

I chuckled, even though it made my chest ache. "You sure you're retired?" I shook my head as she hoisted all the bags up with ease. "Or doing training when no one is looking?"

Aunt Bess winked at me. "I packed some cookies and food for the flight. You keep your strength up and do what Nan told you." She held my gaze then led me down the corridor. "You rest, you feed yourself up, and you shower."

"You heard her?" I smiled at her as we reached the top of the stairs. Then I felt someone watching, so I turned. Lindsey and Jessie's staff waved at me amidst moving their belongings into the rooms.

"Yeah, feels real good to hear her again," Aunt Bess whispered and a gentle breeze fluttered over us. "You think they got enough room for all the slaves you broke out?"

"Guess so. There's a lot of buildings and a whole town nearby. Be nice to see the factory start back up." I smiled at the image of the original Kälteblau sign all spruced up and shiny.

"I'm gonna head back to the cats," Aunt Bess said, cheekiness in her eyes. "And make sure Grimes ain't trashed my house."

"You got it," I said and Jessie hurtled into me as I reached the bottom landing. I winced at the heaviness in my chest. "Some place to fix up, huh?"

Jessie squeezed me. "You need to come visit, a lot. Mom will want to see you."

"Uh huh." I smiled down at her. "And I got to check if you're trying to outgrow me."

Jessie nodded, a big beaming smile, hair jutting out at all angles and eyes full of awe. "You are awesome."

I punched my fist to hers. "Back at you, Mousey."

Huber nodded to me as he strode in, bringing a gust of snow. He held out his hand and shook mine, clearing his throat. "On behalf of my family . . . Thank you."

"Hey, I weren't the one hacking systems." I squeezed Jessie's shoulder. "Just glad I could tag along."

Stosur poked her head out of the dining room. "And you understand that you're considered part of the family now?"

I looked up at Aunt Bess who nodded. "They like cookies."

"I mean it," Stosur said, a smile in her eyes. "If you need us, we're ready."

I nodded and headed out of the door before I started getting misty. Aunt Bess strode off ahead, and I slowed as Frei cut into my path.

"You shot several guards at speed in the dark," she said, all General Frankenfrei. "Impressive." She walked to me and gave me the squishiest cwtch I'd had in a while. "You're a blessing, a real blessing."

I soaked the words in, seeing the truth glitter all around as she said it. "Guess Nan knew who you were all along, huh?" I pointed up at the badge over the door. "Icy."

Frei laughed. "Rest, please."

"Kinda have to." The chopper started up, and I swallowed. "Ain't sure about the flight though."

"Renee will take care of you," Frei said, her voice soft. "And I told you she wouldn't be mad."

"I ain't sure what she is 'cause I can't see nothing about her aura now." I could only catch glimpses of everyone else's.

"Then do something normal for once . . ." Frei smiled up at me and squeezed my hand. "Ask her."

I headed to the chopper, got wrapped in another cwtch by Aunt Bess, and climbed on, hoping no one could see how misty eyed I was getting. Renee was already on board, and I hovered outside the door. I weren't sure if I could look at her, let alone sit in a small space with her for hours. I was guessing hours anyhow. I weren't real sure where we were going.

Aunt Bess shut the door, and I steadied myself as I headed into the cockpit. I stuck on my headset and belted up, knowing Renee was looking at me.

"You darted Jäger while he was running," she said, all Commander Black. "Nice shooting, Lorelei."

I glanced at her. Renee's accent. Every bit of it washed through me and eased my worries and that wriggle went nuts in my stomach. I shrugged.

Renee eased the stick and the chopper slid upward. She'd ripped her long nails off, her hair was scraped back, no makeup, and she looked so much more beautiful for it. "You got to Theo, you protected Frei and helped us ensure that we got every slave to safety. Let alone solving the mystery so Frei's whole family got their freedom." She smiled enough her energy fizzled about. "That's some fantastic work."

I shrugged again.

"And . . . you convinced a whole lot of people that you were your cover to exceptional standards." She nodded my way. "Why don't you check in your pant pocket."

I frowned and checked them, only to find nothing.

"Side pockets."

I tapped them and felt a box. I pulled it out and opened it. "I don't really think it's a good idea for me to be reading medals."

"It's yours," Renee said, a soft smile on her face. "Frei will pin it on officially when we head back to base." She shook her head then let out a gentle sigh. . "And . . . I'm not mad at you so stop looking so worried."

"You ain't?" I stared at the medal. No name but I felt Frei and Renee's love from it. Reassurance and love.

"Never." She slid on her aviators.

My throat ached and my chest tightened so I tucked the medal safely in my pants. "Where are we going, back to base?"

Renee peered over her aviators at me, her gray eyes full of affection. "We're heading to meet my mom."

I grinned. "You mean it?"

"I mean it, Lorelei." Renee swung us to change direction. "Only fair, as I get to spend time at yours so much."

"You're always welcome there." I folded my arms. More welcome than she realized.

"Good." She had a half smile on her face, her eyes shielded by the lenses.

"I still ain't sure how we pulled it off." I rubbed the back of my neck, enjoying the feel of Renee just being Renee and doing something she loved.

"I've been thinking about that," she said, swinging us to switch the flight path. The snow blanketed the ground below but the sun shone off it, making it almost shimmer from height. "Goodness blossoms when someone like you is around."

"Me?" I asked. Didn't get how I'd helped. I'd just done my job and, like always, got folks half-drowned and passed out.

"You," Renee whispered, a shimmer falling from her lips, and I caught a glimmer, just a faint glimmer of her aura firing its light show. How I loved that light show. "A good seed." She beamed my way. "Stands for a noble heart."

About the Author

Jody has been everything from a serving police officer, to recording artist/composer and musician until finding her home in writing. She lives in sunny south wales with a "lively" golden retriever and other furry friends.

Oh, and she has a slight affection for cake . . .

Website: http://www.jodyklaire.com
Facebook: www.facebook.com/jodyklaireauthor
Twitter: @jodyklaire

The Above & Beyond Series, Book 6

BLACK RIDGE FALLS

TEASER

Keep moving . . . just keep moving.

I couldn't catch enough air to breathe; each gasp sucking my stomach concave, pulling at my ribs. My legs were like dragging boulders but I had to keep going. Couldn't see for my eyes watering with the effort, throat ached, chest ached. Renee gripped hold of my hand but my sweat made it slip free. Pain shot through my head—

Smash—Running, need to run . . .
Smash—Gunfire, ping, ping, ping.
Smash—Calls, shouts, a strangled yelp.

My knees buckled and I lurched to the floor, snow tingling at my swollen fingers.

"Aeron, please, we have to move," Renee whispered. A plea, a desperate plea, as she eyed the rocks above the clearing, holding her breath. "Up."

I pulled myself to my knees but every muscle, every nerve below was numb, unresponsive. "Get to cover . . . please . . ." Heartbeats, one, two; one, two, loud and hammering. "You need to get to cover."

Pain hit me again—

Smash—Where do I run?
Smash—Legs sore, tired, need to keep going.
Smash—

I slumped onto my front, the pulse in my head screaming at me, vision blurry . . . then stillness, that gut wrenching stillness.

No.

Adrenaline shot through me, I lunged at Renee but she dodged, drew her gun, fired—

Bam.

Bam.

Someone behind me grunted. I gripped hold of her waist and threw us into the undergrowth, slope dipped, rocks, stones, scraping, scratching; steeper, stones rattling, rocks catching skin. I held onto Renee, she gripped me with one hand, trying to catch hold of something, anything to slow us.

I slammed out my hand . . . a rock—

Drop—the ground fell away, Renee clung on. I couldn't hold us, so swung us inward—*crunch*—knees buckled, back jarred, folded, crumpled, rolled, and Renee slammed onto me with an "oof."

"Are you okay," she wheezed, feeling over me, checking over me.

I caught her hands in mine. "Quit ticklin'." I tried for a smile.

"How can you still smile?" she muttered, rolled off me, and dragged herself under the overhang. "I don't know how we didn't fall."

I turned over my shoulder and jolted: sheer drop, like looking at the ground from a chopper, clouds swirling around the mountain below. I shuddered out a breath, turned back to Renee, and my breath caught; panic, worry, pain whimpering out in a sob.

"You got hit." I scrambled over, dragging my unresponsive feet, and pressed my hand to the wound as she tied a bandage around it. "Why'd you move?"

"If I hadn't fired, you would have been hit in the chest," she muttered, blood covering her hands. "Reacted too slow."

The wound oozed, and I swallowed back the pain throbbing through from it. "I need to fix it, it's deep, you need to be fit—"

She gripped my hands. "No. You can barely stand."

"You got a hole in your leg." I tried to free myself but she held on, her gray eyes full of dullness and pain.

"Aeron, listen to me," she held my gaze. "I'm a soldier, it's part of the job. I got shot." She pointed to her leg. "It's venal. If it was an artery, it wouldn't stop."

I remembered something about that in boot camp. "You gotta lie flat . . . and you need . . . ice?" I looked around, the overhang didn't have any snow so I crawled to the edge and stuck my hand out.

Bam.

I snapped my hand back and clutched a clump of snow, staring at the space on the ground where the bullet had hit.

"They know we're hiding here," Renee said, her jaw muscles flexing. "We have to move."

I went to put the snow on her wound but she stopped me, and took it from my hand and placed it to the wound. "No healing."

"So, lie flat and I'll keep pressure on it." I motioned for her lie down but she shook her head.

"We have to keep moving . . ." She swallowed, her throat flexing. "They'll find us here."

I looked back at the drop and tried not to buckle over with worry. I was sick, real sick; Renee's wound needed help; we were being pursued, shot at and now we were stuck on a ledge high up on the mountain. The clouds above and the clouds below cut us off, swirled, loomed like they were ready to close in.

I met Renee's eyes and we let out a long, mutual sigh.

Yeah, we were in a pickle, a big one . . . again.